DARK DIVIDE

Sonja Stone

Holiday House   New York

Text copyright © 2018 by Sonja Stone
All Rights Reserved
HOLIDAY HOUSE is registered in the U.S. Patent and Trademark Office.
Printed and Bound in May 2018 at Maple Press, York, PA, USA.
www.holidayhouse.com
First Edition
1 3 5 7 9 10 8 6 4 2

Library of Congress Cataloging-in-Publication Data

Names: Stone, Sonja, author.
Title: Dark divide / by Sonja Stone.
Description: First edition. | New York : Holiday House, [2017] | Summary:
    "Nadia Riley and her team are back for another semester at Desert Mountain
    Academy, the covert CIA training school, where Nadia finds herself in
    ex-recruit and traitor Damon Moore's deadly sights"— Provided by
    publisher.
Identifiers: LCCN 2016058465 | ISBN 9780823438365 (hardcover)
Subjects: | CYAC: Boarding schools—Fiction. | Undercover
    operations—Fiction. | Spies—Fiction. | Schools—Fiction. |
    Kidnapping—Fiction. | Dating (Social customs)—Fiction.
Classification: LCC PZ7.1.S755 Dar 2017 | DDC [Fic]—dc23 LC record available at
https://lccn.loc.gov/2016058465

To Jude, for valor
To Kaitlyn, for honor
To Morgan, for strength

And to Hannah Duncan,
for tenacity, eloquence,
fairness, and justice

1 NADIA RILEY
THURSDAY, MARCH 2

Minutes before committing her third felony of the semester, Nadia enters the lobby of the Scottsdale Ritz-Carlton and immediately turns right, following the predetermined route down the marbled hall. She lowers her chin as she passes reception to avoid the sightline of the cameras mounted above the desk.

At the bank of elevators, she waits for a vacant car. As she's reaching for the button to the seventh floor, an elderly man in a dark suit catches the door. Nadia stalls as he makes his selection.

He presses eleven, then turns to her. "And for you, miss?"

"Twelve, please," she says.

Thirty seconds later on the twelfth floor, Nadia exits the elevator and walks silently toward the stairs. She pushes through the heavy door, then jogs down five flights to the seventh floor.

Before leaving the stairwell, she leans against the wall to catch her breath. Her stomach feels like a snarled fishing line, though her nerves have nothing to do with the mission. She sighs and pulls open the door.

Around the corner at room 760, Nadia slides her keycard into the lock. The lock flashes red and beeps twice. She tries again— still no luck. The third time she slows, carefully inserting the card. A single beep chimes as the light on the lock flashes green. She cracks the door.

"Housekeeping," she softly calls. No one answers, so she slips through.

Inside the room a thick duvet covers the king-size bed. A chocolate rests on each pillow. A small toiletries kit sits on the dresser, a metal briefcase on the bed, a half-empty suitcase opened on the valet stand.

Clever details. Whoever staged the mission did a nice job lending authenticity with the personal items.

Nadia retrieves the memory card from her purse. Her op-specs instructed that she hide the tiny device in the target's possessions, preferably somewhere he'll never look.

She moves to the suitcase on the valet. Running her fingers over the fabric lining reveals the perfect spot—between the plastic back and the metal support bar. She unzips the silk, wedges the storage card into place, and reseals the zipper. The knot in her stomach loosens slightly.

Back at the door, Nadia checks the peephole. A man with a shaved head walks toward her room from the direction of the elevators.

She steps away and taps her ear, bringing her comms to life. "Boy Scout, traffic in the hall. I'll be down in ten."

Jack's voice resonates in her ear. "Copy that. See you soon."

A moment later she leans in for another look, but the peephole's gone dark—something obstructs her view. It takes her a second to realize someone's at the door.

A keycard slides into the lock. Her heart flies to her throat as the door beeps twice—red light.

Bathroom, shower, under the bed. The options race through her mind.

The plastic card slides into the lock again, then a single beep.

The knob turns. He's coming in.

Closet.

Nadia slips inside and pulls the slatted doors closed. She holds her breath as he enters the room, then curses herself for not throwing the deadbolt.

A *thunk* as he moves the briefcase from the bed onto the dresser.

Her eyes widen as she strains to hear over the pounding of her heart. She runs through possible scenarios: she's in this man's room; he came home earlier than expected. But it's a mock mission—she assumed the school booked a room just for this exercise, that the suitcase and toiletries kit were props. Why would they have her break into a civilian's room and plant something in his luggage?

The ironing board hanging in the closet presses painfully against her back. As she shifts her weight, the board brushes the wall. She freezes.

The scent of his cologne hits her a second before his shadow darkens the door. His hand reaches for the knob. He opens the closet.

His face registers surprise, then...what? Recognition?

Six feet, shaved head, broad shoulders, slightly crooked nose. Pale skin, light eyes—blue, maybe. Black t-shirt, jeans, sneakers. Late twenties, muscular, handsome.

Totally normal.

Except for the gun pointing at her heart.

SIX WEEKS EARLIER

2 NADIA
SUNDAY, JANUARY 15

Nadia Riley lowered the car window as her chauffeur pulled up to the gatehouse outside the block wall surrounding Desert Mountain Academy. An armed guard stepped forward with a clipboard and a retinal scanner. After verifying the driver's ocular print, the guard waved them through the iron gates.

After a wintery month-long break in Virginia, the lush grounds were a welcome sight.

Eight buildings were arranged in a semicircle around the outskirts of a sloping lawn, which stretched to the edges of the impenetrable wall encircling campus. Flowerbeds packed with violet and yellow pansies ran along the horseshoe-shaped sidewalk in front of the buildings. Hopi Hall, home to the administrative offices, stood at the lower right of the hill.

Her driver followed the single paved road into the parking lot at the far side of the building, where he drew to a stop.

Nadia took a deep breath as she stepped from the black sedan. Lemon blossoms scented the temperate air with a sweet perfume, and the afternoon sun filtered through the palm trees and danced across the wide stone steps leading to the entrance of Hopi Hall.

"I'll drop your bags at security," her driver said. "We'll deliver them to your room after they've been searched. If you're ready to relinquish your cell phone, I can take that, too."

"Oh, right." Nadia fished through her bag. Desert Mountain Academy allowed minimal unsupervised communication with the outside world. Cell phones were forbidden, the hall phones were tapped, laptops were subject to search and tracking, and—above all else—students were strictly prohibited from discussing the true nature of the Academy with anyone—parents included. Recruits who didn't last were treated to a week-long "deprogramming session" before returning to the outside world. Nadia wasn't sure what that entailed, but was fairly certain she didn't want to find out. "Let me just text my mom so she knows I'm here."

A few seconds later, Nadia powered down her phone and handed it over.

"Looks like she's ready for you." He gestured toward the steps of Hopi Hall as Ms. McGill, the dean's assistant, pushed through the massive wooden doors.

"Miss Riley, welcome back." Ms. McGill hurried down the steps.

"Thank you," Nadia said. "How was your holiday?"

"The dean of students wants to see you right away."

I guess that's enough small talk. "Right, we have a new dean."

"Of course we have a new dean. You nearly killed the last one." Ms. McGill gave her a closed-lipped smile.

Nadia frowned. Was that supposed to be a joke?

Ms. McGill continued. "Her name is Dean Shepard, and she's quite eager to meet the young woman who saved our school."

"That seems like an overstatement," Nadia said, trailing the assistant up the stairs.

"Don't be modest; you're a hero. Enjoy the celebrity while you can." Ms. McGill pulled open the carved wooden door. "Because it never lasts."

Nadia paused briefly inside the foyer as her eyes adjusted to the dim light. She ran a hand over her dark, wavy hair, then followed Ms. McGill down the tiled hall.

The dean's sitting room looked untouched, precisely as it had last semester. A pair of leather chairs sat near the unlit fireplace. Behind her, glass-covered bookshelves lined the wall like sentries.

Across the room, the floor-to-ceiling windows revealed distant Phoenix nestled in the valley to the right, and to the left, low mountains covered with rust-colored rock and sage-green cacti.

"Go ahead." Ms. McGill gestured to the closed door on their right. "I'll confirm that your uniforms have been delivered to your room."

Nadia cleared her throat and stepped forward. The brass nameplate bolted to the door no longer read THADIUS WOLFE. Instead, printed in strong block letters, was SOPHIE SHEPARD. Nadia knocked. A moment later the door opened.

Dean Shepard's red hair, styled in a pixie cut, flattered her delicate features. She wore a cream-colored skirt and matching blazer, tailored to precision for her petite frame.

"Nadia, welcome back. I'm Dean Shepard. Let me be the first to say thank you for all you've done for Desert Mountain Academy. Won't you please sit?"

"It's nice to meet you." Nadia moved into the middle of the room and immediately regretted it. She stiffened, her eyes sweeping from corner to corner. The office had been completely redecorated in a Southwestern theme: a large, rustic desk, brown leather chairs for guests, a deep red rug with textured waves of wheat and gold. Automatic shades for the window, enough to block the light but not the view.

The corner to her right: that's where she'd found Jack's body. In front of the desk: that's where she'd stabbed Dean Wolfe. Between the guest chairs: that's where her heart had stopped.

"Is something wrong?" Dean Shepard asked.

"It's just...the last time I was in this office, I got shot."

"Well, let's see how the conversation goes." Dean Shepard smiled and gestured to the chairs. "Hopefully, it won't come to that."

Nadia laughed and picked the chair on the left. Dean Shepard returned to her seat on the far side of the desk.

"I understand you had an exciting first semester," the dean said. "Naturally I've been briefed, but can you tell me your version of the events that transpired?"

"My version?" Now her back was to the open door. Was it too late to switch seats?

"Everyone filters life through their own experience."

"I guess so." Nadia took a deep breath. "Basically, the CIA had intel that a new recruit—one of the juniors here—was a double agent, but that's all they knew. The double turned out to be Damon Moore, one of my teammates." Pause. "Do you mind if I close the door? It feels a bit drafty."

"Not at all."

Nadia shut the door. "Where was I?"

"Double agent."

"Right." She sat back down, the image of Damon filling her mind. His broad shoulders, his dark brown skin. His beautiful smile and unwavering gaze. He had, at one point, been one of her best friends. Or so she'd thought. "He was working for an organization called the Nighthawks, and he tried to frame me as the double. His on-campus handler was Professor Hayden, our political science teacher. Dean Wolfe was also a Nighthawk. I figured it out, Dean Wolfe shot me, and I stabbed him with a poisoned pen. I think that's about it."

"Why did you confront Dean Wolfe?"

"I didn't have a choice. He was holding my team leader hostage." Referring to Jack Felkin as her team leader felt a little dishonest—a lie of omission. But he wasn't her boyfriend, either, and she wasn't about to launch into the whole we're-thinking-about-trying-a-relationship thing.

"Your actions were quite impressive for a first-year recruit."

Nadia shifted in the chair. "I didn't really think it through."

"You have good instincts."

Or I'm reckless and impulsive. "Thank you."

Dean Shepard sat back in her chair. "Well, I'm here this semester serving as the interim administrator as a favor to Director Vincent." The head of the CIA. "Normally, I run the postgraduate CIA training program at The Farm near Williamsburg, Virginia. I'm sure you've heard of it; it's not a black-ops site."

"I have. So you're a former agent?"

"Officer, technically. And current, not former."

"That's incredible," Nadia said. "What a great opportunity for us."

"I'm glad you feel that way. I'll be implementing several new programs this semester. I think you'll find the new curriculum both challenging and exhilarating."

"I look forward to it," Nadia said.

"Will you be checking your shoulder bag with security, or would you like me to inspect it at this time?"

"Oh, I'm sorry." Nadia lifted her small carry-on from the floor. "I didn't even think about it." She handed it across the desk.

Shepard remained seated as she opened the main compartment of the leather purse. "A scarf, magazine, notepad and pen, motion sickness bracelets—that's unfortunate." She glanced at Nadia. "Passport, wallet, lip gloss. No cell phone?"

"Already turned it in."

"Excellent." The dean swept her hand through the large side pocket before handing the bag back. "Do you have any questions for me?"

"I don't think so."

"In that case, check in with Dr. Cameron before going to your dorm."

Nadia sighed. "Of course." Visiting the psychiatrist was not her favorite task, especially when she wanted to catch up with her friends.

Dean Shepard rose from her chair. "It was lovely to meet you. Don't hesitate to drop by should anything arise."

"Thank you," Nadia said, moving toward the door.

"Oh, I almost forgot." The dean opened a desk drawer and pulled out a postcard. "This came for you a few days ago. I'm sure you're aware that security scans all incoming mail for chemical and biological weapons." She smiled. "It's clean."

Nadia took the card from Dean Shepard's outstretched hand. The picture on the front featured an illustrated map of the

Hawaiian Islands. Scribbled on the back, across from her name and the address of Desert Mountain Academy, was a single word: *Aloha*. She checked the postmark: Honolulu, Hawaii, five days ago.

"It's a little on the nose," Shepard said. "But a lovely gesture."

"You read my mail?" Nadia joked.

"I couldn't help myself. I *am* a spy."

3 DAMON MOORE
SUNDAY, JANUARY 15

Twelve hours before his ex-classmates were scheduled to return to Phoenix for their second semester, Damon Moore stood motionless on a squalid street corner in Las Vegas, Nevada. A cold rain drizzled onto his shaved head. He pulled up the hood of his sweatshirt, keeping his eyes trained on the third story window of the apartment building across the street, where a yellow light seeped around the makeshift curtain and out into the night. Occasionally, the occupant's shadow darkened the fabric.

At 0212, the window blackened. Damon double-checked the security cameras pointing toward the parking lot, kept his head low, and adjusted his gait as he crossed the courtyard. The lock on the front door of the dingy building was already broken. After a quick look up the deserted street, he stepped over the puke on the front steps and went inside.

The lobby smelled like mildew and cat piss. He took the scuffed stairs two at a time, up eight flights to apartment 843. Silence behind the paper-thin walls indicated his victim wasn't walking around. Damon picked the lock and went inside. He heard the shower running, the spray of the water as it hit the plastic curtain. In the dim light of the living room he eased himself between the single reclining chair and the upturned plastic crate that served as the TV stand.

Damon pulled on his leather gloves and crossed into the kitchen. He checked the drawers, grabbed the only chef's knife, and stuck it in the freezer. Inside the fridge he found a block of cheese, a loaf of bread, a container of leftover chicken wings, and the remainder of a six-pack of generic cola. He grabbed two cans, opened one, pushed a dirty plate across the shabby kitchen table and sat down, his back to the wall. The joints of the cheap wooden chair creaked under his muscular frame.

He didn't like the taste of the off-brand cola, but he was thirsty. Probably nervous about the upcoming conversation, what he might find out. And he wasn't about to risk catching a staph infection by drinking tap water out of one of the filthy glasses littering the counter. He silently drummed his fingers across his thigh and waited.

A few minutes later his ex-handler—and former professor of political science at Desert Mountain Academy—emerged from the bathroom with a towel wrapped around his waist. Hayden was halfway across the tiny kitchen before he noticed Damon. His body tensed.

"What's up, professor?" Damon extended the second can. "Have a drink with me."

Hayden didn't move.

Damon set the can on the table. "Come on. Sit down."

"Look, I—I was ordered to kill you. It was you or me." He moved toward the drawer where Damon had found the knife.

"Yeah, I get that. It's not personal."

Hayden opened the drawer.

"Really?" asked Damon. "You think I'm that careless? Seriously, sit down."

Hayden sat. His hand visibly shook as he fumbled to open his drink. "I didn't want to eliminate you. I always liked you. I think you know that."

Yeah, right. "Absolutely." Damon popped the top of Hayden's cola and passed it back to him. "We had a definite rapport. In any case: you shot at me, you missed. No harm done, right?" Damon smiled. "That's not why I'm here."

"Why are you wearing gloves?"

"It's cold out. I'll take them off if it makes you feel better." Damon removed his gloves and folded his hands in his lap. *Guess I'm done with my drink.*

Hayden's face registered relief. "Then why are you here?"

"Roberts has something that belongs to me. I'm trying to get it back." Agent Roberts, the head of the rogue organization known as the Nighthawks—and the man who ruined Damon's life—had gone into hiding. It was time to flush him out. "I need the locations of his safe houses."

"I don't know where Roberts is. And I hope to God he doesn't know where I am." Hayden took a long drink.

"That's not what I asked you," Damon said.

Hayden shook his head. "I have a handful of addresses, same as you. I don't have any information you don't already know."

Damon sighed and looked down. He felt the anger building in his chest, elevating his body temperature and blood pressure. He clenched his jaw and took a deep breath, then slowly exhaled. After a second, he locked eyes with Hayden. "Where is my mother?"

"What are you talking about?"

"After your botched assassination attempt, I thought it prudent to get the hell out of town. By the time I got back to Baltimore, Roberts had taken my mother. Burned down her house. He said we could make a trade, me for her, but I haven't heard from him. It's been *weeks*. Think very carefully: where would he take her?"

Hayden shrugged. "He has a storage unit outside of Phoenix...."

Damon had found the storage unit over a week ago. It'd already been cleared out. Completely empty, except for a single thumb drive, hidden in the glass globe of the light fixture. Roberts' guys must've missed it.

The drive contained two folders. The first, which he'd easily cracked open, held a handful of old, mostly redacted case files, both the Nighthawks' and the CIA's. As fascinating as the intel had been, nothing indicated where he might find his mother. He hadn't yet accessed the second folder, heavily encrypted and labeled EYES ONLY, which probably contained classified CIA files that Roberts had stolen when he quit the Agency.

Damon shook his head. "It was empty."

"Have you tried tracking down his old associates?"

"What do you think I'm doing here?" Damon asked.

"How'd you find me, anyway?"

Damon ignored the question. Hayden was careless. He knew enough to put on light disguise before he left the apartment, but he never changed his gait. The way a person walked was as unique as a fingerprint, and Damon had easily located him after hacking into the national CCTV surveillance system database. Every traffic light with a camera, every convenience store with digital security... they all fed into one place. Big Brother was *always* watching. You just had to know where to look. "Why haven't I heard from him?"

"I couldn't say. The only thing I know for sure about Agent Roberts is this: he wants Project Genesis. That's his endgame."

Project Genesis. The reason the Nighthawks recruited Damon in the first place.

Roberts had explained Project Genesis to Damon, probably about two years ago. Genesis was a covert operation, an advanced weapons system currently in development at the CIA, which had been in the making for over two decades. Once completed, it would forever change the arena of war. Basically it served as a GPS for DNA, capable of locating anyone on the planet—provided the Genesis user had a speck of the target's genetic material and access to the millions of sensors being deployed and systemized worldwide. The DNA—a flake of skin, a tiny hair—was entered into the system, analyzed, and the genetic code uploaded to a satellite. The satellite then communicated with the sensors to track the host within a half-mile radius. From that point, a deployed missile would eliminate the target.

If Roberts got his hands on Project Genesis, he'd become the world's deadliest assassin. He'd be able to handpick his enemies and eliminate them one by one, from thousands of miles away.

Damon shook his head. "What does any of that have to do with me? Why would he be holding my mom?"

"Again, I couldn't say."

Anger flashed back through Damon's chest.

Hayden must've seen it on his face, because he held up his hands and said, "Wait a second—just calm down. I might have a lead."

"Talk fast," Damon said.

"You know the bombing last month at that research lab in Northern Virginia?" He paused and Damon nodded. "That's where Genesis is being developed. I'll bet Roberts was behind it."

"Behind the bombing? If he wants the technology so badly, why would he destroy it by blowing up the lab?"

"Not destroy it, steal it. I think it was a break-in."

"Why do you say that?"

"It happened late at night, minimal loss of life, minimal property damage. If he'd wanted to blow up the entire lab, he could've. And if it had been terrorism, it would've happened in the middle of the day at a heavily staffed building, not at a sparsely populated research lab. Project Genesis is well guarded. Even on a fully staffed day, I bet not more than ten people are allowed access to that room."

"Did he succeed? Does Roberts have Genesis?" Damon asked.

"How would I know? As you can see," Hayden gestured around the worn kitchen, "I'm out of the loop. But I'm guessing not, or one of us would already be dead."

That's a good point. Damon rubbed his forehead. "How does this information help me?"

Hayden shrugged. "Maybe you look into Project Genesis?"

"What for?"

"Bargaining chip?"

"Are you proposing that I steal Genesis from a heavily guarded lab that the entire Nighthawks organization, with their unlimited funds and myriad resources, may or may not have found impenetrable? That's your suggestion?" Damon shook his head in frustration. How was this idiot still alive? "You know what, I don't care about Genesis. I don't care about Roberts, or you, or the Nighthawks or the CIA—I just want to find my mom."

"I don't know anything about your mother."

"You're sure?"

"Yeah, I'm sure. Roberts doesn't confide in anyone." Hayden finished his drink and crushed the can, throwing it in the general direction of the sink.

"That's too bad." Damon sighed and put on his gloves. He pulled the 9mm from under his jacket and pointed it across the table. "Because that makes you useless to me."

4 NADIA
SUNDAY, JANUARY 15

Nadia shoved the postcard in her bag as she closed Dean Shepard's door. She heard the whistling before she located its source: a boy her age, standing on a low stack of books with both hands pressed against the wall of windows. He stopped midtune as he noticed her. His sapphire eyes locked onto hers, and he broke into a wide smile, revealing a dimple. Medium height, blond styled hair, broad shoulders with a slim, muscular build. He wore a light-blue fitted tee, a pair of dark jeans, and cowboy boots.

"Hello, love," he said with a crisp British accent.

She returned his smile. "How's it going?"

"Absolutely fantastic. Except I've been summoned to the headmaster's." His voice dropped as he spoke from the side of his mouth. "That never ends well, am I right?" He hopped off the books and gestured toward the window. "You're probably wondering what I'm up to. Curiosity, mostly. Doesn't open, in case you're interested."

Nadia liked him immediately. "Your accent is perfect. Do you do any others?"

"I'm afraid it's the real deal. I'm called Simon." He extended his hand as he walked toward her. "I'm new here. Sort of on exchange from MI-6's training program."

"Nadia." She shook his hand. "Welcome to the Academy."

"Thanks. I actually arrived last week. I came a bit early as it was a particularly good time for me to leave London, if you know what I mean." Simon winked.

Nadia couldn't imagine what that meant. "Sure," she said, nodding along.

"Apparently, I'm replacing some bloke called Damon. I saw his picture." Simon whistled. "The fit ones are always a bit dodgy, am I right?"

She laughed. "I never really thought about it, but I guess so. You're on Jack Felkin's team?"

"That's right."

"That makes us teammates."

"Well that's brilliant. What good luck running into you. I've already met your roommate, the lovely Libby. I think you'll both find I'm quite handy."

"I suspect that's true," Nadia said, glancing toward the window.

Simon followed her gaze and smiled.

She gestured to the hallway. "I'm on my way to Dr. Cameron's, so I've got to run, but it was really nice meeting you."

"The pleasure is mine," he said. "By the by, we're meeting in the student lounge a bit later for takeaway. You'll be there, right?"

"Takeaway?"

"Pizza," Simon said.

"Sounds great. I'll see you there."

"Looking forward to it."

Down the hall, Nadia pushed through the door of the administration building into the warm sun. In front of the lemon trees lining the wall, a small fleet of black Avalons waited in the parking lot. Though recruits weren't allowed their own cars on campus, the school-owned vehicles were available for occasional student use.

At the bottom of the steps she turned right, away from the massive iron gates leading off campus, and followed the sidewalk up the hill. She passed the junior and senior classrooms before reaching the library, a modern glass-and-steel structure near the top of the hill. Beyond that, at the crest, loomed the Navajo

Building, a stone fortress that held the student lounge on the first floor, and the dining hall and outdoor patio on the second.

Across the lawn on the far side of the campus, a flurry of students moved in and out of the dormitories. The girls' dorm, directly across from the library, was closest to the dining hall, followed by the Japanese-style dojo, and at the bottom of the hill, the boys' dorm.

Nadia turned toward the library. A walkway lined with olive trees meandered along the right side of the building. She stepped onto the narrow path and walked under the canopy of gnarled branches and silvery leaves toward the psychiatrist's office.

Inside, Nadia crossed the narrow waiting room and knocked on Dr. Cameron's open door. "Am I interrupting?"

"Nadia, welcome back. Not at all. I've been expecting you. Please, make yourself comfortable." He gestured to the single, cushioned folding chair at the center of the barren room, then grabbed a yellow legal pad and pushed his office door closed. He rolled his leather chair to her side of the desk. Their knees were three feet apart. Nothing between them.

She'd never really noticed that the office door was the *only* exit in the small room. Nadia glanced at the air vent directly over her head. She could easily fit through, but she'd done a little research over break and discovered that crawling through air ducts wasn't actually a viable plan, despite what she'd been led to believe in movies. The thin layer of drywall under the aluminum vent would never hold her weight.

"You seem distracted. Is everything all right?" Dr. Cameron asked.

"Yeah, I'm fine." Nadia tried to measure the paces between her chair and the door.

"Nadia." Dr. Cameron leaned forward. "What's going on?"

"Do you want to know something interesting?"

"Certainly."

Nadia pointed to the floor space between them. "This never used to bother me. You know, the empty space between people."

"And now?"

"I find I'm much more comfortable with a good, solid piece of furniture between me and whoever I'm speaking to."

Dr. Cameron didn't offer to move.

"I guess because of what happened with Dean Wolfe," she said.

"Why don't you tell me about that?" He settled back into his seat.

"We've been over it. Is it necessary to reevaluate the entire event?"

"I'd like to hear your thoughts now that you've had some time to process; some distance from the trauma."

Nadia leaned forward and rested her elbows on her thighs. "The whole thing seems surreal. Like it happened to someone else." She cleared her throat. "The memory seems dulled. Not vivid. The only real difference in my life is my attitude—my sense of...not personal space, exactly. But I find myself looking for escape routes, not sitting with my back to the door, stuff like that."

Dr. Cameron chuckled.

"Is this funny?"

"Not funny, ironic. Dean Wolfe taught you an extremely valuable lesson, one that generally takes years to learn. The things you've mentioned, the reactions you're having, will only serve to make you a better operative. If you continue on to the college-level program—which I strongly urge you to consider—you'll take several classes solely dedicated to increasing your awareness of the environment. Constant vigilance of your surroundings, beyond knowing the number of exits in a room or how many feet to the nearest door. By the time you leave that program, you'll know if a physical threat is present simply by the hunch of a person's shoulders."

She raised an eyebrow. "So being shot was a gift."

"Yes, given the circumstances and the outcome, I would say so."

"Then lucky me." They sat in silence for a few moments. Nadia studied her fingernails, waiting for the psychiatrist's next probe.

"Are you concerned about the Nighthawks seeking retribution?" he asked.

Nadia didn't look up. She wasn't about to confess that three times during the holiday break she could've sworn she'd spotted Damon. Most recently at the Kennedy Center, where she and her parents had attended the ballet. She'd chased his ghost down the stairs, through the lobby, and ended up outside in the courtyard, shivering in her heels and gown, completely alone. She'd been seeing things.

She shook her head. "I'm of no use to them anymore. The only reason I was targeted was because they were trying to frame me as the traitor. Everyone knows it was Damon, so...no, I'm not." After a beat she asked, "Any word on Hayden or Wolfe?"

"Wolfe is still in a coma. He's at a long-term care facility in Tucson. Hayden's whereabouts are unknown."

Nadia hesitated. "And Damon?"

Cameron paused. "We haven't located him yet. But on that subject, what *about* Damon?"

"What do you mean?"

"He's still at large. Are you concerned?"

Nadia shook her head. "I'm actually not worried about Damon at all."

"Can you tell me about that?"

"If he was going to kill me, I'd already be dead. He was *supposed* to kill me, right? And here I am. I don't think he could do it. He and I were pretty close."

"Have you spoken to him?"

"Of course not. This is conjecture. If I'd heard from him, don't you think I would've reported it?"

"I don't know. You just told me how close the two of you were."

"Not so close that I'd commit treason."

Dr. Cameron scribbled a few notes onto his legal pad. "Have you set any personal goals for yourself this semester?"

"I'd love to not get shot."

Dr. Cameron laughed. "Sure, that seems reasonable. Is there anything else you'd care to discuss while you're here?"

"I think I'm all set."

He handed her a clipboard thick with psych tests. "In that case, please take a few minutes and fill these out."

Nadia sighed as she flipped through the pages. The usual tests: multiple choice, short answer, fill-in-the-blanks, true or false. *Love is overrated; I enjoy manipulating other people's feelings; It's okay to steal if you need the item.* "Have there always been so many?"

"You may complete the paperwork in the waiting room. As always, my door is open should anything arise. I'll see you soon." Dr. Cameron stood.

"Thanks," Nadia said as she crossed the room. "I can't wait."

5 SIMON HAWTHORNE
SUNDAY, JANUARY 15

The moment Nadia left the dean's sitting room, Simon Hawthorne plopped into an oversized leather chair and propped his feet up on the coffee table. He checked his watch, sighed loudly, and dropped his head back against the headrest, staring in frustration at the ceiling, which, incidentally, he found devoid of security cameras.

Given his questionable ethics, he'd visited loads of headmasters, but it was never an activity he enjoyed. At this juncture in his life, each hour spent with the principal was wasted time. He had things to do, people to cheat, places to go.

Speaking of places to go.... A week earlier, before checking in at the Academy, Simon had visited the quaint little town of Cave Creek, where he'd had the foresight to secure a postal box for himself. This was a lesson learnt the hard way, after his previous headmaster had confiscated the kilo of aluminum powder that Simon had ordered online. Simon hadn't actually intended to blow anything up, but he firmly believed in planning for all contingencies, which is why he'd ordered the components necessary for the assembly of an improvised explosive device in the first place. The headmaster, however, hadn't been impressed with Simon's preparedness, and had immediately placed him on probation.

Currently, Simon was expecting a package from an old mate back home—nothing special, only a few odds and ends. He wasn't privy to a school-issued vehicle, as his driver's license wasn't entirely valid, so he'd need to make nice with someone who could drive. Perhaps his new roommate, Alan Cohen. A bit peculiar, that one.

When Simon could wait no longer, he crossed the room and rapped on Dean Shepard's closed door. "Simon Hawthorne, madam," he called. "Reporting as instructed."

"Yes, come in," she answered. As he entered, she continued. "I apologize, I forgot you were waiting. Please, have a seat."

Simon resisted the urge to roll his eyes as he settled into one of her wingback leather chairs. He remained silent as she lifted a thick folder from her desk. Reports, assessments, charges filed, written reprimands. Simon had perused the file before. It made for entertaining reading.

"Do you know what this is?" Shepard asked.

"I haven't a clue," Simon lied.

"It's your file," she said. "MI-6 was good enough to forward it after they kicked you out."

"Technically, I wasn't *kicked out* so much as encouraged to pursue an alternate—"

Shepard opened the file. "Petty theft, cheating, identification forgery—"

"I only added a few years to my age, and strictly for the purposes of obtaining a rental car. Rest assured, I made no attempt to purchase liquor."

"Breaking and entering, hacking, kidnapping."

"That last charge was completely unfounded. Stealing a rival mascot should not qualify as kidnapping, especially when it's a hound that I showered with affection. I vehemently object—"

"Renting a flat in the headmaster's name to host parties," she continued.

Simon quietly laughed. "That was brilliant. It took him *months* to figure it out."

The look she shot silenced him immediately.

"I beg your pardon." He cleared his throat. "In retrospect, it's not as funny as I remember."

"Shutting down London's CCTV surveillance system 'just to see if I could.'"

"Did you know that London has one camera to every eleven people? If that's not a violation of privacy, I don't know what is."

Dean Shepard closed the file and dropped it onto her desk. "Do you know why you were invited to Desert Mountain?"

Simon flashed what he hoped was a winning smile. "My magnetic charm and boyish good looks?"

"I'll take that as a 'no.' Let me explain why we agreed to accept you into our program."

"Yes, madam." Simon straightened in his seat. The truth was, he didn't know. He'd assumed some arrangement between the CIA and MI-6: we'll take your derelicts if you take ours. Or maybe his mum had written it into her contract, knowing perfectly well that her son often colored outside the lines, as it were.

Shepard's eyes locked onto his. "As I'm sure you're aware, your mother placed a condition on the acceptance of her last assignment. That condition was that you be admitted to the MI-6 training program. When you were dismissed, the headmaster found your mother unreachable."

Simon remained neutral as Shepard spoke. He'd known his mum was in trouble. She'd missed her last three check-ins. MI-6 refused to send an extraction team; her supervisor had a list of "plausible explanations" as to why she'd failed to make contact. But Simon knew.

"The agency reported her status as Missing in Action," Shepard said.

He'd deliberately gotten himself booted from the MI-6 program, knowing his mum would be forced to return home.

"After several weeks of searching, well...you know."

That's when they'd changed her status to KIA. Killed in Action.

"Which brings us to why you're here. Your mother was a loyal friend to our agency. Decades ago, at great peril to her own life, she assisted the CIA in the exfiltration and relocation of a Syrian asset. The mission was highly controversial, and she saved not only the life of the asset, but also the life of the CIA officer most closely involved. When he found out your mother had gone missing, he checked up on you."

Simon's ears perked up.

Shepard continued. "Your difficulties at the MI-6 training program likely should've deterred him, but apparently his loyalty, like your mother's, runs deep. He insisted that you be admitted to Desert Mountain Academy."

This was him. The one Simon had been looking for. It had to be. He forced an even tone of voice. "May I ask the name of my generous benefactor?"

She shook her head. "I'm afraid I've only heard his code name."

That's a start, thought Simon.

"Which, unfortunately, I'm not at liberty to share. But I know this." The dean held up her right index finger. "This is what that relationship buys you."

"A finger?"

"A semester. *One* semester."

"Ah. That makes more sense."

"I fully expect that your shenanigans are well in the past."

"Worry not," Simon said. "I'd sell out my own mum to stay out of trouble. You know..." He leaned forward. "If she weren't already dead."

Dean Shepard looked down at her lap, then back up at Simon. "We were all very sorry to learn about her death."

Presumed death.

"As I mentioned, she was a great friend to the Agency. And while I sympathize with your loss, I want to be sure we understand each other."

He nodded. "Madam, I'm grateful for the opportunity you've provided." He'd actually been presented with two options: Desert

Mountain Academy or the United States Military Academy at West Point, but even with the military revoking its Don't Ask, Don't Tell policy, Simon didn't imagine he and the Army were a smart match. Furthermore, at West Point he wouldn't stand a chance of success.

Not with his mission.

This was exactly where he needed to be.

6 NADIA
SUNDAY, JANUARY 15

An hour and a half later, Nadia finished the psychological question-naires. She left the clipboard with Dr. Cameron and headed back down the path, through the shady tunnel of trees. As she reached the sidewalk leading up the hill, someone shouted her name.

She turned, searching for the voice. On the second-story patio outside the dining hall, Jack leaned over the railing and waved. Her stomach flipped as she saw him, and an uncontrollable smile spread across her face. They'd texted every day and talked on the phone a few times, but she hadn't seen him in over a month. And he looked *amazing*.

He wore a fitted white button-down, sleeves rolled to the elbows, jeans, boots. His dark hair, cropped in a military style, set off his sun-kissed olive skin. He cupped his mouth and shouted, "Wait there."

He disappeared from view, reappearing a minute later along the side of the Navajo Building. Weeks of missing him—his arms around her, his lips on hers—evaporated as he quickly closed the distance between them.

Before she could speak, he picked her up and spun her around.

Nadia laughed. "Put me down."

He did, then held her at arms' length while his caramel eyes studied her face. "Hi," he said, smiling. "How are you?"

"I'm good," she said, completely unable to remove the ridiculous grin from her face. "How was Zurich?"

"Incredible," he said. "Except that my father was there."

"Well, it was his wedding. How's your new stepmother?"

"Almost old enough to drink."

"You're *kidding*," she said.

"She's twenty-five."

Nadia laughed again. "Oh, that's brutal."

"You have no idea. It's so good to see you."

"You too." They stood in awkward silence for a moment, both trying to contain their grins, until Nadia asked, "Walk me to my dorm?"

"Of course. So, how's Dr. Cameron?"

She tore her eyes away from his face as they started across the lawn. "The usual. Probing, invasive, low-key threatening." She'd meant it as a joke, but it was a fairly accurate assessment. "Have you met the new dean?"

"Only in passing." He glanced at his watch. "Our sit-down is in twenty. She's briefing all team leaders this afternoon. You?"

"Just before I saw Cameron."

"What did you think?"

"I like her. She normally runs The Farm in Virginia, so she trains actual CIA officers. I guess that makes her qualified to supervise a bunch of recruits."

"She's active CIA, not an administrator?"

"Yeah, why? Is that bad?"

"No, it's just..." Jack frowned. "To be honest, I'm a little worried about next year. I need the dean's recommendation to advance to the college-level training program at Langley. I don't expect an easy pass, but her status as an active officer sets the bar really high. And with Wolfe gone, I feel like I'm starting from scratch, you know? I spent three semesters winning *him* over."

"I don't think you need to worry. Your record is impeccable. Plus, her position might be helpful. Since she runs the postgraduate program, her recommendation probably carries a lot more weight than Wolfe's, right?"

He nodded. "That's actually a really good point. I just hope we hit it off. Otherwise, I'm out of options."

"What do you mean?" she asked.

"Money for college. My dad—" Jack shook his head. "It doesn't matter. Here we are."

As they reached her dorm a light breeze picked up, and the soft desert grasses flanking the entrance blew like purple smoke. The architecture of the dorms, with their smooth, adobe-styled exteriors and exposed wooden beams, was Southwestern classic. Discrete modern upgrades—unique to the Academy—included bulletproof glass in the lobby, security cameras in the hallways, and an emergency lockdown button in the resident assistant's room.

Nadia reached for the door handle. "Thanks for the escort."

"Hang on a second." Jack took her arm and led her off the path. He lowered his voice as a few students trickled down the sidewalk. "Over break we talked about giving us another try. Do you want to go out this weekend? Dinner and a movie?"

Nadia hesitated as a flutter passed through her chest. She glanced down the hill toward the guard station. Historically, their timing hadn't been great.

"Before you decide there's something I need to say." He took a deep breath and waited until the students walking by were out of earshot. "There are times in life when we ignore what we know to be true. When we refuse to listen to our gut—to our heart. Last semester, when I investigated you as the double agent, that was one of those times." He took her hands in his. "I will spend every day of this semester proving to you that I have faith in you—that I have faith in us. That is, if you'll let me." He paused and glanced at the ground. "That sounded a lot less melodramatic in my head."

Nadia laughed, flattered by his words. "No, it was perfect." *Just do it—take a chance.* "Yes, of course I'll go out with you. You didn't even need the sales pitch."

He nodded. "So I made that ridiculous speech for nothing?"

"It wasn't for nothing." Her cheeks flushed as she moved back onto the sidewalk.

Jack's hand rested on the door. Nadia leaned against the glass. He moved toward her, tucking a stray curl behind her ear with his free hand.

She had the feeling he was about to kiss her when a group of senior girls emerged from their hallway and entered the lobby. Jack opened the door for them.

As they passed by, Nadia sighed. "I should go. If I don't unpack in the next twenty minutes, Libby won't be able to sleep tonight."

"Okay. I'll see you guys in a little while. But Saturday night, it's just me and you."

"Sounds great."

He smiled at her as he backed away. "And thank you for giving us another chance. I promise it'll be different this time."

7 JACK FELKIN
SUNDAY, JANUARY 15

Jack Felkin had been ready to return to school almost from the moment he'd left for winter break. After last semester's epic failure, he was eager to reestablish himself as a competent recruit. Just as important, he wanted to prove himself to Nadia, to show her how much she meant to him. But what really drove his desire to return: he absolutely loved the work, and this upcoming meeting with Dean Shepard was critical to his future.

After a quick stop at his dorm to change into something more formal, Jack headed across the lawn to Hopi Hall. He arrived with five minutes to spare, so he took a seat in the waiting room, straightened his tie, and tried to look relaxed.

Over break Jack's father had made clear that unless he chose to pursue medicine, Jack was on his own. The covert nature of the Academy dictated that Jack couldn't divulge the true nature of his studies, but even if he could, his dad—a renowned vascular surgeon—thought doctors were godlike, and everyone else peons. Jack would need to secure an invitation to continue on with the CIA at the university level, and he had very little time to make an impression on the new Dean of Students.

One problem at a time, he reminded himself.

A few minutes later, Shepard's door opened. Jack crossed the sitting room as his roommate, Noah, emerged from the dean's office holding a large envelope.

"How'd it go?" Jack asked quietly.

Noah made the gesture of a knife slicing across his throat. "She said to go on in. Good luck, man."

Jack's stomach tightened as he knocked on the open office door. "Noah said you were ready for me?"

"Please, come in." She waited for him to close the door and take a seat. "I'm looking forward to working with you, Jack. I've heard good things."

"Thank you. The honor is mine."

Dean Shepard wasted no time. "This semester, I'm implementing a new program. Each team leader will complete a Senior Project, a simulated operation, designed by active CIA officers. You will execute a series of mock missions, running your juniors as your agents." She opened her bottom drawer, and then dropped a thick manila envelope labeled OPERATIONAL SPECIFICATIONS: JACK FELKIN onto her desk. "These are your op-specs. Treat this as an eyes-only document; share it with no one. No one on your team should have a complete picture of your endgame. Your general goals are listed in the Objectives section; you may design and execute the individual missions as you see fit, but individual op-specs are, again, eyes-only. For the purposes of this assignment, I am your handler. If you have any questions, bring them to me. You are to discuss the mission with no one else, understood?"

"Yes ma'am." He suppressed his smile—he couldn't wait to examine the file, to design his missions. Shepard was the real deal.

"You have seven weeks to complete your project. Keep in mind that your graduation is contingent upon successful completion of these missions. Any questions?"

"What about seniors who weren't chosen as team leaders? Will they be running missions with…agents?" Only a select number of seniors held the honor of team leader, and Jack didn't like the idea of his juniors learning bad habits from second-rate students.

Dean Shepard leaned forward and folded her hands on her desk. After a moment she said, "Naturally, I wish them every success, but their ability to run missions does not interest me. Their Senior Projects are not contingent on subordinate participation. So the short answer is no, they are not running agents."

His heart skipped. *She's actively looking for recruits for the college program.* "If I may, are you planning to return to Langley after this semester?"

"I am."

Jack smiled. "I'm sure I speak for everyone when I say we're very lucky that you were available."

"Thank you. It's an interesting change of pace for me, as well. Do you have any other questions?"

"I don't think so."

"Okay, then let's meet again in a few days when we're not so rushed. At that time I'll expect an assessment of each member of your team."

"Yes ma'am. I'll schedule with Ms. McGill on my way out." He stood and extended his hand. "Thank you for your time."

Shepard smiled. "My pleasure. I'll see you soon."

After stopping by Ms. McGill's cramped office just off the lobby, Jack raced outside into the fading afternoon light. He fought the urge to rip open the sealed op-specs right there on the lawn, and instead kept a brisk pace as he cut across campus to his dorm.

Back in his room, Jack locked the door and sat at his desk. He grinned and sliced open the envelope.

OPERATIONAL SPECIFICATIONS:
OPERATION ROYAL
HANDLING OFFICER: Jack Felkin, Senior Trainee
AGENTS: (temporary code names to be assigned by handling officer)
HISTORY: Last year, the CIA discovered that a top informant was acting against our interests

as a double agent. He was taken into CIA custody for ongoing questioning at an undisclosed location. After his arrest, his wife and child were admitted to the Witness Protection Program (WITSEC) in exchange for the wife's testimony against him. The child (age four) has an ongoing medical condition that requires frequent visits to the hospital for blood work.

COMPLICATION: Due to the vulnerable nature of online medical databases, records of the informant's DNA potentially may be accessible to hostiles, who could then find a link to the child. As the CIA has concerns for the child's safety, additional security measures must be taken.

MISSION: Reassign the genome sequence (DNA profile) of the child's biological father to a deceased CIA officer.

OBJECTIVE: Protection of a minor; maintaining integrity of WITSEC program.

DETAILS: The CIA has chosen a suitable candidate to pose as the child's father: a CIA officer who died with honors in the line of service and has no known family. Your mission is to exchange the DNA profile of the biological father with that of the deceased agent. As a result of the DNA exchange, the child will be hidden from the informant's associates. Further, should the child later look into his or her family history, he or she will not be able to trace the biological father to renew contact.

SPECIFIC OP-SPECS: See enclosed. To be opened only by acting agent as needed. Not to be read by control.

The folder contained five sealed and numbered envelopes, along with a USB drive and SD memory card. Jack flipped through the remaining pages: operational protocols, comms specs, code words and call signs, instructions for completing the written reports that would summarize each mission. After his initial disappointment that he wouldn't get to read the individual op-specs, he felt a flutter of excitement in his chest. He'd still get to design the technical specs and supervise his agents.

This was it—his chance to prove himself to Dean Shepard, to secure his future. His chance to serve his country, to do something meaningful with his life.

His chance to become a full-fledged member of the Black-Ops Division of the CIA.

8 NADIA
SUNDAY, JANUARY 15

After she and Jack parted, Nadia negotiated through the cluster of girls lingering in the dorm lobby.

Parked next to the sofa across from the resident assistant's desk, she found a rolling refreshments cart, piled with stacks of mugs and an urn of hot cocoa. She grabbed a few biscotti from the open jar and continued down the carpeted hall to her room.

Nadia had just slid her key into the lock when her roommate pulled open the door.

"I thought I heard you!" Libby's Southern accent, especially strong when she got excited, thickly laced her words. "Come here!" She threw her arms around Nadia. Her blond hair, perfectly straightened, smelled like summer peaches.

Nadia grinned and hugged back. "I missed you so much."

"Oh my goodness, me too. Come inside, tell me everything." Libby pulled her across the threshold and shut the door. "How are your parents? Did you see your old friends? How's your wound— has it healed?"

Nadia laughed as she moved farther into the bedroom, immaculate as always. The twin beds, dressed in matching earth-toned duvets, were already made, complete with throw pillows arranged along the headboards. Fresh vacuum tracks lined the cream-colored wool shag between the beds, and the chocolate silk curtains looked recently pressed. "You've already cleaned?" Nadia peeked through the bathroom door. A vase of white lilies resting on the marble counter scented the air.

"'Course I have."

"Why, what's wrong?" Nadia turned to her roommate. Most of the time, Libby's mild case of obsessive-compulsive disorder only served to make her a better recruit, but when she got particularly stressed, her OCD kicked into overdrive.

"Nothing. I'm so excited to be back. I just wanted everything to look perfect so we could start the semester fresh, you know? It's the end of our junior year. This was happy cleaning, not stress cleaning." Libby gestured toward Nadia's closet. "Your bags arrived, so I took the liberty of unpacking. I know it's not your favorite activity."

Nadia crossed the room to the far side of her desk and opened her closet. Libby had arranged her clothes by color, each hanger equal distance apart. "It looks amazing. Thank you." She dropped her bag on her desk chair and grabbed the postcard out of the side pocket to use as a plate for the biscotti. Libby didn't like crumbs. Nadia put the cookies on the Hawaiian Islands, then sat on the edge of her bed. "How's your mom doing?"

Libby wrinkled her nose. "Is that a postcard?"

"Yeah, why? It's not from you, is it?"

"No." She moved to Nadia's side and peered at the biscotti. "You can't eat these now. You know that, right? Who knows how many hands touched that piece of mail." Libby grabbed the small trash can from between their beds. "I'll just toss these." She slid the cookies into the trash and put the card back on the desk, and then sat across from Nadia on her own bed. "I'm sorry, what were we talking about?"

"Your mom."

Libby's face brightened. "She's doing well, thank you for asking. She was discharged from the spa a few weeks ago. Still sober, knock on wood." She tapped on her nightstand.

"You don't have to call it a spa for my benefit, you know." Nadia lowered her voice. "There's no shame in going to rehab."

Libby smiled and met Nadia's eyes. "*Spa*, Nadia. That's the official party line."

"Got it. And how is the senator?"

"Daddy's fine, as usual. He promised to spend less time in Washington and more time in Georgia, at least till Momma gets back into her routine. That took some arguing on my brother's part, but Daddy finally came around." Libby waved her hand. "Enough about me. What about you? How are your parents?"

"My dad's at a convention in Las Vegas, so my mom's probably enjoying the quiet." Nadia scooted back against the wall. "You know, I had all these lies prepared about our classes and the curriculum. I was certain they'd grill me about school over break, but they didn't ask a lot of questions, which is totally not like my mother."

"That's a relief, huh? Fewer lies to tell?"

"Yeah, definitely. It's exhausting weighing every word that comes out of my mouth." Nadia shrugged. "But I guess that's the nature of black-ops."

Libby glanced at the clock on her nightstand. "Oh, shoot—we're due in the lounge any minute now. Do you want to change out of your traveling clothes?" She nodded as she asked the question.

Nadia smiled at her roommate's not-so-subtle suggestion. "Yes, I guess I do," she said, climbing off the bed.

"Wait till you meet our new teammate, Simon. He's absolutely adorable, but I'm pretty sure he's gay."

"We already met. And I think you're right." From her closet, Nadia grabbed the sweater closest to her, a cotton pullover in cobalt blue.

Libby went into the bathroom to freshen up, chatting through the open door. "How's everything with Jack?"

Her cheeks warmed as she thought about him. "Fantastic. We texted a lot over break, and we're going out this weekend." She pulled the sweater over her head and turned to the mirror inside the closet door.

Nadia was Irish on her father's side and Lebanese on her mother's. She had his light eyes, and her mother's dark hair and olive complexion. While Libby made a constant effort to always look her best, Nadia barely remembered to run her fingers through her thick waves once or twice a week. But now, for Libby's sake, Nadia pulled her hair into a bun at the crown of her head, as neatly as she could.

"It's about time," Libby said, joining Nadia in the bedroom. She'd reapplied her candy-apple red lipstick and wrapped a turquoise scarf around her neck, which turned her eyes a clear blue, the color of an iceberg. "You two just couldn't get it together last semester." She grabbed a neatly wrapped present from her desk and straightened the satin ribbon before slipping it into her shoulder bag.

"What's that?" Nadia asked.

"Oh, just a thank-you gift for Alan."

"Seriously? What for?" Alan rarely did anything worthy of a verbal thank-you, much less a gift.

"The present he sent me over break. Didn't you get one?" Libby asked.

Nadia smiled. "I did not. But I'm dying of curiosity."

Libby shook her head as her brows pulled together. "It was the strangest thing."

Nadia followed her roommate into the hall and pulled shut their bedroom door.

9 LIBBY BISHOP
SUNDAY, JANUARY 15

Liberty Grace Bishop, eager for a little peace and quiet, had returned to school a day earlier than required. She'd told her parents she wanted plenty of time to get her room set up before classes started, but the truth was she needed a break from the drama. Her momma, freshly back from rehab, wandered around the house talking about how was she supposed to attend all those dreadfully dull fundraisers without a drink in her hand. Her daddy had spent the past month locked in hushed meetings behind closed doors. Every so often he'd start yelling at his advisors, his deep voice thundering through the walls.

Comparatively speaking, training for the CIA was a cakewalk.

As the girls left their room and headed up the hallway, Libby was struck by a double pang of guilt. First, for thinking ill of her parents, and second, for not being completely forthcoming with Nadia. Libby hadn't exactly lied; she'd just omitted certain details. But honestly, there was no sense in rehashing unpleasantries. The Bishops looked good on the outside, and that was all that mattered.

Libby frowned as they reached the lobby. She loved her family more than anything, but there wasn't a lot of room for her in her parents' world. Both of them commanded center stage, which was fine—Libby didn't need to be the center of attention. But she would occasionally like to focus on her own life.

None of that matters right now, she thought, relaxing her features into a pleasant smile. She was back at school, rooming with her best friend, learning about things that had nothing to do with either of her parents.

Libby opened the lobby door by leaning against it, then followed Nadia into the cool evening air. Streaks of orange and pink clung to the bottom of the indigo sky. A sense of calm settled in her chest as she said, "I'm so glad to be back."

"Yeah, me too," Nadia said, returning Libby's smile.

The girls turned away from the distant lights of Phoenix, which twinkled inside the darkening valley, and headed up the hill toward the student lounge, situated underneath the dining hall. The giant saguaro at the base of the Navajo Building extended its silhouetted arms toward the first stars of the night.

"Have you seen Noah yet?" Nadia asked.

Noah was Jack's roommate, and Libby'd had an awful crush on him last semester. She shook her head. "Not yet, but I'm looking forward to it."

As they reached the Navajo Building, Nadia pulled open the door and said, "Maybe we can go on a double date?"

Inside the empty lounge, slipcovered sofas and overstuffed leather chairs formed a half circle around the massive flat-screen mounted on the wall. A bare dining table sat to the left. After inspecting the surface for crumbs, Libby placed her shoulder bag on the table.

"Can you find a music station?" Nadia asked, nodding toward the television.

Libby wrapped a tissue over the remote and turned on the TV. Before she had a chance to flip from the news, the lounge door opened behind them.

"Am I glad to see you two," Alan said.

"Alan!" Libby circled the sofa to give him a hug. Her arms easily fit around his slim frame. "How are you? I brought you a little something." She reached into her bag and withdrew his gift. "All the way from Savannah."

Alan's face turned a splotchy red, exaggerating the fact that his eyes and hair were the exact same color of hazel brown. "How considerate. I am certain that upon opening the gift, I will be delighted."

Libby smiled at his formality as Nadia squeezed between them for a hug.

"How was your holiday?" Nadia asked.

"Long and dull. I cannot believe this, but I am almost happy to be back." Alan flopped down on the sofa. "What is this? Why are we watching the news? These reporters are extremely biased. You would be wise to gather your information online, where you can choose from whom you wish to—" He stopped midsentence as a high-pitched tone from the TV drowned out his words.

The picture went black for a second before the network's logo appeared, then a *Breaking News* banner scrolled across the bottom of the screen. Nadia turned up the volume.

The lounge door swung open and Simon walked in, carrying three large pizza boxes, with Jack trailing behind him. "Who's hungry?"

"Hang on," Libby said. "Something's happened."

Simon set the pizzas on the table as he and Jack joined the rest of the team.

The anchorwoman came on screen. "We've just received new information regarding last month's explosion at a research facility in Northern Virginia. The FBI now believes that the deliberate bombing was orchestrated by a group of domestic terrorists. As a reminder, the fatal explosion claimed two lives. Originally ruled an accident by the authorities, an investigation into the source of the explosion quickly revealed foul play."

"Oh yeah. We heard about this in London," Simon said.

The report continued with the anchorwoman speaking remotely to the FBI's lead investigator. A minute into it, she cut him off. "Sir, I apologize." His image disappeared from the screen as the cameraman centered the anchor. "I'm being told that Senator Wentworth Bishop of Georgia has an announcement. We're going live to the steps of the Capitol."

Libby held her breath. What on earth could her daddy possibly have to say about this? And why was he in Washington?

The camera cut away to the Capitol building, where he stood atop the windy steps surrounded by his entourage. Floodlights lit the scene.

Alan turned to Libby. "Hey, isn't that your—"

"Shh," Jack said.

Her daddy spoke into the camera. "The frequency of domestic terrorism has reached epic proportions. We are no longer safe within our own borders. The American people should not have to live in fear for their lives, for the safety of their children's lives. These attacks on our freedom, on our civil liberties, on our way of life *must stop now*." He pounded the podium in time with the last three words. "And I'm referring to the fight against enemies both foreign *and* domestic. Rogue fringe groups who wrap themselves in the flag and choose to ignore our democratic process. Whether they be lone gunmen or highly organized groups of ex-military and ex-government. Mark my words." He paused and looked dead at the camera. "Your day has come to an end." The small crowd exploded with applause.

I wonder if anyone else thinks it odd that he had time to set up a podium.

He continued. "I have fought against our enemies from inside the Senate, but after uncovering the truth about this latest attack, I feel compelled to take further action. That is why," he hesitated for one of his dramatic pauses, "I am proud to announce my decision to run for President of these United States!"

Libby's heart dropped as the crowd went wild. She felt like the wind had been knocked out of her.

She'd never admit it out loud, but this was devastating news. Beyond devastating—he'd basically just tossed her future out the window. Dean Shepard wouldn't let her stay at the Academy. Between Secret Service agents and the media attention, there was no way the school could remain clandestine.

He's so selfish.

The thought brought a fresh wave of guilt. Of course Libby loved her daddy, and if this was what he wanted, she would do whatever necessary to support him. He didn't know Desert Mountain was run by the CIA; it's not like he deliberately set out to ruin her life. But what about her momma? How would she deal with being in the spotlight right now?

She felt her friends watching for her reaction. She must've looked concerned, because Nadia reached for her hand. Libby faked a smile and said, "My goodness. This is exciting!"

Jack touched her shoulder. "Did you know about this?"

"There was some talk," Libby said cheerfully.

"Do you mean to say—is that your dad then?" Simon asked. "I didn't make the connection. That's brilliant timing on his part."

"Indeed," Libby said.

"This will certainly affect your standing as a recruit." Alan said. "How can the first daughter serve in the Black-Ops Division?"

"Alan." Nadia shook her head.

Libby flashed another big smile and shrugged. "Wouldn't I rather live in the White House anyway? I have my whole life ahead of me. My daddy's been working toward this his entire career. I'm so proud of him!" Tears stung her eyes. Her voice sounded erratic, desperate. She couldn't seem to catch her breath.

"Seriously, though, what about the CIA?" Alan asked.

"I'm gonna go to the dorm and call home. Say congratulations." Libby lowered her voice but maintained her smile as she turned to Nadia. "Gimme half an hour?"

Her roommate nodded. "Of course."

"Why must she wait? The phone is in the lobby," Alan said.

"Oi, mate," Simon said quietly. "Not now."

Alan shook his head, confused. "What? I do not—"

"Wait a second," Jack said, nodding toward the television. "I don't think he's finished."

Someone in the audience shouted out a question. "Senator Bishop, who committed this latest act of terror?"

A hush fell over the crowd and her daddy looked right at the cameras. "I have reason to believe that this heinous crime was executed by an alliance of former CIA and ex-military special forces known as the Nighthawks." Libby's heart skipped a beat. "An anonymous source at the CIA has confirmed that certain branches of our intelligence services have been compromised by these traitors at the foundational level—as recruits at the beginning of training. That infiltration ends *now*."

The crowd cheered as the camera swung to the correspondent on site. The newswoman, bundled in a winter coat and scarf, tucked her blowing hair behind her ear. "Thanks to the tireless investigative work spearheaded by Senator Bishop, the American people might finally learn the truth. Live from the Capitol, this is channel ten news."

Libby's breath caught in her throat. Four pairs of eyes burned her face as everyone turned from the television. She could've heard a pin drop.

Jack took a long breath. "What *exactly* did you tell your dad about DMA?"

"I didn't tell him anything," Libby said, looking from Jack to Nadia and back again. "It wasn't me."

"What about your laptop?" Jack asked. "Did he maybe see something he shouldn't have?"

"Of course not," Libby answered. "Security scrubbed my laptop before break, just like everyone else's. I swear on my life, I'm not his source."

Jack's jaw tightened. "Then who is?"

"I have no idea." Libby wanted to say more, to defend herself against his unjust accusations, but what more could she say? She didn't know anything.

Nadia touched Jack's arm. "If she says it's not her, then it's not her."

"He's bound to have connections at his level of government, right, mate?" Simon asked. "He said, 'an anonymous source inside the CIA.'"

"Yeah," Libby agreed. "He knows everybody. He sits on the

Intelligence Committee, he golfs with the Secretary of State, he could've heard about this anywhere." She gestured to the television. "The reporter said he spearheaded the whole investigation—that had nothing to do with me."

Jack shook his head. "This school is completely off-books. Only the highest ranking CIA black-ops officers have clearance to know about the Academy, and none of them would leak intel to a politician. Your father specifically mentioned a traitor—a double agent—at the training level. He's obviously referring to Damon." He locked onto her eyes. "Did you say *anything* about Damon when you were home? Anything at all?"

"No, nothing." Libby felt the heat rise to her face. "I didn't even mention his name."

"Then how does he know about the Nighthawks? How does he know one of our recruits was a double agent?"

"I—I don't know. I swear to you, I didn't say anything. I would *never* say anything."

Jack turned away, like he couldn't even look at her. "Well, he obviously found out from someone."

Libby's eyes stung. What did that mean? Was he accusing her of lying?

She felt a hollowness inside as she realized that Jack's opinion didn't really matter.

After tonight, the administration would never let her stay.

10 NADIA
MONDAY, JANUARY 16

At 5:55 on Monday morning, Nadia's alarm blasted to life. She groaned and pulled her covers over her head. "Turn it off."

"Rise and shine," Libby said cheerfully.

Nadia emerged from the blankets and sat up. "How are you feeling?"

Libby switched on her bedside light. "Much better, thank you. Thanks for talking me off the ledge."

Nadia smiled. "It wasn't that bad." Last night when Nadia returned from the lounge, Libby had pretended to be okay, but Nadia could tell she'd been crying. After a little coaxing, they'd ended up talking for a few hours. Libby was terrified she'd be forced to leave the Academy. At least Nadia had convinced her that Jack didn't think she was a traitor.

Libby got up and immediately made her bed. "Lemme just brush my teeth," she said, closing the bathroom door behind her.

Nadia forced herself out of her warm bed and into her *gi*, the martial arts uniform required at the dojo. In a few days, her body would sync back into the rhythm of predawn workouts, but this morning, not so much.

After securing her hair into a messy bun, she and Libby rushed next door to the dojo. A faint, white sheen of frost covered the lawn. Before they entered, they slipped off their shoes and lined them up with all the others along the wall, then slid open the *shoji*, the bamboo-and-rice-paper doors.

Her mentor, Hashimoto Sensei, waited in the lobby. He was compact and powerful, with a neatly trimmed goatee that matched the salt-and-pepper of his cropped hair.

Nadia grinned and bowed. "Good morning, Hashimoto Sensei."

"Good morning, Sensei," Libby said, bowing.

"Libby-san, Nadia-san, welcome back. Find your place on the mat so that lessons may begin."

To their right, the polished bamboo floors of the long hallway led them to the main room of the dojo, a large, open space lined with blue mats. Much of the junior class had already arrived, but Nadia and Libby found spaces together toward the front. Simon moved up to join them, dragging Alan along.

A few minutes later, Sensei entered the room. The students drew to attention as he strode to the front. As Nadia waited for his instruction, she realized this was the first time in weeks she hadn't felt the need to look over her shoulder. Whether it was Sensei's presence or the familiar safety of the dojo, she couldn't say.

His dark eyes studied the class for a moment. "One hundred snap kicks. *Hajime!* Begin!"

The students counted off in Japanese as Sensei circled the room, assessing their form. After snap kicks came jumping jacks, then sit-ups, push-ups, and blocking drills. Twenty minutes in, Nadia realized that her stamina was still on winter break. A brutal hour later, he ordered the students to sit *seiza* on the mat. The juniors moved as one body, kneeling together, then resting back onto their heels.

Sensei resumed his place at the front. "Dean Shepard has implemented several new programs in the curriculum. This semester you begin specializations. These lessons will be provided in addition to basic coursework. Specializations include, but are not limited to, the study of forensics, field medicine, cryptography, communications, cybersecurity, analysis, and so on. In order to keep field teams small, you will each be assigned multiple specializations. Your specializations have been selected based on previous testing—your standardized scores, personal aptitude tests, and Dr. Cameron's assessments. Before you leave, pick up your individualized assignment card with me."

Simon called out, "Can I train as an assassin?"

The few laughs he received were quickly silenced by Sensei's posture. "The CIA does not engage in wetworks, or assassinations, so I am afraid you will be forced to develop skills of the intellectual variety."

"But what if I'm attacked?" Simon asked.

Sensei circled the room. "Simon-san, you are new to our program. Please be advised I do not encourage questions; I will tell you what you need to know. Furthermore, do not disrupt my lessons by shouting out comments." Hands clasped behind him, he strolled back to the front of the room. "Having said that, it is quite likely that at some point in your life, you will be attacked. If your life is ever in danger, you must use necessary force. To succeed, you must first know how to *administer* necessary force. Your fellow students spent last semester learning self-defense, weaponry, and survival skills. We continue that training this semester. But we do not employ a 'kill-squad.' No one is tasked as an assassin."

"What a shame," Simon muttered. Nadia shot him a look. Sensei really didn't care for interruptions.

"Additionally, the new administration has created a Senior Project for each of your team leaders. These projects require your participation. Be advised, your leader's graduation rests on successful completion of these missions. Treat these assignments with the respect and diligence you would any instructor-assigned project. Do you understand?"

Simon's arm lifted toward the air and Nadia elbowed him. "It's rhetorical," she whispered. He dropped his hand.

"Lastly," Sensei said. "Dean Shepard will begin issuing survival course orders in the next few days, so be alert for your notice. That is all. See me in the lobby for your cards before your morning run."

As they joined the long line of students waiting to see Sensei, Simon asked, "What's this about a run? Isn't it nap time yet?"

"How did you train for MI-6?" Alan asked. "Video games?"

"Like you're such an athlete," he answered.

"You boys be nice," Libby said. She turned to Simon. "We have to run a few miles as part of our morning drill. The trails are cut through the desert on the far side of the wall surrounding campus. The scenery's gorgeous."

"Brilliant. I'll try to have a look as I'm puking up this morning's latte," Simon answered.

Nadia laughed. "Right? I'm so out of shape." Though she'd resumed her exercises as soon as possible, she obviously hadn't pushed herself hard enough. Her arms still felt shaky from the push-ups.

"Are we required to endure this torture every day?" Simon asked.

"No, of course not. Only Monday through Friday," Libby answered. "These exercises are considered our warm-ups. We have physical education on Tuesdays and Thursdays. That's when we'll do archery, ground fighting, target practice, things of that nature."

The team moved farther down the hall.

"And the survival course?" Simon asked.

Alan said, "It is the Academy's way of weeding out the weak. They send us into the desert to die."

"Don't tell him that," Libby chided.

"It's not that bad," Nadia said. "It's like camping. With lots of hiking. And the constant threat of death."

Simon nodded. "Sounds like a weekend back home with my mates."

They reached the front of the line.

"Alan-san," Sensei said, handing Alan a three-by-five index card.

Alan glanced at his assignment. "Comms specialist? Is this a joke?"

"This does not mean mastering the art of interpersonal communication," Sensei said. "You will be trained in communications technology." He pointed to his ear. "Comms between agents in the field and those at headquarters."

Alan nodded. "I see. I also received language and translation. That seems a more prudent match."

"Please move along," Sensei answered. He handed Simon and Libby their cards, but paused before releasing Nadia's. "Nadia-san, you performed well this morning."

She bowed her head. "Thank you."

"I am pleased with your progress. Perhaps we will wait to resume our private lessons, and then, only if necessary. Your specialized training will keep you busy." He released her card.

Sensei had been generous with his time last semester, meeting her before sunrise to provide individual instruction. She was grateful, but it had been a lot of extra work. Though she cherished their relationship, part of her was relieved. Nadia bowed at the waist. *"Arigato."* She straightened.

He returned her bow. "Move along."

Nadia caught up with her team outside the dojo. They walked together toward the back gate leading off campus.

"What did you get?" Nadia asked Libby.

"Forensics and advanced diplomacy. How about you?"

Nadia read her card. "Field medicine and cryptography. Simon?"

Simon glanced at his card. "Site-specific entry, which I believe is breaking and entering, and document specialist. I think that's a nice way of saying forgery." He chuckled.

"What is funny about that?" Alan asked.

Nadia said, "I'm guessing Simon's criminal reputation precedes him. Am I right?"

Simon grinned. "On the nose, love. On the nose."

After the two-mile run, quick showers, and breakfast, the girls swung by the dorm to pick up their backpacks. As Nadia closed their bedroom door, Libby turned to her and winced. "I have to tell you something."

"What's wrong?"

"This morning while you were in the shower I went to the lobby for a cup of tea. It was really full, and when I got back to the room it sloshed onto my hand. Obviously, it burned, so I had to set the mug down, but I didn't want to put it directly on the furniture, because you know how hard those white rings are to get out, right? I mean, they say mayonnaise does the trick, but it's simply not true." Libby handed Nadia the postcard from Hawaii. "Anyway, I'm so sorry, but I used this as a coaster and I'm afraid I spilled."

Nadia took the card. "That's it?" Leave it to Libby to feel bad about damaging a piece of paper. "It's no big deal. I don't even know who sent it—I'd forgotten all about it. I meant to ask Jack and Alan."

"I really am sorry."

"Seriously, it's totally fine."

"Thank you. I'll just freshen up and we can go." Libby went into the bathroom and shut the door.

Nadia sat at her desk and studied the illustrated islands, then flipped the card over. Libby's tea had blurred the word *Aloha*. The circumference of the mug remained imprinted on the card in a brownish ring. Perfect half circles over the address, over the hand-written message, but at the center, the circle came together oddly, like two half-moons smushed together. The tea had pooled in the middle of the card, gathering along the blue line separating the address box from the message box.

Why is there a seam in the center of a postcard?

Nadia held the card at eye level and examined the horizontal profile. The card stock felt thicker than it should. She bent it into an arch, first folding the written portion together, then the other way, so that the picture sandwiched itself. The pressure forced the card to reveal its secret: it was comprised of two layers. The top layer gave gently at the upper edge of the center seam.

She pulled a letter opener from the pencil holder on her desk, laid the postcard flat, and sliced down the center. She bent the card again and used her thumb to peel off the top layer. Written underneath she discovered a code. A series of numbers: 125.793.4, 51.805.1, 51.792.7, 360.591.5 // 46.599.4, 95.475.7, 112.329.9 // 138.106.3, 104.16.6, 95.475.7, 183.265.7, 116.446.4, 357.493.9; and so on.

Immediately, Nadia recognized the pattern as that of a book cipher: page number, followed by the line, and then word number. The first set indicated page 125, line 793, word number 4. But that couldn't be right; none of her books had eight hundred lines on a page. She glanced at the bookshelf mounted above her desk. Even her largest textbook didn't have more than seventy lines per page.

She tried subtracting every other set from the previous one; that didn't work. She substituted letters for the numbers and got nothing. She reversed the sets, combined them, added, multiplied, divided....It made no sense.

The bathroom door opened, and Nadia flipped the postcard picture-side up.

"What's the matter?" Libby asked.

"Nothing. Why?"

"You're scowling. You'll get wrinkles if you're not careful." Libby gestured to her forehead.

Nadia smiled. "Perish the thought." She slid the postcard into the top drawer of her desk. As much as she loved ciphers, wasting time on a mysterious code probably wasn't the smartest way to start the semester.

"You ready?" Libby asked, opening the door.

"I'm right behind you." Nadia followed her roommate into the hall. On the other hand, maybe it was an assignment? "Hang on a sec." She dashed back inside, grabbed the postcard from the drawer, and stuck it into her bag.

Either way—assignment or mysterious message—she had yet to meet a code she couldn't crack.

11 ALAN COHEN
MONDAY, JANUARY 16

Alan Cohen sat on the edge of his hastily made bed and glared across the room. Once again, fate had spent her free time mocking him. This time, in the shape of an Englishman. A noisy, handsome, charming competitor; as though Alan needed another challenge.

He rolled his eyes. And who had ever heard of an exchange program for spies? This especially bothered him about his new roommate, because if anyone found out the truth about Alan's family, he would be arrested. It was unfair that Simon was allowed ties to another country's intelligence program but Alan was not. It was not Alan's fault that his grandfather, his *saba*, worked for Mossad. He should not be discriminated against because of his ancestors' lineage, while a non-American was freely allowed to attend Desert Mountain Academy. Were the English more trust-worthy than the Israelis?

But his objections to Simon did not end with his country of origin.

Alan had left for holiday break with the distinct impression that he and Libby had shared a spark. She practically carried him to the hospital after he had been shot. However, over break, she behaved as though nothing had transpired between them, barely even returning his infrequent (but carefully constructed) text messages. But then last night she had given him a present, and it was not difficult to decipher the hidden meaning behind the gift, even for Alan, who tended to be rather oblivious to such things, so he had assumed she felt the same way he did. Until she began flirting with Simon during morning exercises.

Alan generally did not notice the subtle innuendos exchanged between the sexes, but when Libby had asked, "Isn't Simon just the most adorable thing you've ever seen?" he had deduced that she found their new teammate appealing, though he could not for the life of him ascertain why, as Simon was clearly a hooligan.

The instant Simon turned off the shower, Alan moved from his bed and began talking at the bathroom door. "We need to discuss something."

The door flew open, startling Alan.

"What'd you say?" Simon waltzed into the bedroom with a towel wrapped around his waist. "I can't hear a bloody thing over the extractor fan." He reached into the bathroom and flipped the switch.

"No, leave it on or the room will be too humid," Alan said. "I was saying that I understand you are new, and so you could not possibly have this information, but Libby and I are kind of...*good* friends."

"Is that right then?" Simon asked, eyebrows raised.

"It is."

Simon rubbed his wet hair with a hand towel. "Well, I have to say, mate, I really had no idea." He paused, squinted off to the side, then shook his head. "No. No, I don't see it." He returned to the bathroom.

As usual, the conversation was not going as Alan had hoped. "Nevertheless, I trust you will honor the code."

Simon leaned his head out. "The code? What code is that?"

"You know. The thing about brothers. Not moving in on my girl." Alan's face warmed; he knew it must be bright pink by now. He should not have tried the expression *my girl*.

Simon stepped back into the bedroom. He looked rather amused. "Your girl? So you're more than good friends?"

"We are moving in that direction."

"Let me ask you something." Simon sat on the edge of his bed, which he had not bothered to make. "Have you in any way whatsoever indicated these feelings to Libby?"

"Of course I have."

"How?"

Alan glanced down at the floor, then back up at his roommate. Why did Simon insist on putting him on the spot? "I sent her a gift. You know, over break."

"Something romantic then?"

Alan nodded. "Naturally."

"What was it?" Simon cocked his head to the side.

"What was the gift? Well, you know."

"I really don't. Jewelry? Flowers? Chocolates?"

What did it matter? Alan cleared his throat. "Pears."

Simon's eyes brightened as he leaned forward. "I'm sorry, did you say *pears*?"

"Yes, pears. I sent her a box of holiday pears."

"Pears," Simon repeated. He stood and went back toward the bathroom. As he passed, he mumbled, "Well, that's quite extraordinary."

"So we have a deal?" Alan called after him.

He heard Simon laugh. "No worries, mate. She's not at all my type."

It took less than four hours for Simon to break his word.

After third period the students were given a short respite, and Alan's team had gone to the dining hall for refreshments. Now at the conclusion of break, Simon was escorting Libby to their fourth class, political science, while Alan trailed miserably behind. Libby was doing that thing where she laughed too loudly and touched his arm too much.

Alan lagged for a moment to let Nadia catch up. "Can I ask you something?"

"Of course," she said.

He matched her pace, which was rather brisk for such a small-framed person. "Am I crazy, or is there a hidden message in a jar of honey?"

"First of all, those are two separate and distinct questions," Nadia said. "Secondly, what do you mean a hidden message? Like a fortune cookie?"

"No, as a gift."

"I'm sorry, you're gonna have to spell it out for me," Nadia said.

"If someone gives you a jar of honey, might it mean that they think of you that way? Like you are their 'honey?'" Alan put air quotes around *honey* so Nadia would not be confused, as she was not the most intelligent person he had ever met. But she did have an acute sense of people's motivations.

"Um, I'm not really sure there's a deeper meaning to a jar of honey."

"Then why did she give it to me?"

Nadia shrugged. "I don't know. Maybe because you sent her pears? Thanks for the gift, by the way. I guess mine got lost in the mail."

Alan sighed and looked away.

Nadia slowed and put her hand on his arm. "So, how did things go over break? What did your saba say when you told him he'd have to find a new CIA informant?"

He shot her a sideways glare. "I was not his informant last semester, nor will I *become* his informant. And your inflammatory language is unnecessary."

"That's exactly where you were headed." She looked over her shoulder. "Reporting to Mossad is *treason,* and you agreed to keep him abreast of CIA intelligence pertaining to the Middle East. Am I misrepresenting your arrangement?"

Alan scowled in response.

"How did he even find out about Desert Mountain?"

"I did not tell him, if that is your implication," Alan whispered. "He is the Director of Mossad. Mossad and the CIA are allies. I do not know how he found out about the Academy, but he knew long before I did. Again, *I did not commit treason.*"

"So have you told him or not?" she pressed.

"I tried. But he was MIA for the entire holiday. My parents do not even know where he is. He must be undercover somewhere. But I will speak with him, as soon as possible."

"I'm not kidding about this." She pulled his arm so he was forced to stop. "I need your word."

Alan yanked his arm free. "Yes, you have my word." He turned away, hoping that she needed his help someday so he could tell her she was on her own. Then she would know how he felt.

Now more irritated with Nadia than with his roommate, Alan hurried to catch up.

Libby and Simon walked into the classroom ahead of him and found seats together. Nadia moved around Alan to select a seat on the end of a row. Alan stood at the back of the room surveying his choices. One seat all the way in the front, or the one in the middle of the classroom, where he would have to pass a dozen kids all engaged in conversation.

Dean Shepard bumped into him as she entered the room.

"Excuse me, Alan. I didn't even see you there." She walked to the front, where the new teacher was writing his name on the dry-erase board. "Class, I would like to introduce your new political science professor. He's just arrived this morning, so I trust you will be courteous as he acclimates. Please welcome Professor Katz."

Professor Katz carefully placed his marker at the bottom of the board before turning to face the class. There was something familiar about the way he moved. He scanned the rows of students. When his gaze found Alan standing at the back of the room, he stopped. As their eyes locked, Alan's heart flew to his throat.

A clean shave, dark plastic eyeglasses, and bleached hair altered his appearance, but Alan would know him anywhere.

His saba.

12 NADIA
TUESDAY, JANUARY 17

Tuesday morning, after exercises at the dojo and two miles worth of laps around campus, Nadia was ravenous. She grabbed the biggest plate she could find and took her place in the buffet line, eyeing the selections.

She didn't normally like eggs, but the breakfast chef had a knack for making his taste more like cheese and bacon than scrambled eggs. Chicken sausage, whole-wheat toast, and a side of mixed berries rounded out her meal.

Nadia greeted her friends and then, as she'd done at every meal since returning to school, pushed her plate across the table to Damon's old seat: corner of the room, back to the wall. She slid into her chair.

As Nadia got settled, Libby turned to Simon. "How are you finding Desert Mountain so far? Is it very different from MI-6's training program?"

"It's more physically demanding, but your campus is so posh. In London we were crammed into a disused warehouse outfitted with classrooms, a dormitory, and a gymnasium."

"I love London," Libby said. "The shopping is amazing."

"Why are you even here?" Alan asked, glaring at his roommate.

"Because it's mealtime and I'm hungry." Simon raised his eyebrows.

Alan scowled. "That is not what I mean. I do not understand how a member of a foreign intelligence agency was permitted to attend a CIA training school."

"Alan, that's not a very nice thing to say," Libby said.

"What is not nice about it? It is a legitimate concern. Can you explain?" Alan asked Simon.

"Sure, mate. I'd be happy to fill you in. My mum worked for MI-6, which is how I got into *their* training program, but now she's dead."

"Oh, no." Libby covered her mouth.

"Simon, I'm so sorry," Nadia said. She couldn't even think about losing her mom.

"There's more." Simon turned to Libby. "You think your dad's an ass?"

"No." Libby shook her head. "I never—"

"Seventeen years ago, immediately following the risky exfiltration of a Middle Eastern asset, a team of CIA officers spent the summer in London," Simon said. "The mission went sideways, and the asset needed a new legend, an entirely falsified life. My mum stepped in to help, met my dad, and they had a summer romance. Now, supposedly, my mum never told him she got pregnant, but here's the kicker. My father—*who didn't know I existed*—found out she died and got me in here. So apparently, he *does* know about me, only he's never wanted anything to do with me. And still doesn't." Simon's fork clattered against his plate as he tossed it down. "So that's my story."

"That seems very inconclusive. What makes you think it was your father who arranged for your transfer?" Alan asked.

"Excellent question." Simon nodded. "I'm assuming that the CIA officer—the one who got me in here after my mum was *killed in action*—is my dad, right? Because why else would he bother with some bloke he's never met? But you're right, I really shouldn't be here." Simon stood and pushed his plate toward the center of the table. "I *should* be back in England with my mum." He stormed from the table.

"What is the matter with you?" Nadia asked Alan.

"With me? It is not fair that Simon is here," he whispered, his face flushing. "If anyone finds out my family history, I am done."

"Yeah, well. I told you to take care of that," she whispered back.

"I cannot help if my saba is undercover somewhere," Alan hissed. "Or whatever he is doing." Large welts began to form on his neck.

Nadia narrowed her eyes. The physical reaction was a telltale sign of his deceit. "You're hiding something. What is it?"

"Your accusations are making me very uncomfortable."

Libby, likely in an effort to ease the tension, asked, "So Simon's father is CIA?"

"Assuming he is telling the truth," Alan said.

Nadia rolled her eyes. She was about to fire back when Libby rested her fork against her plate and folded her hands in her lap.

"Honey, you weren't very nice to Simon. Must you say every little thing that pops into your head? Can't you occasionally filter? Just run some of this stuff by Nadia and I before you speak."

Alan studied his omelet. "Nadia and me," he mumbled.

Libby sighed. "Can you maybe just try to get along with Simon? Please? For me?"

"For you I will try."

Nadia glanced at Alan. Maybe that's what was bothering him. It would probably take him a while to realize that Simon was not competition for Libby's heart.

A few hours later, after Introduction to Intelligence Gathering followed by an archery lesson during physical education, Nadia's team headed to the library for their afternoon study session.

Besides the dojo, the library was Nadia's favorite building. Revolving doors led into the wide, open interior. Vaulted ceilings added to the dramatic effect of the glass wall that faced the lawn. Mahogany bookshelves lined the other three walls and formed neat aisles throughout the center of the room. Library ladders attached to brass bars provided access to the highest selections. To the left of the entrance, behind a secured counter, a row of locked cabinets held decades-old classified case files. The sign above read AUTHO-RIZED PERSONS ONLY.

At the far side of the main area was the language lab, a glass-walled room equipped with laptops, headphones, and computerized learning programs available for student use—every language, from Arabic to Zulu. Behind that, in a separate, locked room, lived the school's cipher computer. It wasn't available for student use except under special circumstances, or else students would never learn to crack a code.

Nadia had never needed the cipher computer.

"This way," she said to Simon, and led them to the right, down a few open steps to the lower level, where teams gathered at small round tables for group study. Damon had initially selected their spot, so once again, she moved through the clusters of students toward the back corner. She nodded hello to a few classmates as she passed. "This is us," she told Simon, and dropped her backpack on the floor by her chair.

Just as she finished unpacking her bag, Jack arrived. He pulled up a chair, wedging himself between her and Simon.

Jack draped his arm over Nadia's shoulder and whispered, "Hi."

She grinned, feeling her cheeks warm. "Hi."

"I missed you," he said quietly.

"I missed you, too."

"You two are nauseating," Simon said. "I've nothing against your lifestyle, but I shouldn't be forced to witness it. Can't you take this elsewhere?"

Libby laughed. "I think they're cute as little bugs."

"I hate bugs," said Alan.

Jack smiled and moved his arm away. "Noah told me his team is being sent out this weekend for their first survival course. I hate to be the bearer of bad news, but it's a solo."

"A solo? What's that?" Simon asked.

"Instead of traveling as a group and competing against

another team, each recruit is dropped alone in the desert. Your job is to navigate back to campus in a timely fashion," Jack said.

"It's horrifying," said Libby. "Twenty-four hours alone in the desert."

"Mmm." Jack shook his head. "More bad news."

"What?" Libby asked. "Longer this time?"

"I'm afraid so. But at least you'll get rations." Jack turned to Simon. "The good news about the solo is there's no chance of getting shot with a tranquilizer dart. Team competitions can get pretty fierce."

"Is that all you wanted?" Alan asked Jack.

"I also wanted to tell you guys about my senior project."

"We already know," Alan said. A girl from the next table shushed him, and he lowered his voice. "Sensei instructed us to treat your missions with reverence. Do you have anything new to add?"

Jack gave Alan a long look. "As a matter of fact, I do." He opened his notebook and removed a handful of papers. As he passed them around he said, "Here are your temporary code names for the semester. As always, after reading, destroy the document. It's written on flash paper so just drop it in water and it'll dissolve."

Nadia glanced at hers: WOLVERINE.

"Any questions?" Jack asked.

"Yeah," Nadia said, holding up her paper. "Wolverine? Isn't that, like, the most aggressive animal on the planet?"

He smiled. "Quick, fierce, smart, agile, resourceful. Some say aggressive, but I say...appropriately assertive."

Nadia felt her cheeks warm as she smiled.

"I'm SUNFLOWER," Libby said. "I love it! Thank you."

"You're welcome," Jack said. "Yours is truly fitting."

"Shh," said the girl at the next table.

"This is a group study area, is it not?" Simon asked her, more loudly than necessary. He stared at her until she looked away.

"RAPTOR?" Alan whispered. "As in the dinosaur? Because technically, the proper name is velociraptor."

"Not the dinosaur," Jack said. "Raptor as in the stealth fighter plane manufactured by Lockheed Martin."

Alan frowned. "But I am not at all stealthy."

"That's what makes it funny," Jack said.

A small smile tugged at Alan's lips. "I see. You are using irony to highlight the fact that I am not terribly deceitful." He chuckled. "Yes, that is funny." He turned to Simon. "Do you get it?"

"Yeah, thanks. I got it." Simon looked at Jack. "Why am I MAKO?"

"Fastest shark on earth. I'll leave the interpretations to you." He turned to Nadia. "I'm not sure how quickly we'll get started, but I might need a rain check on our date this weekend."

"No problem. Spy games are more fun than dinner and a movie anyway."

Jack stood and kissed the top of her head. "That's why I'm crazy about you. By the way, you have a package. It's probably cleared security by now; you can pick it up at Hopi Hall."

An hour later their study session ended and Nadia walked down the hill to the administration building. As she approached the stone steps leading to the heavy wooden doors of Hopi Hall, she hesitated. After a deep breath, she jogged up the stairs.

Once inside, she felt the quickening of her heart as she moved down the hall. Lingering anxiety from last semester's trauma occasionally snuck up on her. She paused at the entrance to the dean's sitting room and practiced the combat breathing Sensei had taught her. Inhale through the nose for a count of four, hold for four, exhale through the mouth for eight, as though blowing through a straw. He'd told her that her heart rate slowed on the exhale, so the longer she spent exhaling, the less her heart would race. After a few moments, she crossed the waiting room and knocked on Dean Shepard's office door.

"Come in."

Nadia entered, closing the door behind her. "I'm sorry to bother you. Jack mentioned I had mail."

"Yes, this came for you." Shepard held out a small package wrapped in brown paper. "Of course, security opened it and examined the contents, but nothing was removed."

Nadia took the item from Dean Shepard's outstretched hand. She peeled back the paper to reveal a shrink-wrapped copy of Homer's *The Iliad*. She frowned. "Was there a note?"

Shepard shook her head. "Just the book."

"What about the return address?"

"No address, but it was postmarked from Honolulu, the same as your postcard. Did you figure out who sent it?"

Nadia shook her head. "I forgot to ask." Her second piece of correspondence from the islands. "Anyway, thank you." As she reached the door, a familiar scent caught her attention. The whiff of a campfire drifted through the air, and Nadia looked back toward the desk. "Dean Shepard, do you smell smoke?"

13 SIMON
TUESDAY, JANUARY 17

Late Tuesday afternoon, following his team's mandatory study session, Simon strolled down the hill to the administration building. Hopi Hall, quiet this time of day, was draped in long shadows that played across the jute-colored walls. After confirming that no students were lingering in the parking lot, he hauled open the massive wooden door and trotted down the tiled hall.

This jaunt to the dean's office wasn't exactly a *fishing* trip, in that Simon didn't know quite what he was looking for. It was more like lobbing a hand grenade into the lake and hoping something edible floated to the surface.

He approached the sitting room cautiously. Finding it vacant, he selected a leather-bound volume from inside one of the bookcases and tossed it onto a chair by the fireplace. Dean Shepard's office door was closed. He double-checked the ceiling, making sure he hadn't overlooked a security camera the first time round.

Simon removed the plastic bag filled with damp newspaper from his backpack and carefully arranged the soggy pages under the logs in the fireplace. He added a fistful of cotton balls and reached inside the shaft to close the flue. He struck a single match on the back of a matchbook, then ignited the remaining matches and placed the blazing packet beneath the cotton; the flame licked upward.

He grabbed his bag and crouched behind the overstuffed chair closest to the window. From this position, he had a clear view of Shepard's door.

Now to wait.

Two seconds later he glanced at his watch. Waiting was not Simon's strong suit, but this was his first lead in sixteen years.

All Simon knew about his birth father was that he worked for the United States government—though he'd always assumed he was an American spy. His mum refused to say anything more—only that he'd been part of a team flown in from Washington. She'd told Simon that his dad had no idea she'd got pregnant, that she'd never informed him because she didn't want anything from him. She promised Simon that when he turned eighteen, she'd tell him his father's name.

But during Simon's conversation with Dean Shepard, he realized his mum had lied—his father *did* know about him.

Shepard had said the man who'd arranged for Simon to attend Desert Mountain Academy was CIA. Shepard knew his code name. And soon enough, Simon would, too.

The damp paper finally caught. White smoke billowed from the fireplace and began to fill the room. Simon pulled his shirt over his mouth. A minute later the smoke alarm sounded and the dean's door opened. Simon pressed himself against the leather as Shepard and Nadia moved quickly toward the hallway.

A few seconds later, Simon stirred from his spot and stole into the dean's office. Circling the desk, he removed a thumb drive from his pocket. He popped the drive into the USB port of Shepard's laptop and waited as his program uploaded. The fire alarm pulsed its obnoxious horn as the safety lights over the door flashed to the beat.

"Come on," he muttered, glancing from the monitor to the door and back again.

The status bar read fifty, sixty, seventy....

Simon scooted to the office door and peeked into the sitting room: still vacant. He rushed back to the desk as the sirens drew nearer to campus.

The fire brigade responded faster than anticipated, especially considering the Academy was in the middle of nowhere. They must have off-site security close by. *Good to know.*

Ninety, ninety-five...

Simon tapped his foot.

Ninety-six. Ninety-seven.

Shouting outside, then from the lobby.

Ninety-eight, ninety-nine. A thundering of boots running up the hall.

One hundred percent. Simon yanked out the drive and dashed back to the sitting room. He reached the fireplace a fraction of a second before the firefighters stormed the room.

Simon coughed and waved his hands to clear the smoke. "Sorry, mates—my bad. I was in here reading and thought a cozy fire would be so nice. I guess I forgot to open the flue."

"Did you use fresh wood?" a fireman asked, yanking Simon away from the hearth by his arm.

"I'm not certain the newspaper was completely dry. Is that what caused all the smoke? So very interesting." Simon coughed again. "Who knew?"

"Everybody," said the fireman. "Everybody knows that. Go outside and check in with the paramedics."

Simon obediently made his way down the hall. He slipped through the wooden doors as discreetly as possible and inhaled the clean night air. Dean Shepard was by the front gate, speaking with security. She hadn't noticed him at all.

After getting the all clear, Simon returned to his room.

The program he'd installed on Shepard's computer would perform two critical functions. In addition to logging her keystrokes, which would enable Simon to record her usernames and passwords the next time she signed onto the CIA's server, his program also provided remote access, so he would be able to view anything on her screen, whether she'd actually typed it or not.

He'd designed the program himself—well, with the help of a

mate back home, who now happened to be serving time in juvie for an unrelated incident.

He waited an hour or so, then booted up his laptop and logged into the program. He scrolled through Shepard's history and randomly selected a file. The email she'd typed a few minutes earlier materialized onscreen: a reminder to the security guards to carefully track the visiting firefighters and file all log-in sheets at the end of each shift.

He sat back and smiled—*perfection*.

Horrible things happened all the time; surely Shepard would have cause to log on soon enough. And once inside, with a little time and luck, he would discover the code name of the agent who got him into Desert Mountain—his father. From there, Simon was only a hop, skip, and a jump away from righting the scales of justice.

Of course, if Shepard took too long before checking into the black-ops mainframe, Simon would happily speed up the mission by organizing a calamity of his own.

14 NADIA
WEDNESDAY, JANUARY 18

Nadia arrived a few minutes late to breakfast on Wednesday. Through the doorway into the main dining room, she saw Libby and Alan, already seated at their usual table in the back corner. She made her selections and joined her friends. Before sitting she asked, "Do you guys know anyone who went to Hawaii over the break?"

Alan shook his head. "I already told you my holiday was long and dull. Do you not think I would have mentioned visiting our nation's most remote state?"

"Still don't know who sent the postcard?" Libby asked, spreading her napkin across her lap.

"Or *The Iliad*, as of yesterday," Nadia said.

Libby looked over her shoulder toward the entrance. "Where'd we lose Simon?"

"How should I know?" Alan answered. "I am not his keeper."

Nadia glanced at Alan. Knowing he didn't adjust well to change, she asked, "How's it going with Simon? Is everything okay?"

Alan shook his head. "I do not believe we are well suited."

"What on earth is your objection to Simon? He's charming, personable, handsome...." Libby trailed off as she wiped the rim of her water glass with a lemon wedge.

"These are not requisite qualities of a satisfactory roommate," Alan said. "He likes to read in bed, but I need a completely dark room or I cannot sleep. He is loud, slovenly, and apparently feels very strongly about never hanging up his wet towel."

"Speak of the devil," Nadia said, nodding toward the buffet line. As Simon made his approach, his eyes scanned the perimeter of the room, lingering on the exits.

That was the second time she'd seen him case a room.

Simon set his plate and napkin roll on the table. "Guess what I just heard?"

Alan shook his head. "We really do not have enough information at this time to make an educated guess."

Simon laughed. "Good one, mate." Alan stared blankly at his roommate, and Simon said, "Oh, you're serious. All right then, how about this: you're not going to believe what I just heard."

"What's that, honey?" Libby asked, as she straightened his silverware.

Simon smiled at Libby, Alan glared at his roommate, and Nadia once again realized why Damon had always insisted on the corner chair. From this angle, she missed nothing; her classmates walking through the buffet line, groups gathered in conversation at the intimate tables, security cameras on the ceiling, the kitchen staff as they restocked the beverage station.

"As I was leaving Dean Shepard's office, after solemnly swearing never again to touch a match while on school property, I heard something extraordinary."

"You were there last night?" Libby asked. "My goodness. I'm so grateful you weren't hurt."

"I may have been partly responsible," Simon said. "It was touch-and-go for a while."

Nadia raised an eyebrow. "That seems an exaggeration. As I recall, it was mostly smoke."

"Did the sprinklers go off?" Libby asked.

Simon shook his head and leaned toward her. "Contrary to popular belief, sprinkler systems are heat activated. And quite localized—most often individually controlled. The release of water begins when the head actually melts."

"Fascinating," Libby said.

Alan rolled his eyes. "How is that fascinating? Everybody knows that. Just because he has an accent you think everything he says is brilliant."

Nadia shook her head. "I didn't know that."

Libby shot Alan a look and then turned back to Simon. "You said you heard something extraordinary. Go on."

"Professor Hayden." Simon paused and snapped open his linen napkin. "He's the old poli-sci instructor, right? One of the dodgy ones?"

"How do you know about that?" Alan glared at Simon.

"What about him?" Nadia asked, trying to prevent Alan from sidelining the conversation.

"He's dead." Simon dropped his napkin on his lap, formed a steeple with his hands, and lowered his voice. "Murdered."

Libby flinched. "That's awful."

"Libby, he shot at us. It's not that awful," Nadia said, feeling a twinge in her gut. She couldn't quite identify the sensation. Fear? Relief? She turned to Simon. "How did it happen?"

"He was thrown out the window of his flat, which, sadly, was on the eighth floor."

"Oh my God." Libby pressed her fingers to her lips.

"But that was probably not what killed him," Simon said. "By the time he was tossed from the ledge, he'd already been shot."

"Oh my God!" Libby said again.

"And stabbed," Simon said cheerfully.

Libby's eyes widened further. "That sounds a little excessive."

Nadia felt sick to her stomach. "That sounds a little like Damon."

"Do you really think it was him?" Libby asked.

Nadia nodded. "That kind of overkill? Yeah, I'm guessing Damon."

"Of course it was Damon," Alan added quickly. "Who else would it be?" He scratched at his neck, now red and splotchy. "It could not possibly have been anyone else."

Nadia's gaze lingered on Alan. He only broke out in hives when he told a lie, but he obviously hadn't killed Hayden, so what was with the physical reaction? "I agree, a revenge killing seems right up Damon's alley."

"That's not the worst of it," Simon continued. "Inside Hayden's apartment, the police found his right index finger."

The color drained from Libby's face. "Why would Damon cut off Hayden's finger?"

Simon shrugged. "I couldn't begin to imagine."

Nadia shaped her hand into a gun and pointed it at Simon. She bent her index finger and said, "Trigger finger. Any word on Damon?"

Simon shook his head. "Didn't sound like it, but apparently this happened days ago. Shepard was furious she was only now hearing about it."

"Well," Alan said, breathing heavily. "Personally, I am grateful to be alive. Let us not forget that my life was constantly in jeopardy. I am the one who was forced to live with that psychopath."

"But you're not the one he's got a beef with, are you, mate?" Simon turned to Nadia. "You worried you're next?"

Nadia shook her head, irritated by his question. "Why does everybody keep asking me that? Why would I be? If he was going to kill me, he would've done it last semester when he was ordered to."

Simon looked a little surprised. "I was under the impression that you ruined his life."

"How? I didn't do anything to him."

"That is false," Alan said. "You cost him his entire career. He was faced with a choice: follow orders and execute you, or let you live, lose both his traitorous job and his place at Desert Mountain Academy, and become a target himself."

"That's ridiculous." Nadia turned to Libby for confirmation. "Damon and I were friends. He could've killed me, and he didn't."

Libby looked down at her plate.

"Libby?"

She winced as she looked at Nadia. "I'm afraid I agree with Alan on this one. Damon may have once considered you a friend, but when he refused to kill you, his coworkers tried to kill *him*. It's possible he blames you for that."

"Well, that's not fair," Nadia objected, as though her teammates could change Damon's mind.

"Also, I believe Damon helped to support his mother financially," Alan added, his face still flushed. "Which may be why he agreed to betray his country in the first place."

Libby nodded. "I can believe that. He's very serious about family."

Alan continued, "Yes, I am certain Damon is responsible for Hayden's death."

"And now he's on the run," Simon chimed in. "Unemployed and unemployable. He lost his job, his financial security, his safety. All because of you."

"Thanks a lot." Nadia pushed her plate away and sat back, glaring at Simon. "*Now* I'm worried."

"I'm teasing," Simon said. "I'm sure his killing spree's got nothing to do with you."

"One person is not a spree," Nadia snapped.

Libby squeezed Nadia's hand. "You'll be okay. You're safe here on campus, right?"

"I guess you're forgetting the time I got shot in Dean Wolfe's office, huh? Being that it was so long ago? What, like eight weeks now?"

Libby gave Nadia a sympathetic look. "Nothing like that would ever happen again. Lightning doesn't strike twice."

"That is incorrect," said Alan. "There are a number of people who have been struck by lightning more than once. It has something to do with the electricity—"

"What is the matter with you?" Libby asked.

"What?" Alan shook his head. "This is not me talking, Libby. This is science. I cannot change the facts because you find them inconvenient."

Nadia grabbed her plate as she stood. "I'll catch up with you guys later."

"Are you okay?" Libby asked. "You want me to come with you?"

"No, I'm fine. I just need some air."

"I'll come get you before class. We'll walk together." Libby offered a reassuring smile.

At the far end of the buffet line, Nadia dumped the remainder of her breakfast into the trash can and went outside. She kept her head down so she wouldn't have to greet her classmates on their way into the dining hall. Halfway down the hill, she ran into Jack.

"I was looking for you," he said, pulling her off the path around the corner by the girls' dorm. "I have my meeting with Shepard later. How about a kiss for luck?"

She feigned a smile.

"What's wrong?" Jack asked, his eyebrows furrowed.

Nadia relayed the entire conversation about Hayden. When she finished, she sighed. "I'm sorry. I shouldn't have unloaded on you right now. It probably didn't do anything to help your nerves."

"I'm not nervous." Jack rubbed his nose. "Not anymore. I've been preparing."

She smiled.

"What?" he asked.

"I know when you're lying," she said. "You have a tell."

"What are you talking about? What tell?"

"When you lie, you touch your face."

"Seriously?" He laughed. "Thanks for letting me know. I should work on that." He reached for her hands. "Are you really worried about Damon?"

"I don't know." She shrugged. "They made some good points about me ruining his life. I hadn't really thought about it like that."

He gathered her into a hug and kissed her forehead. "Don't worry, I'll protect you."

Nadia pulled away, annoyed. "I don't need you to protect me. I can take care of myself."

His eyes met hers as his face softened. "I didn't mean to imply that you couldn't. I just meant we're in this together. Whatever you need."

Nadia shook her head. "I'm sorry. Thank you, I appreciate your saying that."

"Absolutely." He pulled her back into a hug. "I'm on your side, Nadia. Always."

She leaned into his chest. The warmth of his body radiated onto hers. Just being in his arms relaxed her. "Don't worry about your meeting with Dean Shepard. You'll do great."

He squeezed a little. "Thanks for saying it."

Nadia sighed. *At least I have Jack.*

He kissed the top of her head. "Are you okay? Do you want me to walk you inside?"

"No, I'm fine." She forced a weak smile as he pulled back to look at her. "I'll see you later." Before he answered, she turned away.

Back in her room as she waited for Libby, Nadia unwrapped *The Iliad*. The second she removed the cellophane and opened the book, she realized Homer held the key.

The study edition of Homer's epic poem contained numbered lines: page fifty, for example, had line numbers in the high seven hundreds.

Nadia searched her bag for the postcard. Sitting at her desk, she jotted the numbers down onto a fresh piece of notebook paper: 125.793.4, 51.805.1, 51.792.7, 360.591.5 // 46.599.4, 95.475.7, 112.329.9 // 138.106.3, 104.16.6, 95.475.7, 183.265.7, 116.446.4, 357.493.9. Page number, line number, word number. The first, 125.793.4: *north*. The second: *thirty*.

She finished the first series and read the results: *north thirty three degrees // fifty two feet // twelve point two hundred thirteen inch.*

GPS coordinates, latitude and longitude: N 33° 52'12.213". The second set provided the western degree. All she had to do now was enter the coordinates online to find the location.

Nadia sat back in her chair, tapping her pencil against the desk. She knew exactly what this meant.

Someone had left her a dead drop.

15 DAMON
WEDNESDAY, JANUARY 18

After weeks of waiting, Damon had started to think the worst—that his mom hadn't made it, that she was already dead. But then, two days ago, he'd finally received word that Roberts was ready to negotiate. The overwhelming relief Damon experienced when he hung up the phone was indescribable.

His mother was still alive.

Early Wednesday morning he climbed aboard the spacious Phoenix city bus and headed toward the meet.

Every time the bus lurched forward, Damon held his breath. The frequent stops posed no danger—a jolt wouldn't cause detonation—but knowing this didn't ease his mind. He wiped the film of sweat from his forehead and checked the worn slip of paper in his pocket for the hundredth time. The address scribbled on the note was way downtown, three transfers from where he'd started.

The air brakes hissed as the driver pulled to the curb. He opened the doors, and the smell of sweat and diesel momentarily dispersed as chilled air rolled into the cabin. A woman boarded, wrinkled skin and gray hair, and she eyed Damon as she shuffled down the aisle. With his muscular build and shaved head, he knew he looked intimidating—that was the point, but still. She clutched her purse closer to her chest. The driver began to close the doors.

"Hold up," Damon called. He couldn't take it anymore. "Let

me out here." He climbed down the steps and onto the sidewalk. Even in its sketchiest neighborhoods, Phoenix was cleaner than Baltimore, where cigarette butts and fast-food wrappers littered every gutter.

Damon's black jacket, zipped to his neck, was too heavy for the desert morning, even in January. He thrust his hands in the pockets, cast his head down, and took the last two blocks on foot.

A half block from the destination, he slowed. He'd arrived early to check out the area. He found a dumpster across the street to use as cover.

The warehouse, situated in the middle of the block, appeared to have only one usable entrance. There was probably a garage door around back; a loading zone. A line of windows, which provided ventilation and light during the day, ran high along the top of the building, accessible via the fire escape. That meant the interior held a mezzanine office. A single streetlamp stood close to the main entrance, next to the chain-link fence.

Damon crossed the street with quick strides and banged on the door. His left hand returned to his jacket pocket, where it clutched the cylinder wired to the vest.

He didn't recognize the man who answered. "What." The bulge from the man's firearm created a lump under his black sports coat.

"I'm here to see Roberts."

The man stepped back and let Damon through.

The second he'd cleared the entrance, Damon unzipped his jacket, revealing the vest strapped to his torso. Thick packets of C-4 circled his middle.

The guard reached toward his sidearm.

Damon held up his hand, thumb pressed on the dead-man's switch of the detonator. "You shoot me, we all die."

The man's right hand hovered near his hip. "Okay, just calm down."

"I am calm. Get me Roberts."

"Wait here," he said.

Damon scanned the open space of the warehouse as the guard

climbed the metal steps leading to the upper office. The single mezzanine window overlooking the loading area was dark with blinds. As expected, the back wall had a garage-sized door, for loading and unloading trucks.

"Soldier." Footsteps rattled the stairs and echoed lightly across the concrete floor. Agent Roberts, the man who had kidnapped Damon's mother and burned down her house, strolled toward the main level, followed closely by his hired gun. Roberts carried a tactical briefcase in his left hand; his right hand casually trailed along the metal railing. His expensive suit was overkill in this neighborhood.

"Where's my mother?" Damon asked.

"Somewhere safe." Roberts reached the concrete floor.

"What took you so long to contact me?"

"I wanted to be sure you'd be ready to negotiate."

Damon moved forward. He matched Roberts in height and exceeded his build. Damon was solid muscle—he also had youth on his side. "Well, I'm here. You said you'd trade me for her, so where is she?"

"Yo." The hired gun took a tentative step toward Damon. "You need to step off."

"That's not exactly the arrangement," Agent Roberts said.

"Well, what exactly *is* the arrangement?"

"Step off," the guard repeated.

Damon turned on him, pushing his face into the guard's. "I'm about two seconds away from snapping every bone in your body." He squared his shoulders, stared him down.

Roberts took a deep breath. "Everyone, relax." He turned to Damon. "These histrionics are completely unnecessary, as was wrapping yourself in C-4. This is a business meeting. I have something you want; you have something I want."

Damon glared at the guard for another moment, then addressed Roberts. "Go on."

"A few months ago, you claimed to have evidence implicating the Nighthawks as a terrorist group," Roberts said. "I believe your exact words were, 'If you take me down, I will drag all of you down with me.'"

"That does sound like something I would say." Damon had never trusted Roberts. As an insurance policy against becoming their fall guy, he'd carefully assembled incriminating evidence against the Nighthawks organization: photographs, documents, fingerprints....

But Roberts neglected to mention the thumb drive Damon had recently found in the storage unit. He probably didn't even know it was missing.

"I'll need those files."

"Then you'll release my mother? Just like that?"

Roberts nodded.

"Show me proof of life."

Roberts looked to his guard. The man hesitated for a half beat, then pulled a Polaroid from his jacket pocket and handed it to Damon.

Damon felt the rage swell inside his body as he took in the picture of his mother, tear-stained cheeks, dirty hair, holding a copy of today's newspaper. He narrowed his eyes and, for a split second, considered lifting his thumb. He took a deep breath through his nose before he spoke, forcing himself to maintain control of his voice. "If you hurt her..."

Roberts held up a hand. "Let's not."

Damon shoved the picture in his back pocket. "You've had her for six weeks. She's seen you—she can identify you. You can't let her go. And how do you know I won't make copies of those files? You're not gonna let us walk outta here."

"First of all, your mother hasn't seen me. She's been kept in a safe house with another agent. I have no reason to kill her. Secondly, those copies will be of no use to you because you are going to do something else for me, and this errand will provide me sufficient leverage against *you*."

"What's the errand?"

"I need someone brought in."

Damon shook his head. "I don't follow. How does that buy my freedom?"

"You can't very well turn me in to the CIA when you're guilty of kidnapping."

"Bring you someone." Roberts nodded and Damon asked, "Dead?"

"I said kidnapping, not murder."

"All right." Damon's eyes passed from Roberts to the guard and back again. "Who do you want?"

Roberts clasped his hands together. "I want Nadia Riley."

Damon studied Roberts' face in the yellow light of the warehouse. A wind kicked up outside, pressing against the windows and rattling the panes of glass. The gusty breeze swept under the garage door and along the floor, making the hairs on Damon's legs stand. "What do you want with her?"

"What concern is that of yours?"

"She doesn't know anything."

"I didn't ask you what she knew. In any case," Roberts said, "you owe me an agent, don't you?"

Damon frowned. "I don't know what you're talking about."

"Hayden's dead. That makes me a man shy."

"It seems to me that whoever killed Hayden did you a favor."

"How do you figure?"

"He wasn't worth a pinch of—"

Roberts interrupted. "Nevertheless, I'm a man down."

"Technically, you're two men down. You recall you took a shot at me? I'm not exactly toeing the company line." He glared at Roberts. The lack of response annoyed him. After a moment, Damon said, "Nadia won't turn, you know. You're wasting your time trying to recruit her."

"I don't intend to recruit her," Roberts said.

"Then why do you want her?"

"Soldier, let me ask you something: What is your objective here? Why are you asking questions that don't pertain to your mother's safety?"

Damon narrowed his eyes. He didn't like being part of a mission without understanding its endgame—especially with someone as untrustworthy as Roberts. Sure, Roberts wanted Project Genesis, but what did that have to do with Nadia? On the other hand, the man made a valid point. She was someone else's problem. "I bring you Nadia, and my mom and I go free?"

"And your files."

"And my files," Damon said.

Roberts nodded. "That's it."

Damon paused for a beat. "I'll let you know when I get the package."

"Last item of business." Roberts knelt down and opened the plastic case he'd been holding. A medical gun sat nestled in the foam lining. "I need to inject you with a tracking device."

"How do I know it's not lethal?" Damon asked.

"You don't. Now turn around."

Damon held up the detonator as a reminder. "Maybe I'll stick around for an hour. See if I keel over."

"Be my guest." Roberts pulled Damon's shirt away from his shoulder and injected the device. Damon winced as it embedded into his flesh.

"You're all set," Roberts said.

Damon zipped his jacket and backed toward the door, the bodyguard following closely. He held up a hand. "I'll show myself out."

Outside, he hurried down the street and around the corner. When his line of sight no longer included the warehouse, he leaned against the stucco wall running along the sidewalk. His shoulder throbbed. He really hoped it wasn't poison.

Damon pushed off the wall, faced away from the street, and removed the corded detonator from his pocket. The knuckle of his thumb ached from pressing the button so long. With a steady hand, he detached the trigger wire.

Nadia Riley. What did Roberts want with her?

It didn't really matter. If that's who Damon needed to secure his mother's freedom, so be it. He exhaled deeply as he started for the bus stop.

Looks like we're gonna have a reunion.

Two hours after the meet, as Damon was leaving the hardware store with a bag of supplies, he received a phone call. He picked up, expecting to hear Roberts on the other end. "What do you want?"

A digitally modified voice spoke into the line. "I have a proposition for you."

"Who is this?" Damon looked around the busy parking lot. No one seemed out of place. He checked over his shoulder.

The robotic tone continued. "You can call me Mr. Green."

Damon scoffed. Had to be one of Roberts' guys. "What do you *want*?"

"I've wired fifty thousand dollars to an account in your name. I'll text details of how to access the money, as well as instructions for collecting the remainder of your fee—an additional four hundred and fifty thousand dollars."

Half a million? "Who the hell is this?"

"Should you accept, the funds will be made available immediately upon completion."

Is this for real? Damon narrowed his eyes. "Five hundred grand, just like that?"

"Just like that."

He pressed his lips together and looked toward the cloudless sky. After a moment he asked, "And who exactly do I have to kill?"

16 NADIA
WEDNESDAY, JANUARY 18

After cracking the cipher, Nadia met back up with Libby. The juniors filed into the building designated for their studies, sandwiched between the senior class building and Hopi Hall. The classrooms, bright and spacious, were comfortably appointed with cushioned chairs and generous desktops. Large windows supplemented warm overhead lighting, and each soundproofed room was outfitted with a flat-screen television mounted to the wall.

Their chemistry teacher had assigned a research paper on poisoning methods. The student who uncovered the least traceable poison got to skip the first exam. Their next class, right across the hall, was Computer Science and Information Systems, followed by Psychology, Nadia's favorite. She took her seat as Dr. Sherman introduced their first unit of the semester, psychological warfare.

"Psychological warfare encompasses an array of behaviors and techniques, from the relatively benign to the highly dangerous," Dr. Sherman said. "For example, the law of reciprocity. This technique is extremely common, and most of you will use it frequently while establishing relationships with possible assets." She paced the aisles as she spoke. "You buy a drink for someone, they feel obligated to chat with you."

"Well, that seems reasonable," Simon said, not bothering to raise his hand. "I'm happy to chat for free drinks."

"All right, that's enough." Dr. Sherman quieted the peals of laughter. "Simon, I suspect you'd be willing to chat *regardless* of free drinks."

Nadia, smiling at Simon's light blush, raised her hand. "Can you give an example of something more serious?"

"Certainly. Another technique is the 'us against them.' Here, you establish rapport by uniting yourself with your target. For example, say you approach a potential asset at a political rally. You might begin by saying, 'They don't understand what it's like for us. These politicians, they don't live in the real world, not like you and me.'" Dr. Sherman moved back to the front of the room. "Some psychological warfare is not so subtle: threats to colleagues or loved ones, for instance."

"Like a tiger kidnapping?" Nadia asked.

"Exactly. For those of you who don't know, a tiger kidnapping occurs when one person is held hostage in order to force a second person to do something they would not otherwise agree to do."

"Like what?" Simon asked.

Nadia turned toward him. "The son of the bank manager is kidnapped to force his father to break into the vault."

"Great example," Dr. Sherman said to Nadia. "Where did you learn about tiger kidnappings?"

"My father teaches criminology. He specializes in high-value kidnappings and political assassinations."

"Excellent; perhaps you'll choose that topic for your report." Dr. Sherman glanced at the clock. "Speaking of, everyone, I want fifteen hundred words on a specific method of psychological warfare by Monday. Be prepared to explain your method to the class."

"I see we've got a teacher's pet," Simon teased as they gathered their backpacks.

Nadia shook her head. "Wait'll you hear me butcher Mandarin Chinese this afternoon. You'll see my areas of expertise are extremely localized."

Alan glanced up and nodded. "As her former tutor, I concur."

"Thanks, Alan. I can always count on you for backup," Nadia said, rolling her eyes at Simon.

By fourth period, political science, her forearm ached from note-taking. Professor Katz waited as the students settled in. Poli-sci still wasn't Nadia's favorite, but after two days she already liked Katz much more than she'd ever liked Hayden.

As class progressed, she realized it wasn't just her—everyone seemed to enjoy his teaching style. Well, everyone except Alan, who sat and scowled, arms crossed, eyes trained on his desk.

About twenty minutes into the lecture, Nadia leaned toward him and whispered, "You're gonna fail if you don't contribute. Participation is, like, forty percent of our grade. Did you not read the material? Do you want to look at my notes?"

"Mind your own business," he hissed. "It would be a sad day indeed if I needed *your* notes."

"Alan, Nadia," Professor Katz said. "Is it necessary to separate you?"

Nadia glared at Alan before turning to the front of the room. "No, Professor. Sorry for the interruption."

"As I was saying," Katz continued. "Recruitment methods of potential assets." He paused to write on the whiteboard. "Follow the MICE acronym. The most effective ways to turn an asset are money, ideology, coercion, or ego." He pointed at each letter in the acronym as he listed the methods.

Nadia copied the notes into her notebook.

"Ideology includes patriotism and religion," Professor Katz explained, as he paced the aisles like a giant bear. "Coercion most often takes the form of threats and blackmail. Both personal threats and threats to colleagues or loved ones are common. Certain individuals can withstand torture, but will cave if their partner is at risk of bodily harm. Coercion is the least effective of the methods, as your asset will turn on you at the first available opportunity. Ego works only on those concerned with their own self-importance. This is not an attractive quality, eh?" He stopped at Nadia's desk. "Tell me, Miss Riley. Which of these four is your weakness?"

Nadia looked at the whiteboard and then shook her head. "I have no financial responsibilities, so I don't need money. I believe in democracy, so I'm happy with my country and stand ready to defend it. I don't have any secrets, so blackmail's not an option, and I'm not a narcissist, so I don't respond to flattery....I guess I can't be turned."

"Oh, my dear." Professor Katz tipped his head to the side and studied her intently. "Everyone has secrets." His gaze stretched longer than was comfortable, but Nadia refused to look away. Finally, he smiled and continued down the aisle. "Mr. Hawthorne?"

"Money," Simon quipped. "Hands down. My loyalties are most flexible—available to the highest bidder."

Professor Katz chuckled along with the class.

As Nadia turned around to smile at Simon, her eyes fell on Alan.

His face was covered with violent red hives.

After Arabic, Nadia decided to investigate her dead drop. But she wasn't about to trek miles away from campus to verify the mysterious code without some sort of backup.

Jack wasn't an option. As much as she'd love to ask for his help, she knew he'd be forced to report the cipher. Things were going well between them, and Nadia didn't want to jeopardize that—especially on an errand that might turn out to be a hoax. Alan wasn't terribly useful and couldn't keep a secret to save his life, and Nadia had no intention of putting her best friend in harm's way, so Libby was out. Which left Simon.

After a campus-wide search, she found him in the dining hall, reclined in a chair, feet propped up on the linen tablecloth, eating a chocolate pudding cup. "I need your help with something."

He looked up and slowly licked his spoon. "I'm kind of in the middle of something."

"It's top secret," Nadia said.

"Only I'm terribly busy."

"I should warn you, we might get expelled."

Simon jumped up. "Why didn't you say so in the first place? That sounds like fun." He tossed his snack—spoon and all—into the trash can. "What's the mission?"

Nadia laughed. "You're a sociopath. You know that, right?"

"Right, so we're not on a schedule?"

"Good point. Come with me." They exited through the main door leading to the terrace in front of the back wall.

According to her calculations—and the satellite photos readily available online—she'd find the dead drop a few miles from campus. The highest peak of the surrounding mountain range would serve as her guide.

Nadia started toward the gate. The heavy chain and padlock securing the back of campus were removed during daylight hours; right now, they sat in a heap on the ground.

"Where are we going?"

"Just a short walk." As she stepped off campus, Nadia paused and surveyed the running trails. Satisfied they were alone, she moved off the path, making sure to step only on the rocky portions of earth, and not on the tender plants that struggled against the desert.

"Are we meant to leave the trails? I seem to recall this is expressly forbidden."

"It is, so don't make it a habit."

After another dozen steps, he asked, "What's this all about?"

"No questions, please."

"I'm quite curious by nature," he said.

She shrugged. "I guess we could exchange information. Why don't you start with the fire?"

"An unfortunate accident."

Nadia stopped and turned around. "I am ninety-nine percent sure the sitting room was vacant when Shepard and I left her office. Which begs the question, where were you hiding?" She held up her hand. "Wait, no, forget that. I don't even care. Why were you *there*?"

Simon scowled, opened his mouth, then sighed and looked at

the ground. He lifted his head, his clear blue eyes locking onto hers. "I needed Shepard out of the office so I could toss her desk."

Nadia narrowed her eyes, watching for a lie. "Why?"

"She said she knows my father's code name. I was looking for information."

His pupils were appropriately dilated. His body language remained open, his breathing regular. He seemed to be telling the truth. And after the story he'd shared about his mother, could she blame him? In his shoes, she'd certainly go to any length to find a familial connection. "Is that it?"

"That's all I care about. Finding my father."

Nadia nodded, then turned and started walking again. "Can I do anything to help?"

"Thank you for asking. I don't believe so, but I'll let you know should something arise. I trust I can count on your discretion?"

"Sure, as long as you're straight with me."

Simon chuckled. "Well, I can't pretend to be *straight*, but I was being honest."

Nadia laughed. "Fair enough. So did you find anything?"

"I'm afraid not." After a few minutes of silence, Simon said, "You know, I do appreciate your support. As a gesture of goodwill, please consider my personal laptop at your disposal."

"Thanks, but the library is fully stocked."

"Ah, but mine is entirely untraceable. Bouncing wifi, ghost IP addresses, the whole delightfully elusive package."

She stopped and turned to him. "What possible use would I have for that?"

He seemed surprised. "What a deplorable lack of imagination. I can think of a million uses."

Smiling, Nadia resumed their hike. "See, that's the difference between us. I'm not the kind of person who needs an untraceable laptop."

"Suit yourself." After a few minutes of silence, he asked, "Where exactly are we going?" She didn't answer, so he continued. "Can you at least tell me why you brought me along?"

"Oh, you know," Nadia said, without slowing her gait. "Girl wandering through the desert alone. Can't be too careful."

"Right. I've watched you in jujitsu, so I know that's not it." After a brief pause he said, "All right. You'll tell me when you're ready."

Nadia slowed long enough to reorient herself. The low-growing brush forced them to walk a serpentine path. It would be easy to move a few degrees off track.

He maintained his code of silence for three solid minutes. "So what's Alan's story?"

"You'll have to be more specific."

"There's something odd about the way he speaks. Why's he so defensive? And hostile? He got even worse after classes began—did you notice? What's he hiding? I know it's something big. I can tell."

Nadia shrugged, grateful that Simon couldn't see her face. *Not much. His grandfather is the head of Mossad, but besides that, totally normal kid.* "He's multilingual. I think he has trouble with contractions. He's also very literal."

"Hmm. You do like your secrets. I suppose that's good news for me."

They neared the destination and Nadia stopped. "I need a minute. Can you wait here?"

He narrowed his eyes. "For what? Is this some kind of hazing ritual? Abandon the new guy in the desert?"

"I have to pee. You can come if you want, but I don't think our friendship is quite there yet. Also, we're about two miles from campus. If you can't find your way back from here, you're probably in the wrong line of work."

"I suppose I'll wait here." Simon examined his cuticles.

"Excellent," Nadia said as she slipped into the brush.

She found what she believed to be the proper location, but without knowing what she was looking for, it was difficult to tell. Nadia searched the ground, under the bushes, checked for something tucked among the branches. Nothing.

After a few minutes, Simon called, "Are you quite well?"

"Yeah," she yelled. "Almost done." She was about to give up when she noticed a softball-sized piece of obsidian on the ground. The black rock resembled a large chunk of glass. Obsidian was perfect for flint knapping—it made the sharpest knives—but it wasn't indigenous to the low desert. She kicked it aside and found an arrowhead underneath, pointing north.

Nadia moved a few paces deeper into the desert. Hidden in a stand of chaparral she found her dead drop: a large manila envelope tacked to a skinny tree trunk.

She stood to the side and used a stick to lift the package away from the bark. The backside looked clean, so she ripped it off the nail. Was this an assignment?

"Hey," Simon yelled. "Let's move."

She tucked the package inside her waistband. Adjusting her shirt over the envelope, she retraced her steps. "Ready to head back?" She started toward campus.

"You walked two miles into the desert to relieve your bladder? Are you quite mad?" he asked, falling into step behind her.

"At least I'm not an arsonist."

Back on campus Nadia and Simon parted ways at the girls' dorm. She jogged down her hallway, hoping that Libby was still at the library. To her delight, their bedroom was vacant.

The second she closed the door, she peeled the package off her sweaty back and placed it on her desk. Using a letter opener, she sliced along the seam of the manila envelope and removed the contents, which included a single, slim folder. Stamped across the front were the words DESERT MOUNTAIN ACADEMY, NEW RECRUIT: CLASS OF 1990. She sank into the chair and opened the file.

Printed at the top of the intake form, the recruit's code name: JERICHO. With quick fingers she flipped through the remaining pages. Initial test scores, psychological assessments, research papers, commendations. Jericho's records were exemplary across the board—sharpshooting, intelligence analysis, foreign language, martial arts.

Nadia frowned. *Why would someone send me an old recruit file?*

She turned the final page of the admissions packet. Clipped to the back of the folder, she found his photograph.

Nadia took a closer look at the picture and gasped.

It can't be.

Staring back at her was the unmistakable smile of the man she'd known her entire life.

Her father.

17 JACK
WEDNESDAY, JANUARY 18

Two hours before his scheduled appointment, Jack laced up his running shoes and headed toward the back gate to hit the trails. His future rested on the whims of the new Dean of Students, and it was imperative that he consistently make an excellent impression. The best way to clear his head: work up a sweat.

He started slow, focused on his cadence, his breath. The late-afternoon air dried the initial beads of perspiration from his forehead. He picked up the pace and fell into a rhythm. After a few laps, his body switched to autopilot, allowing him to mentally prep for the meeting.

Shepard would ask about his team to evaluate his assessment skills. Liberty Grace Bishop, youngest child of Senator Wentworth Bishop, was loyal, patriotic, eager to please. Diagnosed with mild obsessive-compulsive disorder, but nothing serious enough to interfere with her training last semester. She was a team player, easy to get along with, thoughtful, inclusive.

Simon Hawthorne, the new guy, fell at the opposite end of the spectrum. According to his psych profile, he had a high stress tolerance, low empathy, and experienced little guilt. He was impulsive, and thrived on interpersonal conflict. Simon had a proclivity toward seeking adventure outside the law.

Jack rounded the corner by the gate and began another lap.

Alan Cohen, intelligent, multilingual, extremely obtuse regarding interpersonal relationships, but he seemed to be trying. Alan had tutored Nadia last semester—he'd done a great job helping her catch up.

Jack's stomach flipped as he thought about Nadia. Dedicated, driven, intelligent, athletic, determined, beautiful. He would have to tone down his comments about her so he didn't seem biased. He tried to think of something negative to say. Occasionally she held a grudge, and she could be a little stubborn. He smiled. *Okay, a lot stubborn.*

His pace increased as he considered the most important issue, the one he really didn't want to mention to Dean Shepard: Senator Bishop's public declaration about the Nighthawks. What if his intel *had* come from Libby? Jack's job was to protect his team, but not at the expense of his nation's security.

Nadia was positive it wasn't Libby, but of course she would stand up for her roommate. On the other hand, as he'd unfortunately learned last semester, Nadia's ability to spot lies bordered on superhuman. But how else would the senator have known they'd had a traitor in their midst?

Jack pressed his lips together. No, he couldn't keep quiet about this. He would have to report his suspicions.

His watch beeped, indicating the end of his workout. He slowed to a jog, then took the last half lap at a brisk walk. He'd shower, grab a quick bite, then go impress the dean.

Forty-five minutes later, Jack settled into a guest chair in Dean Shepard's office. He quickly reviewed his impressions of his team one last time, then took a deep breath and folded his hands in his lap. He waited patiently as Shepard perused the folder that described his history at Desert Mountain Academy: commendations, letters of recommendation, awards, exemplary essays.

She closed the file and sat back in her chair.

Jack's stomach twisted as he again thought about Libby. He couldn't wait. "Dean Shepard, before we begin..." He considered his next words. "I'm afraid we may have a security concern. I'm certain it was inadvertent, and I'm not sure the extent of the leak, but I believe Libby accidentally revealed something to Senator Bishop."

"You're referring to his mention of the Nighthawks?"

"Yes ma'am, and the mention of a double agent discovered at the training level." He paused for a beat. "Libby is absolutely loyal, and her parents are clearly patriots. I ask that you consider these factors before making a decision about her future."

After studying him for a moment, she said, "It must have been difficult for you to tell me this."

He nodded. "Yes ma'am, it was. I'm quite fond of Libby."

"I appreciate your candor. Clearly, we have a leak, and we are investigating all potential sources. At this time, the less said about it, the better. Do you understand?"

"Of course." What did that mean? A potential leak here at the Academy? Or a leak in the CIA? Both thoughts turned his stomach. Agents' lives were on the line every day; proper security was paramount.

Shepard leaned back in her chair. "Speaking of fondness...it has come to my attention that you and Miss Riley are engaged in a romantic relationship. Is this correct?"

Jack felt the surprise register on his face. He composed himself, then cleared his throat. "Ma'am, with respect, I'm not entirely comfortable discussing my personal life."

Shepard smiled. "Jack, you're training for the Black-Ops Division of the CIA. You *have* no personal life."

He felt his face burn. "Of course, I apologize. Yes, we are dating. It took a little convincing on my part, but—"

"Before you continue, there's something you need to know. Desert Mountain has instituted a new fraternization policy. Effective immediately, team leaders are prohibited from dating their subordinates."

Jack frowned. "May I ask why?"

Shepard folded her hands on the desk. "It places the newer

recruit in an awkward position. I understand you and Nadia have a history, but this policy is nonnegotiable. Your options are as follows: terminate your romantic relationship and stay on as team leader, or continue dating and forfeit your team."

He shifted in his chair. "Who would take over?"

"That's not your concern," Shepard answered.

"Would I be assigned to another team?"

"Maybe."

"But there's a possibility that I wouldn't be a team leader?" That would significantly hurt his chances for next year—and beyond, for that matter. She'd already told him she wasn't interested in the seniors who weren't leading teams.

"That is correct. Reconfiguring group dynamics is, as you know, not always easy, and never guaranteed. I cannot make a commitment to you at the expense of four other recruits."

Jack nodded. "I understand." He chewed on his lip. "Do you need my answer right now?"

"Perhaps I misunderstood your goals." Shepard leaned back in her chair. "What are your plans for next year?"

"Ideally, I will secure an invitation to continue my training at the undergraduate level."

Dean Shepard looked concerned. "If you truly hope to pursue espionage as your career, you must be prepared to make difficult concessions. Your personal life will *never* come before work."

"No, of course not." Jack nodded quickly. "You're absolutely right."

"So, I will ask you again. What is your decision?"

18 NADIA
THURSDAY, JANUARY 19

At 3:20 a.m. Nadia checked the clock on her nightstand for the millionth time. She still hadn't made sense of the dead drop, and she hated not being able to confide in her best friend.

Was the file real? It was possible the legend had been fabricated, maybe as part of an assignment. If it *was* real, who sent it? Her father's picture had no identifiable scenery—it could've been taken anywhere. But where would someone have gotten an old picture of her dad?

She rolled onto her back and stared at the darkened ceiling. How difficult would it be to find an old yearbook photo? Her parents stood firmly against social media (*that's not how you develop a friendship, Nadia*), and they'd gone to school decades before everything became readily available online. Their generation didn't even have cell phones until well after college, so finding a photo might take some effort. But it could be done.

Nadia sighed, turning toward the wall. Maybe creating a legend about a former recruit was part of Jack's senior project. But why choose her father—why involve her? Then she realized: Jack's assignment included running junior agents. Maybe she was being tested, too. Maybe her mock mission had already begun.

It could be a test of her loyalties—would she call home and ask her father about it? Or a test of her discretion—could she keep a secret? Would she immediately blab to Sensei, or work it out on her own? She wouldn't always have a confidant in the field.

Perhaps it was part of an assignment. Maybe she was supposed to research the file, gather intel, write a report; add to the legend or refute its contents. But for which class? Psychology, maybe? *Ah—psychological warfare.* Shaking one's foundational beliefs in family was a classic technique: isolate your target, alienate her loved ones, turn her into an asset.

No, it wouldn't be for psychology, or everybody would've gotten one. Surely she would've noticed other juniors sneaking off campus or cracking ciphers. It must be part of Jack's senior project, part of the mission he designed especially for her.

Nadia shook her head. Of course the recruit file was fake. Her father would never knowingly send her to a CIA training school. Her mother would kill him—she worried incessantly about Nadia. In fact, her mom hadn't even wanted Nadia to attend last semester, and that was without any knowledge of the actual program. So if her dad knew about the Academy, not only would he be risking Nadia's life by entering her into this line of work, but he'd essentially be ending his marriage. Zaida Riley would never forgive him.

She smiled. It was ridiculous to think that her dad—Professor James Riley, with his sweater vests and tweed jackets—could actually be a spy.

Thursday morning, after Nadia and her classmates had completed drills at the dojo, Sensei made an announcement. Starting today, the students would begin their specializations. Tuesday and Thursday afternoons, previously reserved for team study sessions at the library, would now be dedicated to small, isolated groups learning the specific aspects of tradecraft.

"See your first-period instructor for your schedules," Sensei said. "Class dismissed."

As her team moved toward the lobby, Nadia turned to Libby. "I'll catch up with you on the trail, okay? I need a minute with

Sensei." She lingered in the lobby until the *shoji* doors slid closed behind the last junior. The second they were alone, Nadia started talking. "Sensei, someone murdered Professor Hayden." When he didn't respond, she continued. "I heard it was Damon. Is that true?"

"I received the same information."

"Should I be worried?" She watched his face carefully.

As usual, his expression remained neutral. "You are concerned that he will hurt you?"

"I wasn't until Alan pointed out that I'd destroyed Damon's entire life. But yeah, I guess a little. I don't *think* he would hurt me. We used to be really close."

"Damon is not who you believed him to be."

She nodded and looked at the ground. "I know."

After a moment Sensei said, "I do not expect that he will seek you out, but if he does, you must not trust him. Whether incidentally or by design, associating with Damon puts your life in grave danger. He is a threat to you. Perhaps not an imminent threat, but do not mistake him for your friend." His dark eyes studied her face. "Remember, Nadia-san: a tiger cannot change his stripes."

Sensei's words echoed in her head all morning. She didn't really believe Damon would hurt her—in fact, it was unlikely that she'd ever see him again. Why would he return to the scene of the crime? He was a lot of things, but careless wasn't one of them.

That afternoon after the day's last class, Nadia attended her first specialization, field medicine, held in the chemistry lab. She found a seat next to Niyuri, the sweet girl from Noah's team who'd dated Damon last semester.

"Have you heard anything about Damon?" Niyuri asked.

Nadia shook her head. "Not a word. You?"

"Just the rumor that he killed Professor Hayden." Niyuri leaned closer. "Did you hear how Hayden died?"

Before Nadia could answer, their instructor arrived, carrying a red cooler.

"I am Dr. Clement," she said, setting the cooler on the lab station at the front of the room. "Former Marine Corps captain, former chief of medicine at Massachusetts General. Welcome to my class." She pointed at each of the twelve students as she counted aloud. "Perfect. You—" She nodded to Eric, the boy on the end. "Hand these out, one per student." She gave him the cooler. "Today's lesson: suturing a wound."

Dr. Clement passed around scalpels and suture kits, sterile packages containing prethreaded needles, latex gloves, and alcohol wipes.

As Eric reached their lab table, Niyuri wrinkled her nose. "Is that what I think it is?"

Eric nodded and dropped a pig's foot onto Nadia's desk.

At dinnertime Nadia reconvened with her team in the dining hall. When she reached the buffet line, she was grateful to see lasagna rather than roasted pork. After sitting down, she asked, "How were everyone's specializations?"

"Refreshingly educational," Alan said. "I assembled a transistor radio from a box of spare parts."

"I made a fake ID," Simon said. "The equipment here is much nicer than what I've used previously. Of course, I was working out of my mum's basement with a load of stuff I'd pinched from the hardware store."

Nadia smiled. "How about you, Libby?"

Libby beamed and rested her silverware across her plate. "I had the best afternoon. I discovered that I am going to be an *amazing* spy."

"Of course you are, love, but what happened?" Simon asked.

"Fingerprints," Libby said, clasping her hands together. "Now initially, I had no idea why I was selected for the forensics specialization. I mean, blood splatter analysis? It's repulsive."

"Because of your OCD," Nadia said. "You notice everything. It's remarkable."

"As it turns out, you're absolutely right," Libby said. "But that's only part of it. After our introductory lecture, my forensics unit was instructed to dust the room for prints. Naturally, no one dusts better than I do, even though this exercise involved *creating* dust rather than eliminating it, but after we'd gathered all the prints together, guess which one of us had left no trace of her presence?"

Nadia laughed. "You left no fingerprints because you didn't touch anything."

"You are correct." Libby's smile grew wider. "It was so much fun. I don't think I've ever been the best at anything." She turned to Nadia. "What about you?"

Knowing her germaphobic roommate was a little squeamish, Nadia shook her head. Libby would be horrified to hear about stitching up a pig's foot. "Nothing of interest."

That evening, as the girls got ready for bed, Nadia discovered a note that had been slipped into her bag. After Libby closed the bathroom door, Nadia unfolded the paper and read the printed message: SEV. ZRRG NG ABBA. OYVAQ PBEARE. PBZR NYBAR. She immediately recognized the code as a simple Caesar cipher.

Nadia wrote the alphabet on a fresh sheet of paper. It shouldn't take long to crack the key. The hardest part would be figuring out which letter rotation to use. She started with ABBA—the word contained only two letters, so the vowels were likely internal. Furthermore, the word had to be a palindrome: deed, peep, sees, toot.

She fiddled with the alphabet until she solved ABBA: noon. That meant the code was written in ROT13, or rotation thirteen. *A* was to be replaced by the fourteenth letter of the alphabet; *b* equaled *o,* and so on.

She transcribed the code: FRI. MEET AT NOON. BLIND CORNER. COME ALONE.

Nadia shoved the note into her pocket as her stomach fluttered. Only fourteen more hours till the next portion of her mock mission.

19 ALAN
THURSDAY, JANUARY 19

Normally, Alan would have to force himself to stay awake until one-thirty in the morning, but ever since Saba had slipped him the details for their clandestine meeting during political science, his heart rate had not dipped below one hundred and ten, which made sleeping difficult.

At 0115 Alan climbed from his bed, fully dressed, and slipped out his bedroom door. Once outside in the chilled night air of the desert, he pulled on his shoes and walked toward the wall surrounding campus. The moon was obtrusive; the reflection of the sun cast from its face fell like a spotlight across Alan's shoulders.

His instructions were to follow the wall until he reached the lower left quadrant of campus, and then wait. When he reached his destination, he leaned against the stucco, crossed his arms, and scowled.

Alan's entire family drove him to distraction. Over the holiday, he'd spoken to his mother about Libby. Not because he wanted to, but because she was nosy and discovered that he was sending fruit to Georgia. When he told her Libby seemed less than enthralled, she suggested that Libby might be intimidated by Alan's intellect. Not an impossible theory, but he suspected his mother had said this only to make him feel better.

And now Saba, out of nowhere and for no good reason, had

appeared at the one place that was Alan's own, the one place his intrusive family had yet to control.

Alan scanned the surrounding area, watching for the lumbering shape of his grandfather.

Despite Nadia's accusations, he really had tried to contact Saba, to tell him he would not be his Mossad liaison in the CIA. Now he knew why Saba had been unreachable—he had been preparing to breach Alan's only sanctuary.

It was unfair. For the first time in his life, Alan felt a part of something, like he had friends who cared about his well-being. And now Saba was here to take that away.

As if summoned by the thought, Saba stepped from the shadows.

"Aryeh," he said, addressing Alan by his given name. His hands clamped around Alan's biceps while he kissed both cheeks. "It is a beautiful night, no?"

"Please lower your voice," Alan whispered. Saba's heavy hands remained on Alan's shoulders, like an anchor securing a vessel to shore. Not certain he wanted the answer, Alan asked, "What are you doing here?"

"It is a tragic story. A few months ago, a bomb detonated outside a cafe in Tel Aviv. My people caught the suspect almost immediately, but he was not forthcoming, so they sent for me. Interrogation happens to be my specialty. Eventually, he disclosed critical information relevant to our American allies, which I had to deliver in person. My trip brought me to Las Vegas, and I thought, you know what would be nice? Spending time with my grandson."

Alan's stomach flipped. Before considering the ramifications of his question—or Saba's answer—he asked, "Please tell me you are not the one who leaked confidential information to an American politician?" Saba laughed and Alan shushed him.

"I spoke with our allies in the CIA. What happened after that is beyond my control."

For a single second he considered asking the question that

really weighed on him—did Saba kill Professor Hayden? Alan shook his head. He did not want to know. "You cannot stay here."

"I was concerned for your safety."

"As you can see, I am fine."

"I am also enjoying the opportunity to get to know your friends," Saba said.

Alan felt sick. What did that mean? Was it a veiled threat?

"Alan, Mossad still needs you. We are on course, no?"

A wave of nausea rolled through Alan's stomach. He whispered, "I do not think I can report to you. People know about you. I could be arrested for treason."

Saba sighed and looked around. "This is disappointing news, Aryeh."

Dread filled Alan's chest. He willed himself not to respond, not to offer assurances to his grandfather.

Saba continued. "I need an agent willing to work with Mossad. Israel will have her allies. Obviously, my first choice is you, my only grandson, a member of my family. For this you were sent to the best schools, granted access to the finest tutors." He looked pointedly at Alan. "I will have my agent, Aryeh. Better it should be you, but if you refuse..." Saba shrugged. "I will find another recruit. I will have the best man—or woman—for the job, whatever the cost."

Alan's heart fell as Saba turned and walked away. Whatever the cost—what did that mean? Was someone in danger? Or did Saba mean that he would disown his only grandson and replace him with a more willing protégé?

When feeling returned to his legs, Alan pushed himself away from the cold block wall. As he rounded the first corner toward his dorm, he heard a low whistle from the shadows.

Simon stepped forward, shaking his head. "Oi, mate." He sucked in his breath. "That can't have felt good."

Alan froze. How much had Simon heard? If Saba found out he had been discovered, Simon might be in serious danger—even more than Alan would wish upon him.

Simon threw his arm over Alan's shoulder. "Where does he get off thinking his only grandson is replaceable?" His voice dropped to a whisper. "No wonder you were so agitated that an MI-6 trainee got invited here. You'd be thrown in the clink if anyone learnt your story, wouldn't you? That's not fair at all."

Fear flooded Alan's body. Simon had heard everything. "Why are you following me?"

"Something seemed amiss," Simon said. "Come on. I'll walk with you." They continued toward their dorm. "I have a keen eye for trouble, and I thought you might need backup."

Alan paused. "Would you really have provided backup if necessary?"

Simon slapped his back. "Of course I would. That's what mates do. And we *are* mates, aren't we, Alan?"

Alan smiled. Perhaps he had misjudged Simon. "I suppose we are."

"Brilliant!" Simon opened the lobby door. Barely a beat passed before he said, "Listen, mate. I need a favor."

20 NADIA
FRIDAY, JANUARY 20

Morning classes on Friday seemed to last four times longer than usual. Between lack of sleep the night before and obsessively checking the clock to ensure a prompt arrival at her clandestine meeting, Nadia didn't absorb much information from the lectures.

Something else was bothering her, something about the dead drop, but she couldn't quite put her finger on it. An elusive thought pulled for her attention, like a gnat in her peripheral vision. If she could just get it into focus...

Finally, a few minutes before noon, Nadia jogged up the hill and snuck through the back gate. Per the instructions, she followed the campus wall toward the blind corner on the running trails. As expected, when she rounded the bend, she found Jack waiting. Still, the sight of him brought relief, and she felt the ropes in her shoulders loosen a little.

"Hi." Nadia moved forward to give him a hug. "I feel like I haven't seen you in days."

Before she made contact, he held up a hand and stepped back. "Please, we're here on business."

"Oh, sorry." She smiled. "Are we still on for dinner tonight?"

"No, I'm afraid not."

"Okay." Nadia waited for him to continue. He seemed...off. Distant. "What's up?"

He stood with his hands clasped together, a serious expression on his face. "Thank you for meeting with me."

"Yeah, of course," she said. "What's going on?"

"As part of my assignment, I'm required to set up clandestine meets with my agents, and then file reports summarizing the meeting. So that's what we're doing." He handed her a sealed white envelope and a set of blueprints. "Here are floor plans and op-specs for your mission. Study the emergency exits, memorize the stairwells and elevators, all points of access and egress."

"Got it."

"Do you have any questions?"

"Yeah, I do. Why are you acting so weird?"

"I'm simply trying to maintain professionalism, and I would appreciate if you would do the same. You can go back ahead of me. I'll wait here so we're not spotted together."

Nadia frowned. "Okay." She took a few steps back, then turned and walked briskly toward the back gate. *What was that all about?* Something was bothering him, something to do with her. Was he angry that she'd been so casual? That wasn't really fair—she hadn't known they were meeting as part of his assignment.

She sighed as she stepped back onto campus. Of course it was part of his assignment—why else would he have sent her a coded message? She should've figured it out, been more professional.

Wait a second. Nadia stopped walking. That couldn't be it. After he'd been so affectionate at the library in front of the whole team? No, this wasn't her fault. It was something else.

Nadia spun around and marched back through the gate. She found Jack halfway up the trail.

He raised his arms, questioning. "What are you doing? You were supposed to leave before me as practice for our missions."

"I'm not doing this again. I need you to tell me what's wrong. Have I done something?"

"Other than behaving unprofessionally?" He scratched his nose.

She might've accepted the insult and taken the blame for the strangeness of their interaction if Jack hadn't chosen that exact moment to touch his face. But that was his tell—he was lying. Nadia crossed her arms. "Jack."

He sighed. "It's not you." After a long pause he said, "I met with the dean on Wednesday."

"Yeah, I remember. Did something happen?"

"I don't know how to say this, so I'll just say it." He looked down, then back up. "Dean Shepard has instituted a new policy. She informed me that if we continue dating, I'll be removed as team leader."

Nadia shook her head. "I don't understand."

"We need to break up," he said.

"Seriously? Can she do that?"

"I'm afraid so." Jack met her eyes. "Obviously, I don't want to. She gave me an ultimatum. Of course, I wanted to talk to you about it first—"

"Really?" He was considering *her* over their team?

"But she insisted I answer immediately."

"Oh." A few stray hairs from a loose curl blew across her face. She wiped her hand over her forehead. "Would you get to lead another team?"

Jack's eyebrows pulled closer together. "She couldn't guarantee that would happen."

Nadia looked away, across the open desert. A cactus wren landed on a saguaro to her right, then tipped his head, inquiring. "You told her we would stop seeing each other." A tiny part of her wanted him to say, *No, I told her I don't care about the team. You're the most important thing in my life.* But that wasn't Jack. And one of the things she loved about him was his dedication to the school, to the CIA. If he'd chosen their relationship over his lifelong dream of serving his country—she didn't want that kind of pressure.

"It was an impossible decision. I'm crazy about you, but our team is also very important to me. And if I'm not leading *any* team, I'm sure I won't be recruited for the undergraduate program at Langley. But I can't imagine us not being together."

Nadia was quiet for a second. *So it wasn't an impossible decision. It was a fairly easy decision.*

The worst part was she couldn't even be angry with him. She would've done the exact same thing. Afraid her voice would reveal her disappointment, she swallowed hard before saying, "No, you definitely made the right choice."

"Really?" He took her hands.

She met his eyes and managed a closed-lipped smile. "Of course. You're graduating in a few months. We would've ended it then, right?" She shrugged and pulled her hands away. "Consider us broken up." After a moment she asked, "So you've known about this for two days?"

"I know, I'm sorry. I should've told you right away."

"Is that why you've been avoiding me?"

He sighed. "I just—I couldn't find the words. This isn't what I wanted." He glanced around, then moved forward, reaching for her.

Nadia stepped back as her heart fell. He was already looking over his shoulder. "No need to hug it out." She smiled to lessen the harshness of her statement. "I'm gonna take off. Thanks for the op-specs."

A dusty breeze blew across the desert as she headed back toward the gate.

As she rounded the corner onto campus, it occurred to her that this was her future, this was life in the CIA. Unanswered questions, half-truths, and a constant shroud of fog and doubt over all her interactions and relationships.

Maybe that's why her mock mission involved a faked recruit file about her dad—to start acclimating her.

To illustrate that nothing was ever as it seemed.

On Saturday morning Nadia woke, buried under her covers, to the sound of Libby tiptoeing around their bedroom. Without moving, she said, "I'm awake." The metal curtain rings slid across the bar, the window squeaked open, then the scent of fresh air reached her nose. She emerged from her blankets and squinted against the light.

Libby shot her a sympathetic look. "Are you okay?"

"Yeah, I'm fine. I'm sorry I was in such a bad mood yesterday."

"No, don't be." Libby rushed to Nadia's bed and sat on the edge. "You had every right. I can't believe he did that to you."

Nadia sighed and looked away. After a few moments she said, "I know he made the right decision. Rationally, I completely agree with him. But I think about us constantly missing our moment and I get bummed. Then I swing right back to the fact that if he *had* forfeited the team, that would've made me really uncomfortable."

Libby interrupted. "You know, you are allowed to have mixed feelings about this. You're allowed to set aside logical, rational thought and just feel bad. And angry. And sad."

"That doesn't seem like the best use of my time," Nadia said.

"Yeah, I guess it's a blessing that we're kept so busy." Libby moved onto her own pristine bed. After a moment she said, "I gotta be honest, I'm surprised how much I loved my forensics seminar." Her shoulders slumped forward as her voice took on a wistful note. "I know I've only attended one specialization, but I feel like I've finally found my niche."

Nadia studied her roommate. "Are *you* okay?"

Her face brightened. "Of course, why do you ask?"

"I don't know," Nadia said. "You just looked sad for a second."

"Not at all." Libby popped off her bed. "Get dressed and we'll go to breakfast. Maybe blueberry pancakes will help us both feel better."

Together they headed to the buffet in the dining hall and over to their usual spot, where Alan and Simon were halfway through their meal. Nadia slid her plate across the table.

"We heard about you and Jack," Simon said. "I'm sorry, love."

"Our timing has never been very good," she answered, sinking into her chair. *Timing. The timing is off.* Something deep in her subconscious clawed for her attention, but she couldn't quite reach it. She sliced into her pancakes.

Simon continued. "I don't understand. Why don't you just date on the sly? You know, keep it from Shepard."

"Jack doesn't break rules," Libby said, spreading her napkin across her lap. "Not ever."

Nadia shook her head. "Even if he did, I'm not interested in sneaking around. And honestly, it's not a big deal. We'd barely gotten back together, and he's graduating at the end of the semester...." She shrugged and studied her plate.

"I find your maturity refreshing," Alan said. "And since you seem comfortable discussing the matter, I am curious to learn if anyone has received their assignment from Jack?"

"I don't think we're supposed to compare notes about our missions," Libby said.

"Agreed," said Simon. "But for the record, no."

Nadia took a bite of pancakes in lieu of mentioning that she had, in fact, received hers. She'd immediately studied and memorized the hotel floor plans, as well as her op-specs. Her mission involved planting physical evidence on an enemy agent to suggest that he'd tampered with a digital database.

"Nor have I," Alan said. "However, our instructions were to make them a priority." He turned to Nadia. "As such, I believe the timing of this breakup could not have been better. Your focus can remain solely on schoolwork and this mission, and that is good for us all, as we are occasionally graded as a unit."

Nadia shot Alan a look—to which he remained oblivious—as she stuffed another bite into her mouth.

"Timing is never good for a breakup, you nit," Simon argued.

The nagging thought from before began to crystallize. It was the timing. Nadia set down her fork.

The postcard with the dead drop coordinates had arrived before the semester started, before Jack was assigned a senior project, before any of them knew about the mock missions.

It couldn't have been from Jack.

So who sent the file?

21 SIMON
MONDAY, JANUARY 30

Another week passed without word of the mock missions, but on the last Monday morning of January, Simon found a note slipped into the pocket of his *gi*. This thoroughly impressed him, as he'd not noticed anyone brushing against him. He was more impressed still when he realized the note was from Jack, whom he hadn't even seen yet. It contained, Simon assumed, the location of his dead drop: *576.5 KUTSU*. He instantly recognized the Dewey decimal classification.

That's why, at the conclusion of chemistry class, Simon thrust his backpack into Alan's arms and announced, "I'm off to the loo. Drop this in computer science for me?" Before his roommate could answer, Simon dashed down the hall.

He sprinted next door to the library and quickly located the referenced volume: a book entitled *Human Genetics: Variations and Anomalies*, by E. Kutsunai. Inside the front cover, Simon found a slim envelope. Printed in pencil on the exterior of the envelope were instructions to meet his handler near the front gate on Sunday morning at 1000 hours. *Wear a sports coat and tie.*

He shoved the book back on the shelf and tore open the envelope seam. The flimsy square of flash paper inside described an infiltration mission—Simon would get to use his breaking and entering skills. He was much relieved, as these particular skills tended to rust when not properly exercised.

Just as he finished reviewing the op-specs, Dr. Wilson, the ever-present librarian, came round the corner holding an armload of books. "Simon, why aren't you in class?"

Forced to dispose of the evidence, Simon slipped the note into his mouth. The paper dissolved against his tongue as he called, "Just on my way. Lovely to see you." He darted round her in the narrow aisle.

Late that evening, after a rigorous study session, he offered to escort Libby back to her dorm. Alan had left an hour earlier, and when Nadia disappeared into the language lab, Simon insisted they call it a night. They packed up their bags and headed across campus.

The lack of progress regarding his familial mission had begun to take its toll, and he'd spent the last few days frustrated and agitated. As Libby prattled on beside him, he realized he'd been so self-involved he hadn't bothered to ask about *her* father.

To remedy his thoughtlessness, Simon interrupted her mid-sentence. "I've been meaning to ask how your dad's campaign is coming along."

Libby shrugged. "I haven't spoken to him since last week."

"If you don't mind my saying so, you seemed a bit bothered by the whole thing."

Libby smiled. "Not at all. I couldn't be happier for him. Or more proud."

Simon nodded. "My mistake. Clearly I misread your signals." He snuck a glance as Libby frowned. "If you change your mind and want to talk, I'm available." They reached the girls' dorm and Simon rushed to open her door.

"Thanks, but there's really nothing to talk about. I'll see you tomorrow."

He continued down the walk, mentally reviewing the plan to ruin his own father's life. He hadn't figured out the details, but the highlights included outing his father as a spy, exposing him as a child abandoner, and anything else Simon could think of before the time came.

As he strolled through the lobby of his dorm it occurred to him all of his teammates had family problems. Well, except Nadia.

Down the hall, Simon unlocked his bedroom door. Alan sat unmoving at the edge of his bed, scowling at the tiled floor. "Oi, what's wrong?" Simon slammed the door. "You look like you swallowed a pickle."

Alan shook his head. "I did not have a pickle. I am confused about a conversation I had with a girl."

"I can sort that for you." Simon sat cross-legged on his bed and opened his laptop. "Give me the details."

Alan sighed. "Her name is Penelope, and we are lab partners in our language and translation specialization unit. We were in the middle—"

"Is she cute?"

"What?"

Simon enunciated. "Is she attractive?"

"I suppose her features are pleasant enough. But her appearance is irrelevant. As I was saying, we were engaged in a reasonable discussion about the history of bioweapons in the Middle East—"

"What do bioweapons have to do with language and translation?"

"Nothing. This was a post-class discussion. If I may continue." He paused to glare at Simon.

"A thousand apologies. Please, go on."

"As I was saying, Penelope misspoke, I corrected her, and she seemed to get very agitated. I asked what was wrong, and she said, 'I just think it's interesting that—'"

"Hold on a second. Did she literally say, 'I just think it's interesting,' or are you paraphrasing?"

"That is literally what she said," Alan said. "Why? Does that mean something?"

"Okay, well that was not actually your first mistake, as the conversation had already taken an unfortunate turn, but for the record, when a girl says, 'I just think it's interesting,' it's time to abort the conversation *immediately*." He snapped closed his laptop. "It's a trap."

"I do not understand," Alan said.

"I just think it's interesting that you said you didn't care for Trisha, and now I see you staring at her all the time. I just think it's interesting that you said you didn't feel like going out tonight, but when your mates call, you're out the door. I just think it's interesting that you claim to not be much of a pisser, and yet here you are puking up vodka on my Manolo Blahniks."

"I did not understand what many of those words meant," Alan said.

"'I just think it's interesting' is girl code for 'I'm about to tear you a new one and you will never see it coming.' Also be warned of the oblique, 'I just think it's funny how . . .' Whatever follows, be assured, she most decidedly does *not* think it's funny."

"Why can they not just say what they mean?"

Simon's computer chirped. "Now that I *don't* know," he said absently, unfolding the laptop. The tone indicated Shepard had logged on to a site requiring multiple security checkpoints.

"How is anyone supposed to communicate?"

"It's a learned skill," Simon said. He scanned through Shepard's history. When he realized that—as usual—she'd done nothing more than log in to her email, he silently cursed. *Might as well have a peek while I'm here.* She'd sent a number of emails discussing the security of a database he'd never heard of, called CIADIS. "What is this?"

"What is what?" Alan asked.

Simon looked up. "Hmm?"

"You asked, 'What is this?' What is what?"

"Have you ever heard of CIADIS?"

"Do you mean CODIS? That is the acronym for the Combined DNA Index System, which is like AFIS—the Automated Fingerprint Identification System, but for DNA. It is an online database of the genetic material of criminals, law enforcement agents, childcare workers, and so forth. Perhaps CIADIS is CODIS for the CIA."

"Oh my God, I'll bet you're right. Mate, you're a genius."

Alan nodded. "Yes, I am."

"This is exactly what I need." To find his father, Simon could enter his own genetic sequence and then search for a match. "How quickly do the programs locate a match?"

"Not quickly at all. DNA is extremely complex, and crawling the database is quite time-consuming. You would probably need a specially written program."

Simon frowned. At least it was a place to start. "Cameron did a cheek swab on me when I arrived. Where does he keep the student DNA database?"

"How would I possibly know that? And why would I care?"

Simon sighed. It would be safer to retake the test than to try hacking into the school's database. DNA files were likely heavily guarded and encrypted; no sense in raising flags that needn't be raised. "You know what we need?"

"Light-blocking curtains?"

"A bro day." Simon opened a browser, searched for at-home DNA kits, and ordered one to be overnighted to his post office box in Cave Creek.

"I do not know what that is."

"This weekend you and I will go sightseeing, just the two of us. We'll have lunch, do a little shopping, explore a new town—hey, how about Cave Creek? Never been, but I hear it's a real slice of the Old West." As he finished placing the order, an alert flashed in the lower left corner of his screen: *Keyword Detected*. He'd set an alarm for any mention of his name.

"Why do we care about the Old West?" Alan asked.

"It's what mates do. And you do want to be mates, don't you, Alan?"

Alan seemed to consider the question before answering. "I *am* enjoying the camaraderie."

"Then it's settled." Simon opened the alert and double-clicked the file. A direct message from Dean Shepard to CIA Director Vincent read: *In response to his inquiry, please tell JERICHO that Simon Hawthorne seems to be settling in. I'll keep you both updated.*

Simon's heart all but stopped. There it was, in black and white.

His father's code name.

Jericho.

22 NADIA
FRIDAY, FEBRUARY 3

The next few weeks of classes kept Nadia mercifully busy, but as she fell asleep each night, her thoughts inevitably shifted to Jack. It had been almost two weeks since their breakup, and things were still awkward between them. They couldn't seem to find their new level of relational intimacy. Should she meet and hold his eyes? Smile? Be strictly businesslike and professional? When they bumped into each other in the library or dining hall, she spent so much time trying to figure out how to act that she barely spoke. Her friends obviously picked up on the lingering tension; everyone seemed uncomfortable when they were together. Well, Simon and Libby. Alan neither noticed nor cared.

She'd received no more coded messages, nor had Jack further discussed her mission. She'd laid to rest the file about her father, deciding it was part of Jack's project. Maybe Dean Shepard, eager to establish her new program, had jump-started the missions prior to the students' arrival. Or maybe team leaders had been briefed on senior projects over break, giving them time to design their op-specs. In any case, Jack would read her in as she needed to know. Which she really wasn't looking forward to—it was bad enough spending time with him when they *weren't* alone.

As a result, Nadia was almost relieved when, on the first Friday morning of February, she woke to find a survival course order had been slipped under their door, and her name was printed across the top.

> This weekend is your first survival course.
> This is a solo mission lasting three nights and
> four days. You will be driven to an undisclosed
> location in the desert. Your mission: navigate
> back to campus by 2100 hours on the final
> day. You will be issued one water bottle, a wool
> blanket, a small ration of nuts, and a field knife
> (see Hashimoto Sensei to secure your weapon).

Nadia searched the floor for Libby's notice. "Wait—why didn't you get one?"

"I don't know," Libby said. "Let's check with the boys. Maybe they're going one at a time, too."

Alan and Simon were already at the dojo when the girls arrived. Neither had received an order. After all the students had assembled themselves on the mat, Sensei entered the room.

"Those of you who have been called to the survival course, see me after morning exercise. Snap kicks. *Hajime!*"

A brutal hour later, Nadia waited in the lobby as her teammates left the dojo to begin the several-mile-long run around campus. After a few minutes, Sensei joined her.

"Why is no one else here?" Nadia asked.

"Dean Shepard has issued a change of plans," Sensei said. "You will depart individually for your solo survival courses. Teams will be divided, and the courses will be staggered. You will leave on Saturday, a student from another team leaves on Sunday, and so on."

"What? Why?" Nadia asked. "You never mentioned this to me."

"Nadia-san, please forgive me. Dean Shepard likely did not realize she was required to secure your approval."

Nadia's face burned as she bowed her head. "I beg your pardon, Sensei. Of course she isn't. But Noah's team all went out together. Why did she suddenly make this drastic change? It's reckless."

"Reckless?" A hint of amusement pulled at Sensei's mouth. "Last semester, when your team completed the solo survival courses at the same time, what was the physical distance between each of you?"

"We were about eleven miles apart."

"And what do you suppose a teammate could do to assist you from eleven miles away?" Nadia didn't answer, so he continued. "You successfully completed your solo without a safety net. As with most things in life, you had the illusion of safety, not actual safety. Do you understand?"

"Hai," she said miserably.

"I remind you: fear is nothing more than a chemical response to stimuli. You cannot control external stimuli, but you can control your reaction. You will be no more vulnerable than you ever were."

She stared at the polished floor. "I just don't understand why she's breaking up the teams."

Sensei's words, more measured than usual, came slowly. "I believe Dean Shepard is currently in negotiations with Secret Service."

"This is because of Libby?" Nadia looked up. Sensei remained silent. "They don't want her to go?" Still nothing. "Shepard is fighting with them, right? And to avoid the appearance of conceding, she's decided to send us out one at a time."

He lowered his chin slightly. "That is one possible theory."

"But Libby hasn't even been assigned her own detail yet," Nadia argued. "Obviously, she's not in any danger."

"Campus is quite secure. But perhaps the service feels the far side of the wall is another matter." He straightened. "Now, I will retrieve a knife from the weapons room. In case of emergency, you may use the knife to make a bow drill. As always, fire is permitted only under the most dire circumstances. We do not wish to inadvertently spark a wildfire. Do you remember the password to the covert-ops room? It is the same as last semester."

"*Hai*, Sensei. *Abunai*," she said. It was a Japanese word, a warning that meant *danger*.

"Excellent. Please retrieve your tracking device while I select a field knife."

Nadia trudged back down the hall to the mat room, then took the north hallway to the covert-ops room. Sensei followed. Farther down the hall was the shooting range, with the secured weapons room tucked in back.

She entered his password to the covert-ops room, and the metal door clanged as the lock released. Inside, recessed wall panels concealed the equipment. Nadia pressed one of the wooden panels, and the door clicked open, revealing packed shelves. She'd chosen the wrong panel; this cupboard contained single-shot handguns and other covert weapons.

Her eyes fell on the row of poisoned pens: her lifesaver. In front of the pens, the jar of liquid latex that Sensei had painted on the back of her hand last semester during a lesson. After shaking hands, he'd peeled the film from her skin. A perfect impression of his thumbprint remained on the rubber sheet.

She smiled and lifted the print from the shelf.

"That is not the correct cabinet," Sensei said.

Nadia quickly replaced the print and closed the door. She turned to her mentor, who pointed to the other side the small room.

A few minutes later, back in the lobby with her tracking device, Sensei handed her a lightweight nylon backpack, a wool blanket, a knife, a water bottle, and a bag of peanuts and raisins.

She held up the small bag of rations. "That's it? For three days?"

"It takes three minutes to die of blood loss, three hours to die from exposure, three days to die of dehydration, and three weeks to starve to death. You will be hungry, but you will survive. I will see you in a few days."

I certainly hope so. Her stomach knotted as she bowed.

*　　*　　*

Saturday morning, as the girls dressed for breakfast, their resident assistant, Casey, knocked on their bedroom door. In her arms she held a lush bouquet of pink and white blossoms—tulips, lilies, ranunculus, peonies. "These came for you," she said to Libby.

"Oh my goodness, thank you! They're probably from my daddy. He thinks every girl should get flowers 'just because.'" Libby's smile froze as she read the note attached to the flowers.

"Is something wrong?" Nadia asked.

"No ma'am, right as rain. Let me go freshen the water in this vase and we'll head out. You need to calorie-load before your survival course. Who knows when you'll get your next decent meal."

Later that morning the white van carrying its single passenger rambled along a series of bumpy, dusty roads. Nadia closed her eyes and leaned against the headrest. After an eternity, her driver pulled along the shoulder.

"This is it," he said. "See you in a few days."

"Thanks for the ride." She gathered her pack and climbed from the van.

Nadia felt uneasy from the moment she stepped onto the desert floor. Bad enough she'd been tossed out here alone, but to make matters worse, a strong and constant wind blew across the open land, kicking rough, hazy sand high into the air. The particulates shrouded the sun and blocked the horizon, severely diminishing visibility. In the vast wasteland of desert, limited vision was extremely unsettling. It was only two in the afternoon, but the darkness surrounding her made it feel much later. She hiked along the low base of a small mountain range, following the rocky ridge in lieu of the skyline.

The wind picked up, muffling the typical desert noises of quail calls, crunching gravel, dry leaves blowing across the earth. She lowered her head to protect her eyes from the sand and continued on.

A few hours later, fatigued and thirsty, Nadia reached a

rapid, narrow stream. She filled her bottle and, seeking protection from the scratching wind, crouched beneath a desert willow. She rubbed her eyes, trying to clear the sand. Resting her head against the trunk, she surveyed the landscape. Still cloudy with the dust storm, and now the sun was setting. She was thinking about making camp when, forty feet away, a covey of quail flushed from the earth and shot into flight. They flew haphazardly out of formation.

Chills covered her arms. The birds knew they were prey.

So where was the hunter?

She rose quietly from her spot and eased farther into the brush. She headed uphill, hoping for a better vantage point. When she reached an outcropping of rock halfway up the hill she paused, looking down onto the stream. The dust blew thick across the desert floor.

She wasn't searching for a rattlesnake or a coyote. She was looking for something taller, more sinister, and much more deadly.

She was looking for Damon.

23 DAMON
SATURDAY, FEBRUARY 4

Two weeks after their initial meeting, Damon got the go-ahead from Roberts.

"My man inside tells me your target's up in the rotation. Her survival course starts Saturday, so keep a sharp eye."

For this reason Damon was parked along a dirt path halfway up Coyote Mountain with his binoculars trained on the only road leading away from Desert Mountain Academy. He'd been waiting for hours, and if Roberts had received bad intel, he'd come back next weekend, and the one after that.

Damon found himself curious about Roberts' inside man. Had he missed someone last semester? Or was the inside man one of the newcomers to the Academy—maybe the new dean or political science professor? Whoever it was, he obviously didn't have the strength or ingenuity to deliver Nadia to Agent Roberts. This worked out well for Damon; if he still served a purpose, his mom would—at least temporarily—be kept alive.

The wind picked up, and along with it the dust. Visibility lessened, and the crispness of the mountain range farthest from his position faded. After another twenty minutes, he couldn't see the range at all.

At a little past 1100 hours, Damon's patience paid off. The

white van carrying his ex-teammate pulled into view. He loaded his gear back in the car and left the spotter's nest.

Damon moved through the mountains using unpaved access roads. Occasionally he stopped to get a line of sight on the van, then continued his pursuit from a safe distance. This went on for a few hours before the van pulled over to release the first passenger. Damon zoomed in, expecting to see some random student, maybe his replacement.

Instead, he saw her.

Nadia jumped down from the running board and turned to grab her gear. She pulled a lightweight rucksack from the cabin and threw it over her shoulder. Damon tightened the range of the binoculars. The van pulled away, temporarily obstructing his view.

Not in a million years would Damon have guessed she'd be first out of the van. The driver would drop the next person off a few miles away, then the next, and so on. She used to want the safety of a teammate on either side. *Good for her.*

When Nadia reappeared, he held his breath.

She dropped her pack along the road and pulled the ponytail holder out of her hair. Her long, dark waves blew across her face. She turned into the wind, then gathered her hair together and twisted it into a loose bun. The wind picked up and blew her clothes against her body.

She'd stayed in shape over the holiday.

Damon watched until she was out of view, then packed up and waited for another hour. He drove toward the spot where she'd gotten out, pulling off the road into a stand of chaparral. It was a good location: the brush thick, the dust storm thicker.

He double-checked his bag: handcuffs, Glock, two cell phones, GPS, four bottles of water—one opened, a couple power bars, knife, duct tape. Damon locked the car, placed his keys on the front left wheel-well and arranged a military-grade desert-colored camo net over the car.

The wind and sand had already erased Nadia's tracks. No

matter, it wouldn't be hard to figure out what went on in her head. He knew she had a lousy sense of direction—and she knew it, too, which meant she'd use a landmark. No way she'd stumble off into the desert when she couldn't see the horizon. He followed the base of the low-lying hills.

In less than two hours, he caught sight of her through the haze. She wasn't making great time, but still moved at a decent clip. She hiked for another hour before stopping to rest. Twice he had to slow down to let space grow between them.

As she bent to fill her water bottle, Damon crouched on the desert floor, well hidden by the low growing plants. He watched her stretch, her lean body lengthening toward the sky.

She sat under a tree. Her face was hidden, and Damon felt a strange ache. He wanted to see her eyes. He inched forward, straining his neck, and carelessly disturbed a covey of quail. They exploded into the air—straight up, left, right, feathers beating wildly as they flew. Damon's legs shot out behind him as he hit the dirt, face down.

He held his breath. He didn't dare look up. The flapping of wings receded across the sky, and still he remained flat on the ground.

No way she'd missed that.

Damon maintained his position. He checked his watch. 1715. He closed his eyes and breathed as gently as he could, desperately trying to keep the dust out of his mouth.

Mercifully, as he waited, the wind began to die. At 1800 hours Damon eased into a crouched position. He brushed himself off, then rose to resume the trail. It was dark now, and she'd be a whole lot harder to find.

The dust had ebbed, leaving instead a clear sky filled with glistening stars. He pressed through the chilled night air, walking slowly and quietly across the terrain. She wouldn't have gone far. Not this late.

An hour later he spotted movement. He ducked down and watched. Nadia spread her blanket out onto the ground. Before she lay down, she removed the knife clipped to her waistband and tucked it under a nearby bush. On the ground she rolled over once, pulled the blanket over her shoulders, sat up, tucked the bottom of the blanket toward her knees, lay back down, and continued rolling.

Priceless. Damon smiled. *She dropped her weapon and then rolled herself into a burrito.*

Four hours later Damon unsheathed his knife and prepared to make contact.

24 NADIA
SATURDAY, FEBRUARY 4

"Wake up."

The whispered words pulled Nadia from sleep. A heaviness pressed against her chest, squeezed the air from her lungs. It must be a dream, but the sharpness of detail—the weight, the warmth—it felt too real. She tried to move but found her arms pinned at her sides.

"Wake up," he said again, a little louder this time.

She opened her eyes. A body stretched across her own. She felt the cold metal of a knife blade against her throat. Moonlight shone on the shaved head leaning toward her. A breeze rustled the branches of the Palo Verde tree silhouetted against the sky.

Damon. He'd come to kill her.

"Did you miss me?"

Fear shot through her body. She opened her mouth to scream. Damon clamped his hand over her open lips, partially covering her nose, suffocating her. Panicked, Nadia thrashed under him.

"Knock it off," he said, adjusting his hand.

She inhaled deeply, the chill of midnight burning her nostrils.

"I'm gonna move my hand," he whispered. "You will not scream. Do you understand?"

She nodded under his weight. He moved his arm and she sat up, kicked off her blanket, desperately tried to free herself from her wool cocoon. She scrambled backward, feeling around for her knife.

"Please," Damon said, holding up her knife. "Not my first rodeo."

"What do you want?" In the darkness she scanned the ground, searching for anything to use as a weapon. Dead leaves and a few branches gathered at the foot of a sage bush to her left. Nadia lunged for a branch.

Just as quickly, Damon pounced, spreading his body over her. He pinned her down, his arm across her throat, his legs lead weights on hers. "Knock it *off*."

She struggled under his weight. "It wasn't my fault!"

"*What* wasn't your fault?"

She tried to roll to the side, to push him off.

"Stop it," he demanded through gritted teeth.

"Everything that happened to you. I didn't turn you in. They already knew."

Damon moved his head closer toward her. He looked at her mouth, then to her eyes. He whispered, his breath hot against her lips. "And how does that help my current situation?"

"Please don't kill me," Nadia said.

Damon released his chokehold. His arms straightened as he lifted himself into a push-up position.

Nadia struck the inside of his right arm at the elbow, then rolled out from under him as he collapsed. She scrambled to her feet and raised her arms, one hand blocking her face, one across her stomach—Sensei's fighting stance.

Damon sat up, brushed the dust from his legs, then rested his hands on his thighs. "Put your hands down. If I'd come to kill you, you'd already be dead." He relaxed his posture.

After a minute or so, she lowered her hands. The cold began to seep through her clothes. She grabbed her blanket and wrapped it around her shoulders. "So what do you want? Just stopped by for old times' sake?"

"I came to ask for your help."

She laughed. "That's how you ask for help? Holding a knife to my throat?" She shook her head. "Whatever you need, the answer is no."

"Nadia, I'm desperate. And I only used the knife so you wouldn't scream in my ear."

"Damon, you're a traitor. You tried to frame me for treason. There is no way I'm helping you with anything."

"Just sit down and let me explain." Still on his knees, he clasped his hands together, pleading.

She looked at the horizon, now blacker than the night sky, and remembered something Dean Wolfe told her last semester about Damon, how he'd given everything up to save her life. She sighed and sat down in the dirt. "I'll listen, but I'm not going to help you."

Damon reached into his bag and pulled out two bottles of water. He opened one and handed it to Nadia. "You want a power bar?"

She hesitated. Outside snacks were definitely not in keeping with the spirit of the survival course. She smiled as she realized the absurdity of that thought—consorting with known traitors was also probably frowned upon. "I'd love one. Peanut butter?"

"With chocolate." He tossed it over.

She ripped open the package. "All right, let's hear it."

He dropped his eyes for a moment, then looked back at her. "It's my mom. She's being held hostage by the Nighthawks."

Oh no. Nadia paused, the power bar at her lips. She took a slow bite, studying him. Damon's ability to deceive was unparalleled. He was the only person she'd ever met without a single tell. Could she trust anything he said?

"The agent in charge—his name is Roberts—is going to kill her unless I bring him some files."

"I know who he is." Nadia took a long drink, still uncertain about the legitimacy of his story. "I'm sorry about your mom, but what does this have to do with me?"

Damon sat quietly for a few minutes. Finally, he answered. "Well, the problem is, I need to get on campus."

Nadia felt lightheaded. *I must be more tired than I thought.* "To get your files?" None of this was making sense. "I don't understand. Where are they? The library? Why would you need my help? Just break in yourself." *Did I just tell Damon to break into the school?*

"Because you're the only one who can get into the dojo. Into the firing range. The weapons room."

Nadia swayed a little. She put an arm out to catch herself.

Damon squinted at her. "You okay?"

"Yeah, I'm just...I feel a little dizzy."

"Maybe you're dehydrated. Finish your water."

Nadia nodded and chugged the bottle. "Why are your files in the dojo? When were you ever in that room?" Her words slurred together. Her tongue wouldn't form the right sounds.

"I may need one other thing."

"Like what?"

"Something that belongs to me." Damon rooted through his bag. "I have to get it back."

"If you want..." Her voice trailed off. What was she saying? "Um...my help you, uh, you need to tell me exactly what you want."

"No, Nadia. I don't."

"Hmm?" Her vision blurred as Damon removed a handgun from his bag.

"I don't *need* to do anything. That's the benefit of being the man with the gun."

She fell forward into Damon's open arms.

25 LIBBY
SATURDAY, FEBRUARY 4
(TWELVE HOURS EARLIER)

For weeks now Libby had been walking on eggshells, waiting to be summoned to Dean Shepard's office to receive news of her dismissal. Uncovering an act of domestic terrorism had been a blessing for her daddy, but a curse for her.

Leave it to him to turn tragedy into opportunity. For a few seconds after his announcement, she'd wondered if he'd fabricated evidence to implicate the Nighthawks. Not really, but a little. He was ambitious, but he wasn't crazy. And anyway, if the Nighthawks weren't behind the bombing, how would he even have learned about their existence?

The timing of the revelation certainly was fortuitous, as he'd been talking about running for president for a while. But he'd promised to wait until the next election cycle. That way she'd be out of school, her momma would be settled back in to her routine.... He'd promised. And like a fool, she'd believed him. She should've known, all those meetings with his advisors. He'd never intended to wait at all.

After lunch on Saturday, Libby pushed through the doors of the dining hall into the hazy afternoon, nodding to the pair of senior girls walking toward her. All she'd wanted was a place of her own, away from her debutante mother and politician father. Out of the spotlight, where she didn't have to sit still and look pretty all the time. A place where she could make a change in the world, quietly and with grace. She'd found that place here at the Academy.

She shook her head, trying to focus on the task at hand. A few hours ago, her marching orders had been hand-delivered to her dorm room, affixed to a beautiful bouquet of flowers. So now, as instructed, Libby crossed the lawn to meet Jack at the southeast corner of campus, otherwise known as the parking lot.

With each step forward, with each issued order, a new thrill rolled through her. Every day that passed without getting called to the dean's office felt like a tiny victory.

She arrived at the meet right on time. Jack stood between the lemon trees, his back against the wall, a garment bag folded over his arm.

"This is for you. Be ready by six o'clock," he said, handing her the opaque bag. "Op-specs are inside."

Libby grinned and whispered, "Where are we going?"

"We're going to a party," Jack said, as he walked away.

The whole way back to her room, Libby imagined the gorgeous gown tucked safely away in the garment bag. She wondered if he'd included a wig and shoes. No matter, she had strappy heels in both black and nude to match any color dress. Maybe the party would be at the state capitol. Her experience chatting up politicians was second to none.

The instant she reached her bedroom, Libby hung the bag on the closet door and pulled open the zipper. Her mild disappointment at seeing the hotel uniform quickly faded; she'd still get to work undercover, it would just be as a coat-check girl.

For the next few hours, she struggled to contain her excitement. At five-thirty she waited for Jack in the parking lot. He arrived a couple minutes past six, having just returned from town. Recon, she imagined.

On the drive in, Jack handed her a small package. "Here are your comms. Just touch it to wake it up."

"Okay." Libby opened the wooden box and lifted the tiny earpiece that would allow them to communicate. She tucked the device into her ear.

"The protocol for the exchange is as follows." Jack glanced at her. "Your contact will say, 'The manager wanted me to confirm that you're here until eleven.' If he's okay to pick up the package, you answer, 'Yes, till eleven.' If he needs to abort, you say, 'I'm only scheduled until ten.' Got it?"

"Got it."

"You read the op-specs?" he asked. "Think you can handle it?"

"Yes." Libby looked out the passenger-side window and smiled. The desert raced by and her stomach flipped as she said, "I'm ready."

A few minutes before seven o'clock, Libby strode through the main hall of the Scottsdale Oasis Resort and into the ballroom. She took her place in the coat-check closet and smiled as the doctors and scientists attending the Annual Biomedical Research Convention thrust their light coats and wraps across her small countertop.

"Thank you," she said, handing the claim tickets one at a time. "Enjoy the party. Thank you."

As ordered, she checked the pockets of every single jacket. It took two hours before she completed the second part of her mission—acquiring an ID badge from a high-level employee of Gentech Labcorp.

As her customers drifted away from the coat check toward the bar, Libby palmed the ID card and touched her ear to wake the comms. She turned slightly from the window so it didn't look like she was talking to herself. "Boy Scout, this is Sunflower, do you copy? Over."

"Sunflower, this is Boy Scout. I read you loud and clear. Ready for your relief? Over."

"Affirmative. I have the item."

Jack told her to be on the lookout. An agent would be along to gather the card. They'd make a copy on-site and return the badge, at which time she would replace it.

A moment later, wearing a waiter's tuxedo and looking handsome as could be, Simon rounded the corner and headed straight to the coat check. Libby tried to hide her delight, as they weren't supposed to know each other.

He rested his empty drinks tray on the counter. "The manager wanted me to confirm that you're here till eleven. Is that right?"

Libby placed her hands flat on the surface. "Yes, till eleven."

"Brilliant," he said. Libby moved her hands away, revealing the palmed card. Simon lifted the card along with his tray. "Back to it, then. I'll bring you a bottled water."

Twenty minutes later Simon returned with a bottle of water on his tray. He placed a cocktail napkin on the counter, then set the bottle on top. Libby slid the napkin into her hand as she took a drink. She returned the plastic ID card, tucked between the napkin layers, to its proper pocket.

A few hours later, the three of them drove back to campus together. Of course Simon had offered her the front seat, but Libby wanted to sit in the darkened back and think about the mission: small, simple, meaningless. And the most exciting experience of her life.

Her eyes stung and she looked out the window, across the unlit desert.

She was really gonna miss this.

When Libby returned to her dorm, she found Casey waiting at the front desk, her bright red curls framing her head like a lion's mane. "What are you doing up so late?" Libby asked, knowing their resident assistant preferred early morning hours.

"Sweetie, your mom called. She said it was really important that you get back to her tonight."

Libby's stomach fell. "Why? What's wrong?"

Casey shook her head. "She didn't say. Today's code to call off campus is 4-5-4-6. It resets at midnight, so you have to call right now. I'll give you some privacy, but knock on my door if you need me."

As Casey left the lobby, Libby circled around her desk to the telephone. She should've asked if her mother sounded drunk. Bracing herself, she dialed home.

The line picked up on the first ring. "Liberty?"

"Yes, Momma, it's me. What's wrong? Is it Daddy?"

"Honey, nothin's wrong."

Libby frowned. That was obviously a lie, but her momma didn't sound like she'd been drinking. "Then why am I calling you at two a.m. eastern time?"

Her momma sighed. "Listen, there's something I need to tell you. Your daddy would'a done it himself, but he had to get back to Washington."

Libby's stomach churned. Something bad was coming.

"A long time ago, there was an incident between your daddy and me. Now, it's ancient history, we've worked through it, and all has been forgiven."

"Momma, please. I can't take the suspense, and you're really scaring me."

"You know your daddy loves you, right? And he loves your brother, and he loves me. And I love him."

"Momma," Libby said sharply. Were they getting a divorce? They would never do that—certainly not during an election year.

"Your daddy had.... There was a short time in our marriage when he was seeing another woman."

Libby felt nauseous. She sat down in Casey's chair.

"The *only* reason I am telling you about this is because someone called the house making some empty threats."

"What are you talking about? What kind of threats?"

"They said if he doesn't drop out of the election, they're going to the press with the affair. Well, you know perfectly well your father is like a dog with a bone, and all that did was rile him up even more."

"Is he in danger?"

"Of course not. I just wanted to tell you myself. In the unlikely event that the caller follows through, we didn't want you hearing about it on the morning news."

Libby felt like she'd been kicked in the gut. All this time she'd resented her momma for drinking so much, for making things so hard for her daddy—who was just the sweetest man alive. But maybe this was why she'd started drinking in the first place.

For a second Libby thought she might be sick. She pressed her hand to her mouth.

"You still there?" her momma asked.

She took a deep, steadying breath. "Yeah, I'm here. But it's late and I need to go."

"Are you okay?"

"I'm okay. How about you? Are you okay?" What she really wanted to ask was, *are you gonna drink over this?*

"Honey, I'm fine. We've gotten through a whole lot worse together; we'll get through this. Call me in a couple days?"

"Yes, Momma, I will. Tell Daddy I love him. Love you." Libby hung up the phone and rested her head in her hand.

A moment later Casey's door opened. "Everything okay?"

Libby jumped up and threw a smile on her face. "Yeah, everything's great. Well, my brother broke his ankle skiing, so that's not great, but he'll be fine. He's always doing stuff like that."

"I'm glad to hear it," Casey said. "I was a little worried. Sleep tight, okay?"

"I will, thank you. You too."

Libby was halfway down the hall before she remembered that the phones were tapped. Every Desert Mountain employee with clearance had just witnessed the airing of Senator Bishop's dirty laundry.

26 NADIA
SUNDAY, FEBRUARY 5

Nadia struggled to open her eyes. Her lids felt heavy, stuck together. Every muscle ached, like she'd been shoved in the trunk of a car all night. Her head throbbed—it took a minute to remember what had happened.

Sunlight poured across the popcorn ceiling from a small, grimy window high on the wall. Was it Sunday? Or had she been out for an entire day? Did the school know she was missing? She wasn't due back until Tuesday. How long had she been gone?

My tracking device. Had Sensei checked her beacon yet?

With effort she lifted her head. She didn't recognize the queen-sized bed, the small room. Under the blanket her wrists were handcuffed together. As her eyes adjusted to the light, she searched for a weapon—anything heavy or sharp to use on Damon at the first available opportunity. Nothing. She tried pulling her hands apart, but the restraints wouldn't give.

Frustrated and angry, she dropped her head onto the pillow.

A few minutes later she heard footsteps outside the bedroom door.

Damon entered the room and offered a small smile. "How are you feeling?"

"How am I *feeling*? Are you out of your mind?"

"Scoot over." He pushed her toward the center of the bed and sat on the edge, then gently pressed two fingers along her throat. "Your pulse is good," he said. "I know you don't wanna be here, but if you pay attention, you might learn something. So here's your first lesson: don't ever accept a drink from someone you don't trust."

"I *did* trust you."

"That was your first mistake. You know what they say, once a traitor, always a traitor."

"That's 'cheater.' Once a cheater."

"Potato, potahto," he said.

"Uncuff me. I have a splitting headache. Where's my bag?"

"Yeah, sorry. That'll go away. It's the Datura—I might have used too much for your size. It's hard to gauge with plants. Why do you want your bag?"

"You drugged me?"

"A little bit," he said.

"Uncuff me!" Her head pounded and she instantly regretted raising her voice.

"Not until we get some things squared away."

She scowled. "I need my bag."

"I already tossed your tracker." He leaned back and folded his hands in his lap. "I'm sorry I drugged you. And restrained you. But sometimes you can be stubborn, and I need your undivided attention."

Anger rose in her chest. Without her tracker, she had no shot of being rescued. She'd have to do it herself. She tried again to loosen her wrists, which already felt raw from wrestling against the restraints.

"I need you to listen." Damon placed a paper clip and a safety pin on her blanket. "I have a plan, and I can't do it without you."

She narrowed her eyes. "What makes you think I would *ever* agree to help you?"

"For starters, I'm the only person in your entire life who's had the decency to be honest. You got my dead drop?" He propped her pillows against the wall, then gestured for her to move back.

"Oh, please. The faked recruit file? I should've known it was from you." She pressed her feet against his thigh and tried to push him away. He didn't budge. *"Move."* She kicked at him.

With one hand, Damon grabbed her ankles and swung her legs off the bed. "You can throw a tantrum if you want, but the faster we get through this mission, the faster you get rid of me."

His reasonable reaction infuriated her—she wanted a fight, a way to release the anger building inside her body. She held out her chaffed wrists. "Take these off."

He nodded toward the paper clip and pin. "Open them yourself."

"How?" When he didn't answer she rolled her eyes, unfolded the paper clip, then bent the tip to make a tiny loop. She bit down on the clip to tighten the hook, then inserted the makeshift key into the lock. "I don't know what the locking mechanism looks like." Again, no response. She shoved the clip into the hole.

He took a deep breath. "The file I sent you is real. I can prove it."

"I'm sure you can. I just have to complete a series of treasonous crimes first, right? Then you'll tell me everything? Offer more fabricated evidence?"

"I'll show you proof long before the treasonous crimes begin."

She scowled at the handcuffs. "I can't get them. It's too hard."

Damon scoffed. "It's a whole lot easier than the training I went through."

Against her will, Nadia felt a flicker of curiosity. "What, am I supposed to thank you for your graciousness?"

"You want to hear about my first time?" She refused to answer, but after a moment, he continued. "Roberts had these agents working for him, ex-special forces. Those guys beat the hell out of me. But this was one of my lessons." He nodded toward her wrists. "Getting out of handcuffs. So they put me in this cinder-block room with a concrete floor. There was one chair—wooden, straight-backed—and they sat me down. Duct taped my feet to the legs, cuffed my wrists behind the back of the chair. The guy dropped a straight pin, a safety pin, a paper clip, and a pair of reading glasses on the ground. Left one bottle of water near the door. Said he'd be back when I got myself out. It took me two days."

"That explains your lack of hospitality."

He smiled. "Right? The worst part was having to knock myself over in the chair." He mimed the forceful movement. "I dislocated my shoulder. Then I figured out how to open the water bottle behind my back, but the only way I could drink it was to dump it out and lick it off the floor."

Nadia sighed. "So which tool was most effective?"

"The reading glasses. Snap the arm off the frame and use the protruding metal."

"Second best?"

"Figure it out yourself." He stood and left the room.

Five minutes into the task, her neck began to ache. Another ten minutes made her fingers raw. The paper clip wasn't working, so she moved on to the safety pin. She pulled it open and twisted the sharp end into the tiny lock. It slipped in her fingers, and she accidentally bent the tip into a right angle. A tight rope of knots formed across her shoulders. She stretched her arms toward the ceiling.

Nadia rolled her neck from side to side before shoving the bent pin back into the lock. Twenty minutes later, fingers aching, she was about to give up. Then the lock clicked open. She threw the cuffs against the wall and rubbed her wrists.

Damon popped his head inside the door. "It's about time. Now take a second to figure out how you accidentally freed yourself, just in case you ever need to repeat the performance. Look at the angle of the pin."

"Yeah, I got it."

"Seriously, look at the angle." He pointed to the safety pin. "You never know—it might save your life one day."

27 SIMON
SUNDAY, FEBRUARY 5

A few weeks ago, as he wasn't endowed with the virtue of patience, Simon had convinced Alan that a jaunt to Cave Creek was of paramount importance to their friendship. While his roommate browsed an independent bookstore, Simon had slipped next door to the post office. Inside a reeking stall in the men's room, he'd swabbed his cheek, sealed the prepaid package from the genetics lab, and popped it back in the post.

Naturally, he'd ordered a rush on the DNA sequencing. The results were to be sent via encrypted email. Problem was, until he discovered Shepard's credentials for the CIA mainframe, he couldn't access CIADIS and, therefore, would have nothing with which to compare his results. This he found absolutely maddening. He'd never been closer to learning the truth about his father, and each day he was made to wait seemed longer than the last.

As a result, Simon had been forced to formulate a contingency plan. It would commence within the next twenty-four hours, and might or might not get his roommate arrested for treason.

Sunday morning, a few minutes before ten, Simon straightened his tie as he walked toward the guard station. He'd chosen a light blue oxford, yellow and cornflower blue striped tie, and a navy jacket, along with a crisply pressed pair of khakis.

As he reached the end of the sidewalk, Jack pulled round in a black Avalon. He rolled down the passenger-side window and said, "Get in."

"I ate my op-specs," Simon said, climbing into the vehicle. "What's my mission?"

Jack waved to the guard as the iron gate swung open. "Look in the glovebox."

Inside, among a few other items, Simon found a USB memory stick and the Gentech ID badge he'd copied while assisting Libby's mission.

Simon held up the memory stick. "What's this? Are we adding or extracting?"

Jack shrugged. "My op-specs said not to open it."

"So what?"

"So I follow orders, and you should, too. That stick has wifi capability. My handler will receive an alert the moment it's plugged in."

"Live a little."

Jack ignored him and continued issuing instructions. "You're the nephew of Barrett Lyle. She's the only European working at the lab, so she's the one we're going with."

"Is she even English? We don't all sound alike, you know," Simon said, mildly insulted. "And what should I do if she's there?"

"Gentech is closed on Sundays. You won't run into your aunt."

Twenty minutes later the boys pulled into the deserted parking lot of Gentech Labcorp, a sleek ten-story building with loads of dark, tinted glass and brushed stainless steel.

Jack parked the car and handed Simon his comms. "Your distress word is *tumble*. If you get caught, say the word and I'll pull the fire alarm."

"You've nothing to worry about. I do this sort of thing all the time."

Simon crossed the lot and pulled open the glass doors leading into the bright lobby. The security guard looked up from his station, situated in the center of the atrium.

"Can I help you, son?"

"Yeah, I hope so. My aunt works upstairs, fifth floor. Friday afternoon she forgot her briefcase. The problem is she's driven to Tucson for the week, but her medication is in her bag." Simon patted his heart a few times. "It's her ticker. I told her, just go to the emergency room and get a new prescription. She spent the next twenty minutes lecturing me on patient abuse of emergency rooms." Simon raised his voice an octave, mimicking his imaginary aunt. "'They're not drugstores, Nigel! This is why healthcare costs so much. People taking advantage of the system.'" He rolled his eyes. "'All right, Auntie,' I said. 'I'll pop round to your office and fetch your bag.'" Simon checked his watch. "So I get to spend my Sunday afternoon driving to Tucson because my aunt can't be bothered to trouble an actual physician. What are they paid for, that's my question. Am I right?"

The guard nodded once. "What's your aunt's name?"

"Barrett Lyle. You know her? Not the warmest woman in the world."

"I thought she was German."

"Marriage relations," Simon said. The man hesitated and Simon shrugged. "Know what? That's fine. Can I borrow your phone? I'll ring from here and let her know you're not able to send me upstairs. It'll save me the drive to Tucson, and I still get credit for making an effort. That's what I call a win-win." He moved toward the desk and reached for the phone. "What's your name then? Cause she'll want to know. And brace yourself for her fury. But no matter what she says, I'm on your side. When she complains to your boss, I'll tell him it wasn't your fault."

The guard rested his hand over the receiver and sighed. "Go ahead. The elevators are down that hall. You have the keys to her office?"

"Sure do. Thanks, mate. I'll be back in a jiffy." Simon speed-walked to the lift. As the doors closed, he touched his comms. "Boy Scout, I'm in."

"Copy, Mako. Take the elevator to the fifth floor, then the stairwell up to seven. That's where the mainframe is stored. Over."

The doors opened, and Simon stepped into the darkened hallway. He followed the exit signs to the stairwell, then jogged up the steps to the seventh floor.

The room that housed the server took up half the floor. Simon swiped his ID badge through the security lock. Inside the darkened, windowless room, the bank of computers glowed with soft greens and blues. It wasn't much light, but enough to navigate the area.

He searched the equipment until he found the section labeled BACKUP. His instructions dictated that he plug in the USB drive here, as it likely wouldn't be noticed before Jack could destroy the evidence. Simon inserted the drive and waited for the tiny green light, indicating that he'd properly placed the device.

A few seconds later, he was back in the hall, racing toward the stairwell. On the fifth-floor landing, he pushed through the door and sprinted back to the lift.

A minute later the doors opened into the lobby. Simon thrust his hands in his pockets and whistled as he stepped from the cabin. "Thanks again," he said, moving quickly toward the door.

"Wait," the guard ordered.

Simon froze. *Tumble.* How to work that into a sentence? He turned toward the man and smiled. "Yes?"

The guard narrowed his eyes. "Where's the briefcase?"

"Ah." Simon pulled a prescription bottle from his pocket and gave it a shake. The breath mints rattled against the plastic. "This is really all she needs. If she wants something else, she can get it herself."

28 NADIA
SUNDAY, FEBRUARY 5

Nadia tossed her blanket aside. She had no intention of heeding Damon's instructions to study the handcuffs. Instead, she scrambled out of bed and followed him into a narrow hallway. Ten steps later the hall opened into a kitchenette and dining room—they were in a trailer. She scanned the surfaces for weapons: a coffee pot, a flashlight, a box of matches. Nothing heavy enough to knock him out—just heavy enough to piss him off.

Without asking she opened the window over the tiny kitchen sink to survey the landscape, trying to assess her location. The sun, almost directly overhead, reflected off the native cacti and low-growing bushes of the Sonoran Desert, so she knew he hadn't taken her too far from school. The trailer, parked in a small clearing, appeared to be isolated. "Where are we?"

"Off the grid." Damon turned on the light over the kitchen sink.

"Then how do you have electricity?"

"Gas-powered generator."

Tacked to the wood-paneled walls were photographs, memos, sticky notes, shards of maps. The worn linoleum floor peeled up at the corners. Across from the kitchenette was a small dining table piled with papers. Damon sat on one of the attached benches. He slid open the window above the table, then unrolled a USCG topographical map and studied the terrain.

Two pictures taped to the refrigerator grabbed her attention. The first was Professor Hayden, wearing a baseball hat and dark sunglasses. A thick black X had been drawn across his face. She didn't recognize the man in the second photo. "Who's this?"

Without looking, Damon answered, "That's Roberts."

Agent Roberts, the head of the Nighthawks. The man who'd tried to frame her for treason.

"By the way, this is for you," Damon said. In his extended hand rested a tiny metal key. "It's for the cuffs."

She took the key, a small cylinder with a short, blunt right angle at the very end. "What am I supposed to do with this?"

"Look at it, that's what. You didn't bother looking at the angle of the safety pin, did you? That was lesson number two. Here's lesson number three." He grabbed the bottle of water sitting on the table across from his seat, then tossed it to her.

"How stupid do you think I am?" She hurled the bottle back at him, even though her mouth felt like sandpaper. Maybe the tap water was drinkable.

Damon caught it in midair. He sighed and handed it back. "Check the seal. It's not broken."

Nadia examined the intact seal, then started to twist off the cap.

"Squeeze it first," he said.

"What?"

"Squeeze the bottle."

Her eyes narrowed, studying him. "Why?"

"Check for syringe holes. In the future, your next move would be to wet your lips and wait for half an hour. If they tingle or start to turn numb, it's poisoned." He turned back to his map. "But don't worry, you're of little use to me dead. At this point, anyway."

Nadia cracked open the bottle and took a long drink, annoyed that Damon's lessons interested her. She leaned against the refrigerator and crossed her arms. "You said you had proof that my dad's CIA."

Damon glanced up. "Operation Cyprus."

She shrugged. "What's that?"

"Operation Cyprus is the file you get to read after we've completed our mission."

Nadia scoffed. "I knew it. You don't have anything. You forged the recruit file."

"I didn't. And as soon as we get back I'll prove it."

"Why do I have to wait?"

"Because I need you to focus on the mission in front of us and not be thinking about your dad."

"I can often hold up to two thoughts in my head at once," she said, glaring at him.

Damon leaned to the side and pulled a piece of paper from his back pocket. He held it out to her.

"What's that?"

He averted his gaze as a shadow crossed his face.

Nadia took the paper—a folded photograph. She slid into the bench seat across from him and unfolded the picture. The woman, dark brown skin, black hair, tear-stained cheeks, gripped a newspaper as she stared blankly into the camera.

Nadia's stomach churned. Damon's mom.

She glanced at him. His eyes were on the map spread across the table, but his shallow breath led her to believe his thoughts were with the picture. She tried to ignore the sudden surge of compassion she felt toward him. After a moment, she said, "I'm sorry this happened to her."

He looked up. "If you don't help me, it'll be your mom next."

Anger flashed around her heart. She slammed her hand on the table. "Do *not* threaten me."

Damon's mouth tightened as his nostrils flared. "It is not a threat. It is a fact. And just to clarify, I'm not the one endangering her. You are."

"What are you talking about?"

He rubbed his face with both hands. After a moment he asked, "Have you ever heard of Project Genesis?"

Nadia shook her head.

"Basically, it's a GPS for DNA. Upload your target's genetic fingerprint, and a satellite locates them anywhere on the planet. After that, a guided missile takes them out. Roberts wants Project Genesis. He tried to steal it—remember the bombing last month in Northern Virginia?"

She nodded. "Yeah, Libby's dad mentioned it when he made his big announcement."

"Exactly. That's where they're developing Project Genesis. And it's only a matter of time until Roberts gets his hands on the technology."

"What does this have to do with me?"

"You know the DNA samples Dr. Cameron collects from all the recruits? He destroys the physical sample, but our sequence is kept in a database. Since we're minors, the student database is housed on campus. When we turn eighteen, a copy of our DNA is sent to CIADIS to be stored with all the other CIA officers."

"What's CIADIS?" she asked.

"CIADIS is the genome encyclopedia of the entire Central Intelligence Agency. The DNA database of everyone who works for the CIA."

"And that's stored at Langley? At CIA headquarters?"

"No, actually. CIADIS is housed at a biomedical data storage facility in Phoenix, called Gentech Labcorp. But that's irrelevant, because *you* can access the student database and delete our DNA *before* it's uploaded to the main server."

"Why don't you just break onto campus and do it yourself?"

He shook his head. "Won't do me any good. You're the only one who can get to it."

"What makes you think I can get to it?"

"It's in the weapons room at the dojo."

She frowned. "Why would the database be in the weapons room?" Damon, evidently exasperated by her stupid questions, sighed loudly. Nadia narrowed her eyes. "I'm sorry, are my questions annoying you? Maybe you should've kidnapped a smarter sidekick."

"Yeah, well, you're all I've got." With a light nod, he added, "You're my muscle."

"*I'm* your muscle? Solid plan."

He took a deep breath. "Do you remember last semester, the first time Sensei took us into the shooting range?" When she nodded, he said, "Did you notice the filing cabinet against the wall in the weapons room?"

"I was a little distracted by the arsenal. I just saw a bunch of weapons. What makes you think that's the database?" she asked.

"Why would he need a filing cabinet in a weapons room? Also, it's the most secure spot on campus."

Nadia shook her head. "So why do I need to delete your DNA? How does that help your mother?"

"Because of Project Genesis. As long as my DNA is on file, I'm not safe. Whether the weapon is controlled by Roberts or the CIA, I've got a target on my back. And I want out. As soon as I rescue my mom, I'm done. She and I disappear. And destroying the student database is the *only* way to make that happen." He paused for a beat. "I would also like to point out that as long as the database is intact, you're not safe, either."

"Me? Roberts barely knows I exist."

He pursed his lips. "Are you willing to consider the possibility that your dad's recruit file is real?"

"Not at all. You've shown me zero evidence. And where did you supposedly get that file?"

"I found a zip drive that belonged to Roberts. *He* had the file on your dad. I just printed you a copy. Try to make that one of the two thoughts you can hold in your head at any given time, because that information will be extremely relevant in a few hours." He paused. "Just for argument's sake, pretend your dad's file is legit. If Roberts can get to my DNA in the student database, he can get to yours, too—and your dad's. And if he can find you and your dad, he can probably find your mom." Damon held up the picture of his mother. "That's what I meant when I said your mom might be next."

A stab of fear pierced her heart. He made a valid point. But why would Roberts have a file on her dad? Why would he bother with them? She shook her head. "He doesn't know my family, and I'm guessing he doesn't care about any of us. He tried to set me up because I was a convenient scapegoat, not because he personally dislikes me."

Damon opened his mouth like he was going to say something, but seemed to change his mind. He went back to his map. A minute later he looked up and leaned toward her. He locked onto her eyes. "I swear on my mother's life that your father is CIA. The second we get back I'll prove it, and you'll be *thanking* me for letting you delete our DNA." He sat back, resumed his work.

Nadia rested her head in her hands. Was any of this true? Could her father really be CIA? If he was, did her mom know? No, no way. Her mom wouldn't have signed up for this kind of life, and she *never* would've allowed Nadia to join. If she found out that her husband had recruited their only child...

Nadia sighed. Why was she still considering this? If Damon had proof, he'd have shown her by now. So why couldn't she let it go?

She leaned back in the narrow bench seat and crossed her arms. "No offense, but if you want me to break into the Academy and tamper with government-owned equipment, you need to give me a little more than just your word."

"Offense taken," he mumbled.

"I'm not kidding. I won't do it."

Damon met her eyes. He stared at her in that way of his—scrutinizing, analyzing, unblinking. She didn't flinch.

After a minute he said, "I won't show you the whole file, not until we get back." He crouched on the floor and reached under the table. Nadia stuck her head underneath as Damon opened the built-in cupboard tucked below his bench seat. After rifling through a black backpack, he tossed a photograph onto the table, then took the pack and disappeared into the bedroom. A second later he returned, empty-handed. "Go ahead." He nodded at the table.

She glanced at the picture. Two high school boys standing on a bright green lawn in caps and gowns. Graduation day. She looked back at Damon.

"Closer," he said.

As Nadia turned her eyes back to the photograph, a warm rush moved through her body. Her heart sank as she took in her father's face. She started to say, "You could've gotten this anywhere," until she recognized the other kid.

Her dad stood with his arm thrown over the shoulder of a tall, slender boy, impeccably groomed even then. Marcus Sloan, the recruiter who had invited her to Desert Mountain Academy. The man her father pretended never to have seen before.

It was true. Her father was CIA.

And he knew about the Academy.

29 ALAN
SUNDAY, FEBRUARY 5

Alan could not decide which was worse: his Mossad-agent grandfather lurking around campus jeopardizing Alan's freedoms, or his charlatan roommate who, upon discovering the family secret, immediately blackmailed Alan into committing a series of horrific crimes.

Presently, Alan sat at his desk in his dorm room, fingers poised over Simon's laptop, racking his brain for Saba's password.

"Hack the back door," Simon said nonchalantly, as though Alan's relationship with his grandfather did not rest on this mission remaining undiscovered. "It's no big deal."

Simon, Alan decided. *Simon is definitely worse.*

Alan swiveled in his chair. His roommate lounged across his bed, bare feet propped up on a pillow, flipping through a men's fashion magazine. "If it is such an easy task, why do you need my help?"

"Because I don't speak Hebrew." Simon dropped the magazine and rose from the bed. He pulled his desk chair next to Alan's. "Look, I can probably get into Mossad's mainframe, but we'll need your grandfather's credentials to hijack a drone. Can you translate once we're in?"

"Of course I can, but I am still unclear as to why you need a military drone."

"Hand me the laptop."

Alan pushed the computer across the desk and waited while Simon tapped away at the keyboard. After a few minutes, Simon passed it back.

"There." He returned to his bed. "Now hook me up. I want a flyover at noon. Just as Shepard leaves for lunch."

Alan had learned Hebrew before English, so negotiating the menu to locate Saba's nonlethal arsenal required little mental effort. "If you are so curious as to where she eats, why do you not just follow her?"

"I don't care where she's going. I want her to see the drone."

Alan turned back around. "You know it flies several miles above the earth, right?"

Simon dropped his head back against the pile of pillows. "Oh, shite. I didn't even think of that. Can you set it to fly lower?"

Alan sighed and glared at his roommate. "I will do my best."

Simon smiled. "I really owe you one, mate."

An hour after redirecting the Israeli drone, Alan received a coded message under the door instructing him to attend a clandestine meeting later that afternoon. Convinced that Saba had already discovered his transgressions, Alan nearly burst into his office to confess. But it was Sunday, and he did not believe that Saba kept office hours on Sunday. So when Alan arrived at the specified location—a small grove of olive trees behind the library—he was infinitely relieved to see Jack waiting for him, and not his grandfather.

"How's it going?" Jack asked.

"What do you mean? Have you heard something?" Panic filled his chest. Maybe Simon had lied—maybe his laptop was *not* undetectable.

"What are you talking about?"

Alan swallowed hard. "Nothing, why? What are *you* talking about?"

Jack narrowed his eyes as he handed Alan an envelope. "Your op-specs are in here. Use the cipher computer in the library. Dr. Wilson is expecting you. Questions?"

"My mission is to crack a code using the cipher computer?"

"You're using that computer because it's not monitored. It's barely used, so security doesn't bother with it. That's all I can tell you right now. Read your op-specs; following directions is part of the assignment. Understand?"

Alan nodded slightly, still woozy from the rush of stress-induced cortisol he'd experienced.

"Give me three minutes, then go to the library. Good luck."

As Jack receded around the building, Alan leaned against the gnarled trunk of the closest tree. He checked his watch and took a few deep breaths. He could not do this—how did people live with the constant deceit? What was he doing here, at a black-ops training facility?

This was a horrible mistake. He closed his eyes and waited.

Two minutes later he pushed himself off the tree, rounded the building, and entered the library.

Dr. Wilson escorted him down the hall behind the language lab and unlocked the door to the cipher computer. "Lock up when you're done," she said, turning on the light.

"Yes ma'am." Alan closed the door and sat at the tiny cubicle, which filled the windowless room. He pulled the trash can close to his chair—the jumping nerves in his stomach had left a lingering nausea, and he was afraid he might vomit—and then ripped open the envelope Jack had given him. His instructions were to open a private browser and follow an IP address to an encrypted portal, where he was then to upload a DNA sequence through a surreptitious backdoor entry point.

Alan carefully followed the directions, grateful that his mission did not require him to leave campus. He opened the portal, which led to an external drive that had been manually installed in the mainframe of a place called Gentech Labcorp. He searched for the target of his mission, a deceased agent by the name of Milo Riazotti, then painstakingly entered the provided data. Next, in accordance with the written op-specs, he erased his browsing history, opened the hard drive, and manually deleted the last hour's worth of activities.

Lastly, Alan opened the cipher program, entered the coded message included in his documentation, transcribed the message, and powered down. The last step of his assignment was to destroy all paperwork, including the transcribed message. Apparently, he had only entered a code in case the librarian got curious. If she checked the history, she would see that Alan's assignment involved cracking a difficult cipher.

On his way out of the library, Alan stopped at the men's room. After pressing a damp wad of paper towels against the back of his neck, he locked himself in a stall and dug the flash paper from his pocket. He dropped the pages into the toilet and watched as the genetic sequence—the entirety of a human being—dissolved into nothingness.

If only it were so easy to disappear.

Less than twenty-four hours after Alan betrayed his grandfather, at a few minutes past 0300 on Monday morning, his roommate's computer stirred to life. With his eye mask firmly in place, Alan did not notice the soft blue light, but the quiet beeping was enough to pull him from slumber. He sat up and slid the mask onto his forehead, rubbing the sleep from his eyes.

The laptop screen flashed a message: *Video Available for Download*.

"Hey," Alan said. "Wake up." He lay back down as Simon sat up.

"Oi, what do you want?" Simon's voice was cross, which Alan found somewhat ironic, as it was his project rousting them in the middle of the night.

"Your drone. It is on its way back to Israel."

"What?" The bedcovers rustled and Simon's feet hit the floor. "No, I said noon!"

Alan opened his eyes. *Uh-oh*. He had not thought to change the time zone. Feeling his face flush, he sat up, grateful for the dark. "I did exactly as you instructed. According to the Israeli drone, it *is* noon."

"It's three o'clock in the bloody morning!"

Alan was not about to admit to Simon that he had made such an elementary mistake. "There is a nine-hour time difference between here and Tel Aviv."

"I'm aware of that," Simon declared. "Why would I want a bloody drone in the middle of the bloody night?"

"I cannot begin to imagine why you want the things you do."

"Of course I meant Phoenix time—I specifically told you I wanted Shepard to see it when she left for *lunch*!"

Alan lay back down and pulled the covers around his neck. He slid the satin mask over his eyes. "You really should have confirmed these details in advance."

30 NADIA
MONDAY, FEBRUARY 6
(40 MINUTES EARLIER)

At 2:20 a.m. Nadia watched the moon as Damon drove toward campus. She rested her head against the cool glass of the passenger-side window. It had taken several hours for the nausea to pass, for her heart to stop racing. Now her adrenaline had temporarily dipped, leaving her exhausted and depleted.

She needed to see the rest of that file. She'd scrutinized the photo, examined the shadows, the pixels. It was either real, or a flawless forgery. But knowing Marcus Sloan didn't necessarily make her father CIA, did it?

Of course it did. And to think otherwise was foolish and naive.

She turned toward Damon. "Why did you send me that file?"

"I thought you deserved to know the truth."

"I don't believe for a second it was an act of altruism, so I'll ask again, why did you send me his file?"

Damon's hands tightened around the wheel. "You and I are both pawns in someone else's game. How are you not outraged by this?" His nostrils flared as he clenched his jaw. "You deserve the truth. You deserve the chance to make your own decisions, and not be forced—or tricked—into espionage. I'm sick of being used. I want *out*. And if I can't delete my DNA, I don't stand a chance."

She narrowed her eyes. There was something else. "Tell me the rest."

"That's all you get right now." He glanced at her.

Nadia scowled. A moment later she asked, "So how do I disable the database?"

Damon unzipped the breast pocket of his jacket, reached inside, then handed her a thumb drive. "Insert this into the USB port, then double-click the icon. The worm will do the rest. It's completely fool-proof. Just turn on the mainframe and start the program."

"Cyberespionage for dummies." Nadia tapped the thumb drive against the back of her hand. "So I'm erasing the entire history of everyone who's ever attended Desert Mountain?"

"As I said, you'll thank me later."

She looked out the window and frowned. "Listen, we may have a problem. The weapons room has a biometric security lock, and I can't get in without Sensei's thumbprint."

"So kill him and cut off his thumb."

"I don't really see that happening."

"You're fairly resourceful. You'll think of something." Damon adjusted the rearview mirror. "What are you gonna say if you get caught?"

"I won't get caught."

"If you do, I'm coming after you. And that will not end well for the other guy."

She closed her eyes. Why would her father send her to the Academy if he knew the truth? Would she have picked this life for *her* child?

After a few minutes, Damon said, "You're distracted, aren't you? That's why I didn't want to show you the file."

"I'm not distracted," she lied.

"What were you thinking about?"

A beat. "Puppies."

Damon smiled and they continued in silence.

Fifteen minutes later he pulled off the road. "We're about a half klick out. We'll go on foot from here." He popped the trunk.

Nadia stepped from the car into the chilled night air. A million stars punctured the blanket of black that stretched overhead.

"You know what to do?" he asked.

"Yes."

"You have the thumb drive?"

"Yes." She looked away.

"Look at me."

Nadia narrowed her eyes and slowly turned her head. "What?"

"I'm scanning you for tracking devices when we get out. You don't want me to find one. And don't get some idea that you're gonna alert Sensei that we're on campus so the CIA can catch their traitor. Do you understand?" He waited for her to nod, then pulled a rifle from the back of the trunk.

She shook her head. "What do you need that for?"

"Just in case you *don't* understand." He attached a silencer and secured a laser scope to the side rail.

"Leave it. You won't need it."

"Ain't your mission. Move."

"If you kill anyone, I'm done."

"If you're done, my mom is dead. And you will never learn the truth. We haven't even scratched the surface of your father's lies." Nadia crossed her arms and scowled. Damon rolled his eyes and said, "I don't kill for sport. This is a last resort. Let's go."

She followed him through the brush. As the back wall of campus came into view, Damon grabbed her arm. "Put this in your ear." He handed her the tiny comms device. "Now you can hear me, and I can hear you. You get in any trouble, I'll come get you. From the time you hit the dojo, we've got maybe ten minutes to get out." Damon held his hands together to boost her up the wall.

Nadia pulled herself to the top and crouched down. Her eyes scanned campus for movement. All was still, so she stretched onto her stomach and offered Damon a hand. He grabbed her wrist and, a second later, was beside her on the wall. Silently, he jumped the ten feet to the campus side, where he held out his arms. She eased down onto him.

Damon held her against him for a split second as their eyes met. Nadia looked away.

"Good luck," he said.

"I don't need you to wish me luck."

"I admire your confidence."

Nadia moved swiftly along the back of the buildings, hidden in the shadows. When she opened the door to the covert-ops room, a silent alarm would sound in Sensei's sleeping quarters. After triggering the alarm, she'd still have to make it into the weapons room and back to the wall before Sensei found her.

She reached the dojo and slid open the *shoji* screens. She raced down the hall, across the mats, up the north wing. At the door to the covert-ops room, she typed in the code: *abunai*. A soft clang of metal, and the lock opened.

Nadia slipped inside and tapped her comms. "I'm in."

Damon's voice crackled in her ear. "Roger that. All's quiet out here."

Nadia opened the cabinet closest to the door and breathed a sigh of relief. Sensei's thumbprint on a thin sheet of latex, right where she'd left it.

She carefully lifted the print and laid it over her thumb. Next to the latex print were a selection of lock-picking kits; she shoved one into her pocket.

Back in the hall, she moved two doors down to the shooting range. She entered the code, pressed her latex-covered thumb onto the keypad, and held her breath.

Clang. The lock released.

Nadia sprinted the width of the shooting range toward the locked door at the back of the room. She repeated the entry procedure and stepped into the weapons room, then clicked on her penlight.

Pegboards lined all four walls. Fixed to the walls were the weapons: groups of swords, knives, and daggers; long-range and assault rifles; handguns in every caliber, both revolver and semi-automatic. She shone her light along the lower part of the room until she reached the filing cabinet, nestled between a column of Japanese katana swords and Swiss hunting knives.

The chest was locked. Nadia held the penlight in her mouth and used the lock-picking kit to open the top drawer. The built-in CPU hummed quietly as she flipped up the screen. The cursor blinked a bright blue light in the darkened room. She ran her fingers along the edge until she felt the USB port, then inserted Damon's thumb drive and double-clicked.

While she waited for the worm to load, she searched the shelves for a tranquilizer gun. She loaded the magazine and tucked the weapon into her waistband. Damon might have information she needed, but she didn't have to trust him. He still wasn't telling her the whole truth. It probably wouldn't come to it, but this way, she could leave when she wanted.

Back at the computer, Nadia checked the status. A single box had appeared onscreen: *Press to Run*. She clicked the button. Within ninety seconds the pixels on the screen had bled together into a sheet of black. She ripped the drive from the port and rushed from the room, closing the door behind her.

Nadia secured the shooting gallery and ran toward the dojo entrance. Outside she sprinted along the back wall, around her dorm, and past the dining hall, until she reached her starting point. Damon wasn't there.

They didn't have much time before Sensei would reach the weapons room and investigate the break-in. He knew there was only one person who could get in. He would realize she wasn't on her solo, alert the guards, and then—

"Where are you?" she whispered frantically. The hands of her watch glowed through the darkness. Nine minutes. They'd been on campus for nine minutes. How long since she'd opened the covert-ops room door? What would she say if she got caught?

"Nadia?"

She froze. *Oh no.*

"What are you doing here?"

Jack.

Slowly, she turned away from the wall. "Hey, what's up?"

He let out a short laugh and raised his eyebrows. "'What's up?' What are you doing back so soon?"

"I'm not. I mean, I *am*, but I'm still on my solo." Nadia shifted her gaze away from his face and scanned the area behind him. "I had a special assignment." No sign of Damon.

Jack stepped toward her. "I never came back to campus during a solo."

"Yeah, Dean Shepard's changing things up, I guess."

"What's the assignment?"

"I can't really talk about it—you understand. Listen, I have to go. We'll catch up when I get back, okay?"

Jack took her arm as his eyes searched her face. "Are you okay?"

"Yeah, I'm fine. I'm just really tired." She gently freed herself.

His eyes narrowed. "Seriously, what's going on?"

"Nothing." She smiled a little. "It's just—it's none of your business. I don't mean to be rude, but I'm not allowed to talk about it. If Shepard had wanted to read you in, she would've. I really do have to go."

Jack looked toward the wall. "How did you get in here?"

Nadia followed his gaze to the securely padlocked back gate. "What are *you* doing here?" She checked her watch—eleven minutes. "It's almost three."

"I was working in the documents lab. I lost track of time."

"You must be tired, too. You'd better get going. I'll see you later, okay?" She waved her hand gently in the direction of the dorms, hoping to usher him away.

"I really feel like something's going on. Tell me why you're on campus."

Pleasantries weren't working. Making up excuses, explaining herself—she was out of time. *Plan B.* She glared at him, deliberately added an edge to her voice. "Can you please—for *once*—mind your own business?"

His face fell. "Hey, I just wanted to make sure you were okay."

"You want me to be okay? Then leave me alone. I don't really want to talk to you."

"Wait—what are you talking about? I still consider us good friends. Don't you?"

Nadia shook her head. "I don't think so."

"What did I do?"

"Seriously?" She moved forward and jabbed her finger into his chest. "You told Shepard you'd break up with me, then you lied to me about it."

"I didn't *lie*—"

"It was a lie of omission."

"Damn, girl." Damon's voice crackled through the comms in her ear. "He is one cold son of a—"

"Shut up," she snapped.

"I didn't say anything," Jack said. "What is wrong with you?"

"Go away," she said.

"Come on, you know I had no choice." He put his hand on his heart. "I didn't want to break up with you. I'm crazy about you."

Her heart pounded harder. If only she could tell him the truth—that a woman's life was on the line, that every word her father had ever spoken to her was a lie, that if she didn't complete this mission her own mother might pay the price.

But that was the thing. Lives were at stake, and she didn't have time to explain. "You have a funny way of showing it."

"Listen, I should've said this sooner, but that night at the Fall Dance—"

"Right. When you were *assigned* to date me so you could spy on me?"

"No, it wasn't like that! When I'm with you, being with you—it's like...I feel like I've just robbed a bank, you know? Like I'm smarter than everyone else, and the luckiest guy in the world."

His words made her ache, but she couldn't focus on that now. She shook her head. "You gave me up. You didn't even fight for me."

"That's not fair. It was my only option. My entire future hung on this one decision."

"And you made it. Don't act like it's up for discussion."

Jack sighed. "Listen, ever since I can remember, I've only wanted one thing: to serve my country. Nothing has ever interfered with that goal. Until I met you. Nadia, I'm crazy about you, and that terrifies me. You're obviously angry with me. We need to talk about this."

A small red light flashed into view. She tried to follow it with her eyes. It flicked across his jacket sleeve and onto his left flank. Behind him and to his left, a tiny glow shone from the bushes. The light reappeared and remained stationary: the crisp red dot of Damon's rifle scope.

Damon spoke through her comms. "We don't have time for this jackass and his soul-searching. Get out of the way. I'm gonna take him out."

"No!" Nadia hooked the back of her leg behind Jack's knee, pulling his leg forward as she shoved hard against his chest. Jack fell flat on his back.

"I just . . ." He struggled for breath. "Wanted—to talk."

"Nadia, *move away*," Damon said into her ear. "I can't have him following us."

Fifteen minutes. An eternity.

Nadia pulled the tranq gun from her hip and pointed the muzzle at Jack's torso. She hesitated.

"Tick tock," Damon said.

"Wait, no!" Jack gasped. "What are you—"

Chirp, chirp. Two in the stomach.

Jack reached for the darts. "You shot me." His eyes closed as his body relaxed.

Damon crawled from the bushes, his rifle slung across his back. Nadia bolted toward the wall, Damon right behind her. He hoisted her up. At the top, she lay on her stomach and extended her arm.

"You are *unbelievable*," she whispered fiercely. "I told you not to bring your gun."

Damon jumped to the far side of the wall, then held out his arms. "Come on."

She dropped her full weight on him, knocking him to the ground.

"Get off me." He easily pushed her to the side. "And give me that tranq gun." Without waiting for an answer, he reached behind her and took the Beretta. "What's done is done. He's fine, so let's go."

They sprinted the half kilometer back to the car and Damon drove them into the night.

31 DAMON
MONDAY, FEBRUARY 6

Damon drove the first few miles without headlights. When they reached the main highway, he glanced at Nadia in the passenger seat. He felt the anger thrumming out of her. "Listen," he said. "About Jack."

"Don't you dare." She spat the words.

"I just wanted to say I'm sorry."

"You're sorry?" She turned on him. "About what, Damon? That I lied to him? That you threatened to kill him? That I had to shoot him?"

"No, I don't care about any of that. I'm sorry he didn't fight for you," Damon said. "I would've fought for you."

"That would carry a lot more weight if you weren't currently blackmailing me."

"Maybe." He shrugged. "On the plus side, this turn of events eliminates the awkward love triangle we had growing between us."

Nadia snapped her head around and Damon smiled. A tiny flicker of amusement crossed her face before she turned away. "You're delusional. And just to be clear, I only said those things to Jack so he'd go away. I totally agree with his decision. Breaking up was the only rational option."

"Ah, young love. Who among us hasn't said, 'I wish my relationship were more rational.'"

"Seriously, Damon, what is the matter with you? A sniper's rifle? You have a real flair for overkill. Anyone ever tell you that?"

He shook his head. "You're the first."

She continued her rant. "Like with Hayden."

"I imagine a whole lot of people wanted him dead."

"But you took it upon yourself."

"Here's the thing about Hayden: I don't like to be double-crossed. You might wanna keep that in mind."

"Why did you bother asking for my help if you were planning to threaten me anyway?"

"You know what they say, you catch more flies with honey. But rest assured, if honey doesn't work, I'll use brute force." He glanced at her. "And since when is this a blackmail scenario? I thought we were a team. You and I working together, just like old times."

"You're kidding, right? You won't tell me the truth about my father until I commit acts of treason, you threatened Jack's life—"

"Jack's a big boy. He can take care of himself."

She settled back into the seat, crossed her arms, and glared through the side window. "You sent me that code, *The Iliad*, my father's recruit file—it's like you're playing a game with my life. You're toying with me."

"I'm not toying with you. I knew you'd have to examine the evidence for yourself. And I couldn't very well mail the file to your dorm room. Sending the book was risky enough. Why do you think I forged a Hawaiian postmark?" He shot her a look. "And what was your plan, by the way?"

"What are you talking about?"

"The tranq gun." She didn't answer, so he continued. "You were gonna knock me out, then force the information from me?" Still no answer. "Do you have any idea what it's like to torture someone? It's *horrific*." He glanced at her, then back at the road. "I'm glad I spared you that experience."

"Yeah, you're a prince." She turned further away.

"And I have every intention of keeping my promise. You'll get the file."

The mile markers ticked by, and the silence continued.

If she was this angry already, he needed a new plan. It wasn't his fault Jack had materialized in the middle of the night. It's not like Damon deliberately sought him out to shoot him.

He shook his head. By threatening Jack, Damon had lost a lot of ground on this mission. Appealing to Nadia's sense of justice might no longer suffice. She wanted to know about her father, but that would only take him so far. Damon was pretty sure she knew he wouldn't hurt her, so threats were futile. She might respond to threats to others, people she cared about—Libby, maybe. But the best motivators were revenge and money.

Or love.

If he hadn't gotten greedy, maybe he could've made the exchange already. But when he got the fifty-grand down payment from Mr. Green, all Damon could think about was setting up a nest egg for himself and his mother. So he'd decided to kill two birds with one stone.

Ideally, he didn't want to hand Nadia over to Roberts. There had to be another way. She was sharp—together they could come up with some plan where she, Damon, and his mom could all walk out of that warehouse together.

He drove through the darkness, choosing large, overlapping routes to disorient her. It turned out not to be necessary, because she fell asleep. An hour later he pulled up to the trailer.

"Hey," he whispered, gently stroking her forehead. "Nadia."

She woke with a start. When she saw him, a cloud passed over her face. She exhaled.

"We're here. Are you hungry? I'll make you breakfast."

Nadia scowled. Her signature look. "We had a deal. You said you needed me to get into the dojo, which I did. I don't want breakfast; I want information. Give me what you promised so I can get out of here."

"Stop worrying." Damon got out, circled the vehicle, and opened her door. "I'm sure I'll have you back in time for prom."

32 NADIA
MONDAY, FEBRUARY 6

When he passed the plate of scrambled eggs and toast across the table, Nadia almost forgot they weren't friends. His eyes were soft, sweet like they'd always been when he looked at her.

"I'm sorry." His fingers brushed against hers as he offered his apology. "I know you don't really like eggs, but I also know that you need protein in the morning or you feel sick."

She couldn't believe he'd remembered such a tiny detail. Silently, she ate her breakfast while Damon prepared his plate. It took him a good twenty minutes to realize she wasn't speaking to him, which thoroughly annoyed her. Finally, after finishing his breakfast, he asked, "Is something wrong?"

She narrowed her eyes. "Yeah, something's wrong. You pointed a gun at Jack. You were gonna kill him. I'm not okay with that."

"I wasn't gonna kill him." Damon cleared their plates from the table. "I knew the second you saw the laser you'd figure out a way to get rid of him. I was just helping to motivate you." He leaned against the sink to face her. "I wouldn't shoot your boyfriend."

Nadia's gaze fell to the table. She swept a few crumbs onto the floor. "Good."

"Even though it sounds like he's not really your boyfriend anymore."

"I want to see Operation Cyprus," she said.

"First thing in the morning."

"It *is* first thing in the morning." She pointed out the window at the rising sun.

"I mean after we sleep for a few hours." He sat down and rubbed his face. His eyes were bloodshot.

"That wasn't our deal." Under the table, she nudged him with her foot. "Show me the file."

"Fine." Damon sighed as he dragged himself up. "But then we're cool, right?" he asked, walking to the bedroom.

"You made me shoot Jack with enough tranquilizer to stop a charging elephant," Nadia called after him. "So no, we're not cool." She pictured Jack lying by the back wall, unconscious in the cold night air. Images flashed before her: his smile, his laugh...the pained expression on his face when she told him she didn't want to speak to him anymore. Her eyes burned and she pressed her hands against them.

Compartmentalize, she told herself. *It's all just noise.*

Damon retuned with his backpack and placed it on the table. "Listen, are you sure you want to see this?"

"According to you, my father lied to me about his entire life and knows a lot more about mine than he let on." Nadia reached for the pack. "Yeah, I'm sure."

Before she made contact, he snatched the bag. "I'll get it." He rifled through the contents, then handed her a large manila envelope and a tactical flashlight. "You'll need this."

"What else is in there?"

"None of your business. I'll give you a minute."

She waited until he left before opening the envelope. Inside she found a black, unmarked folder. The folder contained a single sheet of blank black paper.

Sunrise had flooded the narrow space, so Nadia pulled the roller shade down over the dining room window. She clicked the black light feature on Damon's flashlight. Words materialized in fluorescent blue. Her heart skipped as she read the name *Jericho*.

She scanned the document—it described a failed mission.

OPERATION CYPRUS, ███████

CLASSIFIED: EYES ONLY

RELEVANT FILES: ███████

OPERATIVES: Black Sheep, Archer, Jericho, Lincoln

POST-MISSION ASSIST: Nightingale

OBJECTIVE: ███████ of ███████, declared a national threat

RESULT: FAILURE. ███████ incomplete. ███████ opted for ███████ (see file number ███████).

SUCCESS: Negative. <u>MISSION FAILURE</u>.

BLACK SHEEP: debriefed, deported.
ARCHER: compromised. No longer field-eligible.
JERICHO: requests legend for SWANDIVE.
LINCOLN: injured. Medical leave required.
NIGHTINGALE: success.

OPERATION BRIEF: ███████ acted independently and against orders. While instructed to ███████, the ███████ ███████ of ███████ ███████, ███████ instead ███████ the target, claiming the target can be further used as an ███████ to the United States of America. As part of the continued ███████ operation, ███████ will ███████ ███████ to ███████. ███████ asserts with certainty that ███████ shall remain unaware of the ███████. ███████ assures the agency that he will maintain ███████ by any means necessary, including ███████.

Nadia turned the page over, but it was blank. "This tells me nothing," she said aloud. She reread the document, then carefully ran the black light across the back of the page to see if she'd missed anything.

Damon opened the bathroom door and strolled back down the hall.

"This is it?" she asked. "This is all you have?"

"Are you kidding? That's everything." Damon picked up the black paper in front of her, then set it back down. He lifted the empty folder. "Where's the picture?"

She frowned and double-checked the manila envelope; a photograph had slipped from the file. Nadia shook it onto the table. Three men and a woman, early twenties, and an older man standing together in front of Buckingham Palace, smiling, arms draped over each other. An old team, no doubt.

Damon yanked on the bottom of the roller shade covering the window. As it sprang up, light spilled into the room.

Turning her attention back to the photo, she scrutinized the team. Her father and Marcus Sloan. Standing next to Sloan were a man and woman whom Nadia didn't recognize. But the older man... there was something familiar about his face. Her throat constricted as she placed him. A dark-haired, younger version of her new political science teacher, Professor Katz. But there was more. Why did he look so familiar—like she'd known him more than a few weeks?

Her hand flew to her mouth as she realized. Decades ago, when this picture was taken, young Professor Katz was the spitting image of Alan.

His saba.

"Right?" Damon asked.

"Do you know who this is?" Nadia asked, pointing to Katz.

"I assume it's Alan's grandfather. It looks just like him. Which means your dad worked with Mossad. Or Mossad worked with the CIA."

Of course Damon hadn't made the Katz connection; he wouldn't know Saba was on campus. She pointed to the couple. "Who are these two?"

"I don't know the woman, but that's Agent Roberts."

"What?" Nadia's heart pounded harder. Roberts used to be on

a team with her father? She looked from the picture in her hand to the one on the fridge. Now that he'd pointed it out, she could see the resemblance. "How would my dad know Agent Roberts?"

"Roberts is ex-CIA," Damon said.

She looked out the window, across the empty desert to the low mountains on the horizon. Damon sat down across from her. She felt him watching, felt the color rise through her cheeks, felt her nostrils flare.

Nadia flipped the picture over and examined the paper, hoping for signs of forgery, though her gut said it was real. How would Damon have gotten a twenty-year-old picture of Alan's grandfather? She felt sick to her stomach.

She stood and began pacing up and down the small trailer. "What was the mission? Operation Cyprus—what was it? It's so redacted I can't tell."

He shrugged. "Don't know, don't care. Roberts is ex-CIA, and apparently, he used to work on a team with your father, Marcus Sloan, and Alan's grandfather. That's all I know." After two more passes up and down the small walkway, Damon said, "Please sit down."

Nadia sat. Her head began to ache, a low throbbing at the back of her skull. "This is why you warned me about Project Genesis and the student database. Roberts *does* know my family. My father, at least."

"I told you you'd thank me for destroying it."

Her thoughts raced too quickly to follow—Roberts, her dad, the Nighthawks, the CIA, Alan's grandfather. Were she and Alan deliberately placed together? Was Saba on campus to protect them, or to finish what Roberts had started? She looked at Damon. "Is my dad in danger?"

He shook his head. "I don't know. Roberts and your father used to be teammates. Last semester, Roberts chose *you* as his fall guy. He probably wouldn't have done that if he and your dad had parted on good terms."

That made a lot of sense. Nadia looked back at the team photo. "How did you even meet Agent Roberts?"

Damon hesitated. "He found me. In Baltimore."

"Why'd you agree to work for him? The money?" When he didn't answer, she continued. "Because you're a smart guy. There are a lot of ways you could make a living without committing treason."

"It wasn't about the money."

"What, then? Not ideology. I know you don't buy into the Nighthawks' dogma."

"He said he would help me find someone."

"Who?"

Damon sighed. "Do you remember me telling you about my brother? The hit-and-run?"

"Yeah, of course."

"Well, what I didn't tell you was that the guy's lawyer got him off on a technicality." His jaw tightened. "After killing my little brother, he walked out of the courtroom a free man."

"Oh, Damon. I'm so sorry. I had no idea."

He pressed his lips together. After a moment, he said, "Roberts found the driver."

It took her a minute to understand. Roberts found the driver, then Damon went to work for Roberts.

Roberts killed the man who'd killed Damon's brother.

He stood, opened the fridge, rooted around for a bit. When he closed the fridge his anger had vanished. Like he'd just placed it on a shelf and shut the door. "You want a soda? I have root beer." He smiled.

Nadia shook her head. "No thanks."

His smile faded as his eyes moved to the window. Buried under the lightness lay the heavy guilt she knew he still carried for his brother.

She had no right to judge the choices he'd made.

Damon sat back down. "I'll do whatever I can to keep your father safe, but I can't do it without you."

"What do I need to do?"

He leaned across the table. "Help me get my mom back."

She met Damon's eyes. "How does that help my dad?"

"Because the second she's safe, I'll kill Agent Roberts."

33 JACK
MONDAY, FEBRUARY 6

Jack woke in the infirmary, a small, sterile room with two single cots tucked behind Dr. Cameron's office behind the library. His brain felt too big for his skull. A wave of nausea washed over him as he tried to sit up; he quickly abandoned the idea and remained as motionless as possible.

The last thing he remembered was finding Nadia on campus. He'd asked her to talk. She'd shouted *no*, then shot him.

He'd just wanted to talk.

Beyond the fabric screen that offered his bed the illusion of privacy, he heard the nurse on the phone. "Yes ma'am, he's waking up."

A minute later she came around the divider to check his vitals: blood pressure, heart rate, temperature. As she finished, Dean Shepard arrived.

"Do you know the penalty for underage drinking at Desert Mountain Academy?" Shepard asked from the doorway. "Immediate expulsion, no questions asked."

"I don't drink." His head throbbed.

She moved to his bedside and stood over him, hands clasped together. "Can you explain why your classmates found you passed out in the middle of campus?"

"With respect, Dean Shepard, were you not informed of the

two tranquilizer darts sticking out of my stomach?" Every word raked his throat and pounded against his head.

"I was; you are not the first student to engage in an illicit game of tranq-tag. I can only assume that for you to make such a poor decision, one that jeopardizes your entire future, you must have been intoxicated. With whom were you playing?"

"Are you kidding?"

"Do I sound like I'm kidding?"

"Of course not, I beg your pardon. I was shot—" Jack hesitated. He didn't want to say Nadia's name. It couldn't be that simple—she wouldn't just shoot him. Something else had to be going on. "Did you pull the security tapes?"

"The camera situated along the back wall was deliberately electrocuted, which badly damaged the video. The tech department is working to extract and repair the digital file, but it will take some time. Who shot you?"

Jack looked at the ceiling. The next words out of his mouth would determine his future. If he lied and got caught, he'd be kicked out. If he told the truth, Nadia might be declared an enemy of the United States of America. A cold chip of ice wedged itself into his heart, causing stabbing pains with each beat.

Time to sell her out. Again.

"Jack," said Dean Shepard. "Who shot you?"

He took a deep breath and looked Shepard in the eyes. "The last thing I remember was leaving the documents lab." He shook his head. "I have no idea who shot me."

34 NADIA
MONDAY, FEBRUARY 6

After a few hours' sleep, Nadia and Damon reconvened over an early dinner of frozen waffles and bananas. Halfway through the meal, Nadia said, "I don't mean to be insensitive, but what's the plan here? What's our timeline? How are we getting your mom? I need to get back to school."

Damon poured more syrup on his waffles. "Tomorrow night. We'll go to the warehouse where I met with Roberts. He's only got one body man, and you and I will both be armed. I give him his files, we get my mom, and the three of us leave together."

Nadia raised her eyebrows. "Just like that."

He nodded. "Piece of cake. I mean, we'll iron out the tactical details, but yeah. Pretty easy."

She pushed her waffles around the plate. There was more to it—something he wasn't telling her. Her eyes moved back to his face. Damon had always been an extraordinary liar. She never saw his tells, his reveals. It was just this feeling she had. "These files he wants—they're the same ones you showed me? The ones you found on his thumb drive?"

"No." Damon shook his head. "Roberts probably doesn't even know the thumb drive is missing. It's something from last semester. They...wanted me to do something, and I refused. They threatened me, and I told them I had evidence against all of them—against their whole organization. And that if I went down, I was taking them with me."

"What did they want you to do?"

He glanced up at her, then back to his breakfast. "Kill you." He said the words matter-of-factly.

Nadia opened her mouth, but found no words. His decision to spare her life had made him a target. Finally she said, "Well... thanks. For not doing that, I mean." After another minute she said, "But I feel like there's something else. Something you're not telling me."

"Nope, that's it." He finished his waffles in three bites before putting his sticky plate in the sink. "I do need one more tiny favor." He opened a few cupboards, then placed a small bowl and a bottle of rubbing alcohol on the table.

"I'm kind of in the middle of the last favor you asked for."

"I need you to remove a tracking device." From under the kitchen sink, he retrieved a substantial first-aid kit. "You'll have to cut it out of me, so I'll need stitches when you're done."

Nadia frowned. "Yeah, I'm not doing that."

"You are," he said, pulling his shirt over his head. His abs tightened as he tossed the shirt to the side. He grinned. "Not bad, huh?"

She rolled her eyes. "Yeah, you're a perfect ten. I'm still not performing surgery in this cesspool."

"Sutures are easy. Exactly like sewing."

"I'm a little insulted. What about me gives you the impression that I can sew? Because I'm a girl?" She'd already practiced on the pig's foot, but she had no intention of easing Damon's mind.

"Because you're clever," he said. "I'll talk you through it." He sat beside her on the bench, his back turned, and reached over his shoulder, pointing to the spot. "It's here."

"Wait, I have to wash my hands." She pushed him out of the way to get to the kitchen sink. Nadia ran the water for a decade before it turned hot. She meticulously cleaned around her fingernails, then lathered the lemon-scented soap up to her elbows. After a few moments she asked, "How exactly did you find out about my father?" With her elbow, she turned off the faucet, and then grabbed a fistful of paper towels. "You weren't entirely clear on that point."

"I was researching Roberts' old case files. I thought if I could find out about his previous missions—who he knew, where he went—maybe I could get a lead on my mom."

She returned to her seat, doused a cotton pad with alcohol, and swiped it across his shoulder.

Damon continued. "When I found the file for Operation Cyprus, I recognized your dad from the picture in your dorm room. The one with your parents in front of the dogwood tree."

Nadia's face warmed. Of course; Damon had broken into her room. Now he'd read files about her father. He knew a lot about her family. She placed her hand on his back. Her fingers, pale against his dark skin, lightly traced the muscles between his shoulder blades as she felt for the tracker. Above his right scapula, she found a small, hard lump. "Here?"

He nodded and turned slightly toward her, his face an inch from hers. She held her breath as he said, "Make a single, shallow slit. Try not to hesitate or it'll hurt more." A few seconds passed before he turned away. "Roberts also had a handful of Desert Mountain recruit files on the thumb drive. I don't know the common denominator, but I'm guessing they're all people whose DNA he wants. Anyway, your dad was one of them."

She opened the first-aid box and found the suture kit and a syringe of lidocaine. "Do you want me to numb it first?"

"No, I'm allergic to lidocaine. That's why I have epinephrine in there."

"What happens if you take it?" she asked.

He turned all the way around and looked into her eyes. "I die. So how about you don't?" He picked up the syringe and tossed it onto the kitchen counter, well out of her reach.

"I wasn't going to try it." Nadia opened the sealed scalpel pouch. She brought the tip of the blade to Damon's skin. "Do you have a scalpel or should I use this steak knife?"

He jerked away. "Yes, I have a scalpel."

"I'm kidding. Relax." She pressed her left palm against Damon's shoulder and used it to stabilize her right wrist.

"Remember to breathe," he said.

She took a deep breath, exhaled, and made the cut, slicing into his skin. It took more pressure to get started than she'd anticipated, but once the knife was in, the sharp blade easily severed his flesh. There was a lot more blood than she'd expected. "Paper towels," she said. Damon leaned forward, grabbed the roll from the counter and passed it over his head. She pressed a wad of towels against his shoulder, then examined the cut. "I can't see anything. There's too much blood."

"You have to feel for it."

Nadia doused her fingers in alcohol. Tentatively, she slid her index finger into the wound. Damon gasped and she hesitated.

Through clenched teeth, he said, "Keep going."

The squishy stickiness felt like raw meat. Her fingers found the tracker, hard and warm, buried inside. Slick, elusive. She couldn't get a grip. She tried squeezing it out. Damon groaned. Finally, the tracking device slipped from the cut: a small metal capsule, no markings, no flashing beacon. She set it on the table and leaned around to look at Damon. His face had paled. "Do you want a drink?"

He shook his head. "Just finish."

"The sutures will hurt."

"Compared to what just happened? I think I'll pull through."

Piercing his flesh with the threaded needle turned her stomach. The thread kept catching on his skin, separating it from the muscle, forcing her to pull harder. With her left hand, she pressed on either side of the cut. Her right hand drove the needle in, out, around. She sewed a total of three evenly-spaced stitches.

Damon rested his head in his hand. "How's it look?"

The flesh met cleanly, which meant his scarring would be

minimal. "Not bad." She cut the thread and dropped the needle into the bowl.

Between ragged breaths he said, "Thank you."

"No problem."

Damon picked up the tracking device and examined the capsule. Carefully, he twisted the two pieces apart. Inside was a small metal cube and what looked like a vitamin—a yellowish gelcap. "That son of a bitch," he muttered.

"What's wrong?"

Anger flashed across his face. "Do you know what this is?" He held up the gelcap. "A cyanide capsule. Agents used to get these sewn inside their cheeks so if they got captured, rather than divulge any information, they'd bite down, breaking the capsule. It's a suicide pill. Roberts injected me with a remote-controlled kill switch."

"So after you deliver your files, he kills you."

"I don't know if he'd use it if everything went according to plan, but if I was a no-show, certainly. And it would look like a suicide."

"I don't think I'd have the courage to take my own life," Nadia said.

"It doesn't take courage. Suicide is the coward's way out. I would *never* do that." He reassembled the capsule. "I'm sure Roberts is tracking my movements." He stood, swaying, and put the tracker in the pocket of his jeans. "I don't feel so well. I think I need to lie down for a couple minutes. Do you mind?"

Nadia shook her head.

"You have to come with me," he said.

"Seriously?"

"Please. I need to rest, and I won't be able to do that if you're not with me."

She rolled her eyes. "Fine." She pushed past him, stopping at the sink to wash her hands. In the bedroom she sat on the edge of the bed until he settled in, then stretched out beside him. "What if Roberts comes for us?"

His breath, still rapid, revealed his pain. "He won't."

"But what if he does?"

"He wants the exchange on his terms. He won't come here. He can't control the outcome." His teeth started to chatter.

Nadia sat up. "It's really cold in here."

"It's from the pain—it'll stop."

"No, it's actually cold." She covered him with the blanket. "I'm gonna turn up the heat."

"No, don't. The generator's old and very temperamental. Every time I mess with it the power shuts off, and I'm too tired to go outside and fix it right now. We'll have to make do." He paused for a moment. "You know, they say the best way to preserve heat is to strip down—"

She narrowed her eyes. "Don't even finish that sentence. I'll fix it if it goes out." She scooted out of bed and adjusted the thermostat attached to the wall. Back in bed, she slid under the covers.

"For the record, I didn't kill Hayden." He paused for a beat. "I just thought you should know."

Nadia twisted around to look at him. "Seriously? He was stabbed, shot, thrown out a window, and his trigger finger severed from his body. You're telling me it wasn't you?"

"Lie back down so I can spoon you. It wasn't me."

"Yeah, right."

"I thought about killing him. I mean, fair's fair—he tried to kill me. He was probably responsible for my mother getting kidnapped. But I didn't kill him. Somebody beat me to it."

"He was dead when you got there?"

"Not exactly."

"Then what, exactly?"

Damon exhaled, then said, "I thought Hayden might know where Roberts was holding my mom. He didn't, and before I got around to putting him out of his misery, three guys busted through the door. Israelis. Mossad."

Of course. Mossad. "Because Hayden accidentally shot Alan."

She felt his head nodding behind her. "Why'd they let you live? At the time Alan was shot, you were still working with Hayden."

"One of the agents asked my name. I told him the truth, and he said, 'You took care of Alan after he was shot.' I said, 'Hell, yeah. Alan's my boy.' They told me to be on my way, so I bolted."

Nadia smiled. "So Alan saved your life."

"Seems like. The irony, right?"

She hesitated. "Did you meet his grandfather?"

"No, these were young guys." After a second he said, "Listen, I couldn't have taken out the tracker without you. I'm sure Roberts would've eventually killed me. I appreciate your help, and what it means for you, personally. The treason, and whatnot. If we get caught, I will swear on a stack of Bibles that I held you at gunpoint this entire time. Whatever I gotta do to keep you clean in this."

"I think that ship has sailed."

"Nah, you're still good," he whispered. Then, "I can smell you on my pillow."

"What?"

"My pillow smells like you."

"Oh. Sorry."

"I don't mind." He exhaled the words.

She felt him shivering. "Are you sure you don't want some water?"

He wrapped an arm around her and pulled her close, burying his face in her hair. "I'm good," he whispered. "Thanks, Nadia."

"You're welcome," she whispered back.

35 ALAN
MONDAY, FEBRUARY 6

Alan had not slept in days. A thick black cloud pressed around him from all sides, slowly smothering out his oxygen, darkening the sun. He could not think or eat or breathe. The dark circles under his eyes had grown so large that Libby suggested he visit the nurse. His entire world was about to implode, and it was all Simon's fault.

Just before lunch, Simon, completely oblivious to Alan's anguish, burst through their bedroom door, grabbed Alan, and swung him around, then kissed each cheek.

Alan scowled. "Why are you so happy?"

"I knew we were destined to be lifelong mates, and your brilliance confirms my razor-sharp intuition," Simon said. "Initially, I was thoroughly annoyed at your inattention to detail, but as it happens, I believe you've done it!"

"What have I done?"

"Did you hear the news about Jack? He got caught playing an illicit game of tranq-tag, and he's refusing to name his cohorts."

"Aside from the fact that you clearly relish in others' misery, why does this news delight you?"

"Good one, mate." Simon sat on his bed and opened his laptop. "Our commandeered drone flew overhead on the exact night that Jack so spectacularly violated the rules. Either someone up there adores me, or I'm the luckiest bloke on earth. Can you imagine?

I wasn't going to bother watching the bloody video, and then this!"

"I still do not understand your glee."

"Ha, glee." Simon chuckled. "If I can identify his compadres, his brothers-in-arms, I'll have something to trade with Shepard."

Alan's heart began to race. "What do you mean, a trade with Shepard?"

Simon scooted over on his bed and tapped the recently vacated spot. "Come on, then, let's see what we've got." He pulled up the video and pressed *play*.

Alan sank down next to him, praying to see nothing more than a coyote. To his horror, the drone had captured the entire assault, which, inexplicably, starred one Nadia Riley.

"What is *she* doing there?" Simon asked.

Alan, unable to avert his eyes, watched the scene unfold.

Nadia stood by the back wall as Jack approached. He grabbed her arm; she threw him to the ground.

Then she shot him. Twice.

At that point, Simon laughed out loud. "Oh, this is better than I could've imagined." He played it again.

"Why did she shoot him?" Alan asked.

"Because my guardian angel is a very hard worker."

"I do not know what that means."

"Doesn't matter. I've got business to attend to, so if you'll excuse me." He elbowed Alan off the bed. "Now that I have something to trade, I'm going straight to Shepard."

"No, you cannot do that," Alan said, his voice panicky. "Why would you do that? We will both be expelled." What he meant was, *If Saba finds out you were involved, he may kill you.*

"Worth it, mate. Totally worth it." Simon grinned.

"Do you dislike Nadia? Is that why you are turning her in?" Alan thought he might be hyperventilating, but Simon failed to notice.

"Nadia's lovely! It's only that Shepard has something I need." He held up his laptop. "So I'll make a trade."

"A trade for what?" To conserve energy and maximize lung capacity, Alan rested on the edge of his bed.

Simon smiled. "For Jericho."

He stuck his head between his knees. "What is Jericho?"

"Not what, mate, *who*. Jericho's my father." Before Alan could respond, someone knocked on the door. "S'open," Simon called.

Noah stuck his head inside. "Alan, Professor Katz just called the hall phone. He wants to see you in his office immediately."

Alan took a shaky breath as he sat up. "Right now?"

"That's what 'immediately' means," Noah said, and ducked back out the door.

"Simon, I beg you," Alan said. "Do nothing until I return." His roommate did not answer. "Please, Simon. *Promise* me."

Simon rolled his eyes. "Till you get back? All right, I can agree to that."

Relief flooded Alan's body. "Thank you."

"But then you'll owe me one."

"Yes, fine." Alan scowled as he moved toward the door. "Once again, I will owe you one. Provided I live through the next half hour."

Alan trudged down the hall and through the lobby of his dorm. He dragged his feet across the lawn, the desperate dread growing inside him like a cancer, making simple movement difficult.

He entered the junior classroom building and headed toward Saba's office. His pace slowed considerably as he drew closer. He froze when he heard Saba's voice through the closed door.

"When will we send a team to retrieve our little bird? We all owe Nightingale a debt of gratitude."

Alan listened for a response, but none came. Saba must be on the phone. He waited a few more minutes to be certain the call had ended. Finally, unable to stall further, he knocked.

"Enter," Saba called.

"You requested me?" Alan asked, his voice wavering. He sat across from his grandfather in the cramped, windowless office. The room smelled of garlic. Remnants of Saba's dinner lay wounded in the trash can: wilted lettuce, scraps of beef. Alan's attention drifted to the world map tacked to the wall.

Saba rocked back and forth in his desk chair. "Something unusual has happened."

Alan forced his eyebrows to rise. "Oh?"

"It seems one of Mossad's drones flew over campus in the middle of the night. An agent contacted me to see if I needed more information and assistance. Imagine his surprise when I knew nothing of the mission."

Alan opened his mouth, closed it, then tried again. He stammered, then managed to say, "That is unusual."

"Indeed," Saba said. "Alan." He stopped rocking and leaned across the desk. "We both know I did not task this drone."

"No?" Alan could manage no other words. Speaking was difficult without oxygen in the lungs.

"No." Saba paused for an excruciatingly long beat. "Perhaps you will now explain why you hacked my credentials and infiltrated my account?"

Alan felt the prickly heat rising from his chest to his neck. A second later his face began to burn. His scalp itched, and he slipped his hands under his thighs to avoid scratching.

He could come clean right now, tell Saba that Simon had discovered his presence on campus. Tell Saba that Nadia had shot Jack. This information would interest Saba very much, as he seemed to have an affinity for Nadia that Alan did not understand.

Alan frowned. It might also incriminate her. He did not yet have enough information to ascertain her motives for shooting Jack, an action that Alan did not find entirely objectionable.

Somewhere beneath the anxiety, he felt a small flicker of anger. If Saba had not come here, none of this would have happened. He was the one who put Alan at risk. Alan took a deep breath and slowly exhaled.

It was time to choose a side: Saba or Nadia. Mossad or the CIA.

Alan dropped his eyes to the desktop. "I do not know anything about it."

A horrific silence followed. Alan had lied and Saba knew it. The people standing outside the building probably knew it. He kept his eyes cast down and thought about prime numbers.

"Alan, you understand nothing is more important than family, correct?" Saba did not appear to actually want an answer, so Alan remained mute. Saba continued. "Second only to family is country. You are American, but your country is Israel. I will ask again: what do you know about the rerouted drone?"

"Nothing," Alan said.

After what seemed like an hour of silence, Saba said, "This is disappointing news. Thank you for coming. You are dismissed."

He could not feel his legs as he waded from the building. They grew so weak that he had to stop when he reached the dining hall. Unable to continue, he slumped against the exterior wall and slid onto the ground. His head dropped to his knees, and he concentrated on not dying.

Some time later, hours maybe, Libby approached. "Are you okay? What are you doing out here?" She knelt beside him. Alan raised his head and she gasped. "You're white as a sheet. Come inside—lemme get you some juice."

Libby took his arm and walked him into the dining room, which was quiet and dark between meals.

"Is it your blood sugar?" She handed him a small glass of orange juice.

He shook his head.

"Well, what then?" Her brows pulled together as she leaned closer and touched his forehead.

"Simon," he whispered.

"What did he do?"

Alan did not immediately answer. Breathing still presented difficulties. This unfortunate event made clear to him that he would never work as a field agent. Not that anyone had ever thought he would. Finally, he said, "He found out about Saba. That he is Mossad."

Libby sat back. "Oh no. How? What happened?"

"He blackmailed me. He made me do something and Saba found out and he just confronted me and I lied to him—but of course he knows I lied, because I am quite possibly the world's worst liar." Alan leaned his head against his open palms.

Libby remained silent for a moment. "You lied to Saba?"

"Yes." His head pounded, the ache thumping with his heartbeat as the blood pulsed through his temples.

"Alan," she said.

He looked up. "What?"

"Just now you lied to Saba?"

Alan squinted at Libby. "Yes, just now. Are you not listening?" She was not the most intelligent girl he knew, but these questions were pedestrian even by her standards. "But you are missing the point—"

"Where is he?"

Uh-oh. "Hmm?"

"Your saba," she said firmly. "Where is he?"

Alan slammed his head down on the table. In his mind's eye, the intricate web unraveled. Black threads that had been securely woven together now untangled, and as they did, they wrapped themselves around him, binding him in a smothering cocoon.

He sighed. Another lie was futile. "Professor Katz."

36 NADIA
MONDAY, FEBRUARY 6

Nadia's eyes fluttered open. In the darkened room, the air felt cold and deathly still. She sat up to check the clock on Damon's nightstand. When she couldn't find the time, she realized the power had gone out. Damon lay beside her, lightly shivering. He slept on his side, curled up, facing her, one hand pressed against his forehead like a little kid. His eyelashes, long and black, brushed against his cheeks like whispers.

He looked deceptively innocent.

She pulled the blanket higher around his neck, then lay back down and closed her eyes. A second later they opened again. What was she missing?

Damon had to relinquish his incriminating files to Agent Roberts, at which time Roberts would release Damon's mom. But if it was such a simple exchange, why did Damon need Nadia at all? Was she the best choice to serve as backup?

The mattress shook slightly as his shivering increased. Nadia slipped from the bed to search for extra covers. Inside the small closet she found an army-green wool blanket. As she dragged it out, she uncovered Damon's backpack hidden beneath.

After gently covering him, Nadia grabbed the pack and tiptoed from the room, easing the door closed behind her. Down the hall, she searched the table with her hands until she found the flashlight.

Without taking them from his pack, she leafed through the files. The last one, an empty envelope, had the name JERICHO printed across the top. In a similar typeface right beneath her father's code name, a string of numbers: 78655986. She was about to work on the numeric code when she noticed a cell phone in the bottom of the bag.

Nadia dug it out and set the bag aside. She powered up the phone, then swiped across the time, 0921. Of course the phone was password protected. She dragged down from the top to read the recent notifications: a single message, sent from a Phoenix area code. *Exchange 2100 hours. Same location. See that the package is conscious.*

She frowned. Conscious? But Roberts wanted Damon's files.

Nadia turned her eyes to the window. Moonlight shone across the desert, exposing each ripple in the sand, casting long shadows from the saguaro and chaparral. A cold fear wrapped around her heart as the meaning of the text sank in—the exchange wasn't for paperwork. The trade Damon had arranged with Roberts had nothing to do with his files. It had to do with the person he was taking to the meet.

To secure his mother's freedom, Damon planned to sacrifice Nadia.

A rising anger in her chest assaulted the fear, pushed it down, tucked it away. Heat spread through her body as her blood pressure rose, her heart rate increased. Then the adrenaline kicked in—she stormed down the hall, climbed onto the bed, and punched Damon in the back.

"You lied to me," she yelled.

"Ow—watch the stitches! What is the matter with you?"

"You're planning to trade me for your mother—you're taking me to Roberts to have me killed!"

"Calm down." He pushed himself into a seated position. "I don't know what you think you know—"

"Save it. I read your messages. This is nothing more than a hostage exchange."

"He's not gonna kill you. If you read my messages then you know Roberts specifically demanded that I deliver you alive."

"Are you kidding me right now?"

"I wasn't going to do it! I was just waiting for the right time to tell you. Roberts *thinks* I'm going along with his plan. He really does have only one guard. He won't expect me to double-cross him—not when my mother's life is on the line. I'll pretend to hand you over, but you'll be armed. We'll get the drop on him."

Rage welled out from the anger. She felt it in her hands—envisioned wrapping them around Damon's throat, watching as his veins popped, his eyes bulged. "You lied to me this whole time." Afraid she might further assault him, Nadia scrambled to her feet. "I'm leaving." She flicked the light switch, then remembered the generator had died.

"Okay, just stop." He climbed out of bed and moved toward her. "You have to know I'd never do anything to hurt you." He wrapped his arms around her and kissed her forehead. She tried to push him back. "Nadia, I love you."

"Get off me." Nadia shoved him away. "How stupid do you think I am? I don't believe a single word that comes out of your mouth."

"Hang on a second. I know you're angry." Damon reached for her again. She smacked his hand as he said, "But this is a *good* thing. I'm glad you found out. I didn't know how to tell you without creating panic, and now you know. We can move forward with a plan."

"You completely manipulated me." Nadia felt around on the floor for a pair of socks. She pulled them on and searched for her sneakers.

"I would like to point out that I *helped* you. By destroying the DNA database, you have eliminated a significant risk to both yourself and your father. So, you're welcome."

"That was completely self-serving. Don't pretend it had anything to do with protecting me. Any benefit to my family was incidental." She dropped to her hands and knees to feel under the bed. "Where are my shoes? Get me a light!"

"I don't know. If you could just calm down—"

"Calm down?" She glared at him. "Let's recap. You drugged me, kidnapped me, forced me to break-and-enter, convinced me to destroy CIA property, made me shoot someone, insinuated threats against my parents—"

"Okay, but some of that was for you."

"You're insane. Like, literally insane." Nadia pressed her palms against her temples and turned away. "Why am I even talking to you?"

"And let's be honest," he said. "You can't tell me that shooting Jack wasn't just a little bit fun."

"I don't even know what to say to you right now. I am *so angry*." She pushed past him into the hallway, still searching for her shoes.

Damon followed close behind. He opened a kitchen cabinet and removed a hurricane lamp, then set the lantern on the table and lit the wick. "Listen, I still need your help to get my mother back. If we work together, I know we can come up with a solid plan—something we're both comfortable with. If I show up without you, Roberts will kill her."

She found her sneakers under the dining table. Dropping to the floor, she shoved them onto her feet and roughly tied the laces. "You absolutely betrayed me—again. You're on your own."

"I had no choice," he said.

"We always have a choice! That's *all* we have."

"You think you have choices? We're all pawns, Nadia, every one of us. Me, Alan, Libby, and especially you. Even more than you know."

"What are you talking about?"

He hesitated.

"You said 'even more than I know.' So what is it?" When he didn't answer, Nadia stood and leaned over her bench seat. She grabbed the empty envelope with her father's code name from Damon's backpack and held it up. "What does this code mean?"

He swallowed and snatched the envelope. "Nothing. It doesn't mean anything. It has nothing to do with you. Or your father."

"Liar," she mumbled, pushing past him. She stepped into the kitchen to get a bottled water for the road, turning her back on him.

His steely fingers closed around her bicep. "I can't let you leave. I need you, Nadia. He will *kill* my mother."

A steak knife sat to the left of the sink. Nadia grabbed the knife and swung around, slicing at his torso. Damon dodged her attack and snatched his Glock from the top of the refrigerator, taking aim at her chest.

Just as quickly, he raised his hands in surrender, pointing the muzzle toward the ceiling. "I'm sorry—that was reflex. I'm putting the gun down." He eased his weapon onto the table. "Please, put down the knife before you get hurt."

"No." She took a step back and bumped into the kitchen sink.

Damon inched toward her. "Put it down, seriously. I put down my gun, right?"

"Stay back," she warned, her arm extended.

In one smooth motion Damon grabbed her wrist and twisted, pressing his fingers into the tendons that gave strength to her hand. The knife fell from her grip as she cried out in pain. He turned her body away from his and placed her in a chokehold.

He spoke softly into her ear. "I need you to calm down and listen to me. Will you do that?"

She weighed her options. Sensei taught her to escape a chokehold, but then what? In a hand-to-hand fight against Damon, she'd get her butt kicked. Maybe she could reach his gun, but did she really want to shoot him? Would she even be capable of shooting him?

He relaxed his muscles, so the chokehold turned into more of a bear hug. "Will you listen?"

Then she noticed the syringe of lidocaine, wedged along the backsplash behind the sink. "Yeah, I'll listen."

He released her and took a step back. "Let's sit down. Do you want me to make some coffee or something?"

Nadia snatched the syringe from the counter. She bit off the safety cap, spun around, and plunged the needle into Damon's chest.

He gasped and yanked out the needle. His mouth fell open as he looked from the syringe in his hand to Nadia's face and back again. Immediately, his breathing became labored and he grabbed his throat. He half-sat, half-fell to the floor, taking sharp, strangled breaths.

She hadn't expected to incapacitate him so quickly.

Nadia raced to the bedroom for the handcuffs. Back in the dining area, she secured one of Damon's wrists to the table leg before dropping the EpiPen at his feet. He fumbled for the epinephrine. She yanked open the trailer door. He flailed behind her, wheezing.

Her foot hovered over the doorjamb. A second later she shut the door, crouched beside him, and administered the antidote. Nadia waited.

In less than a minute his respiration returned to normal.

Damon looked up at her. His voice weak, he said, "I'm the only person who's ever told you the truth." He paused for a beat. "I didn't want to point this out because your life is already unraveling, but do you honestly think Sensei didn't know about your dad? Or Dr. Cameron? Or the dean? Everyone lied to you. Everyone but me."

She stood, moving out of reach.

"Wait—there's more. If you stay, I'll tell you the rest."

She crossed her arms and waited.

"I lied about the student database."

"What are you talking about?"

"Someone hired me to destroy the database—it wasn't about my DNA. It was about someone else's."

She shrugged. "Yeah? Who hired you? Who was it about?"

He shook his head. "I don't know. He called himself Mr. Green. And he offered me a ton of money. Enough that I didn't care about his real name."

"Mr. Green? Are you kidding me?" Another stall tactic. "Goodbye, Damon." She opened the door.

Behind her, the scrape of metal as Damon racked his gun. She turned to him.

"You know as well as I do, Nadia, I can drop you before your foot crosses that threshold. I don't want to do it, but I will if I have to."

Nadia stared at him. Seconds passed. The night air circled her, pushing its way into the stale room. The gun remained steady. Damon didn't blink.

"So shoot me," she said, and walked out the door.

37 LIBBY
MONDAY, FEBRUARY 6

In the darkened dining room, Libby gently tapped her index finger on the top of Alan's head. "Sit up. Are you telling me that Professor Katz is your grandfather?"

Alan looked toward the ceiling. "Yes. And now he knows I rerouted a Mossad drone for Simon—"

"Why did Simon want a drone?"

"I can only assume it was to further his own investigation."

"What investigation?"

Alan shrugged. He looked disgusted. "He has determined that an agent known as Jericho is his father. He wants Jericho's given name. But when he saw Nadia on the video—"

"He saw Nadia?" Libby sat forward. "Where? What video? She's not due back till tomorrow."

He sighed loudly. "Yes, I know. The video recorded by the drone. Simon saw her shoot Jack—"

"Wait—Nadia shot Jack?" *She* was playing tranq-tag? That didn't make any sense.

Alan slammed his hand on the table. "Why do you keep interrupting me?"

She cleared her throat. "I apologize. What happened? Where is Nadia? Is she here?"

"It appears that she snuck onto campus in the middle of the night and shot Jack by the back gate. That is all I know."

"Come on then," Libby said, dragging Alan across the dining room to the main entrance, which faced the back wall. She shoved open the terrace door and herded Alan toward the gate: the alleged scene of the crime. "Tell me everything that happened."

Alan sighed heavily. "Jack and Nadia were somewhere in this area."

"Here?" Libby asked, situating herself.

"No, more like here." Alan led her to the correct spot. "You be Nadia, I will be Jack. He grabbed her right arm—" Alan grabbed Libby's arm. "And she wrenched it away." He paused and stared at Libby, gesturing with his head to her arm.

Libby rolled her eyes and yanked her wrist free.

"Then she threw him to the ground...." Alan paused as he eased himself onto the desert floor. "And shot him twice in the stomach." He stood and brushed himself off. "It happened very quickly. It really was quite impressive. Then the drone moved on."

Libby frowned. "Why would she do that?"

"Perhaps she finally came to her senses?"

She shot Alan a look. "Was she alone?"

"I believe so."

"So the gate was open?"

Alan paused. "No, now that you mention it, it was not."

"That wall's ten feet high. Nadia's five three."

"So?"

"So how'd she get in?" Libby asked. Nadia couldn't have scaled the wall by herself, but where had her accomplice been? Why hadn't Alan's drone captured anyone else?

Libby turned around, her back to the wall. She pictured Jack walking up, interrupting the jailbreak, slowing Nadia down. If someone had assisted Nadia from the far side of the wall, Jack would've seen them. The person would've been waiting on top of the wall, ready to hoist her up. So whoever helped her escape had also been on campus.

Was this part of Nadia's mock mission? An assignment issued by Dean Shepard? There had to be an explanation. Why would she sneak onto campus just to shoot Jack? She hadn't been *that* upset about the breakup.

Libby scanned the area, searching for anything out of place. Between her OCD and the forensics training, she ought to figure something out. Besides the chaparral bushes along the back wall, the area was clear.

The bushes.

Libby walked along the wall toward the chaparral. As she closed in, the clue revealed itself like a neon light. The tiny plants growing in the shade of the bush had been crushed. She crouched against the wall and looked back at the clearing. From this spot, Nadia's accomplice would've remained completely out of sight. "Alan, over here. Look at this."

Alan meandered toward the bushes. "What am I looking at?"

She pointed under the chaparral. "The disturbed earth. Someone was here."

He shook his head. "I do not see disturbed earth."

"Right here—it's plain as the nose on your face." Her eyes trailed along the top of the wall until they reached the vacant camera mount.

Simon's video held the key.

Libby stood. "I wanna speak to Simon."

"I appreciate your loyalty, but I have bigger problems than my roommate."

"Alan." She leaned toward him. "It's not for you."

Alan frowned. "Fine. I believe he is in our room."

Libby stayed on his heels as they left the back wall and rushed down the hill to the boys' dorm. At the entrance, she said, "Tell him to bring his laptop. I intend to watch that video."

A few minutes later, Alan reemerged from the hallway, Simon in tow.

"Hello, love. To what do we owe the pleasure?"

"You know perfectly well why I'm here. Show it to me."

"I can't do that," Simon answered. "Your roommate has committed a crime. I have a civic responsibility to relinquish the film to Dean Shepard."

Libby stepped forward. Simon stood a few inches taller, but not so much that she couldn't look in his eyes. Alan was easy to manipulate; Simon would not be. She considered her best play. Flattery? Blackmail? Bribery? Then it came to her.

Smiling sweetly, she began. "Simon, as you know, my daddy might well be the next President of the United States. I would like you to take a moment to consider the implications of what it might mean for you personally if the daughter of the president was in your debt."

Simon's poker face revealed nothing, but Libby knew he was smart enough to use his tiny little fish—the video he'd acquired—as bait, and not as his entrée.

"Looks, cunning, and a crooked moral compass? Darling, if I weren't gay, you would be my dream girl," Simon said.

"Wait—you are gay?" Alan asked.

"Of course I'm gay. You didn't know that?"

"Simon," Libby said sharply. "Do we have a deal?"

Simon pursed his lips, exhaled loudly, and nodded. "The terms are satisfactory. I'll fetch my laptop."

Four minutes later the trio sat huddled on the sofa in the boys' lobby. Simon zoomed in on the footage to get a close-up of the scene. The detail was remarkable, even in the dark of night. Libby watched as Nadia threw Jack to the ground. As he lay in the dirt, she pulled her weapon and fired into his stomach.

"There you have it," Simon said. "Guilty as sin."

Libby shot him a look before she remembered he was doing her a favor. She relaxed her face and asked, "Does it show her leaving campus?"

Simon shook his head. "It flew away before that. We had a few technical difficulties." He glared at Alan.

"Can you run it through an infrared filter?" Libby asked.

"I might be able to. Let me see." Simon fiddled with the settings.

Libby turned to Alan. "Go get Jack."

"A 'please' would not be unwelcome," Alan mumbled as he left the lobby.

"I think it's ready," Simon said.

"Lemme see." Libby didn't dare so much as blink as Simon played the video.

I knew it! That same thrill of excitement rolled through her as her suspicions were confirmed. "Did you see it?" she asked breathlessly.

"See what?" Simon asked, rewinding the file.

"Wait a second," Libby instructed. "Here they come."

The boys emerged from the hallway and Jack asked, "What do you need? I have a splitting headache."

"What happened last night?" Libby asked.

"I don't remember."

"You lied for her, didn't you?" she whispered.

"I don't know what you're talking about."

Lying was totally out of character for Jack. If he'd lied to the dean, that meant Nadia was in serious trouble. "Did you know she wasn't alone?"

The color drained from Jack's face. "What?" He sat on the edge of the coffee table in front of Libby. "How do you know that?"

"Simon has a video. Someone else was there, hiding in the bushes along the back wall. The video doesn't show the other guy, but it proves she wasn't alone." She elbowed Simon. "Go on."

Through the infrared filter, they watched the video. Jack's torso glowed red, his limbs bright orange, indicating normal, relaxed blood flow. Nadia, however, cast an entirely different heat signature. Her arms were blue and her fingers black, which meant her heat was concentrated in her core. A sure-fire sign of fear.

"Watch." Libby leaned closer to the laptop and held her breath.

Jack grabbed Nadia; she pulled away. And right before she

threw him to the ground, a tiny flash of light hit Jack's body. "There—did you see?" She tapped her fingernail against the monitor. "Simon, go back."

He rewound and played the film frame by frame. "You couldn't counter her throw?" he asked Jack.

"She's very quick," Jack snapped.

Just before Nadia moved in, a beam of red light hit Jack's left flank.

"You guys saw that, right?" Libby asked, her eyes jumping from Simon to Alan to Jack. "Right?"

"I saw it," Jack said.

"There's a scope trained on you," Libby said.

"Yeah, I said I saw it." He asked Simon, "Can you zoom out to cover the whole area?"

Simon complied, and they watched the scene again. Another heat signature appeared on screen, red and orange and larger than Nadia, tucked behind the bushes along the back wall. Perfectly relaxed.

Simon froze the frame and nodded at Libby. "You were right, love."

"Who is that?" Alan asked.

"That's gotta be Damon, right?" Jack asked quietly.

Libby sat back and crossed her arms. "Well, Jack," she said, not bothering to hide her satisfaction. "It seems that, once again, Nadia saved your life."

38 NADIA
MONDAY, FEBRUARY 6

Nadia slammed the door to the trailer, silencing Damon's threats. Fury had replaced the lingering fatigue of the past few days, and she took off in a dead sprint. She knew the general direction of the road, and this patch of desert was barren enough that the waning moon provided sufficient light. Cold air pulled into her nostrils, energizing her.

Any remaining sentiment she'd had toward Damon had vanished when he admitted the hostage exchange. Every word out of his mouth was a calculated lie, a manipulation. He'd had the nerve to put his arms around her, to touch his lips to her skin.

Less than a mile later, she realized her pace was unsustainable. She slowed to a brisk jog.

As her feet pounded against the packed earth, she wondered about Jack, about how long he'd been stranded in the cold, unconscious by the back wall. Had he realized yet that she'd been protecting him? Or did he hate her—did he think she'd betrayed him, her school, her country?

Trusting Damon had been a mistake, and she had no one but herself to blame. But getting romantically involved with Jack had also demonstrated poor judgment. It was easy to make promises when nothing was on the line. But she'd learned last semester where his loyalties lay, and they weren't with her.

Another half mile found her speed-walking. She cursed herself for forgetting the water—and not grabbing the backpack with Damon's files. Or his knife, for that matter.

I can't believe I trusted him.

Panting now, she slowed again.

What had he meant about her being more of a pawn than she thought? Nothing, probably; he was trying to get inside her head. Pique her curiosity so she'd stay and help. She was *his* pawn. Going along with his plan, thinking her parents' lives were at stake. She'd believed they were in mortal danger, and she would've done anything to protect them. She did, in fact—she committed treason. Consorting with a known traitor, destroying CIA property.

Nadia stopped walking. She would've done anything.

Just like Damon and his mother.

She leaned forward onto her knees and extended her exhales to slow her pounding heart.

Damon had broken the law to protect his mother; Nadia had broken the law to protect her parents. To achieve his goal, he'd lied to Nadia. To achieve hers, she'd lied to Jack. She had no moral high ground on which to stand.

She looked back. The distant silhouette of the trailer cast a black rectangle against the inky horizon. She couldn't assist in his mother's rescue without further committing treason, and there was no way she would voluntarily surrender to Roberts, but she could at least help Damon formulate a plan. But should she?

Her eyes searched the sky, as though answers could be found in the ocean of stars overhead. He didn't deserve her help.

But maybe his mother did. Nadia knew what it felt like to be used by the Nighthawks.

She groaned out loud and started back toward the trailer.

Ten steps later a concussive boom vibrated through her body. A fraction of a second after that, a blast of heat reached her skin. Fifty yards in front of her, flaming debris rained down onto the desert floor.

When the sky cleared, she searched the horizon. The black rectangle had morphed into a raging bonfire.

The explosion had obliterated the trailer.

Nadia wandered through the desert, moving away from the explosion, until she found a paved road. She trudged for hours before spotting a car. Once again berating herself for not grabbing a knife on the way out, she flagged down the driver. The car stopped, and she tentatively approached the passenger side. To her relief, two women occupied the vehicle.

She lied about a hike gone wrong and asked for a ride to the nearest gas station. Forty minutes later she placed a collect call to the switchboard at Desert Mountain Academy.

"Code name?" the operator asked.

"Wolverine," Nadia said.

"Please hold while I connect you."

After a few seconds a man picked up. "Yes?"

"I need someone to come get me."

"Location?"

"I don't know." She turned around to read the storefront. "Mike's Quick Stop."

"We'll be there in a few hours. Sit tight."

Nadia waited on the curb, arms wrapped around her knees, as far from the door as she could manage. To distract herself, she tried to decipher the numeric code written on the envelope beneath her father's code name. The numbers floated to the sky, jumbled together; she couldn't concentrate enough to attach any meaning.

Behind her closed eyes she saw the flash of the explosion, the trails of orange and red as the fiery debris rained down from the sky.

There was no way he survived that explosion. Not after she injected him with lidocaine, weakened him, restrained him. If she hadn't left the trailer when she did, she wouldn't have survived, either.

Nadia pushed the images aside. Launching herself off the curb, she paced rapidly alongside the building. She just wanted to go home.

It took her a second to realize that home meant school. She wanted to go back to school.

As the first rays of sunrise streaked the sky, her driver pulled in front of Hopi Hall. Libby, Alan, Simon, and Jack waited on the steps. As Nadia left the car, Libby rushed forward to give her a hug. Like little ducklings, Alan and Simon followed.

"Are you okay?" Libby asked. "We've been so worried about you."

Nadia nodded. "I'm glad to be back," she said, her eyes stinging. She stopped talking so she wouldn't cry.

"Sensei and Dean Shepard are inside," Libby said. "We'll wait out here for you."

"But I am hungry," Alan said. "Can we not meet at breakfast?" Libby shot him a look, and he shook his head. "We will wait."

"Of course we will," said Simon. "Welcome back, love."

Nadia smiled and continued up the steps.

Jack stood at the top, deep concern etched in his forehead. "I'm so glad you're okay."

"I'm sorry I shot you," she said. "Damon—"

"I know. I know what you did for me. Thank you."

Her eyes burned, and she willed herself not to cry. Her lip quivered as she thought about Damon. She'd killed him. And what would happen to his mom? Nadia pressed her hand over her mouth.

Jack stepped forward and wrapped his arms around her. He rested his chin on the top of her head and pulled her close. "It's okay," he whispered. "You're okay."

She nodded against his chest.

"Do you want me to go inside with you?" he asked.

Nadia moved back and shook her head. "No, thanks. I'm fine."

"Then we'll talk later." Jack opened the door for her.

Sensei waited in the foyer. As the heavy door closed behind her, Nadia bowed to him and burst into tears.

He moved forward quickly, leaning down to look at her face. "Are you hurt?"

She shook her head.

He straightened. "Then your tears are wasted energy. We only have a moment. Dean Shepard is expecting you." He lowered his voice. "Tell me, why did you destroy the DNA database?"

"Damon," she answered, as she fought down the tears. "He convinced me that my parents were in danger—and I think he may be right. He said it was the only way to keep them safe. I thought I had no choice." Nadia dropped her eyes to hide the half-truth. That was most of it, but she'd also gone along with his plan because she wanted information.

"Did he want to erase his own DNA?"

"Yes, but he also said someone hired him to destroy the entire database. He didn't know who."

"Is this why he came for you? Because you were the only one able to access that room?"

Nadia sniffed and wiped her nose on her arm. "No, that was just an added bonus. Roberts has Damon's mother. Damon told me Roberts is holding her prisoner until he returns some files that he stole last semester—some evidence against the Nighthawks— and that he needed my help to get her back. But it turns out it was a hostage exchange—Roberts wanted to trade *me* for Damon's mother." Nadia shook her head. "I know, you warned me not to trust him, and I shouldn't have." She took a shaky breath. "I think Roberts planned to kill him. Damon's tracking device had a remote-controlled suicide pill—cyanide."

Sensei studied her closely. "Why is Agent Roberts interested in you?"

"I don't know." *Revenge against my father?* Nadia dropped her voice to a nearly inaudible whisper. "Do you know Project Genesis?" He shook his head so slightly she wasn't sure he'd actually done it.

"We must not keep the dean waiting." He gestured down the hall. When they reached the sitting room, he stopped in the doorway. "We will speak more after you have rested."

Again, her eyes filled with tears. "Sensei, why didn't anyone come for me?"

"Every effort was made to find you. When I discovered you had accessed the secured rooms, I alerted Director Vincent. He dispatched a team that followed your tracking device to your campsite, but they found no trace of you. Before the director generated another lead, you telephoned." His intense eyes bore into hers. "Nadia-san, had we the slightest notion where to find you, we would have come." He bowed slightly then turned to go.

Nadia felt the quickening of her heart. She grabbed Sensei's sleeve. "Wait. Please."

He studied her, concern clouding his dark eyes. "You are very troubled."

Afraid to say the words, she whispered, "The trailer exploded. He was inside."

"Nadia-san—"

"He's dead, Sensei. Damon is dead. I killed him."

39 DAMON
MONDAY, FEBRUARY 6

The instant Nadia slammed the trailer door, Damon reached into the cupboard under her bench seat at the dining table and rummaged through his duffel for the spare handcuff key. After freeing himself, he grabbed an empty rucksack from the closet. He shoved his Glock, hunting knife, two sets of spare license plates, passport, a wad of cash, cell phone, the thumb drive he'd stolen from Roberts' storage unit, and the tracking device Nadia had cut from his shoulder inside the bag, then kicked out the window above the dining table.

Before climbing out, he eased his rifle and the vest packed with C-4 onto the desert floor.

Damon dropped the ten feet from the window to the ground. He wedged the vest against the gas-powered generator and sprinted a hundred yards away from the trailer.

Nadia would've gone in the opposite direction, toward the road. He didn't follow. At this point, the only way to stop her would be brute force, and he'd just discovered that wasn't an acceptable option. He needed another plan. Even if Roberts hadn't said not to kill her, Damon knew he couldn't do it. Not even for his mother.

He found a chaparral large enough to catch the shrapnel, slid underneath, then set up his rifle. He sighted his scope on the detonator attached to the vest. If he missed, if he severed the cord instead of striking the switch, the C-4 would be useless. Damon exhaled and pressed the trigger. He was another hundred yards away before the debris hit the earth.

Hayden hadn't known anything about his mother, and Damon's sole bargaining chip had just bolted. The last man who might be able to help was currently convalescing in a medically induced coma.

It was time to wake him up.

A few hours later, Damon boosted a rental car from the parking lot of the Hilton Condominium Vacation Properties in North Scottsdale and, after swapping out the plates, headed south. He reached Tucson before sunrise on Tuesday morning, hit the Shop-Mart for supplies, then got to work.

At 0500, dressed in navy blue scrubs with a fake ID clipped to his waist, Damon entered the front door of the Catalina Foothills Long-Term Care Facility and immediately headed to the nurses' station. He picked the youngest, a cute twenty-something with a blond ponytail, and flashed his most disarming smile.

"I'm Jordan Phelps." He carefully set his duffel bag on the floor. "The new orderly."

An older nurse approached. She had that no-nonsense look of a seasoned professional, someone who'd trained hundreds of nurses over the years. She peered over the rim of her reading glasses. "I didn't hear about a new orderly."

Damon didn't bother flirting. "Yes ma'am," he said courteously. "The temp agency called this morning. I guess the complaints about understaffing finally got through to the powers-that-be, because your human resources director sent a request." Damon consulted the note in his pocket. "Mr. Hernandez?" He shoved the fake note back into his scrubs. Using an actual name was risky, but Damon had researched the facility and learned that HR, along with the rest of corporate, was headquartered in Phoenix. The nurses probably had minimal contact with the administrative staff. "And I'm very grateful. I've been out of work for a while. You know what it's like."

"Well, it better not come out of the nurses' pay." She appraised him for another moment and then nodded. "You can put your bag in the break room. Start at the end of the hall. Grab the janitor's cart out of the closet and work your way up, room by room."

"Yes ma'am," Damon said. "Thank you."

Down the hall, before he entered the break room, he slipped into the supply closet. He removed the teddy bear, the houseplant, and the canvas knife roll from his duffel. Those items he tucked onto the janitor's cart. Across the hall, he threw his now-empty bag into a locker, and wheeled the cart into his first room.

Two hours and sixteen scrubbed toilets later, he found his target. The name written on the chart hanging in room 117 said John Seacrest, but Damon would've recognized his face anywhere.

Thadius Wolfe: former dean of students at Desert Mountain Academy, former CIA, current Nighthawk, and soon-to-be victim of one *very* disgruntled employee.

From his cart, Damon removed the nanny-cam teddy bear and stuck it on the built-in bookshelf across from the bed. He arranged the houseplant beside it: close enough so that no one would pick up the stuffed animal, but not so close that the leaves would block the camera lens. After Damon left, Wolfe would send for someone. They'd discuss the Nighthawks. Damon might learn where his mom was being held.

He unrolled the canvas knife bag and removed the syringe of adrenaline tucked inside.

The safe way to bring someone out of a medically induced coma was to slowly wean them off sedation while simultaneously warming their body back up to ninety-eight-point-six. Since Damon had neither the time nor the inclination to revive him safely, he folded the cooling blanket away from Wolfe's chest, drove the needle into his heart, and squeezed the plunger.

Immediately the cardiac monitor registered an increased heart rate. Damon shoved the syringe into the medical waste can on his cart and returned to the bed. Wolfe's eyes shot open.

"Where is my mother?" Damon asked.

Wolfe's eyes darted wildly around the room.

"Hey," Damon said sharply. "Roberts has my mother. Where would he keep her?"

The machine beeped faster. Wolfe's heart pounded, whether from fear or adrenaline or a combination, Damon couldn't say. He snapped his fingers in Wolfe's face. "Where is she?"

The overhead announcement clicked on, "Code blue, room one-seventeen. All nurses respond."

"Dammit." Damon returned to his cart as the first wave of nurses rushed the room. He should've disconnected the monitor. "I don't know what happened," he said.

The head nurse came in and ordered him out. Damon dropped his cart off in the janitor's room, threw the knife roll into his duffle, and shoved the plastic container of medical waste on top of that. He'd dump it somewhere else. He pushed through the exit at the end of the hall and jogged to his car, then drove to the parking lot across the street to pull up the nanny-cam surveillance feed on his laptop.

As the nurses sedated Wolfe, he slipped back into unconsciousness.

Now to wait.

A few hours later, Wolfe had a visitor. Damon saw her walk in: large sunglasses, a long white sweater-wrap, a sun hat. He didn't recognize her. But once inside, she took off the light disguise and leaned toward the camera to pull a chair to the side of Wolfe's bed.

Damon's pulse quickened as he placed her.

Ms. McGill, assistant to the dean of students at Desert Mountain Academy, sat down and took Wolfe's hand. She wiped at her eyes, visibly distraught.

"How the hell did I miss that?" Damon sat back in his seat and exhaled. He'd had no idea they were a couple.

Or that she was Roberts' inside man.

As if things weren't complicated enough.

40 NADIA
TUESDAY, FEBRUARY 7

Late Tuesday morning, after a few short hours of sleep, Nadia reported to medical. Security scanned her for tracking devices, the nurse collected blood and urine samples to run a toxicity screen, then Dr. Cameron sent for her. Instead of attending classes, Nadia spent three hours hooked up to a lie detector, fielding questions from both the psychiatrist and Dean Shepard.

Fortunately, their common goal was determining Nadia's complicity in breaking and entering, stealing from the school, and destroying equipment. They had no reason to ask about her father. Her stress response remained consistent throughout the interview, so no red flags. *Yes, when Damon arrived at my campsite, I believed my life was in danger. Yes, when I destroyed the database, Damon was armed and I acted under threat of death to my classmates and colleagues. Yes, I wholeheartedly believed Damon intended to shoot Jack with lethal ammo. No, I did not deliberately kill Damon.*

As the exam ended, Dr. Cameron unhooked the electrodes from Nadia's body, loosened the blood pressure cuff, and slipped the heart-rate monitor from her finger.

Dean Shepard turned off the camcorder. "Well, I'm satisfied that you had no previous knowledge of Damon's intentions, and that you acted under duress." She leaned against Cameron's desk and crossed her arms. "But you must understand, Nadia, once you leave the safety of this institution and complete your undergraduate training, once you are a full officer of the CIA, actions such as those you've recently engaged in will result in a conviction of treason, the punishment for which is the death penalty. Nothing—not even a quest to save your teammates' lives—will excuse that behavior."

Nadia felt her blood pressure rise as anger welled in her chest. "The safety of this institution? Is that what you said?" She lifted the edge of her shirt, exposing the scar near her right hip. "I hate to keep bringing it up, but I haven't been safe since I got here."

Dean Shepard's eyes flitted to her scar, then back to her face. "I'm so pleased you've been exonerated." She turned crisply and marched from the room.

"I know you're angry," Dr. Cameron said. "But you should know: she went to bat for you. Student or not, you assisted a terrorist and essentially stole from the CIA. You destroyed government equipment and wiped the entire DNA history from the Academy's records. The fact that you aren't in shackles leads me to believe that she probably lied through her teeth to protect you."

Nadia looked away. If Shepard lied, it was to protect herself. She turned her eyes back to Cameron. "I'm a minor. Why isn't anyone apologizing that I was kidnapped by an ex-classmate during a school-sanctioned exercise?"

He offered a sympathetic smile. "Welcome to black-ops."

Against her will, Nadia joined her teammates at the library for their afternoon study session. She had work to do, research on her father to conduct, though in her gut she knew that Damon's files were authentic. He couldn't have pulled together images of her father, Sloan, Roberts, Alan's grandfather...

And what *about* Alan's grandfather—whose side was he on? Had he turned, like Roberts? Should she report him to Dean Shepard? Could she, without implicating her father?

Nadia glanced at Alan. Maybe she should talk to him about Saba, though she doubted Alan would know one way or the other if his grandfather had joined the Nighthawks.

No—of course Saba wasn't a Nighthawk. His officers had let Damon live. If he was a bad guy, Mossad would've killed Damon right along with Hayden.

She sighed, tired of having more questions than answers. Though she didn't really care, she asked, "So what did I miss?"

"Yesterday in psychology we talked about Amsterdam Syndrome," Simon said.

"*Stockholm* Syndrome, not Amsterdam," Alan said. "I knew you were not listening." He turned to Nadia. "It is a little complex. In the event of a prolonged kidnapping or hostage situation, the victim often experiences a complete psychic change—one's foundational beliefs are eventually destroyed. The target loses trust in friends and family, and begins to rely solely on the person administering the manipulation."

She jotted Damon's code at the top of her planner: 78655986. "I know about Stockholm Syndrome."

"How? I barely understand it, and I sat through the bloody lesson," Simon said.

"Shh." A cute boy from the next table locked eyes with Simon. "Keep it down, please," he said with a smile.

In a stage whisper, Simon said, "Sorry to disturb."

"My father." Nadia paused. "The professor." *Specializing in political assassinations and high-value kidnappings.* The line played like a recording in her head.

"Nadia, why don't *you* explain it to Simon," Libby whispered. "Because these two had this exact conversation at lunch, and I don't believe I can listen to it again."

Nadia had once asked to sit in on her father's class. He'd been teaching a summer course called *Kidnappings Abroad: A Lucrative Business.* Her dad had refused; he told her it was against school policy, and anyway, wouldn't she rather hang out at the pool with her friends? He'd given her twenty bucks for lunch and dropped her at the mall.

"Go on then," Simon said.

Nadia sighed. "Stockholm Syndrome occurs when a kidnapping victim begins to sympathize with her captors."

"Ah." Simon nodded. "See? When you explain it, it's clear as day."

Nadia turned her eyes to Alan. "What about political science? Did Professor Katz have anything interesting to say?"

Alan's face reddened as the table fell silent. Libby examined her cuticles, Simon busied himself by sorting through his backpack, and Nadia realized that every one of her teammates knew Alan's secret. What on earth had she missed?

And what else did they know?

That night as the girls climbed into bed, Nadia asked, "Why did everyone get weird when I asked about poli-sci?"

Libby's face lit up and she clamped her lips together, like she was trying to contain her excitement. She took a deep breath, held it for a few seconds, and then exhaled her words in one quick stream. "Okay, you know I hate to gossip, but oh my goodness— guess who Professor Katz is? Alan's saba! Can you believe it? I was dying to tell you but you've been through so much, I didn't want to sound petty if you weren't ready to chat." She clapped a hand over her mouth, eyes smiling.

"Wow." Nadia pulled the covers around her legs. "How did you find that out?"

Libby filled her in on Alan's confession, Simon's video, Jack's lie to Dean Shepard. "I promised Alan I wouldn't breathe a word about his grandfather, but of course I didn't mean *you*. I mean, we tell each other everything, right?"

Nadia studied the cream colored rug between their beds. "Yeah, of course."

Libby sighed. "Like the fact that I'm *still* not allowed off campus."

"What do you mean? For your survival course?"

Libby nodded. "I haven't even been assigned my own detail, but Secret Service is already calling the shots. They're fighting with Shepard about having a presence on campus if my daddy becomes the front-runner." She looked away for a second, then back at Nadia. "Promise you won't tell anyone, okay? It's so embarrassing. It's like having a babysitter." Libby's blue eyes filled with tears. "And I know it's only a matter of time till Shepard decides she's had enough."

"I'm so sorry."

Libby shrugged and wiped at her eyes. "In the grand scheme of things, I guess it's not that important." After a moment she said, "No one blames you, you know. For Damon, God rest his soul."

That's because you don't know how it happened. The remorse felt like a dull ache in the pit of her stomach. Nadia lay on her back and stared at the ceiling.

Libby's words didn't touch her; they offered no condolence, no absolution. Nadia knew the truth. If she hadn't injected him with lidocaine, hadn't handcuffed him to the table, he would've gotten out. After a few minutes of silence, Nadia said, "Can I ask you something?"

"Of course."

She turned toward Libby. "Have your parents ever lied to you?"

Libby laughed. "Is that a joke?"

"No, what do you mean?"

"Honey, my daddy's a politician and my momma's an alcoholic." Libby clicked off the bedside lamp. "My life is built on lies."

Join the club. Nadia closed her eyes. Her mind wandered back to the trailer. If she hadn't turned up the heat, the generator wouldn't have gone out. The malfunction probably caused the explosion.

Libby's covers rustled. "Oh, I almost forgot—I have more gossip. Are you still awake?"

Nadia turned toward her roommate's bed. "Yeah, I'm awake."

Libby pushed herself up onto her elbow. "Simon discovered his father's CIA code name. He thinks he's very close to identifying him."

"That's great," Nadia said, tucking her hand under her pillow. "I'm really happy for him."

"I know. Me too."

"What is it? His code name?" Nadia asked.

Libby flopped back down onto her pillow. "He goes by Jericho."

41 SIMON
TUESDAY, FEBRUARY 7

Shortly after discovering that his borrowed drone had captured the fight of the century, it occurred to Simon that such an event—a recruit gone missing on a survival course and another passed out cold in the middle of campus—would likely propel the Dean of Students into some online investigation. Which is why last night, seconds after Alan left for his appointment with Professor Katz, Simon had pulled up the shadow server on Shepard's computer.

The flurry of activity across CIA mainframes had sparkled like Christmas morning. The whole reason Simon wanted the drone was to prompt Shepard to log on to the CIA server. She would've seen the drone flying overhead, grown curious, and investigated. Turns out, he hadn't needed to orchestrate a calamity after all. He'd only needed a bit of patience.

Only a high-ranking member of the CIA would've had the clout to secure Simon's position at Desert Mountain. That meant his father's DNA *had* to be in CIADIS. And soon enough, Simon's would be, as well. And the instant the program located a match, he'd know Jericho's name.

Shepard's log-in and password were buried in code, but he'd filtered the information through a specially designed program. He'd then repeated her steps to log on to CIADIS.

As soon as he heard back from the lab, he'd enter his own DNA, and then...

He was so close it hurt.

On Tuesday after lunch, Simon stopped by his room to swap out textbooks and check his computer. He waited until Alan left for class to retrieve the laptop from his satchel, and then immediately opened his email. He'd received one from the lab. His breath quickened as he clicked on the correspondence.

He skimmed the results, then copied his gene sequence and pasted it into the CIADIS database. His finger hovered over the button for a millisecond before he hit *search*. A progress bar appeared in the middle of the screen.

Simon went into the loo to splash cool water on his face. With shaking hands, he hung up his wet towel, which he'd forgotten to do earlier, then walked back to his desk to check the status bar. Point-zero-two percent.

Simon groaned out loud. "This'll take a bloody year." He clicked the info button and read the message: *Search initiated. Program running. Select YES to continue running search in background, NO to exit.* "Yes," he said aloud, clicking the green button. *Check back for results.*

He snapped closed his laptop and left for class.

The remainder of Tuesday lasted approximately seven hundred years. At 10:15, after watching the status bar for a solid hour as it crawled from seventy-three to eighty-four percent, Simon went to bed.

A few minutes before midnight, his computer chirped to life. Two seconds later Alan's pillow landed on his face.

"Oi," Simon called. "Take it easy."

"Silence your laptop," Alan demanded.

How Alan had heard the alarm over his jet-engine white-noise machine was anyone's guess, but Simon felt he'd antagonized his roommate enough in the past few days. "Right you are. My apologies." He threw back the blankets and returned Alan's pillow. "I'll take it to the lobby." He grabbed his laptop and a sweatshirt and plodded from the room.

Down the hall, the lobby was vacant. Simon sat on the sofa and opened his computer. The alert flashing in the dock made his stomach flutter—this might be it. He clicked on the notice and read *CIADIS: Results Available*.

Simon's breath caught in his throat. He'd waited sixteen years for this.

The nerves in his stomach bound themselves into a cannonball-sized knot as he opened the file. And then, as he processed the message, pain seared like a knife stabbing into his gut.

Simon reread the notification flashing on his screen.

Match Found: Subject Deceased.

His heart fell as he scrolled through the report. His father, a CIA officer, had died over a decade ago.

Hollow platitudes drifted off the screen: heroically in the line of duty, a treasure to his country, the thanks of a grateful nation.

But Jericho had only recently secured Simon's admission to Desert Mountain Academy. *This can't be right—it's a mistake.*

Simon closed his eyes and slouched back against the couch. Jericho *wasn't* his father. So who was he? His dad's old partner? A friend of his mum?

"You can't sleep either?"

Simon opened his eyes. "Jack. I didn't hear you come in." He felt absolutely numb. "No rest for the wicked, I suppose."

Jack paced the floor in front of the lobby desk. "I'm worried about Nadia. Do you think she's okay?"

Simon looked at the ceiling. "She seems no worse for the wear."

"I really screwed up."

"With Nadia? I'm sure it's not too late," he said flatly, not bothering to lift his head.

"No, Dean Shepard. I lied to her." Jack's stride quickened. "And it was a *big* lie." Back and forth, back and forth.

"What choice did you have? You couldn't sell out your girl."

Jack stopped abruptly and slumped onto the sofa next to Simon. After a moment, he said, "Are you okay? You don't look so good."

Simon heaved himself to an upright position and hoisted his feet onto the coffee table. He wasn't sure he had the energy to tell the story. How could he possibly relay the simultaneous feeling of terror and euphoria as he'd clicked open the file? And then to read that his father had died in the line of service over a decade ago, never having met his son?

No matter. Simon had oodles of practice compartmentalizing. He knew how to bury the pain, tuck it away in a little box, and set it on a shelf in the back of his mind.

"What's up, man?" Jack asked.

After a heavy sigh, he said, "I found my father."

"Hey, that's fantastic," Jack said. "I didn't realize you were looking for him."

"He's dead."

"Oh. I'm sorry, man."

"It doesn't matter, does it? It's not like I knew him."

Long pause. "Do you want to talk about it?"

Simon shrugged. "I don't know very much. Just that he was CIA and he died in the line of service."

"Your dad was CIA? No kidding?"

"Mmm. The report said he died a hero, so I guess *that's* something to celebrate." Simon assumed his mocking tone adequately conveyed his contempt.

Two countries, two parents, two deaths. And one abandoned orphan.

42 NADIA
WEDNESDAY, FEBRUARY 8

After a fitful night's sleep, Nadia woke before dawn. The memory of her roommate's words flashed through her consciousness before Nadia had fully opened her eyes. Simon might be her brother. Her heart felt sick—was it possible?

Was any of this possible?

She pulled on her *gi* and rushed through the dark morning, arriving at the dojo an hour before the other juniors were due. After bowing in, she greeted her mentor. "You said we would talk after I rested?"

Sensei invited her into the meditation room. They stepped onto the *tatami* mats and sat across from each other on small *seiza* benches.

"When we spoke last night, I recalled hearing about Project Genesis. Due to the highly classified level of the project, I did not wish to speak to you in the administration building," Sensei said. "I returned to the dojo and contacted an old friend familiar with Project Genesis. He confirmed that there was much controversy surrounding the project, as well as the mission that was initially run to destroy it."

"There was a mission to destroy Project Genesis?"

"It was called Operation Cyprus."

Nadia's stomach sunk. Operation Cyprus was tied to Project

Genesis. Her father was waist deep in this quagmire. "What kind of controversy?"

"It seems Project Genesis did not originate in the United States. It was initially developed in Syria. When we learned of the project, the CIA sent a team to Syria to eliminate the creator of Genesis and destroy the technology. But on arrival, the team found the developer eager to cooperate. The lead officer of the operation disobeyed orders and commanded the team to extract the developer to be used as a CIA asset. The team members of Operation Cyprus suffered much discord in the process. They were not in agreement regarding the extraction. Some wanted to follow orders and execute the scientist, others felt the technology and its creator were too valuable to lose. In the end, both were extracted. And in exchange, the developer handed over all the original project files to the United States."

Nadia's voice sounded thin to her ears as she asked, "Do you know who served on the team?"

"I do not."

"So the CIA *does* perform assassinations?"

He shook his head. "Performing an assassination and eliminating a terrorist are not considered one and the same. This scientist was developing a weapon of mass destruction. It is my understanding that the CIA does *not* assassinate nonterrorist targets."

She hesitated before asking the next question. "How long have you been teaching at the Academy?"

"I do not answer personal questions."

"Sensei, please."

He paused a moment. "This is my fourteenth year."

Nadia exhaled with relief. He'd never taught her father. He hadn't lied. After a few seconds she said, "I think my father attended the school."

Surprise crossed his face; he quickly regained composure. "Why do you believe this?"

"I saw his recruit file. And I'm pretty sure he was part of Operation Cyprus."

"Ah," Sensei said, nodding slightly. "This explains why Agent Roberts demanded you in exchange for Damon's mother."

Nadia frowned. "What do you mean?"

"Why would Roberts be interested in an untrained recruit with no insider knowledge or connections? Why *you*?"

She shook her head. "I don't know. Roberts also worked Operation Cyprus. He knows my dad. Maybe he—" She stopped talking.

Agent Roberts. Operation Cyprus. Project Genesis.

It all clicked together.

"Roberts wants Genesis," she said. "He thinks my dad can locate the developer—the asset. He wants the scientist to recreate the technology. Damon was using me to get to his mother; Roberts was using me to get to my dad. It *was* a hostage exchange, but not for me—he wants my father. A tiger kidnapping."

"*Hai*," Sensei agreed.

Nadia dropped her gaze to the space between their knees, to the textured mats woven so tightly together it was impossible to see where one ended and another began. Again, she thought about Simon. What if he figured out Jericho's identity? What if he exposed her dad? Simon was shrewd; she'd need to keep her distance until she knew more. She looked back at Sensei. "My father lied to me about everything."

Sensei's dark eyes studied her as his face softened. "Do not judge too harshly, Nadia-san. If this is true, I am certain your father had good reason to keep you in the dark. As you well know, in the CIA, we do not always get to choose with whom we share our secrets."

A few hours later, just before breakfast, Dean Shepard visited the girls' dorm. After everyone had gathered in the lobby, she made an announcement. "Students, your attention please. A week from next Tuesday is the first Republican debate. As many of you know, Senator Wentworth Bishop of Georgia has announced his intention to run for president. Regardless of personal politics, this is an extraordinary opportunity for our community to observe democracy in action. Attendance at the debate is mandatory. Please arrive in the student lounge no later than six o'clock."

Nadia glanced at Libby. Her roommate, clearly in campaign mode, nodded politely, thanking the many well-wishers.

After the lobby emptied, Nadia said, "I'm so sorry. I didn't even ask how it was going with your dad." They walked slowly toward their room.

Libby shook her head. "You've just been through the most traumatic event of your life. You get a pass." Her voice dropped. "Just promise me you won't leave my side during the debate. When it comes to my daddy, people either love him or hate him, and I never know which way it's gonna go. I might need a bodyguard to get me out of there."

Nadia smiled. "Don't worry. I've got your back."

Halfway down the hall, Casey called from the lobby. "Nadia, phone's for you."

She jogged back up the hall and took the receiver. "Hello?"

"Nadia Riley?" The computerized voice on the other end of the line sent chills down her spine.

"Who is this?" she asked.

"Tell Liberty justice is coming." The line went dead.

Nadia's hand shook as she replaced the telephone. Fear washed through her as she realized that once again, campus offered only the illusion of safety.

Beneath the fear bubbled something else. It took a second to identify, but then—

Relief. She felt relieved.

That phone call, the robotic voice, it was exactly like the one she'd received last semester. The call meant to frame her as the double agent. The call placed by Damon.

She hadn't killed him. Damon was alive.

And apparently, he wasn't finished with her.

Despite her plan to avoid him until she'd uncovered more information, after lunch, Nadia got caught walking with Simon back to their dorms. Halfway down the hill, Simon asked, "All right, what is going on with you? You've been dodgy all morning. What's on your mind?"

She felt sick keeping her suspicions from him. If they were siblings, he had a right to know, didn't he? But she couldn't tell him. She had no way to anticipate his reaction. And until she knew more about her father.... *Keep your mouth shut. Give him something else.* "I have a hypothetical question. If you thought Alan was in danger, but you really weren't sure, would you tell someone, or keep it to yourself?" They reached her dorm and she stopped.

Simon narrowed his eyes. "Why do you ask?"

"No reason," Nadia answered. "Just making conversation."

"Interesting conversation," he said. "All right. Hypothetically speaking, what's your indication of danger?"

"I don't know." She shrugged. "Say, a vaguely threatening phone call."

Simon seemed to consider. Finally, he shook his head. "No, I guess not. No sense in worrying everyone before I knew something definitive."

She nodded. "Yeah, that makes sense."

"Unless, of course, the call came over an open line."

"What do you mean?"

"The hall phones, for example. Aren't the lines monitored?"

"Yes, but I don't know if security listens regularly, or only when they have cause. What does that have to do with anything?"

"Normally, I'm wholeheartedly anti-authority, but..." He shook his head. "In that situation, I guess I'd probably take it to Shepard. If security heard it and I *didn't* report it—well, that looks bad for everyone, eh?"

With her professor's permission, Nadia ditched Mandarin Chinese that afternoon, and instead copied Libby's class notes before she fell any further behind. She sat outside on the upper level of the Navajo Building, on the patio facing campus, and transcribed page after page, enjoying the normalcy of the warm sun on her shoulders. After an hour or so, Jack joined her.

"Why aren't you in class?" she asked.

"Follow-up at medical. That was a pretty heavy dose of tranquilizer you gave me." He handed her a glass of iced tea and sat down.

"Beats a bullet."

He smiled. "I wasn't complaining." After a moment he said, "Listen, your mock mission is scheduled for the twenty-third, but I've decided to ask Dean Shepard if we can postpone. I'll need to get an extension on my project, but under the circumstances, I don't think she can object."

"I appreciate the thought, but I don't want special treatment. And to be honest, I'd love to focus on something other than the last few days."

He nodded. "Okay, if you're sure."

"Of course. It's still weeks away. If I can't focus by then, I probably shouldn't be here."

Jack leaned back in his chair, propping his feet against the metal railing. "Man, what a gorgeous day, huh?"

Nadia shot him a glare—which he missed because he wasn't even looking at her. She found it annoying that Jack seemed totally fine with everything, that he spoke to her just as he would to Libby or Alan. She didn't expect a big dramatic scene, but he could act a little sad about breaking up.

As she turned the page in Libby's notebook, a sheet of flash paper as thin as an onion skin fluttered from the spiral-bound pages. Like any good spy, Nadia scanned the assignment, picking up the key words: *medical convention, ID badge, Gentech Labcorp.* "Are these Libby's op-specs?"

Before she finished reading, Jack snatched the paper from the notebook and said, "You aren't supposed to read that. Libby should've destroyed it."

"Gentech Labcorp—you know what that is, right?" Nadia asked.

"No, and I don't care." He shoved the paper into his pocket. "My job is to execute missions, not research companies."

Nadia leaned forward. "I appreciate that, and typically I'd agree with you, but you've heard of CIADIS, right?"

"Sure, the CIA's Combined DNA Index System. It's the online genetic database of all employees. What about it?"

"CIADIS is stored at Gentech Labcorp."

He shrugged. "And?"

"Did you know that when we turn eighteen our DNA results are transferred from the campus database to Gentech for permanent storage?"

"So what?"

"So you don't think it's an odd coincidence that you've been assigned to tamper with CIADIS at the exact same time Damon forced me to destroy the student database?"

"First of all, I'm not *tampering* with anything," he said.

"Aren't you?"

"Second of all, that's the definition of a coincidence—an odd occurrence of events. You're seeing patterns that aren't there."

"I study cryptography. I don't invent patterns where there are none—I spot patterns that already exist."

"Nadia, think about it. It makes sense that our mock missions would be at a CIA facility, right?"

She looked away, across the field and over the wall to the rocky desert. Jack made a good point. But two unrelated missions involving DNA databases? That had to be more than a coincidence. After a few moments, she asked, "What can you tell me about your senior project?"

He shook his head. "Nothing. I can't tell you anything. Dean Shepard specifically instructed me not to discuss the mission as a whole." He stood and grabbed his full glass of iced tea. "You've been through a lot. I don't mean to sound unsympathetic, but I think you should let this go. There's no connection between my senior project and your time with Damon." He nodded toward her glass. "Do you want a refill before I take off?"

"I'm all set," she said.

"In that case, good luck with your studying. I'll see you later."
Jack walked away, disappearing into the dining room.

Nadia tapped her pen against the table. A hard knot had formed deep in her gut. Despite the logic of Jack's argument, she was unconvinced. He wouldn't share mission details, but Simon was not so scrupulous, and Alan couldn't keep a secret to save his life.

She'd find out what she wanted to know soon enough.

43 DAMON
THURSDAY, FEBRUARY 9

Damon knew the second Wolfe's heart monitor flatlined that Ms. McGill would be out for blood. It had taken less than an hour. The problem, of course, was that as far as McGill knew, Wolfe lay dead because Nadia had stabbed him with a poisoned pen eight weeks ago. It would take days for an autopsy to confirm an adrenaline injection. For now, if McGill had a fraction of Damon's lust for revenge, Nadia was in imminent danger. He needed to keep an eye on McGill.

She'd cried over Wolfe's bed for most of the night. Then she got up, wiped her eyes, pulled on her sweater, and marched outside. After placing a single phone call that lasted approximately twenty-five seconds, she drove north toward Phoenix. Damon followed as McGill stopped at every ATM in the valley. As the sun rose, she pulled into the parking lot of the Malt-Shop Diner in north Tempe, donned her sunglasses, and went inside.

Damon had a clear view of her booth through the window. A few minutes after she arrived, a man joined her: six-two, muscular, shaved head. He looked like ex-military.

McGill slid a fat envelope across the table. The man peeked at the contents and then tucked it inside his jacket. She leaned forward, pounding her index finger on the table as her lips formed angry words.

Damon recognized the situation immediately. McGill had just hired a hitman.

Twelve hours later, in response to McGill's rash breakfast decision, Damon stood in her kitchen and reviewed his next move.

Her house was nicer than he'd expected. The open floor plan allowed a clear view through the living room and into the back yard. A high, stuccoed wall surrounded the property, as with most houses in this neighborhood, providing maximum privacy. McGill had left the windows open, which granted Damon easy access, and the evening breeze ruffled the gauzy sheers. Outside, the pool blazed with the reflected orange and pink light of the setting sun.

The kitchen, small but well equipped, was immaculate. The counters were clear of everything except a half-empty bottle of red wine. *Perfect.*

He pulled on his lambskin gloves, checked the cupboards for an unopened bottle of wine, the drawers for a corkscrew. Satisfied he had everything he needed, Damon removed the cork from the open bottle, emptied the ampule from his pocket into the wine, and replaced the stopper.

Down the hall in McGill's bedroom closet, Damon found a few of Wolfe's dress shirts and a suit. His robe hung alongside hers on the back of the bathroom door. Damon checked the medicine cabinet, found what he needed, then went back into the bedroom. The only item on her dresser was a framed picture of the two of them standing in the desert, Wolfe's arm around McGill's shoulder.

It was strange to see them like this. Not only because Damon had had no idea about their relationship, but because he knew Wolfe as a coldhearted killer. He'd never pictured him with a personal life.

This was a lesson Damon would need to consider when he had more time—not only that he'd missed Wolfe's vulnerability, but what personal relationships meant for him moving forward. Relationships were the reason he was in this mess. Other people were always the chink in the armor. Everyone he cared about became a liability. Therefore, the more people he cared about, the weaker he became. He could take care of himself, no problem. It was all the other dead weight that made him susceptible to attack.

The garage door slammed shut, and McGill's shoes clicked across the tiled kitchen floor. He slipped inside her walk-in closet, leaving the door cracked. A kitchen cabinet opened and closed, and liquid sloshed into a glass.

A minute later she came into the bedroom, glass of wine in hand. She stepped out of her heels and continued to the bathroom. He debated moving from his position, but before he'd decided, she emerged wearing her bathrobe. Back down the hall toward the kitchen.

He checked his watch. Four, five more swallows. Seven minutes, tops.

Six minutes later he heard the thud as her body hit the floor. He moved from the closet, down the hall, to the edge of the living room. She was on her back looking at her hands. The tingling must've started. Next: chills, sweats, numbness. Muscle paralysis. Eventually, she'd stop breathing—if her heart didn't give out first.

Damon stepped from the shadows. He knelt down and took her hand.

She tried to say his name, but it came out as a hoarse one-syllable whisper.

He leaned toward her ear and said, "Aconite. It's very quick."

Confusion in her eyes as she tried to form words.

"Nadia," he said.

Anger replaced the confusion. McGill tried again to speak.

"The drug," Damon whispered, "has a common name that you might know. I thought it an appropriate choice."

Her eyes lost focus, so he moved closer.

"It's from a lovely flowering plant called *wolfsbane*. But no need to panic, I have the antidote." Damon patted his jacket pocket. "Tell me where to find my mother, call off the hit on Nadia, and it's yours. Deal?"

She whispered something.

"What?" he asked, moving closer still.

"See..." She breathed out the word. "You...in hell."

A rush of anger washed through him. Was she really that vindictive? He dropped her hand and stood. "I have no doubt that's true."

After leaving her side, Damon began his search. In her home office, a small room just off the kitchen, he found her computer. She hadn't bothered to log out, so he checked the schedule labeled *Desert Mountain Academy*. It only took a moment to locate the time and place. He exhaled, relieved. He still had time. All he had to do now was beat Nadia to the destination.

He returned to McGill's bathroom to raid the medicine cabinet for the sleeping pills he'd seen earlier. He would have to ease a small handful down her esophagus and into her stomach. Fortunately, McGill's fridge was stocked with bottles of water. He'd tip up her chin, which would open her throat—the same way he would if he were administering CPR—then drop the pills in and follow with a gentle stream of water.

Between the wine and the pills, the medical examiner would have no reason to run a toxicity screen for anything unusual. But even if he did, aconite was extremely difficult to identify.

He left the open prescription bottle on the floor next to her body.

He found her photographs in her bedside chest. Damon flipped through the stack: McGill and Wolfe dressed in evening wear at a charity event, the pair drinking cocktails at a pool party, sitting together at an outdoor café. He arranged one of the pictures in McGill's lifeless hand, tucked another inside his jacket, and returned the stack to her bedroom.

Lastly, Damon opened the new bottle of wine. He served a generous amount into a fresh wine glass, swished it around, then dumped the contents into the kitchen sink. To make it look like she'd had a lot, he poured another three-quarters of the bottle down the drain. He corked the wine, setting the bottle on the granite countertop. He took the poisoned bottle of wine and the tainted glass and placed them in a paper bag, which he would take with him, just in case she was assigned an overeager investigator.

A final once-over satisfied him that all details had been addressed.

44 NADIA
FRIDAY, FEBRUARY 10

Despite her best efforts to focus on catching up, the next few days found Nadia struggling to keep her mind on her classes and specializations. Dozens of unanswered questions plagued her waking thoughts and embedded themselves into strange and vivid dreams.

Was Simon her half brother? He couldn't be—he'd made a mistake. But how else would Simon have learned Jericho's name? Did he know Jericho was *her* father?

And what *about* her father? Why had he kept the truth from her? Nadia felt they'd always had an open and honest relationship. Now she realized she'd been completely misled.

And Damon—did he, a known traitor to the United States, somehow fit in with Jack's senior project? If he did, then either Damon was working in the interests of his country, or she and her teammates were working against those interests. But neither of those options made sense.

Maybe Jack was right—maybe his project and Damon's objective to destroy the database weren't related. Maybe she *was* seeing patterns that didn't exist.

For the time being, she found herself frustratingly stuck in the purgatory of the unknown.

*　　*　　*

By late Friday morning, Nadia had reached her breaking point. After political science, she caught Simon's eye and asked him to walk with her. She slowed to create distance. When their classmates were halfway up the hill, Nadia said, "Libby mentioned you had a lead on your dad. How's that going?"

Simon frowned and he shook his head. "Not well, I'm afraid."

"What do you mean?"

He cleared his throat. "I discovered my father's given name." She held her breath as he continued. "Apparently, he died in the line of duty."

Nadia's heart seized. "What?" Simon always heard news before anyone else—had he received intel about Jericho? "When?"

"About ten years ago." Simon dropped his gaze.

Nadia exhaled so forcefully that Simon shot her a glance. "I'm so sorry. I can't imagine how disappointed you must feel. Did you just find out?"

"I got the report on Monday, only I haven't been up for talking about it." He shrugged. "It doesn't make much sense to mourn the loss of something I never had."

She wanted to know why Simon believed Jericho had died ten years ago, but she didn't know how to ask without rousing suspicion. "If you ever want to talk..."

"It was good of you to ask," he said. "You know, it's funny. I had this revenge fantasy—I wanted to get even because he'd abandoned me, but now that I know he's dead, I just feel...sad."

Her heart pounded faster. *Ask the question.* "What was his name?"

Simon looked past her as he answered. "Riazotti." His clear blue eyes filled with tears. "His name was Milo Riazotti." He turned away.

Nadia frowned as she followed Simon up the hill.

What the hell is going on?

The rest of the day's classes bled together. Nadia, fatigued and distracted, had to force herself back to the present about a million times. She needed more information, but how could she conduct research on the CIA's Black-Ops Division?

As they were leaving Arabic, their last class, Nadia put her hand on Simon's shoulder. "Hang on a second, okay?" She leaned against him and slipped off her shoe, shaking out an imaginary stone. "Go ahead," she said to Libby. "We'll meet you at the library."

When her classmates were out of earshot, she pulled on her shoe, then glanced around to make sure they were alone. "I need a favor."

"Yes, I assumed you weren't only using me for balance. How can I be of assistance?"

She tried to look casual. "Can I borrow your laptop?"

"Of course. As I mentioned, it's at your disposal." He dropped his bag to the sidewalk and unzipped the pouch. "I trust your interest is covert?"

"It's personal. If your help is contingent on—"

"Steady on, I'm only making conversation." He handed her the computer, then fished for the cord. "Password is *Tiresias*. I'll swing by your dorm a bit later and fetch it back. Shall I convey your regrets to Alan and Libby? I assume your research supersedes our study session."

"That would be great. Thank you." She hugged the computer against her body as the compressing squeeze around her heart slightly lessened.

"Listen, about earlier," Simon said. "Thanks for asking about my dad. Saying the words out loud seems to have lifted a bit of weight."

"I'm glad." Nadia offered a half smile. She didn't dare ask about Jericho. They resumed walking. "So have you already completed your mock mission?"

"Yeah, you're the last one."

"What did you have to do?"

Simon looked at her quizzically. "Why do you ask?"

She shook her head. "Just curious. Mine's coming up and I'm a little nervous, I guess. Can you tell me or not?"

Simon shrugged. "Yeah, what do I care? You'll be fine, there's nothing to it. Jack had me break into this place called Gentech Labcorp using an ID badge Libby stole on *her* mission. I plugged a wifi-enabled thumb drive into the mainframe. That's it."

"What was on the drive?"

"I dunno. Boy Scout refused to toss it."

"Shocking." Nadia rolled her eyes. "Jack wouldn't bend the rules? I can hardly believe it."

"Listen, love, I know you're hurt, but if it's any consolation, I believe he's hurting, too."

She opened her mouth to tell him to mind his own business, that he didn't know what he was talking about, but before she spoke, he grabbed her wrist and glanced over his shoulder.

"Hey," he whispered. "Did you hear about Ms. McGill?"

"No, what about her?"

"She didn't show up for work, so Shepard sent security to her place to check if she was all right. She'd overdosed on sleeping pills. She's dead."

"Oh my God, that's horrible. I had no idea. How'd you find out?"

Simon shrugged. "Secrets are ten a penny. I have a knack for hearing things, I suppose."

"Poor Ms. McGill. I guess you never really know what someone else is going through." She sighed and held up his laptop. "Thanks for this. I won't be long."

A few minutes later, locked in her bedroom, Nadia booted up the computer.

She opened a private tab in the browser and paused for a second—where to begin? Part of her knew that researching her father was a waste of time. After reviewing Operation Cyprus and seeing the photographs, she had no doubt the files were real. Furthermore, the CIA wouldn't allow anything sensitive to be posted online, right? So this exercise was likely in vain. Still, she felt compelled to look for clues, hints about what she'd missed. How could she not have realized her father was CIA?

In the search box, Nadia typed the name of the town where

she'd gone to sixth grade, along with *CIA satellite office*. She knew it was a long shot, but she had to start somewhere. Nothing relevant, so she included the year she'd lived there.

That yielded results, but unfortunately, nothing useful. Apparently, a government official had died in a freak accident; sensational headlines dominated the first page. She deleted the search and tried another town, the one she'd lived in during her fourth-grade year.

That resulted in another splashy headline: *Visiting dignitary dies moments before scheduled speech*. She sat back and frowned at the screen.

She went back further, started at the beginning—Michigan, where she was born.

A year after her birth, a Supreme Court justice from Ann Arbor was killed in his home during a break-in. After that, her family moved to Belize. A few months later, a congressman, well known for his love of scuba diving, disappeared into the Blue Hole just off the coast. The press reported malfunctioning equipment. Los Angeles, California, a whistle blower from the NSA died of a heart attack while crossing the street. He was thirty-seven years old. Corpus Christi, the untimely death of a former FBI agent. According to the medical examiner, he drowned in his swimming pool.

Nadia's heart pounded as she read the reports. Guam, upstate New York, Pennsylvania, Maryland....Everywhere she'd ever lived, page after page of unsolved homicides. Death after mysterious death.

And always a few short weeks before her father packed up the family and moved again.

Nadia pushed away from the desk—she couldn't catch her breath. She stood to straighten her torso, expand her lungs.

They'd lied—the CIA had lied to Sensei, to the recruits. They *did* employ assassins. Assassins who killed American citizens, on American soil.

Maybe her dad was an expert in political assassinations not because he'd studied them, but because he'd performed them.

Her mouth watered as a cold sweat broke across her body. She dashed into the bathroom, threw open the toilet lid, and vomited. The heaving continued long after her stomach emptied; painful, uncontrollable spasms. She sat on the floor, pressed her forehead against the tiled wall, and closed her eyes.

As soon as she could move, Nadia pulled herself to a kneeling position. She grabbed a washcloth from the vanity drawer and held it under a cold stream of water. A few seconds later, she shut off the faucet and wrung out the excess water, then slid back down the wall and covered her eyes with the cool cloth.

And then something else occurred to her. Her eyes opened as another wave of nausea flooded her body.

Maybe they hadn't lied. Maybe the CIA *didn't* perform assassinations.

Maybe her father wasn't CIA.

Maybe, just like Agent Roberts, her father was a Nighthawk.

45 DAMON
SUNDAY, FEBRUARY 12

Damon's ringing cell phone pushed its way into his sleep. Eventually, it woke him, and when it did he came up quick. In that hazy moment between sleep and consciousness, he had no idea where he was.

He fumbled for the phone. "Yeah." Then he remembered—he was at a rest stop off the highway, camped in the bushes behind the restrooms.

Someone using a voice modification program spoke into his ear. "I know where to find your mother."

Damon's eyes narrowed. "Is that right?"

The computerized voice continued. "She's being moved to a safe house near the Louisiana State University stadium. I'll text the address and date of arrival."

He couldn't tell if this was the same caller as before. The modification software skewed voice, tone, and inflection. "Who is this?" He searched the surrounding area, peering through the dark for any movement. His hand found the gun in his bag. His fingers wrapped into place.

"A friend."

"I don't have any friends," Damon said.

"Very well. Then let's just say we have a mutual enemy. The sooner Roberts goes down, the better."

"Mr. Green?" The background noise ceased, and Damon realized he was alone on the line. He checked his call history but, as expected, the number of the last incoming call was blocked. A minute later Damon got the text: an address in Baton Rouge. She'd be there a week from Tuesday.

He hoisted himself from the ground and paced in quick, nervous strides. The lead might be bogus, moving him further from his mom. Was that a risk he was willing to take? But it might be legit. Roberts had no shortage of enemies. If Damon could get his mom back without trading Nadia, so much the better.

And what *about* Nadia? He might still need her, alive and unharmed, and McGill's hitman was still on the loose. Could he trust the information he'd seen on McGill's computer?

He dropped to his knees to gather his belongings. He didn't have the luxury of choice.

When Nadia escaped, Damon had lost his leverage, and for the first time in his life, he was out of ideas.

46 NADIA
MONDAY, FEBRUARY 13

On Monday morning Nadia forced herself out of bed and into her *gi*. She'd spent most of the weekend studying in the library, pausing only to eat and sleep. Libby assumed that her stress-induced fatigue was a result of her time away with Damon, but the truth was, Nadia couldn't reconcile what she'd learned from her research.

Her father couldn't be a Nighthawk. If he was, Roberts would've picked someone else as his scapegoat last semester. He wouldn't frame the daughter of a colleague. Furthermore, Roberts wouldn't need to order a tiger kidnapping—he'd just call Jericho himself. But what about the trail of bodies in her father's wake?

The CIA didn't sanction hits, and no way were all those people declared terrorists. The timing of the deaths coupled with the timing of her family's constant relocating did not bode well, but her dad *couldn't* be an assassin. This was a man incapable of streaming a movie without a written tutorial.

She had reached one comforting conclusion. After careful consideration, Nadia decided not to worry about Damon's voice-modified phone call regarding Libby. His approach was a classic technique—threatening her best friend in an attempt to compel Nadia to help rescue his mother. But Damon didn't know he'd made an empty threat. No one but Nadia knew that Libby was on lockdown. The only remaining question was whether or not to report to Dean Shepard that Damon was alive.

Late that afternoon Professor Shaheen, the Arabic instructor, distributed a test. Since Nadia had missed a few classes, he sent her to the library to review.

She sat alone at her team's usual table, but rather than review the notes, she stared at Damon's code scrawled across the top of her planner.

Her need to decipher the message bordered on obsessive. She'd tried everything: a Vigenère cipher, a skip-sequence cipher, no cipher at all—was it a phone number? A bank account? Coordinates? She didn't dare use the cipher computer.

Fifteen minutes past the hour, Jack showed up. "How's it going?"

"Never better. You?"

"Good." He slid into the seat next to her. "Listen, the more I think about your mission, the more I think we should postpone. I'm worried about you."

His caretaking irritated her. He wasn't her boyfriend, and coming from her team leader, it indicated a lack of confidence in her abilities. "If you don't think I can handle myself, just say so."

"Don't get defensive. It's not that at all. You've had a rough month." He lowered his voice. "Do you want to talk about what happened with Damon? I hope you know that I'm still here for you."

Yeah, whatever. "I'm not really comfortable discussing my personal life with you."

"Being kidnapped by a traitor doesn't exactly constitute a 'personal life.'"

"I wouldn't know," she said. "I don't have the best luck when it comes to relationships."

His jaw tightened. "I know you're angry with me. And I regret that I can't share my op-specs with you, but those are the rules." After a moment, he asked, "Do you feel like I didn't protect you? Is that why you're mad?"

Anger rose in her chest like the swell of a wave. She leaned toward him and whispered, "I don't need you to protect me. And why would you? As you may recall, you're not my boyfriend, so back off."

Jack looked away.

Nadia glared at the table, furious with herself. What was wrong with her? Ending their relationship had been Jack's only option, she knew that. It was just the way he'd done it. Unilaterally making the decision, and then pretending to discuss it with her. She shook her head. "I'm sorry—I didn't mean that."

After a few long, uncomfortable minutes, Jack spoke as though nothing had happened. "Are you all caught up with your schoolwork?" Before she could stop him, he scooped up her planner. He pointed to Damon's code. "What are you doing with this?"

"Trying to solve it." She reached for her planner, and he moved farther away.

He frowned. "There's nothing to solve. It's not a code. It's a case file number."

Nadia met his eyes. "What?"

He dropped the planner on the table and nodded toward the long row of locked cabinets near the main entrance, the Authorized Persons Only section of the library. "It's a restricted case file number."

"How can you tell?"

He shrugged. "I've studied some of them as team leader. The first two numbers state the location of the mission—in this case, it was executed in the Middle East. The next three indicate that this file is *highly* classified. Like, eyes-only, burn-after-reading classified."

"Why does the CIA keep highly classified documents in a school library?" she asked. "Why aren't they at Langley?"

He smiled. "Get this. Since its opening in 1961, CIA headquarters has been hacked, bombed, and broken into over two hundred times. Know how many times Desert Mountain Academy has been breached? Once. By you, the other night. The files are hidden in plain sight." He nodded toward her planner. "So where'd you get the file number?"

She rubbed her forehead. "I saw it written somewhere and assumed it was a cipher. I thought it would be fun to solve. I guess that explains why I haven't made any progress." Her eyes wandered to the restricted access area.

Well, I definitely can't report Damon's phone call now. Breaking into the library would be difficult enough without Secret Service crawling all over campus, and if Nadia reported the full message about the threat to Libby, Dean Shepard's desire for privacy would certainly be vetoed. *I'll wait till I get the file, then I'll talk to the dean.*

Jack smiled. "That's how you spend your free time?" When she didn't answer, he pushed back from the table. "Look, I'm sorry you're upset with me. But you don't get to tell me you completely agree with my decision, then get angry with me for making it. And I'm sorry you don't agree with my principles and my work ethic, but it's my senior project, not yours. I was instructed not to talk about it, and I won't." He stood. "Regarding your mission, please review your op-specs and be ready to go in two weeks." He turned away.

For a brief second she thought about stopping him. He was right about everything. She *was* angry, and she was being completely unfair—and childish. She would never want him to pick their relationship over his life's goal.

And logic dictated that his senior project was, in fact, completely fictional. It had to be. Her gut feeling about a connection between his assignment and Damon's directive to destroy the student database was likely a result of something else—like the drama with her father. It made perfect sense that the CIA would use an affiliated facility like Gentech. That way, if the students got caught during their missions, the CIA could cover it up. There would be no police record of breaking and entering. Why would a student team be given an actual CIA assignment? They weren't trained; they didn't know what they were doing. If his project was actually relevant or mission critical, the CIA would've assigned it to an active officer. Her suspicions from earlier were completely unfounded.

But her annoyance with him wasn't about any of that. His constant questioning of her ability and skill was insulting. She'd literally saved his life *twice* now.

Still, he was her team leader—he'd earned that position. She should apologize and put this animosity behind them.

Instead, she turned her eyes to her planner. Why would Damon have the number to a restricted case file? And what did it have to do with Jericho?

More importantly: How could she get her hands on it?

Her heart beat faster as the answer crystallized in her mind. In a few days, she'd have the perfect opportunity. The library would be closed, and every student on campus accounted for.

A week from Tuesday. The night of the Republican debate.

47 LIBBY
TUESDAY, FEBRUARY 21

Since the entire student body had been ordered to attend her daddy's first televised debate, Libby arrived early to the student lounge to ensure she'd get a front-row seat. That way she wouldn't see any eye-rolling if her daddy went off on one of his tangents. She'd dragged Nadia along, but her roommate wasn't being terribly helpful, as she'd been distracted and agitated for days. After all she'd been through recently, Libby couldn't blame her, but Nadia's tension wasn't helping Libby one lick. To relax, Libby had spent the previous hour scrubbing their room from top to bottom. Unfortunately, the sense of calm that arrived in conjunction with an immaculate bathroom had already dissipated.

As the lounge started to fill, Libby faced the television, not the door, so people wouldn't have to say nice, obligatory things. Simon sat to her right, Nadia to her left, and Alan plopped down on the floor at her feet. Jack arrived and stood behind her, which she found comforting, even though several students complained that he was blocking their view. He told them to move if they didn't like it and rested his hand on her shoulder.

Nadia fidgeted beside her, chewing her lip and frowning. Libby felt the energy and her anxiety increased. "Why are you so nervous?"

Nadia smiled and breathed out. "I don't know. I'm sorry. It's probably not helpful right now, is it?"

"No, not really," Libby muttered.

The pundits came onscreen. "Welcome to the first Republican debate, coming to you live from Baton Rouge, where the Louisiana State University auditorium is nearly full." They continued warming up, talking about this and that, while butterflies beat around inside Libby's stomach.

Jack leaned forward and asked Nadia, "Did you do the reading we talked about? Are you all set for next week?"

"Seriously?" Nadia turned around. "You really have no faith in my ability to execute this mission."

"What are you talking about?" Jack asked.

Libby pressed her lips together. *Was this really necessary right now?* As politely as possible she asked, "Is there any chance y'all can talk about this later?" Libby asked.

Nadia, ignoring Libby's request, continued. "I just think it's interesting—"

Alan's face lit up. "I know what that means!"

Simon sucked in his breath and shook his head. "Not now, mate."

"I just think it's interesting that you've asked me that question *three separate times* now." Nadia lowered her voice. "You gave me my op-specs *weeks* before my mission. You obviously don't think I'm capable of doing my job."

Libby's heart rate increased. Animosity made her so uneasy. Jack's hand tightened on her shoulder. She was about to say something placating when Nadia shot from her seat.

"Nadia, wait," Simon said. "Do you remember that thing we talked about?"

She shook her head. "I'm fine. I just forgot my sweatshirt. I'm going to get it." She turned to Libby. "Do you need anything?"

Libby could tell Nadia was angry. If she weren't in the middle of her own crisis, she would've accompanied her roommate outside for some fresh air. Maybe tried to reason with her while they were at it. Libby and Nadia both knew none of this was Jack's fault, but Nadia couldn't seem to stop taking jabs, swiping at him like a wounded animal.

Libby sighed. Even though her hands were like ice, she said, "No, but please hurry back. They're gonna start any second now."

"Don't worry—I'll be quick."

Alan glanced at Nadia. "Get something with color. You look like a ninja dressed in all black."

"Thanks for the fashion tip," Nadia said over her shoulder.

Libby turned back to the television and waited.

48 NADIA
TUESDAY, FEBRUARY 21

Nadia pushed aside her irritation with Jack as she stood in the shadow of the dining hall and scanned the open lawn. With all the students sequestered in the lounge, campus was deathly still. The library, which had closed early to force attendance at the debate, loomed dark and quiet across campus. Satisfied she was alone, Nadia grabbed the messenger bag she'd stashed earlier in the bushes and jogged across the unlit lawn toward the parking lot behind Hopi Hall.

The third car she tried was unlocked. Nadia popped the trunk and held a black t-shirt over the tiny lightbulb so the guards wouldn't notice the illumination. After locating the repair kit, she removed the small crowbar from its case. She eased the trunk closed and sprinted up the hill toward the library.

She paused for a moment, then stepped forward and jimmied the crowbar between the library door and its frame. The edge of the metal bar hooked the lock, and with a small *click*, it released. Tucking the crowbar into her bag, she slipped inside.

The sign to her left read AUTHORIZED PERSONS ONLY: the restricted access case files. She climbed over the counter separating the files from the main collection and crouched down. Blood pounded through her ears, roared like an ocean. She controlled her breath, extending her exhales to slow her heart. The white noise quieted, and she turned to the filing cabinets. The drawers were arranged sequentially; she found the one labeled 78011145-78674558.

Behind her, the security camera swept the room. She waited for the blind spot, then started picking the lock. Ducked back down as the camera returned, tried again. It took longer than it should've.

Finally, the lock released. Nadia opened the drawer and removed the file.

The black envelope, sealed along the seam, was dense with pages. She sliced open the top and fished through her messenger bag until her fingers found the flashlight.

The cover page read CLASSIFIED. EYES ONLY. Nadia slid the metal clip from the packet. She turned the page and scanned the next document, a mint-green marriage license, entitled *Certified Copy of an Entry of Marriage Pursuant to the Marriage Act of 1949*, issued to James Riley and Zaida Azar from the General Register Office, England. Two years after their wedding date.

Nadia frowned. They'd renewed their vows in England? *Who cares?*

Under the marriage license, she found a photograph. Her mother in a white dress holding a newborn, her father in a tuxedo, smiling lovingly at his bride. Another couple flanked her parents. Nadia immediately recognized the woman from the Operation Cyprus file. And standing next to her mother, a very young Senator Wentworth Bishop.

"This makes no sense," she whispered, sliding the picture to the back of the pile. The next showed her father hugging the woman she didn't know. His lips were pressed to her cheek and she laughed into the camera. Handwritten on the back in deep blue ink, *James and Maggie, Hyde Park, London*. Then another photograph of Libby's dad with the woman. Written across the bottom were the names *Wentworth Bishop and Maggie Pearle*. Then the senator with her mom; her mom and Maggie; Maggie holding the baby. Nadia flipped that picture over: *Nadyya with Auntie Maggie*.

The next pages were stamped across in black ink: LEGEND. A second marriage certificate, issued from the state of Florida, with the anniversary date her parents had always celebrated. Photographs of her parents striking different poses in front of a green screen, followed by a stack of pictures with famous landmarks and empty scenery. Then the two stacks photoshopped together: copies of the pictures she'd seen all her life. Her parents in Italy, the Greek Islands, Majorca. In front of the Eiffel Tower, the Leaning Tower of Pisa.

Nadia pushed the photos aside and found her birth certificate. Nadia Soraya Riley, born in Ann Arbor, Michigan. Tucked underneath, a second birth certificate, issued to Nadyya Soraya Azar, born in Damascus, Syria. She gasped and pressed her palm over her mouth.

Her heart quickened as she turned the page: EMERGENCY PROTOCOL. That section contained false names, social security numbers, bank statements, passport photos. Her mother's, her father's, and her own.

She held her breath. If she didn't move, if she didn't breathe, if her heart could just pause for one second maybe it would all make sense.

It's fake, she told herself. *It has to be.* But somewhere deep inside, she knew the truth.

Is he even my father?

49 LIBBY
TUESDAY, FEBRUARY 21

Libby's eyes stayed glued to the television as the cameraman swept around the auditorium. The lens locked onto her parents. Her daddy looked very presidential in a dark charcoal suit, light blue shirt, and navy and red striped tie. His tanned skin accentuated his white smile, the clear blue of his eyes. Her momma wore a knit dress in just the right shade of red—blue undertones, never orange. A matching cashmere wrap rested on her arms.

"Is that your mum, then?" asked Simon. "She's very smart looking."

"Thank you."

"Quiet everyone," Jack called. "They're introducing the candidates."

Libby barely heard the introductions. Her daddy received the most applause. She glanced toward the door for Nadia, but as the debate started, her attention turned back to the television.

"Senator Bishop, can you elaborate on your plan to tighten security and reduce acts of domestic terrorism?" the moderator asked.

"Yes, Scott, I can, and I'm so glad you asked." Bishop gave him a boyish grin and the audience laughed. "My opponent seems to have the ignore-it-and-it'll-go-away attitude toward domestic terror. We have suffered attack after attack on our soil, and I for one won't stand for it any longer." The crowd exploded with applause.

"Congressman Moss, would you care to respond?" the moderator asked.

Her daddy smirked while the congressman spoke. He looked down at the podium and shook his head—not much, just enough. He raised his chin and smiled, amused.

Congressman Moss noticed and turned to her father. "Senator, if you wouldn't mind keeping your contempt—"

"Keeping my what, Congressman? My thoughts to myself? I assure you, sir, I am." Her daddy smiled and stepped away from his podium, toward the congressman.

"Now, gentlemen," the moderator began.

Before he said another word, a *pop-pop* sounded, the camera jarred, and cries from the television audience filled the student lounge. On screen, Secret Service agents rushed the stage and swarmed the candidates, tackling them to the ground. The camera stilled and zoomed in toward the stage. Her daddy was on the floor, an agent draped over his body. Three more agents lined up in front, partially blocking the camera's view, but when the agents shifted, Libby saw the blood.

Reporters broke in, voicing over the scene. "We're coming to you live from Baton Rouge, where tragedy has just struck the Republican debate. We don't know what's happening, but it seems—oh wait, we're hearing something now."

Libby waited as the excruciatingly long pause dragged on.

"We're being told that Senator Bishop has been shot."

Libby's heart fell to her stomach.

"I repeat: Senator Wentworth Bishop of Georgia has been shot in the chest."

50 NADIA
TUESDAY, FEBRUARY 21

Panic built inside Nadia's body as flashes of light sparked in her peripheral vision. It was all true—the recruit file, Operation Cyprus, her parents' legend. They lied to her about *everything*—her entire *life* was a lie.

Icy tendrils wrapped around her heart. She wasn't even an American.

Blood pulsed back through her ears, thumping a techno beat. After a few deep breaths, the noise began to quiet, but then rushed back louder than before. It seemed to come from outside of her. *Whoosh-whoosh-whoosh-whoosh.* The beating got louder.

Then the flashing lights.

Nadia shot up from her position and turned toward the glass wall. A fierce white light strobed through the library as the beating continued. Helicopter blades—it was a helicopter.

Oh, this is not good.

Her hands shook as she shoved the file inside her messenger bag. Had she set off a silent alarm?

She catapulted over the counter and pressed herself against the entry wall.

The beating of the blades slowed as the chopper lowered to the lawn. She scanned the interior walls for an escape—a window, a hiding place—but she knew there was only one way out.

No, there was always another way out. A fire door. An alarm would definitely sound, but she was out of options.

She'd make a break for the side entrance. As long as she could get to the emergency exit before they surrounded the building, she'd be clear.

Nadia glanced through the main door to estimate her time. The helicopter landed on the lawn, headlights flooding the guard station.

She expected the squad of agents to rush the library. Instead, the well-formed team raced toward the student lounge.

Nadia ran.

Twenty seconds later she was coming up on the lounge, but from the wrong side—she was supposed to be in her dorm.

Nadia reached for the handle as the door burst open. Four men in dark suits raced toward the helicopter. Libby, sandwiched in the center of the suits, jogged to keep pace.

Jack pushed through the door and sprinted toward the security guards. "Libby," he called.

A fifth agent jumped from the helicopter and rushed Jack. "Stand down!"

"Wait—" Jack moved forward, and the guard threw him to the ground.

"Stay!" he barked, then climbed into the chopper as it lifted from the lawn.

Libby was wheels up before Nadia could speak.

Simon and Alan spilled from the lounge.

"What happened?" Nadia asked, rushing to help Jack up.

"That was excessive." He brushed himself off and scowled. "Come here." He took her elbow and gestured his team away from the lounge entrance, then looked at Nadia. "Senator Bishop was shot."

Nadia's hand flew to her mouth. *No.* The phone call—it was about the senator. "Is he alive?"

"We don't know," Jack said. "Two minutes later Secret Service arrived."

"Where were you?" Alan asked.

Her breath caught, just for an instant. Nadia pulled the sweater from the bottom of the messenger bag. "I went to get this."

Simon's eyes narrowed as he looked from her face to the bag and back again.

"Are they taking Libby to see her dad?" Nadia asked, turning her body away from Simon.

Jack shook his head. "They didn't tell us anything." He nodded toward the sidewalk as the guards from the front gate approached. "Maybe they can fill us in."

"We're on lockdown," the first guard said. "Return to your dorm rooms immediately."

Jack stepped forward. "Any word on the senator?"

The guard shook his head. "Not yet. I'm sure your resident assistant will keep you posted." His eyes moved away from Jack. They stopped on Nadia's face. "Let's move, people."

Did he know about the library? Nadia waited for him to look away. *No, there was no silent alarm, or they'd be searching the building. No one knows anything.* A second later she turned toward the dorms and bumped into Simon, who'd planted himself in her path.

"You and I have something to discuss," he said quietly.

"I don't know what you're talking about," she said.

He grabbed her wrist. "You always carry a tyre lever?"

Nadia yanked her hand free and shoved the crowbar deeper into her bag. "Like I said, I don't know what you're talking about. And mind your own business."

"This is my business. You involved me. That *hypothetical* phone call you asked me about—you never reported it, did you?"

No, and if Senator Bishop is dead, I will never forgive myself.

Nadia pushed past him. "Leave me alone," she said, and speed-walked to her dorm.

She rushed through the lobby and jogged down the hall. The instant the door closed behind her, she buried the file between her mattress and box spring.

*　　*　　*

Nadia paced for hours as she waited for a report.

Every twenty minutes she opened her bedroom door to make sure Casey was still manning the phones. Her excursion to the library felt unreal, like a dream. Maybe she'd misunderstood. The dual marriage licenses, her duplicate birth certificates, the forged photographs of her parents' life together.

And who was that woman? And how did her parents know her best friend's father? Were they all here by design? Were they all—like Damon said—just pawns in someone else's game?

Her thoughts rushed in like pounding waves. First, *my father's deceit got me shot and kidnapped.* He'd knowingly sent her here to become a spy. Next, *everything they ever told me is a lie.* Then, *how much does Mom know?*

Lastly, *he might not even be my father.*

She was dying to retrieve the file from its hiding place, to spread out the evidence, to examine the documents and photographs for meaning and authenticity. But she didn't dare.

Casey knocked on her door. "Secret Service is sending for a bag. Can you pull some of Libby's things together?"

"How is she? How's her dad? Is he alive?"

"She's been taken to a safe house. That's all I know."

"Did she get to see him? Is she coming back? How much should I pack?" Nadia asked.

"I don't know. A week's worth, maybe? If I hear anything about her dad, I'll pass it along. Bring her bag to the lobby when you're done, okay?"

"Wait—Casey, before you go, there's something I need to tell you." Nadia described the telephone call. "I didn't take it seriously. I knew Libby wasn't allowed off campus, so I thought she'd be safe. I—I'm pretty sure the call came from Damon."

Casey hesitated. "Everyone assumed he died in the explosion. What makes you think it was him?"

"Do you remember that robotic-sounding phone call I got last semester? The voice modification sounded identical, and that turned out to be Damon." Nadia shook her head. "I didn't think for a second Libby was actually in danger. And it never occurred to me it might be about her dad. I'm so sorry." Tears stung her eyes.

Casey patted her hand. "No, sweetie, it's not your fault. I'll call Dean Shepard and pass along the information, okay?"

Nadia nodded. "Thank you."

After Casey left, Nadia painstakingly folded her roommate's favorite outfits. Knowing it was important to Libby, she included the shoes and accessories that she'd seen her wear with each selection. She gathered Libby's makeup and skincare products, packing them separately in case the agents were careless with luggage. The very last thing she tucked into the bag was Libby's container of sanitizing wipes.

51 SIMON
TUESDAY, FEBRUARY 21

Simon and Alan, on strict orders to return to their room, walked silently down the carpeted hallway of the boys' dormitory. Around them students chattered about the shooting, about the chopper on the lawn, about the fate of Libby Bishop. Through their closed bedroom door, Simon heard the chirping of his computer; an alert had been sounded.

At this point he barely cared.

Once inside, Simon turned on his bedside lamp and threw a magazine onto his pillow.

"You are not planning to leave that light on, are you?" Alan asked.

"It's seven-thirty," Simon answered. "It's not bedtime, mummy."

Alan scowled. "Can you at least silence that irritating alarm? It sounds like a cricket has been let loose." He slinked into the loo, closing the door forcefully behind him.

Simon unfolded his laptop. If he hadn't been so curious, he would've let it chime for a bit longer, as he did not particularly care for Alan's tone.

He checked the alert from Shepard's database. His remote access program allowed him to see her screen, and she was flipping through documents at an alarming pace, closing each mere seconds after opening. Of course she was logged on right now—she was looking for intel on Libby's father.

The documents flashed across his monitor, one after another, faster and faster until—one stayed visible for almost thirty seconds. Simon took a screenshot right before the screen went black. She'd found what she wanted and shut it down.

He clicked to examine the picture of the document—a memo time-stamped just moments ago, marked NO EYES, meant to be burned in the room after reading. Someone screwed up—it never should've been online.

His mouth fell open as he scanned the words and realized what it meant: Shepard had found the shooter. And it was a name Simon knew.

A new alert caught his attention, a flashing in the dock of his screen. He clicked it open. Before the meaning of the message fully registered, Simon's heart flew to his throat.

The words flashed red, over and over and over. *CIADIS: Error—Duplicate Match Found—Profile Repeat.*

Duplicate match? How could that even happen? Simon launched the genetic database. His heart pounded fiercely against his ribcage, threatening to burst from his chest. *This can't be right.*

He read the name three times.

It had to be a mistake.

52 NADIA
WEDNESDAY, FEBRUARY 22

On Wednesday morning Nadia forced herself into a cold shower in a desperate attempt to clear her mind. All night she'd thought about her lying father. And Libby. And Libby's father, and Damon, and the awful fact that if she'd reported his threat, maybe none of this would've happened.

Just before breakfast Casey knocked on her bedroom door.

"How's Libby?" Nadia asked. "Any word on the senator?"

Casey shook her head. "I still haven't heard. Dean Shepard wants to see you in her office. Maybe she has news."

Nadia sprinted to Hopi Hall. Jack, already seated in the dean's office, nodded hello as she arrived.

"Please sit," Dean Shepard said. "Thank you for coming. I have troubling news. Normally, this information would be reserved for Libby's team leader, but in light of Nadia's recent experience on her survival course, I thought it prudent to include you both in this conversation. We've discovered that Damon is responsible for the attempted assassination of Senator Bishop."

It felt like a kick in the stomach. If Nadia had spoken up about the call sooner. . . . How could he have done this to Libby? "How certain are you that it was Damon?"

"Extremely. After we received your intel about the phone call and realized that Damon was still alive, we checked flight records and local traffic cams around the senator's venue. Under an alias, Damon booked a flight to Baton Rouge a week before the debate. Traffic cameras spotted him a few blocks away, mere hours before the senator arrived on scene."

"Why would Damon shoot Senator Bishop?" Jack asked.

"We believe Damon tried to eliminate the senator as a way to get back in with the Nighthawks."

Nadia chewed her lip. So that was his new plan to get his mother back.

"That makes sense," Jack said. "After the way Senator Bishop attacked the Nighthawks in his announcement speech."

"As a result, Damon Moore has been placed on the CIA's kill list."

"Wait—what's that?" Nadia asked.

"A list of approximately seventy people that its agents are allowed to kill on sight with absolutely no repercussions," Jack said quietly.

Shepard nodded. "That is correct."

"I thought the CIA didn't perform assassinations?" Nadia asked.

"We don't. Shoot-to-kill orders are not considered assassinations by our government," Shepard said.

"That seems a very gray line." Nadia sighed heavily. "Any word on Senator Bishop? Or Libby? Do you know when she'll be back?"

Shepard shook her head. "I don't know about Libby. Senator Bishop is in critical condition. He was immediately taken in for surgery after the shooting, but his doctors are tight-lipped. I'll let you know as soon as I hear anything."

"I'm so sorry." Nadia dropped her gaze, studied her clasped hands resting in her lap. "If I'd come to you sooner, this might not have happened."

Dean Shepard offered no reassuring words. "I've shared this information with you in the strictest confidence. You are not to discuss any of this once you leave my office. Are we clear?"

"Yes ma'am," Jack said.

"Yes ma'am," Nadia echoed.

"You are dismissed."

She walked quickly through the sitting room to avoid a conversation with Jack. She felt awful about screwing up and didn't want to face him.

"Hey," he called after her. "Wait up."

Why had Damon warned her in advance? Why had he given her a heads-up? If she'd reported the call like she should've, additional security would've been dispatched to the senator's venue.

Jack jogged to catch up. "This isn't your fault. You aren't responsible because Secret Service dropped the ball. Seriously. They should always assume a clear and present danger—that's their job."

Nadia frowned as they crossed through the foyer. "I don't need you to coddle me. I know I screwed up."

"Should you have reported the call? Absolutely. Is it your fault the senator was shot? Of course not. He declared war on the Nighthawks on national television."

She sighed. "Listen, I appreciate the gesture, but we both know I messed up." As she stepped outside, the brilliant sunlight pierced her eyes.

That evening, Nadia remained in the library long after her brain stopped working. The thought of her empty room depressed her. Finally, when she could no longer stay awake, she headed across the dark lawn.

Outside Nadia's dorm, Simon accosted her. "You scared me," she said, pressing a hand against her chest. "That's a good way to get stabbed."

"Steady on," he said. "I know perfectly well you haven't got a knife."

"What do you want?"

"I need to know what the dean told you."

"Why do you care?" she asked.

"I'm interested in what happens to Libby."

Nadia narrowed her eyes. "Why? What's with your sudden interest in my roommate?"

"Of course I'm interested. I'm not heartless, and I resent the implication. Now tell me what Shepard said."

"I can't. She swore me to secrecy."

"I'll tell you what: if you tell me her secret, I will keep yours."

"If you're referring to the phone call, I already reported it," Nadia said. "Beyond that, I have no secrets."

"Really? No secrets at all? You weren't in your room last night during the debate." Simon spun her around so she faced the library. "Shall I ask Dean Shepard about the after-hours policy?"

"You're blackmailing me?"

He shook his head. "It doesn't have to be like this. We can have an open, honest exchange of information."

"I'm not allowed to tell you."

Simon rocked back on his heels and crossed his arms. "Then yes, I'm blackmailing you." After a moment, he shrugged and turned away. "Suit yourself, love."

"Wait." She couldn't possibly explain her trip to the library to Dean Shepard. Not yet, anyway. Nadia looked across the lawn, then back into Simon's brilliant blue eyes. "She said it was Damon. Who shot Libby's father."

Simon squinted at her. "But you're skeptical."

She shook her head. "No. I mean, I understand his motive. It's just—I'm surprised, I guess. He's not usually so careless. He was caught on tape a few blocks from the shooting."

"It so happens I'm privy to a bit of information myself. Would you like to trade?"

"What do you want, and what do you know?"

"I know Damon's been framed."

She studied his face intently but saw no signs of deceit. "What makes you say that?"

"Not so fast. I need to know where the student DNA files are kept and how to access them."

Nadia's heart raced. Why did Simon care about the database?

He believed his father was dead. Fear gripped her as she wondered whether he had learned the truth. Did he know they might be siblings? Maybe he'd decided that Jericho *was* his father, and that he'd attended Desert Mountain. Maybe Simon wanted to compare their DNA.

Simon moved closer and whispered, "In exchange, I'll give you the code name of the agent responsible for shooting Bishop. And it's not Damon."

"How would you possibly know that?" she whispered back.

He smiled. "It's what I do."

Nadia looked back across the darkened lawn, considering. She'd destroyed the student database. Simon wouldn't find anything. She had nothing to lose in this exchange. "Okay. Tell me what you know."

"Come closer," he said. Nadia leaned in and Simon moved her hair away from her ear. With his other hand, he shielded his mouth.

"Enough with the theatrics," she said. "Give me a name. Who shot the senator?"

His lips brushed against her skin as he breathed the word. "Jericho."

A rushing sound filled Nadia's head. Words pushed through the white noise; Simon was still talking. Afraid she might pass out, she pressed a cool hand to her forehead and then leaned forward onto her knees.

"I'll tell you another thing," he said. "If Bishop's not actually dead, Jericho's in a world of trouble."

"What do you mean?" She forced herself to straighten.

"An assassin who fails to eliminate his target? Are you mad?" He gave her a questioning look and then shook his head. "It's your turn, love."

How did Simon have access to a presumably classified mission? More importantly, was it true?

"Where's the student database?" he asked.

Had her father shot Libby's dad? But in the wedding photos, they'd looked like best friends.

"Oi," Simon said, elbowing her in the ribs. "Database."

"Uh, it's in the weapons room. In the dojo. At the back of the shooting range."

Simon whipped a small notepad and pencil from the side pocket of his messenger bag. "How do I get in?"

Was her father an assassin? Was he a traitor? Maybe Senator Bishop was the traitor. Had the CIA made another exception to their rule and placed Libby's father on their kill list?

Simon snapped his fingers in Nadia's face. Instinctively, she snatched his hand, twisting it into a wrist lock. He hit his knees and cried out. "What the bloody hell is wrong with you?"

"Oh, Simon—I'm sorry, I wasn't thinking." Nadia helped him up. "Um, you can't get into the weapons room without Sensei's thumbprint and password, but it doesn't matter anyway, because I destroyed the database."

"You destroyed the entire student database?" he asked slowly.

"Yeah."

"And you didn't think to mention that before we struck our deal?"

"You didn't ask." Nadia turned away before he responded, pushing through the lobby doors of her dorm. She didn't trust herself to spend another second with him—not right now. Her face might reveal her fear.

"Nadia," Casey called from her desk. She replaced the telephone on the receiver and said, "Good news—Senator Bishop is out of surgery. It's still touch-and-go, but his operations went well."

Relief flooded her body. "How's Libby?"

"Still at the safe house. If I hear anything else, I'll knock on your door. Try to get some rest. It's been a rough couple days."

"Thanks for letting me know," Nadia said, as she headed down the hall.

Inside her bedroom, anxiety quickly nudged out the relief. If her father had been tasked to kill Bishop, was his life now in danger?

No, her dad hadn't shot Bishop. It was Damon. Simon had made a mistake. Damon had no other reason to be in Louisiana. And her dad wasn't a killer.

Isn't he?

Assuming the library files were authentic, Nadia didn't know the first thing about either one of her parents. He might not even be her biological father—not that it necessarily mattered, except that he'd lied about it. Maybe he'd manipulated her mom, as well.

She shook her head. There was no way the man who raised her was an assassin. But Damon, he would do anything to save his mother.

On the other hand.... Nadia sat on her bed. The CIA wouldn't have realized Damon was the shooter if Nadia hadn't reported his cryptic phone call. That's what prompted them to search for him in Baton Rouge. Again she wondered, why would he have told her his plans in advance?

He wouldn't. Damon would never show his hand.

What if the CIA sanctioned a hit on a presidential candidate, then framed an at-large, known traitor? They'd come out clean, and they'd have a valid reason to kill Damon.

Someone else had placed that phone call. Someone who expected her to report the message to the authorities immediately. Someone who thought she could be used, she could be played, just like a pawn.

Someone like Jericho.

53 LIBBY
WEDNESDAY, FEBRUARY 22

Libby woke, disoriented and unsure of her surroundings. The windows were dark, and the bed wasn't familiar. Then she remembered lying down for a quick rest around four in the afternoon. She sat up, pushed the heavy blankets aside, and checked the clock on the nightstand: it was almost ten o'clock.

Her daddy had been shot. That's why she was here, in a snow-dusted cabin near Sedona, Arizona. Her momma'd flown out to be with her. Secret Service wouldn't let them go to the hospital where her daddy was being treated. They wouldn't say why; security issue, probably.

She crawled from the bed and stepped into the hall, following the voices toward the living room.

"Mrs. Bishop, please," the doctor was saying. "It's perfectly safe."

"I'm not gonna tell you again," her momma answered.

Libby stepped around the corner. "What's going on?"

Her momma looked small, wrapped in a fluffy bathrobe in the dimly lit room, curled up in a chair by the fire. Libby automatically checked for a glass on the chair-side table to see what she'd been drinking. Sparkling water.

"Dr. Patterson is insisting I take something to help me sleep." She turned to the doctor. "That is an option no longer available to me."

"Administered under my care in limited doses, there really is no risk—"

"Thank you, Dr. Patterson," Libby interrupted. "I believe my momma has expressed her wishes. That'll be all." Her heart pounded. She'd never spoken so forcefully to an adult—certainly not a physician. She crossed the floor to stand at her mother's side.

He gathered his supplies, tucking the pills into a small bag. "I'll be in my room if you change your mind."

As he left, her momma reached up and squeezed Libby's hand resting on her shoulder. "Thank you."

"I'm really proud of you," Libby said. She sat in the over-stuffed chair opposite her mother. "Any word from the hospital?"

Her momma shook her head.

"He'll be okay," Libby said, even though she didn't know. "He's too stubborn to die."

Her mother laughed—a quick burst of air that sounded like a bark. "That's true. He'll pull through. He'll somehow spin this into votes and end up winning the election."

Libby frowned. "He promised me he was gonna wait."

Her momma reached forward and swatted her arm. "Don't make that face. You'll get wrinkles." Libby rearranged her features and her mother leaned back. "Your daddy has always been a man who does what he wants. He's used to getting his own way."

Libby glanced at her momma, but saw no bitterness on her face. "Why do you put up with it?"

"Honey, one day I will likely be the First Lady of the United States of America. His ambition is an evil I can live with."

She waited a long moment. "I'm sorry about what he did." She stared at the fire but felt her momma watching her.

"You're gonna have to be a whole lot more specific than that."

"The affair." Libby looked over. She could tell that her momma was about to shoo it away, tell her another pretty lie, but at the last second, her face fell and she nodded.

"Your daddy's a good man. I'm sorry you had to find out. I hope you don't hold it against him."

Libby chewed on her lip, worked up her courage. She was raised not to talk about unpleasantries. "When did it happen?"

Her momma waved the question away. "Forever ago. When I was pregnant with you."

"When you were pregnant?" Libby's stomach churned.

"It was a stressful time," her momma said. "We were new to Washington. He'd just been selected to serve on an elite intelligence committee." She smiled. "He thought he was James Bond, finally privy to top-secret information inside the Beltway. His first assignment required him to spend the summer in London. I didn't go with him. We were young. We thought we were immune to infidelity, that the separation wouldn't take its toll. The other wives warned me, encouraged me to go along, but your brother was just a toddler and I was so tired that first trimester."

"Why'd you stay with him?"

Her momma looked squarely at Libby. "Because, honey. I love him. And he loves me."

She studied her momma's unlined face, her perfect hair. Even here under all this stress she was the picture of grace. After a minute Libby said, "It's his fault you became an alcoholic."

"No, it's not." She laughed a little as she added, "Much as I'd love to blame him. Remember Nana and her mint juleps every afternoon? Probably something I was born with." She leaned forward and patted Libby's knee. "You too, by the way. You need to be careful. Runs in families."

"Who was she?" Libby asked. "The woman."

"Does it matter?"

"I don't guess so." The popping of the logs in the fireplace filled the long silence.

"She was an intelligence officer," her momma said. "She worked for MI-6. A few of our people were in danger, and she jumped right in to help. That's all I know."

"How'd you find out?"

Her momma smiled a little. "He told me. The guilt ate away at him. He begged my forgiveness and I gave it. Took me a while, but I did. Far as I know, he's been faithful ever since."

Libby turned back to the fire. Her eyes stung as she watched the blue and orange flames dance over the wood. She rubbed her face.

Something her momma had said tugged for her attention. Then it hit her. "Wait a minute. Did you say MI-6?"

54 NADIA
THURSDAY, MARCH 2

For the next week, Nadia reviewed every minute of her life in obsessive detail, replayed every interaction with her parents, analyzed every casual exchange. She studied her reflection in the mirror, desperately searching for her father's features.

If she hadn't destroyed the student DNA database, she could've learned the truth once and for all. Compared James Riley's DNA with her own—and with Simon's.

How much did her mother know? How complicit was she in the deceit? Did she know the true nature of the Academy? No, she couldn't possibly.

Out of anger, Nadia considered calling her parents. Telling them, "I know everything." Then she'd hang up before they could mollify her. But of course, she couldn't; the lines were tapped. Until she knew more about her family....It was possible she wasn't even an American citizen. She contemplated the consequences if she were found out.

Late Friday afternoon, after eight solid days of complete radio silence regarding all things Libby, Nadia forced her thoughts away from her family, Simon, and her roommate. Instead, to prepare for her mission, she reviewed the op-specs Jack had given her over a month ago.

Her task involved planting physical evidence on a rogue

employee who'd sold secrets to an enemy nation. Now that she'd accepted Jack's senior project as fiction, she had to admit that the fabricated backstory added a touch of excitement.

After committing the floor plans to memory, she filled her bathroom sink and dropped the papers in the standing water, still troubled that she'd seen patterns where none existed. If she couldn't trust her gut, she wouldn't make a very successful spy.

And an unsuccessful spy was a dead spy.

A few minutes later, her op-specs thoroughly dissolved, she drained the sink and headed toward the parking lot to meet Jack.

As they drove toward the Scottsdale Ritz-Carlton, Nadia wanted to apologize, to explain to Jack that she didn't understand why she was so angry, but her pride wouldn't let her. Finally, when she could no longer stand the silence, she turned toward him and asked, as casually as possible, "Do you think Shepard was telling the truth about the CIA not sanctioning executions?"

He frowned, as though considering. "You mean like does the CIA assassinate people?"

"Yeah, exactly. Wetworks."

"I don't think so." He shook his head. "I believe they used to, but now that everything is hackable and surveillance is everywhere, I don't think our government could get away with it even if they wanted to. Why do you ask?"

Nadia looked at her hands and shrugged. *Because my dad is CIA, and everywhere we've lived there's been a suspicious, high-profile death. And I obviously don't know the first thing about him.* "Just curious."

"I know there's a task squad in place to *prevent* assassinations."

She turned to Jack. "What do you mean?"

"We learned about them last semester. They're called scouts. If the CIA receives intel that a hit's been ordered, they send a man to do recon. After his report is filed, another team moves in to protect the target. It's a tough job with a low success rate. As a group, assassins are pretty tenacious."

A flicker of hope sparked in her chest. Maybe her dad was

a scout. If he'd filed his reports but the CIA hadn't moved fast enough, that would explain the trail of bodies.

That made more sense. No way was the man calling himself her father a field-rated officer. He didn't know how to fight. He didn't even own a gun.

"You sure you're up for this?" Jack asked, pulling into the parking lot of the resort.

"Don't worry, I won't let you flunk." She applied a fresh coat of lip gloss.

"That's not what I meant," Jack said.

Nadia flipped up the visor. "I'm fine. You?"

"Just trying to keep my head in the game." He surveyed the crowded parking lot. "Here are your comms. Remember to only use code names. Never break protocol. Treat this as an actual mission. I have to file a detailed report, and I want it to be absolutely professional."

She inserted the device into her ear. "So I shouldn't hum the *Mission Impossible* theme song as I'm working?"

Jack smiled tightly. "Right. You've got this. Sorry, I just need everything to go smoothly. My final operational report is due tomorrow."

"Cutting it a little close, aren't you?"

"The dates and times were predetermined," he said.

"Stop worrying. It'll be fine. See you in a few." She climbed out of the car and slammed the door.

RIGHT NOW

55 NADIA
THURSDAY, MARCH 2

Minutes from committing her third felony of the semester, Nadia enters the lobby of the Scottsdale Ritz-Carlton, a half hour ahead of schedule. Immediately she turns right, following the predetermined route down the marbled hall. She lowers her chin as she passes reception to avoid the sightline of the cameras mounted above the desk.

At the bank of elevators, she waits for a vacant car. As she's reaching for the button to the seventh floor, an elderly man in a dark suit catches the door. Nadia stalls as he makes his selection.

He presses eleven, then turns to her. "And for you, miss?"

"Twelve, please," she says.

Thirty seconds later on the twelfth floor, Nadia steps onto the midnight-blue carpet and moves silently toward the exit sign. Glancing over her shoulder, she enters the stairwell. She jogs down five flights to the seventh floor.

Before leaving the stairwell, she leans against the wall to catch her breath. Her stomach feels like a snarled fishing line, though her nerves have nothing to do with the mission.

The real issue: her father might be an assassin. Her entire life is a lie.

She sighs and pulls open the heavy door leading to the hall. Around the corner, she finds room 760. Nadia slides her keycard into the lock. The lock flashes red and beeps twice. She tries again—still no luck. The third time she slows, carefully inserting the card. A single beep chimes as the light on the lock flashes green. She cracks the door.

"Housekeeping," she softly calls. No answer, so she slips through.

Inside the room, a thick white duvet covers the king-size bed. A chocolate rests on each pillow. A small toiletries kit sits on the dresser, a metal briefcase on the bed, a half-empty suitcase opened on the valet stand.

Clever details. Whoever staged the mission did a nice job lending authenticity with the personal items.

She touches her ear, bringing her comms to life. "Boy Scout, this is Wolverine. I'm in."

Jack's voice resonates in her ear. "Copy, Wolverine. Proceed."

The light switch by the dresser activates the floor lamp. Nadia retrieves the memory card from her purse. Her op-specs instructed that she hide the tiny device in the target's possessions, preferably somewhere he'll never look.

She moves to the suitcase on the valet. The luggage tag reads OLIVER WESTLAKE. Running her fingers along the fabric lining, she finds the perfect spot—between the plastic back and the metal support bar. She unzips the silk, wedges the storage card into place, and reseals the zipper.

After a visual sweep of the surfaces to confirm she's left nothing behind, Nadia checks the peephole to see if the hall is clear. A man with a shaved head walks toward her room from the direction of the elevators.

Nadia steps away from the door and taps her comms. "Boy Scout, traffic in the hall. I'll be down in ten."

"Copy that. See you soon."

A few seconds later she leans against the door to have another look. The peephole's gone dark—something obstructs her view. It takes her a moment to realize someone's at the door.

A keycard slides into the lock. Her heart flies to her throat as the door beeps twice—red light.

Bathroom, shower, under the bed. The options race through her mind. *Closet.*

The plastic card slides into the lock again, then a single beep. The doorknob turns. He's coming in.

Nadia slips inside the closet and pulls the slatted doors closed just as he enters the bedroom. She holds her breath as his shadow crosses the door, then curses herself for not throwing the deadbolt.

A *thunk* as he moves the briefcase from the bed onto the dresser.

Her eyes widen as she strains to hear over the pounding of her heart. She runs through possible scenarios: she's in this man's room; he came home earlier than expected. But it's a mock mission—she assumed the school booked a room just for this exercise, that the suitcase and toiletries kit were props. Why would they have her break into a civilian's room and plant something in his luggage?

The ironing board hanging in the closet presses painfully against her back. As she shifts her weight, the board brushes the wall. She freezes.

The scent of his cologne hits her a second before his shadow darkens the door. His hand reaches for the knob. He opens the closet.

His face registers surprise, then...what? Recognition?

Six feet, shaved head, broad shoulders, slightly crooked nose. Light eyes—blue, maybe. Black t-shirt, jeans, sneakers. Late twenties, muscular, handsome.

Totally normal.

Except for the gun pointing at her heart.

56 DAMON
THURSDAY, MARCH 2

Damon waits until 1500 hours—the shift change—before entering the ground floor of the Ritz-Carlton through the employee's entrance. He follows the crew toward the locker rooms, then veers left and through the door marked LAUNDRY. He grabs a bellman's uniform from the rack and slips into the restroom to change.

A few minutes later, dressed in his freshly pressed uniform and cap, Damon turns his attention to the maids.

He starts looking on the second floor. Hallway after hallway, then up the flight of stairs to the next floor. Finally, on five, he finds a housekeeper's cart. Damon snatches the clipboard from the cart and goes inside the room.

"Hello?" he calls. The housekeeper comes out from the bathroom with an armload of towels. "I'm sorry to bother you, but today's my first day. Can you help me?" He moves back so she can access the doorway. Less threatening, which will make him less memorable.

"What do you need?" She steps into the hall and deposits the dirty towels into the canvas bag attached to her cart.

He holds up the clipboard and moves to her side. "This guest, can you tell me if they're checking out today?" As she reviews the papers, he cuts the plastic coil securing her master key to her apron and palms the keycard.

"Is this mine?" she asks, indicating the clipboard. He nods.

"You don't need this. Just go down to the lobby and ask the head bellman where you should be."

"Oh, okay." Damon keeps his eyes on the clipboard, scanning the guest registry until he finds the name listed on McGill's computer: *Oliver Westlake, room 760.* "Thanks for your help. The system here is a little different from the last place I worked."

"Good luck," she says, taking a stack of fresh towels into the room.

Back in the stairwell, Damon takes the steps two at a time. He stops on the sixth floor; he'll make it look like he's working his way up. He knocks on the door closest to the stairwell and, when no one answers, uses his newly acquired master key to let himself in. A quick search of the drawers nets fifty-seven dollars and a pair of gold earrings. The safe is locked, and he doesn't bother cracking it. He checks the peephole before moving on to the next room.

All told, Damon hits eight rooms on the sixth floor. Including his take from the Plaza earlier this morning, he's scored about seven hundred in cash, a few pieces of jewelry, and a gold watch. He doesn't take the credit cards or passports. He checks the time, then heads back to the stairwell to get to the seventh floor. According to McGill's calendar, he's right on schedule. And after striking out in Baton Rouge, saving Nadia is, once again, his top priority.

Damon surveys the hallway, making sure he's alone. He takes the 9mm from his shoulder holster and tightens the silencer on the muzzle. Out of habit, he drops the magazine, checks that it's full, reinserts, and racks the slide. He slips the master key into the lock as quietly as possible and pushes open the door.

Nadia lies face down on the navy carpet, fingers interlaced behind her head.

She arrived early.

A shadow moves around the corner by the bed. The dim lamplight catches the glint of gunmetal.

Damon fires two shots before he's taken a full step into the room. Both bullets land near the man's heart. A fraction of a second later, the assassin hits the floor. Damon quickly crosses the room and kicks the gun from the man's hand. The hitman gurgles as his lungs fight for air. He looks at Damon, utter surprise on his face.

Behind him, Nadia stirs. "Stay down," he says gruffly, attempting to alter his voice.

The gunman struggles, gasping for life. Damon points his weapon at the man's shaved head and fires again. The wheezing stops. Damon searches the hitman's pockets until he finds what he needs: the photograph of Nadia that McGill provided. Blood smears the edges.

In the now-empty pocket, Damon places a wad of cash and a few pieces of the stolen jewelry. He moves toward Nadia, stops just behind her. He's about to yank her up, drag her out the door, when he notices the tiny comms device tucked into her ear. *Dammit.*

Jack.

Has she bugged the room? Is anyone else listening? The comms in her ear might be on a live-feed. Jack might've heard everything. Damon shakes his head—he doubts it, she probably turns them on as needed. But if she doesn't check in, Jack will come looking for her. Damon briefly considers destroying the comms, but that'll result in a stream of static, which will certainly attract Jack's attention. He might assume the equipment malfunctioned, nothing more, but that's a gamble Damon can't afford.

Make a decision. Damon plucks the device from her ear. He presses his foot against her shoulder. Using the same altered tone as before, he says, "Count to one hundred."

She starts counting and Damon leaves the room. He drops her comms by the door.

He sprints down four flights of stairs before she bursts into the stairwell and yells after him. He pushes himself harder to reach ground level, silently willing her to follow. If she doesn't, Damon will miss his last chance to save his mother.

He hits the landing and pushes open the side door to the parking lot. Damon tosses the remaining jewelry and the watch inside the dumpster by the door, then shoots back inside, tucking himself beneath the stairs.

Then he waits.

57 NADIA
THURSDAY, MARCH 2

For a few seconds it seems like part of the drill, part of the mock mission. Plans go sideways all the time. She needs to train for situations like this. But then she remembers this is Jack's mission, not hers, and comms are off, and unless he saw this guy enter the room—which she knows he hasn't, because he's parked at the far end of the lot—something has gone terribly wrong.

Blood roars through her ears—she barely hears the man say, "Face down on the floor, hands behind your head."

Nadia kneels on the carpet. Even if he didn't have a gun pointed at her, he isn't close enough to strike. She lowers herself onto her stomach and laces her fingers behind her head. Her heart pounds against her ribs like a hummingbird. She puts her head to the ground.

This has to be about her father. His lies have gotten her killed.

Metal scrapes metal as he racks the slide on his gun.

A soft beep filters through the noise in her head—is that the door? Then two muffled chirps—shots from a silenced gun. She holds her breath and waits for the searing pain.

It never comes.

A thud as a body hits the ground.

Nadia lifts her head an inch off the carpet.

The man with the gun lies crumpled on the floor. The wet

wheezing of his breath churns her stomach. A second man stands in front of him: bellman's pants, black leather loafers. Before she raises her head further, the second man says, "Stay down."

Her eyelids close against the soft light of the room. The cloying floral smell of the carpet cleaner overpowers the odor of burnt smoke from the fired gun. She wonders if Jack will fail his mission, or if she'll see him again.

This shouldn't have happened. He should've had her back.

Seconds, minutes, hours later, a weight presses into her shoulders. Then the second man speaks again. His voice has changed, softened. "Count to one hundred."

It sounds like an old friend, like something from a dream.

"One, two, three," she begins. The bedroom door closes. The voice, its gentleness, reminds her of something, but the memory is elusive and the room is closing in and the dead body lies a few feet away and she can't breathe.

She focuses on the numbers.

When Nadia reaches ten, she looks up at her lifeless companion. Dark liquid seeps into the carpet, spreading from his body like spilled ink. Still counting, she pulls herself up and crawls toward him. His open eyes are fixed on the ceiling, unmoving. His head is turned away from her; he has a bullet hole behind his ear.

Somewhere in the corner of her thoughts, she realizes she should be more upset. The body, though...it looks fake. Like in the movies. Again she considers that this is part of the drill.

But two tentative fingers on his neck confirm death.

This guy had been ready to kill her. He'd pointed his gun, ordered her down, and racked his slide.

Then the bellman saved her life.

Nadia stops counting and pushes herself off the floor. If the bellman wanted her dead, she'd be dead. Without checking the peephole, she throws open the door—elevators to the left, stairs around the corner to the right.

She turns right and sprints down the hall, reaching the corner just as the stairwell door closes. Nadia follows the bellman down the stairs; he hugs tight to the inside, his gloved hand gripping the railing. Something about him seems familiar. His concise, deliberate movements, the smooth speed he uses to navigate the stairs. *No.* It can't be.

"Hey!" she yells.

He gains speed, increasing the distance between them. When she reaches the third floor landing, a flash of light from the streetlamp outside floods the stairwell as he pushes through the exterior door and out into the night.

Taking the steps two at a time, Nadia forces herself to move faster.

As she hits ground level at full velocity, someone tackles her from behind. She's thrown to the ground under the weight of her assailant. Nadia fights against his force before she registers what's happened.

"Stop it," Damon says. "I'm not here to hurt you."

"Said the spider to the fly." She struggles against him, tries to free an elbow, a knee, anything to land a blow. He wraps his legs around hers, pins her arms against her torso. Even at maximum exertion, she can't move an inch. She feels Damon relax slightly, just enough so she's not crushed.

"When you settle, I'll let go," he says.

"You just killed someone!" She keeps fighting, more out of spite than any thought she can overpower him. Her muscles fatigue rapidly. After a few minutes she sighs, and then relaxes her body.

"That's better," he says.

"I see you're still alive."

"Nothing gets past you."

"Get off me," she demands.

He slowly releases his grip, and she scrambles to her feet. He rolls onto his knees. "And you're welcome for saving your life, by the way."

She opens her mouth to argue but stops herself. Reluctantly, she says, "Thank you." Then, after a beat, "Was that about my father? Did you know about my family? Why didn't you tell me?"

"Why didn't I tell you? Because I care about you. I *never* wanted you to see that. I was hoping to spare you." He sighs. "And no, that had nothing to do with your family."

"Then who—"

"Here." Damon pulls a stack of pictures from his jacket pocket. He hands her the one on top, a couple sitting in the window at a restaurant. It's taken from outside, like a surveillance photo. Ms. McGill and the dead man upstairs. Nadia glances at Damon.

"She ordered a hit on you. I followed her and she met with this guy." He gestures to the picture. "She paid him for the contract on your life. I watched her do it. See?" Damon passes her the remaining pictures.

She flips through three more of McGill and the hitman. But the last is a close-up of Nadia, the picture taken on her first day at school—the day she met Dean Wolfe and learned the truth about the Academy. McGill must've found it in Nadia's recruit file. The edges are smeared with blood.

Damon continues. "McGill gave that one to the assassin. I just took it off his body. That's his blood."

Nadia drops the stack and wipes her hands on her hips. "I don't understand. Why would McGill want to kill me? And how did you know about it?" Is this another one of his manipulations?

"Dean Wolfe," he says, as though that clarifies everything.

"What about him?"

"Look." Damon flips through the stack. "Here—it's stuck." He peels two pictures apart and holds one up. Wolfe and McGill on the deck of a cruise ship, arms around each other. "I went to the hospital in Tucson to try and wake him. I thought he might know where my mom's being held. Let's just say it didn't go as well as I'd hoped. McGill came to sit vigil as he died. I could tell they were together, so I followed her, figuring if she was anything like me, you'd be in big trouble."

"Why would I be in trouble?"

He makes a face like it's obvious. "Because you're the one who put him in a coma."

"Wait—so you also killed Wolfe?"

"What is this, confession? Are you my priest? I followed her, she met with this guy, so I followed him."

"Ms. McGill didn't OD, did she?"

His gaze doesn't waver. "She refused to call off the hit. So it was you or her. That's easy math."

Nadia rubs her forehead. Damon killed McGill to save her life?

"I didn't mean to kill Wolfe," he says. "It was an accident."

"I'll be sure and mention that at your parole hearing."

Damon smiles for a half second, then his expression turns serious again. "I came here to save your life. I knew about the hit, and I stopped it. But I also came to ask for your help."

"You shot Libby's dad," Nadia says, not believing it, but so hoping it's true. "Wasn't that enough to get your mother back?"

"Please. If I had taken that shot, Bishop would be dead. I was framed."

She looks away for a second. *I was right—we were both set up.*

Her face must've revealed something, because his eyes narrow. As he studies her, he says, "You know who framed me, don't you?"

"Of course not, but I do enjoy the irony of someone framing *you.*"

"Who was it? Was it Roberts? How did you find out?"

"What were you doing in Baton Rouge?"

After a beat he says, "I got a phone call. An anonymous tip about my mom. Obviously, it turned out to be bogus."

The phone call, an anonymously delivered message, same as hers. She lets out a tiny laugh and shakes her head. They both got played.

"You think this is funny?"

She shrugs. "I don't know what to think."

He stands and straightens his bellman's vest. "Please help me get my mom back. You're all I have."

"I hate to tell you, but you don't have me." Nadia glances toward the exit. Jack will be wondering what's taking so long.

If he comes looking for her...well, she doesn't know how Damon will react. She turns her eyes to Damon and takes a step toward the stairs. "Good luck, man."

"Nadia, I am begging you." His voice catches in his throat.

"You lied to me and manipulated me. The whole time I was with you, you were planning to trade me for your mom. You never intended to let me go."

His voice is low. "That's what Roberts thinks. But you and I know better. We'll get my mom, and the three of us will walk out of there together."

She shakes her head. "I can't help you."

He pulls a photo out of his back pocket and holds it out. The picture of his mother, tear-stained and scared. "Then help her," he whispers.

The photograph breaks her heart—that's his *mother*. Unable to bear the image any longer, she looks away.

Damon moves closer. "Think about it. Roberts won't stop until he gets what he wants. And if he can't get to you, who do you think he's gonna go after next? I guarantee it'll be *your* mom."

Her heart lurches. What if Roberts sends an agent after her mom? Her mother would have no idea how to defend herself.

Damon continues. "And the guy he sends for her probably won't be as careful as I've been with you." He reaches into his pocket and pulls out a small, orange, plastic cylinder. "Take it."

She doesn't extend her arm. "What is it?" He tosses it at her feet; a locker key.

"If you want this to end, you need to help me put him down." Damon nods toward the key. "Meet me there. Tonight." He backs away. "I left Jack's comms upstairs outside your room." Damon pushes through the door into the parking lot.

He can't really believe I'm going to help him, can he? Nadia starts up the stairs, taking them two at a time. Halfway to the first floor landing, she stops. What about his mom? What about *her* mom?

Nadia jogs back downstairs. She snatches the key off the floor before heading up to get her comms.

58 JACK
THURSDAY, MARCH 2

Jack sits in the car chewing his lower lip, leg pumping up and down. He has a nagging feeling he's forgotten something, some mission-critical detail. Every fifteen seconds he checks his watch. What's taking her so long?

He clicks on the comms. "Wolverine, what's your sit-rep?" No answer. His leg pumps faster.

Truth is, he's been distracted since Nadia returned from her survival course. He desperately wants to be there for her, to ask questions, to find out exactly what happened while she was away, but he's afraid of the answers. Last semester he suspected that Damon had a thing for her. What if she has feelings for him? Worse yet—what if Damon mistreated her and then Jack asks a stupid question like, "Are you in love with the guy who just traumatized you?"

He hates that he can't tell her how much he misses her. He hates that he can't hold her. But the rules are the rules for a reason.

A flurry of activity catches his eye during the shift change. Kitchen workers, waitstaff, and bellmen cross the back parking lot to their cars.

What is it—what did he forget? He checked the route, the room, the reservation. The time, the date, the details of the mission. He confirmed that Nadia's comms were operational.

A minute later he tries again. "Wolverine, what's your sit-rep?" Still nothing.

That's when he remembers what he forgot: he didn't check the staff rosters for new and temporary hires. It's standard procedure, like the second thing he should've marked off his list. How did he miss something so basic, so mundane? If this were a real mission, that error might've cost Nadia her life.

Jack shakes his head. *This is what happens when you're emotionally attached to your agents.* Shepard was right to condemn their relationship. Into the comms, "Wolverine, do you copy?"

Finally, Nadia's voice crackles in his ear. "Boy Scout, assistance needed ASAP. Meet me on-site."

"Wolverine, request that you follow protocol and meet me at the extraction point. Over."

"Negative, Boy Scout. Northern stairwell. *Now.*"

Jack curses as he rips the listening device from his ear. Why is she changing protocol? This is *his* mission. He throws the car in drive and tears across the lot, pulling into a parking space close to the stairwell. Jack slams the car door and strides toward the entrance, hoping that someone has left it ajar so he won't have to go around the building to the front. He reaches for the handle as Nadia opens the door.

"What is going on?" he demands.

"We have a situation." She reaches for his hand.

Jack withdraws his hand and glances around. The floodlight mounted over the entrance to the stairs shines on them like a spotlight. "Please try to be professional," he says quietly. "This is a *huge* part of my graduation requirement, and I have no idea if we're under surveillance."

She steps back and glares at him. "Yeah, after what just happened, I'm fairly certain we're not." Turning away, she stomps up the stairs.

"What do you mean? What happened?"

She refuses to answer.

He rolls his eyes and follows her up the first flight. "You're pissed because I won't hold your hand in the middle of a mission?"

"Oh my God," she says over her shoulder, her voice tense. "I had no intention of holding your hand. That's not why I'm upset."

"Then why are you upset?"

Six flights later they reach her floor. She leads him to 760 and keys open the door. Jack waits for her to enter, but she says, "Oh, you first. I insist."

A few steps in, Jack sees the body.

Nine minutes later Jack completes his wipe-down of the hotel room. After a final visual once-over, he turns to Nadia. She stands in the middle of the floor facing away from the body, arms crossed, chewing on the edge of her thumbnail. Frowning, deep in thought.

"What's up?" Jack asks.

Her eyes dart to his face. "Nothing."

"Wait—were you in the closet?" Jack pulls the door open. A single garment hangs inside: a jacket with the Gentech Labcorp logo.

Nadia gasps lightly and Jack turns around. As he does, her eyes shoot from the jacket to his face. "Gentech?" she asks. "Are you kidding me?"

"Let's not jump to conclusions," he says. Nadia moves away, stepping carefully over the corpse. "What are you doing?"

"I'm getting the data card I planted." She reaches inside the suitcase on the stand by the bed.

"I don't know if you should do that. Technically that means I failed to execute the mission."

Nadia turns to him, eyes narrowed, and says, "There is a dead man in this room. We were never here."

Jack nods once and looks away. She's got a good point. He wipes the interior of the closet, then uses his cloth to open the bedroom door. "Come on. We gotta go."

They jog down the stairwell and across the lot to his car. Before he starts the ignition, Jack leans his head against the steering wheel. After a few seconds, he sits back and looks at her. "I am so angry with you right now."

"Wait—*what*?"

"Why did you chase a man who'd just shot someone?"

"You're angry at me? You convinced me these missions were staged. Why was I sent into a civilian's room? CIA-affiliated or not, that seems like a pretty big risk to my personal safety. And why wasn't that room secured? You're the one who was supposed to be on overwatch."

"I know! That's why—" Jack closes his eyes. He takes a deep breath, then looks at her. "You were almost killed. If anything had happened to you, I would never forgive myself."

She looks away. "Well, nothing happened. So go ahead and let yourself off the hook."

Jack berates himself for the next forty-five minutes as they drive home in silence. Back at school, they relay the events to Dean Shepard, and then wait quietly while she makes a few phone calls.

Nadia looks exhausted. She's loosened her hair, and her dark curls spill around her face. Her eyebrows pull together with concern.

What would he have done if she'd been killed? Jack's stomach turns and he shakes his head, trying to lose the thought. The shooter wore a bellman's uniform, which means he was probably on the staff roster. Jack might've been able to prevent all of this—if he hadn't screwed up.

Dean Shepard hangs up the phone and clears her throat. "Well, it's relatively good news. According to my source, both the Plaza and the Ritz-Carlton have suffered a rash of robberies in the past two days. The police believe the dead man in 760 was part of the robbery team, and that he was killed by his partner. Several pieces of stolen jewelry were found on his person. I suspect it was a double-cross. Maybe the dead man tried to take more than his share. The fact that it happened in your room appears to have been an unfortunate coincidence."

Another coincidence. Jack glances at Nadia. She doesn't react to Shepard's words in any way. "How many rooms were hit?"

"Six at the Ritz, thirteen at the Plaza," Shepard says. "Jack, did anyone of concern appear on your preliminary staff check?"

He presses his lips together. For a second he considers lying; it would be so easy.

Lying about who shot him, lying to protect Nadia—that's one thing. Lying to save his own skin is something else entirely. He straightens in his chair. "Dean Shepard, I messed up. I forgot to run the check. It should've been the first thing on my list. I am so sorry, and I totally understand that the oversight will likely affect my final grade." He turns to Nadia. "Most importantly, I'm furious with myself that I put you in harm's way. I don't expect you to forgive me."

For the first time since they sat down, Nadia looks up. As her eyes meet his, Jack feels an ache in his chest.

"This wasn't your fault," she says softly.

"Jack, I appreciate your honesty, but I agree with Nadia," Shepard says. "These missions are meant to be learning experiences. No one expects you to execute a covert operation perfectly while you're in training. You both conducted yourselves professionally and with honor. Nadia, in the future I would prefer that you *not* chase after gunmen without backup, but otherwise, well done. For all intents and purposes, you completed the mission." She turns to Jack. "Are you sure you got out clean?"

He nods, turning his attention back to the dean. "Absolutely. We wiped every surface she may have touched." He doesn't mention that Nadia retrieved her data chip. He'll have to write it up in his final report, but he needs a few hours to decide how the information should be presented.

"Good." Dean Shepard exhales and sits back in her chair. "Let's keep this incident to ourselves. There's no sense alarming the other recruits."

"Will you share your information with the police?" Jack asks. "That hotel staff members are involved?"

"I can't without compromising the Academy. You two would be interviewed, questioned, suspected. My job is to protect you and to safeguard this program. Unfortunately, the police are on their own." She pauses. "It's been a long day. You're both excused."

"Thank you, ma'am," Jack says. He stands and waits for Nadia, then follows her to the sitting room. "Talk about the wrong place at the wrong time, huh?" he asks, as they cross to the hall.

"Mmm," she says.

He steals a sideways glance. It isn't like her to keep her opinions to herself. They reach the front door and he holds it open. "What's on your mind?"

She sighs and looks away, then after a moment locks onto his eyes. "There's something I need to tell you."

59 NADIA
THURSDAY, MARCH 2

Nadia leads Jack down the stone steps outside Hopi Hall. Right or wrong, she hasn't told him about Damon because she knows he'll have to report it, and she hasn't yet decided on her course of action. But something else bothers her more.

At the bottom of the stairs, she turns to him. Quietly, she says, "My op-specs were to plant evidence on the resident of room 760. We both assumed that the data storage card was empty—a prop, right?" He nods and she continues. "What if it wasn't? What if we were sent to frame a guy for a crime he didn't commit?"

"I admit, there are a number of coincidences—"

Nadia shakes her head. "It just doesn't *feel* right. Something else is going on here—something bigger than your senior project." She pauses. "Is it possible you did something illegal? Something that some guy named Oliver Westlake will now take the blame for?"

"Who?"

"The guy in room 760. It doesn't make sense that I would be sent to a civilian's room, and you know it. What if he'd been there? What if we'd gotten into a physical altercation?" After a beat, she continues. "You need to tell me the endgame of your senior project."

"Come here," he says, taking her wrist and pulling her across the parking lot. When they reach the back wall, he glances around to make sure they're alone. "I can't do that. Shepard specifically instructed me—"

"I don't care what she told you. How can you not see that there's a larger issue?"

"You know, everything's so easy for you." Jack shakes his head. "You don't like how the mission's going, so you change up the rules. We don't have the luxury of questioning orders. What if every agent decided for themselves whether or not a mission should be completed? It can't work like that. There's a hierarchy. I'm not given access to all the information. Someone else makes the high-level decisions—someone who knows the whole story, not just the bits and pieces shared with us. I can't break protocol because you have a weird feeling."

Nadia narrows her eyes. "Did you seriously just say that everything's so easy for me?"

"When you join the CIA, you need to decide, yes, I trust the people above me, the ones making the tough decisions. If you can't do that, if you are incapable of following orders, then don't sign up. I hate to remind you, but in this instance, we are not peers. You are not my equal. I'm the team leader. I have the burden of responsibility."

A flash of anger floods her body. She takes a breath, looks away, then back into his eyes. "At what point will you ever stand up and say, *this is unacceptable*?"

"It's not my call," he says through clenched teeth.

"What if she's setting us up? What if Shepard's a Nighthawk? What if your mission is actually real?"

"You sound paranoid. And it's not possible. She didn't even design the senior projects. They were created by active CIA officers."

Oh no.

Nadia's stomach drops. She forces herself to ask the question. "The code name of the agent who designed your mission—what was it?"

"I have no idea. What does it matter?"

She shakes her head and turns away. A chill runs down her spine as the pieces fall into place.

Jericho orchestrated Jack's entire mission—she can't prove it, but she knows it to be true. Jericho is Simon's father. To protect himself, he falsified the DNA results of a deceased agent. In case they got caught, he used his own daughter to frame an innocent Gentech employee.

Jack continues. "And why would the CIA assign an actual mission to a bunch of half-trained recruits? It makes no sense."

"I don't know, maybe it's off-books," she says. "Plausible deniability? So there's no paper trail back to the CIA?"

He looks at her like she's crazy. After a minute, he says, "You've had a very difficult few weeks. I suggest you get some rest. We can talk about this tomorrow."

Nadia turns away. The lights of the dormitories glitter in the darkness. Telling him about Damon definitely isn't an option. Jack doesn't trust her. At the very least, he doesn't trust her soundness of mind. And until she knows exactly how her dad is involved, she can't share any more of her suspicions about his senior project, either. Jack continually chooses procedure over loyalty to her.

She turns back toward him and nods. "You're probably right. I'm just really tired. I'll see you later, okay?"

"You can't tell anyone about this," Jack says. "You know that, right?"

With the strangest sensation of weightlessness, she moves across the lawn, thinking about her father, how he used her. Thinking about Damon and his mom. Worried about her own mother. What if Roberts goes after her?

Inside the lobby of the girls' dorm, Casey's desk sits unoccupied. Nadia sighs; she's dreading another night without Libby. If she could just talk to her, make sure she's okay. Something to assuage the guilt.

Down the hall Nadia unlocks her bedroom door. She rips off her sweater and kicks the shoes from her feet, then pushes the door shut and feels along the wall for the light switch.

Before her fingers make contact, someone grabs her from behind and clamps a hand over her mouth.

60 SIMON
THURSDAY, MARCH 2

Something's rotten in the state of Denmark, and Simon intends to uncover the stinking corpse. He's been lied to—either earlier, about his dad being dead, or more recently, when CIADIS identified a new man as his father. If Simon can't trust the DNA database—if *science* isn't his ally—then he doesn't have a prayer.

That left him one remaining option: check the student database and compare the DNA himself. But Nadia destroyed it, and with it, his only chance to uncover the truth.

As such, she has no one but herself to blame for this current invasion of privacy, which is why Simon feels no guilt as he rifles through her unmentionables.

So far, his search proves fruitless. Inside Libby and Nadia's bathroom, he shines his torch along the baseboards. He checks the shower drain, the wastepaper basket, tosses their drawers for a hairbrush or blow dryer—anything with a scrap of DNA.

He's literally never seen such a pristine bathroom in his entire life.

After fifteen minutes of wasted effort, Simon heads back into the bedroom. He's about to press duct tape along the shoulders of their sweaters when a noise outside catches his attention.

A key slides into the lock. Simon clicks off his torch and ducks behind the door. Nadia walks in, kicks off her shoes. As she's reaching for the light switch, he moves from his position and wraps his hand over her mouth, not to hurt her—only so she won't scream bloody murder.

Before he knows what's happening, Nadia stomps the top of his foot, grabs his elbow, and heaves him over her shoulder. He lands on his back across the tiled floor, sucking for air.

She switches on the overhead and viciously whispers, "What the hell are you doing here?"

Simon gasps and holds up a finger. He rolls to his side. Unable to speak, he mouths, "Help me up." Nadia raises an eyebrow in response. He drags himself off the floor and onto a crisply made bed. "Dear God. I can't breathe. How did Damon get the jump on you?"

Nadia rolls her eyes and goes into the loo, returning with two glasses of water. She hands him one and, without taking her eyes off him, chugs the other. He sips carefully, curious to see whether she's punctured any internal organs.

"What are you doing here?" she asks again.

"DNA," he whispers. His lungs feel rather depleted. "It's your fault I'm here."

"How do you figure?"

"I need to compare DNA. I could've used the database, but you destroyed it, so I'm forced to go old school."

She nods. "I see. You knew Damon was being framed for shooting Bishop because you know he's not Jericho. Because Jericho is the CIA officer who secured your position here."

Simon narrows his eyes. "How did you know that?" *And what else does she know?*

"Jericho is not your father. And I'm not giving you my DNA, so get out."

Why would she even mention Jericho? And why would she think he was looking for information about Jericho in her bedroom? "What a peculiar thing to say." He studies her carefully as she shifts her weight, then transfers the empty water glass from her right hand to left.

"Not really." She turns away to set the glass on her desk. "You said your father got you in here, and then you said you knew Damon was being framed, because the guy who shot Bishop is called Jericho. *Ergo*, that means you know Damon's code name isn't Jericho. The only way you could definitively know that is if Jericho is the code name of the agent who got you here. Simple deductive reasoning. I don't know what any of this has to do with me, and why you're in my bedroom remains a mystery, but I know you're looking for information about Jericho, right?" She crosses her arms. "I am a little confused about one thing: you said you found your father, and that he's deceased. Milo Riazotti, correct? So why are you here, and what are you looking for?" Now she studies him.

"Firstly, there was absolutely nothing 'simple' about your deductive reasoning. Secondly, I was mistaken. My father did not secure my position here, Jericho did. To what end, I don't yet know. But they are not one and the same." It had occurred to Simon that Jericho might be playing him, using him to expose his father, perhaps to ruin his political career. But if that was the case, Jericho was certainly taking his leisurely time. "I believe I've been manipulated."

She looks at her feet. "Really? What makes you say that?"

"Let's just say it's not your DNA I'm interested in."

Nadia's eyes shoot to Libby's dresser, to the framed pictures of her family, then back to Simon. "Seriously?"

"As you know, a few weeks ago my DNA flagged a match in CIADIS."

"Wait—I destroyed the student database. How'd you get a match?"

"I did a takeaway kit with a private lab." He sips his water, works up the nerve to say it out loud, then plunges forward. "The night Bishop was shot, I received another message—an error message indicating a duplicate match. Which means that unless Milo Riazotti was Bishop's identical twin, someone tampered with my results."

"No kidding."

He nods. She doesn't look as surprised as he expected. "I investigated and found a chain of evidence leading to a Gentech Labcorp employee by the name of Oliver Westlake. About an hour ago, someone sent an anonymous tip to the feds and they've issued a search warrant for his place."

Nadia shakes her head. "I knew it."

"Knew what?"

"Jack's senior project. They won't find anything on Oliver Westlake."

"How do you know?"

She pulls a small plastic square from her pocket. "Because I didn't leave the evidence."

"Wait, what?"

"Did you know that CIADIS is stored at Gentech Labcorp?"

"*What?*"

"Your mission was to infiltrate the mainframe. My mission was to frame Oliver Westlake for tampering with the database. Do you see where this is going?"

Simon frowns. *Why would Jack try to conceal my dad's identity?* "I don't—"

A look of understanding crosses Nadia's face. "Of course— *that's* why Jack was given this assignment."

"What are you talking about?"

"This mission—they gave it to Jack instead of an actual CIA team because we all have a motive for keeping quiet. If anything goes wrong, they probably assume we'll lie to protect our parents. Better yet, it could be argued that we were acting independently and for our own gain. I suppose the CIA could deny any involvement whatsoever."

Simon holds up a hand. "Too much, too fast." He takes a breath, hoping she'll do the same. "Now, did you say Jack knows about this cover-up? Did he orchestrate it?"

She shakes her head. "No, he thinks his senior project is entirely fabricated. You think Bishop is your father?"

"I don't know what to think. My mum told me the story of how she met my dad. If he wasn't part of the CIA team, it means everything she told me is a lie. It makes no sense. I don't know when she ever would've met the senator. Do you have any idea what it feels like to discover that every bit of your past is completely false?"

"I have some idea. So you need Libby's DNA to see if Bishop is actually a match."

"Precisely." Simon nods. "If she and I are genetically related, it's settled. And you may or may not be aware that there is not one single blond hair in this entire room. How is that possible?"

"Come on, it's Libby." Nadia hesitates a long moment. Finally, she says, "I might not have her DNA, but I do have a picture of the senator when he was younger. And it was taken in London, so theoretically, he could've met your mom." She moves to the other bed and drops to her knees.

Simon shifts uncomfortably. "Are you praying? Shall I wait in the loo?"

She ignores the question and says, "Coincidentally, I recently learned that everything my parents have ever said to *me* is a lie. And now I want the truth." Thrusting her arm between the mattress and box spring, she extracts a large envelope from the bed. She withdraws several photographs from a folder and hands them over.

Simon takes the pictures, scans the faces, and feels his heart seize. "Where did you get these?" She doesn't answer right away, and he yells, "Where did you get these?"

She scowls and loudly whispers, "Lower your voice. It's from a case file I stole from the library. I found the intel when I was with Damon."

"Nadia." Simon's voice shakes. "Why would Damon have intel about my mum?"

"What? What are you talking about?"

Simon holds up a photograph. His mother, laughing, as a man kisses her cheek. The back reads *James and Maggie, Hyde Park, London.* "Who is this man?"

"That's my father." She hesitates, and then says, "Jericho."

"Jericho is your father?" Simon flips the picture back over. "Nadia—that's my mum!" He taps the photograph.

Nadia eases herself onto the bed opposite him. "Your mom is Maggie Pearle?"

Simon pushes off the bed and paces the small room. "Yes, Maggie Pearle. And Jericho secured my spot here, and Bishop is my father. Your dad shot my dad."

"Okay, stop saying that until we have all the facts."

"Yikes." Simon sits back down. "It seems we all have daddy issues." A few seconds pass before he asks, "May I see the whole file?"

She seems reluctant, but passes him the folder.

He feels her stare as he flips through the documents. She wasn't kidding, her entire life is fabricated.

When he gets to the marriage license, he smiles. His mum's flowery signature is drawn on the bottom of the page. "My mum witnessed your parents' wedding." He finds a picture of his mum holding a baby and raises an eyebrow. "Looks like you witnessed your parents' wedding, as well."

Nadia leans forward, rests her elbows on her knees. After a few moments she says, "I don't think we're here by accident, Simon."

He pulls his eyes away from the file to look at her. "What are you on about?"

Nadia shakes her head. "I don't know exactly, but I think—I feel like we were recruited for a reason. All of us. Like we're playing out someone else's agenda." She glances at the clock on the nightstand and asks, "Do you feel like getting some air?"

"Yes. Only give me a minute. This is a lot to take in."

61 NADIA
THURSDAY, MARCH 2

As Simon reviews the body of lies that is her life, Nadia runs down her list of facts. Her father lied about everything. He conspired to ruin Bishop's career by bringing Simon to the Academy, where Simon would discover his sister, Libby. Bishop launched into damage control and tampered with someone else's DNA profile. Nadia's dad grew impatient and shot him. Apparently, after he was shot, Bishop's DNA was immediately loaded into CIADIS, where Simon got a proper hit.

Her dad knows Libby's father, Alan's grandfather, Agent Roberts, and Simon's mom. And somehow, Damon uncovered the truth and connected the dots.

What about destroying the student database? Did her father mastermind that mission? Was he worried she would discover that he's CIA? Or did Bishop do it, to prevent the link between Simon and Libby? To hide the fact that Simon is his son? Did he hire Damon *and* arrange Jack's senior project? No—Bishop isn't CIA. How would he even know the database exists? On the other hand, he sits on the Intelligence Committee—maybe it's common knowledge.

That still wouldn't explain how Jack got his assignment. It was issued by an active CIA officer. And it would've gone off perfectly if Bishop hadn't been shot and entered into the DNA database. But it *had* to be Bishop, right?

Nadia stands, pulls on her shoes. Her father's callous disregard for her safety—knowingly sending her to a black-ops training facility and blatantly lying to her mother about it—clearly demonstrates that he is unwilling to protect his family. She will not follow suit. She will not abandon her mother, leaving her at the mercy of Roberts' men.

And what about Damon's mom? She's been held captive for months. How does someone recover from that kind of trauma? Damon said Roberts would kill her if Nadia didn't show.

She glances at Simon, still poring over the file, as a familiar anger rises in her chest.

Pawns. Every one of them. One way or another, this ends tonight.

"You ready?" she asks.

"Always," he says.

After checking the hall, she waves Simon through her bedroom door. "Hurry up before anyone sees you." Halfway to the lobby she asks, "Can you check out a car?"

"Will they ask to see my license?"

She glances at him. "I assume so."

He shakes his head. "Then no. But Alan can."

They reach the lobby unscathed and Nadia pushes through the door. "We can't take him. He can't keep a secret to save his life."

"We won't have to. We'll have him check out the car, then we'll drop him before the errand commences."

"But we need him to drive."

"No, we need him to check out a car. I happen to be an excellent driver. I just don't have a license, per se."

Nadia rubs her face. "This isn't gonna work."

"Really, it will be fine." Simon starts down the sidewalk to the boys' dorm. "Alan will be relieved to settle his debts."

Fifteen minutes later Alan drives their black sedan away from the security gate. Nadia watches the guard house shrink in the passenger-side mirror as Simon stretches out across the back seat. Alan pulls onto the highway and accelerates.

After he sets the cruise control, Nadia says, "Tell us about your mock mission."

"I cannot. I was informed that discretion is critical."

"That's fine." She shrugs like she doesn't care. "I already know it was with Gentech."

"How do you know that?" His question sounds like an accusation.

"All of our missions were with Gentech," she says. "Was yours off campus?"

He scowls. "I really cannot say."

Nadia narrows her eyes, studies him. "No, Jack would've had you working from school." Alan's face flushes—she's on the right track. "Tech-specs?" He exhales—slight relief. So it wasn't tech-specs. *Not language and translation, not comms....* Someone had to access Simon's wifi-enabled thumb drive. "You hacked into Gentech's mainframe."

Simon leans forward, over the center console, watching Alan closely.

Alan clears his throat. His Adam's apple protrudes as he swallows.

Bingo. "Let me guess," she says. "Your mission involved replacing the genetic sequence of someone already in the database with a new string of DNA."

Hives appear on his cherry-red neck. "How could you possibly know that?"

"Was it Milo Riazotti?" she asks.

The car swerves and Nadia steadies the wheel. Alan regains control, then asks, "How do you know about my mission? Did you read my op-specs? I destroyed them immediately. Simon, was I talking in my sleep?"

Simon leans back. "No worries, mate. It's not your fault. You did everything right."

Nadia looks out the window across the darkened desert as they continue in silence. For the next twenty minutes she turns the details over and over in her head. Without knowing extenuating circumstances, she finds it difficult to gauge her level of anger at her father. He shot Bishop. But Bishop orchestrated an entire cover-up. Still, an assassination attempt trumps tampering with a genetic database. She shakes her head. Whatever the circumstances, they've all been used. Libby, Alan, Simon, Damon, even Jack. Used to cover up their parents' mistakes. And somehow, at the heart of the conspiracy, lies Agent Roberts.

As they approach town, Nadia asks Alan to pull into the parking lot at a shopping plaza off Scottsdale Road. He eases into a spot at a snail's pace.

"Now get out," Simon tells him.

"What? Why?"

"Faster, please." Nadia scans the lot for surveillance vehicles.

Simon climbs out and opens the driver's door. "We've got something to do and you can't come."

"What am I supposed to do until you get back?" Alan asks as he steps from the car.

Simon gestures to the plaza. "Pizza, bookstore, get your nails done. Whatever. I'll be back in a flash." Alan crosses his arms. Simon says, "The other option is we stuff you in the boot."

Alan scowls. "And then we are even?"

Simon smiles. "As a level."

Nadia leans toward Alan and says, "Thanks for your help."

"Maybe after this you will owe *me* one," Alan mumbles.

Simon chuckles and winks at Nadia. "Let's not push it, mate."

The bus station smells like diesel and greasy French fries. To one side is a small snack bar and sundries shop. Backless benches, bolted to the floor, fill the center of the room. On the far side of the station, Nadia finds the wall of grey lockers. Simon stays on her heels as she slides the key into locker 213.

Inside she finds a small envelope, a burner phone, and a handwritten note: *last number called*. She pulls up the call history and presses send.

Damon answers. "Open the envelope. Go outside and wait for me. If I see any surveillance, I start picking off civilians, got it? And ditch the phone." He hangs up.

Simon's brows pull together, questioning. "What's he on about now?"

"I think this is where you and I part ways." Nadia rips open the seam of the envelope and plucks the tiny comms device from inside. She tosses the cell phone in the trash can and nestles the comms into her ear.

Simon looks over her shoulder and nods toward the entrance. "Ready?"

"Give me a sec." Nadia stops by the shop and purchases a pre-stamped postcard with a picture of a coyote on the front. She borrows a pen from the cashier, scribbles a message and her home address on the back, then hands it to Simon. "Can you mail this for me?"

"'I know about you.' That's the best you've got?"

"We're a little pressed for time." They move through the sparsely populated station and out into the night. When they reach the side of the building, out of the streetlights, away from the parking lot, she asks, "You're clear on the plan?"

"It's a very simple plan. I'm beginning to feel a bit insulted."

Nadia smiles. "Humor me."

"I go back to school, tell everyone Damon popped me and snatched you against your will, cry a wee bit, Bob's your uncle."

She nods. "Don't forget to stop and pick up Alan."

"Oh hell, I'd already forgotten."

"Simon." Nadia waits until he makes eye contact. "Thank you."

His face softens. "No worries, love. I wish you'd let me tag along. If anything happens to you, Libby will see me drawn and quartered."

Her eyes search the parking lot. Across the street, taking up half a city block, is a gas station and convenience store. The bright lights spill into the street. "Not this time." Truth is, she'd love to take Simon. But she knows Damon won't allow it—plus, it's not fair to ask Simon to risk his future, possibly his life. This is her fight as much as it is Damon's, but it's definitely not Simon's. "Maybe for my next act of treason."

"It's a date."

She turns back to Simon. His blue eyes bore into hers. The resemblance, now that she's looking for it, is uncanny. "Are you going to tell Libby?"

He shakes his head. "I'm not sure what to do. What would I even say? 'Turns out your dad dipped his wick in someone else's ink pot. Surprise, I'm your baby brother!'"

"Who's this clown?" Damon says into her ear. "Did he just say he's Libby's brother?"

Nadia looks around. "Where are you?"

"Right here, love," Simon says. "I'm right here."

She shakes her head and mouths, "Not you." She points to her ear.

"Who is he?" Damon repeats.

"He's the new you," Nadia says.

"Did we run out of American teens to exploit? Now we're importing?" Damon asks. "Hurry up and say your goodbyes."

Nadia rolls her eyes and asks Simon, "You ready?"

He nods once and takes a deep breath. "Mmm. Ready."

She steps forward with her left foot and draws back her right arm. Without hesitation, she strikes. The contact with Simon's mouth is perfect.

"Damn, girl," Damon says in her ear. "That was a nice crossover."

Simon's hand comes to his lip, split and already swelling. He wipes the blood and licks the cut.

Nadia winces. "I'm so sorry."

"No worries. I'll tell everyone it was Damon."

"Tsk," Damon scoffs. "I would've knocked him out cold."

"Yes, Damon," Nadia says. "We're all wildly impressed."

Simon leans forward and gives her a hug. "Good luck. Don't be too long."

His embrace lasts longer than it should. "Okay then." Nadia pulls away.

"Wait there and don't say anything," Damon says.

A minute after Simon drives off, a black BMW with heavily tinted windows pulls into the lot. The car rolls up, the window rolls down.

"I wasn't sure you'd come," Damon says.

Nadia shrugs. "I heard you needed a little muscle."

62 JACK
THURSDAY, MARCH 2

Thursday night, an hour after his botched assignment with Nadia, Jack receives a coded message from his handler, Dean Shepard. The final piece of Operation Royal—this part a solo mission—directs him to the Stay Connected Internet Café in downtown Phoenix. From there, he'll spoof an IP address, log onto the wifi-enabled thumb drive that Simon planted at Gentech Labcorp, and then activate the self-destruct code. Lastly, he's to dead drop the entire operational report in a trash can at the first light-rail stop in Tempe by 0100 hours, thereby erasing all evidence of his team's involvement.

He glances at the clock, annoyed that he's getting an assignment minutes after completing the *last* assignment. *I don't know what I expected—this is life in the CIA.* He shakes his head, changes into a fresh polo, grabs a cotton pullover, and heads out the door for a little study time.

After a few hours at the library reviewing the mission and plotting out his route, Jack returns to the lobby of his dorm. He's surprised to see Libby sitting on the sofa. "When did you get back?"

"Oh, Jack, thank goodness you're here." She rushes toward him, hands clutched together. Her clear blue eyes are filled with tears.

"What's the matter? Is it your dad?"

315

"Nadia's gone," she says. "I came back and she was gone. I can't find her anywhere."

Jack sighs. "I can't help you there. She's not exactly confiding in me these days." The lobby door opens behind him, and Simon and Alan join the pair. Simon, uncharacteristically disheveled, sports a split and swollen lip.

"Darling, you're back." Simon wraps Libby into a hug. "We missed you." He pulls away. "What's wrong?"

"What happened to you?" Jack asks him.

"Nadia's missing," Libby says.

Simon shakes his head. "She's not missing. She's just not here."

"Hey—what happened to your face?" Jack asks again.

Simon leans toward Libby. "Listen, I *really* need to speak with you. Privately."

She nods, her eyes wide. "Yeah, we definitely have some catching up to do. But first, where's Nadia?"

Simon shakes his head. "I don't know."

Libby says, "But you just said—"

"He does that all the time," Alan says. "It is maddening."

Jack shakes his head. *It's like herding kittens.* "Will someone please tell me—"

Simon turns to Jack. "I dropped Nadia at the bus station."

"What?"

"She had some errand. Something to do with Damon." Simon points to his lip. "That's what happened here. Oh, but if anyone asks, she was taken against her will."

"How could you leave her with that psychopath?" Jack asks.

"I'm not her mum."

"We have to go after her," Libby says.

"She'll be long gone by now," Simon answers.

Jack narrows his eyes, fists clenched at his sides. "How could you do that? Who knows where he'll take her—or what he'll do to her?"

Simon shakes his head. "Not to worry. I slipped a tracking

device in her pocket. She should be live in about thirty minutes." He winks at Libby. "I set a delay in case she's scanned for surveillance."

"You just happened to have a tracking device with you?" Jack asks.

"Yeah, of course. I always carry a few, courtesy of Her Majesty's Secret Service. Why, don't you?"

"Well, let's go," Libby says.

"Right, when do we leave?" Simon asks cheerfully.

Jack shakes his head. "No way—it's out of the question. She made a decision to risk her life for him. She doesn't get to make that call for everyone else."

"Fine," Libby says. "Then you go."

"I have my final mission in less than two hours. If I don't complete it, I don't graduate."

"Yeah, about that," Simon says.

Before Jack can respond to Simon, Libby jabs at his chest. Jack scowls. "Stop it."

Anger flashes through her eyes. "She is your responsibility. *We* are your responsibility, whether you like it or not. You are our team leader—at the expense of all else, I might add."

Jack's about to fire back when he realizes something: Libby is right. If anything happens to Nadia tonight, can he live with that? If there's the slightest chance that he could've helped her? His first priority should be the safety of his team. He's always done right by his country. It's time to do right by his friend.

Even if it costs him his future.

Jack nods. "You know what? You're absolutely right. She made a stupid decision and put herself in danger, but this is my team, and she's still my responsibility."

"And the love of your life," Simon says.

"Yeah, that too." He glances at his team. "Okay, here's what we'll do." Jack opens his laptop and pulls up a satellite map of downtown Phoenix. "When her signal goes live, I need you running comms," he tells Alan. "Simon, search the map for seldom-used or recently leased buildings and warehouses. When we locate her, I'll need an entry point."

"Got it," Simon says.

"What can I do?" Libby asks.

"Compare their results with live satellite imagery. Use the infrared filter. We're looking for activity in a nonresidential section of the city. Probably a couple guys, mostly stationary—like standing guard, right? So one out front, one in the rear, stuff like that."

"That sounds pretty high-tech. Where can I find a program like that?" Libby asks.

Jack and Alan answer in sync. "Simon's laptop."

63 NADIA
THURSDAY, MARCH 2

Across the street from a deserted-looking warehouse, Nadia crouches behind a blue dumpster as Damon shoves his rifle and a bag of gear underneath. She surveys the layout. A single streetlight casts a beam over the front entrance, narrow windows run high across the top, a chain-link fence surrounds the exterior. "That's it?"

"Yeah, that's it."

She shakes her head. "This is insanity. There's gotta be a better way. You remember the cyanide pill, right? We're walking straight into the arms of the man who wants you dead."

Damon's eyes don't leave the warehouse. "Then I'll try to be particularly charming. Here." He hands her a Glock.

She drops the magazine, checks that it's loaded, then reinserts it and racks the slide. "Listen, my life depends on you, so you better bring your A-game."

Damon scoffs. "Please. Worry about your own self." He readies his gun. "Roberts has a single body man—the guard out front. We'll surround him from the rear. I'll go around the right side, you take the left. You ready?"

"Not really," she mumbles, as she follows him across the darkened street.

They approach from the back of the building to flank the front door. Nadia rounds her corner, leading with the gun. The guard moves toward her, reaches into his jacket. Damon, now standing behind him, whistles. The man turns, sees he's surrounded, and lifts his arms. Damon waves him inside.

Nadia follows after them, her gun raised, finger resting on the trigger guard. Inside, a second man immediately lifts his weapon and points it at her. She aims back and moves her finger to the trigger. "Damon?"

"Roberts," Damon yells. "Get down here."

The office door on the mezzanine level opens and Roberts steps into view. He's older than she expected, and no longer in military shape. The metal stairs clang against his weight as he descends to ground level.

She debates whether or not to move her sights onto Roberts. He's not armed, and the second guard still has a gun pointed at her head, so she holds her position.

"What is this?" asks Roberts.

Damon shifts his aim from the first guard to Roberts. "Where's my mother?"

"Soldier, lower your weapon," Roberts says to Damon.

"Where's my mother?"

"She's on her way. Now lower your weapon."

"No way," Nadia says, answering for Damon. "Not until this guy does." She steps back with her right foot, bracing for the kickback. Her eyes move between Roberts and her target.

Roberts turns his head slightly toward the stairs and lets out a shrill whistle. Two more men emerge from the office, both armed, both aiming at Nadia. He stares evenly at Damon. "You think I didn't expect you to double-cross me?"

"You set me up," Damon says, gun still pointing at Roberts. "You framed me for shooting Bishop. You put a bounty on my head."

"No, I didn't. In fact, I thought you bid on that contract to get back in my good graces."

Nadia narrows her eyes at Roberts. "That was your doing? *You* ordered the hit on Bishop?" He doesn't answer.

Damon continues. "Then who shot him? Who framed me?"

Why is my father doing the Nighthawks' bidding? Her hand shakes. She takes a deep breath, tries to steady her nerves.

"I have no idea," Roberts says. "He has no shortage of enemies. Nor do you, which is probably why someone leaked your name. Make a list of everyone you've screwed over. See if you can narrow it down." He shrugs. "The contract wasn't fulfilled, so I haven't received an invoice. And thanks to the failed attempt instigating additional security and excessive publicity, I've had to revoke the contract." He lifts his chin. "Now, for the last time, lower your weapon, and let's finish our business together."

Damon takes a step back, then lowers his gun.

Nadia shoots him a look. This isn't part of the plan. "What are you doing?"

"Put your gun down," he says. "We're significantly outmanned."

"Are you kidding?" Her heart drops. She glares at Damon. "So you're just giving up?"

"I'll take that," Agent Roberts says, reaching for her gun.

"I'm sorry," Damon says.

"You're *sorry*?" She thrusts the gun at Roberts' midsection. Nadia's eyes move from Damon to Roberts to the four bodyguards, all of whom have their weapons trained on her. "What about your—"

"Enough," Roberts interrupts. "Damon, cuff her to that chair." He nods to the single wooden chair in the center of the near-empty warehouse.

"No, I want my mother. Now."

"She's right outside."

Damon wraps his arm around Nadia's neck. Before she can respond, she's in a chokehold. The muzzle of his gun presses against her temple. "Let me see."

"Or what? You're gonna kill her?" Roberts nods toward Nadia. "Be my guest."

Nadia grabs Damon's forearm, a steel vice against her throat. "No—wait."

"You need her alive or she'd already be dead. Which, incidentally, would've saved me a whole lot of trouble."

"We both know you won't do it," Roberts says.

Damon presses the muzzle harder against her head. "Try me."

"Wait!" she says again.

Roberts raises a placating hand. "All right, enough. Put down your gun." He nods to one of his bodyguards.

The guard raises the garage door at the back of the warehouse and waves his arm. A minute later a silver sedan pulls inside. He opens the rear passenger side. A woman sits on the back seat, bound, gagged, blindfolded.

Nadia's fingers tighten around Damon's arm as she sees his mother. He has to save her.

The guard slams the door before anyone speaks.

Damon's arm flexes, tightening against Nadia's neck as he points to the guard. "Tell him to move the car outside so it faces the street. Leave the driver's side open and come back in."

"We have one more item of business," Roberts says. "Your files?"

"Nadia, inside my bag. Get the file."

With a sick feeling of resignation, she reaches into the messenger bag slung over his shoulder. A quick hand sweep for weapons yields nothing, so she removes the sealed manila envelope.

"Open it and give it to me," Damon says.

She rips the top off the envelope and pulls out the files. Stacks of papers and photographs held together with paper clips.

Damon snatches the papers from her hand. "This is *it*," he says. "We are done." He throws the stack to the ground. The papers slide across the slick floor, spreading out like a deck of cards.

"That wasn't so hard, was it? You can go." Roberts turns to his hired gun. "Cuff the girl."

"I'm happy to do that on my way out," Damon says, dragging her toward the chair. "Sit down." He wrenches her arms behind her back. "I'm really sorry it has to end like this."

A pain shoots between her shoulders and she flinches.

He cuffs her hands. "If it were me being locked up, here's where you'd promise to wait for me." He leans against her body and says, "You'll wait for me, right?"

What is he talking about? Nadia waits until he circles around the chair, until he looks into her eyes. "Did you know about this? That he would have extra security?"

He shrugs. "It occurred to me."

"You're unbelievable."

"What do you want from me? I can't abandon my mother." Damon turns his back on Roberts' men and whispers to her, "Brace yourself."

"What?" Nadia asks.

"She's your problem now," Damon calls to Roberts. "And let me tell you something, she's a handful." He presses his boot against the side of her chair and kicks.

Nadia's chair falls onto its side as her shoulder slams against the concrete floor. She cries out before she can think. Her lip pulses as the taste of blood seeps into her mouth. He stands over her and says, "You wanna know what your problem is?"

"Bad taste in friends?"

"You never think about the angle. It's all angles, Nadia. That's what determines whether you live or you die."

His legs blur out of focus as he strides out the back door and disappears. The screech of tires echoes through the warehouse. The guard lowers the garage door.

Nadia squeezes her eyes closed, hoping her head will stop spinning. When she opens them, Roberts is standing by the stairs in quiet conference with his guards. Roberts glances once in her direction, then strolls up the stairs to the mezzanine office.

Her shoulder throbs from taking the weight of the fall.

Panic creeps through her body. Fingers of fear grow from her midsection up around her heart, down through her legs. Maybe she can break the chair, get free, steal a gun, shoot her way out. Fake a seizure, vomit, have a heart attack. Bribe the guards—with what? She has nothing.

Her father did this to her. And Damon. And she herself—for trusting them.

Nadia spits onto the floor as rage wells in her chest. Anger overpowers the fear. She lifts her head. A sheet of paper from the discarded file sticks to her bloodied lip.

The gunmen relax at their posts. One chats with the driver, the other leans against the front door, messing with his cell phone. Ignoring her. Why wouldn't they? She's completely helpless, cuffed and lying on the floor. In front of a pile of papers that Damon threw to the ground. Right beside her chair.

His voice echoes in her head, the story he told her their first day in his trailer. *The hardest part was knocking over the chair.*

A second later the bare lightbulb hanging from the ceiling high above her turns on, casting a pool of yellow light around her body.

Damon dropped the files on purpose. He doesn't do anything without good reason—every action is premeditated. It's exhausting.

She twists her head to look at the documents. At the far edge of the sheaf she sees it, clinging precariously to a photograph.

A paper clip.

Nadia glances at the gunmen. Finding them still preoccupied, she eases her body backward, a millimeter at a time. Her hands brush against the papers nearest to her. Quietly, with as little movement as possible, bit by bit, she slides along the floor.

The guard by the door glances up. She lowers her head to the ground, relaxes her muscles. Adopts the posture of the defeated. His attention turns back to his phone.

With the tips of her fingers, she pulls the pages toward her, sheet by sheet.

And then she feels it. The paper clip holding the stack together.

Damon brought her here, a lamb to the slaughter. He could've told her about his suspicions; they could've come up with a plan. Instead, he traded her life for his mother's. But he left her a way to escape.

Even so, she will never forgive him.

One paper clip is not enough to redeem a man.

64 DAMON
THURSDAY, MARCH 2

Damon's chest aches as he leaves Nadia handcuffed on the ground. But his mother is tied up in the back of a car behind the warehouse. She's starving, dehydrated...who knows what. He prays that Nadia understood his message.

He climbs into the driver's seat as the garage door closes behind him. Reaching into the back, Damon removes the gag from her mouth, pulling it down around her neck. "Stay down," he says.

"Damon?" Her voice is hoarse, like she hasn't spoken in a while. "Is that you?"

"It's me. Just hang on." The headlights sear through the darkness as he peels out. Two blocks from the warehouse, Damon pulls over and climbs into the back seat. He unties the blindfold and cuts the restraints from her wrists. "Are you okay?" he asks, looking her over.

She throws her arms around him. "Thank God."

Damon holds her as long as he dares, then pulls away. "Mom, we gotta go." They move to the front seat, and Damon continues in the direction of the police station.

"What is going on?" his mother asks, tears running down her face.

"I'm so sorry, but I can't explain right now. I'm taking you to the police." He hands her a slip of paper with the number of the local WITSEC office. "This is Witness Protection. You need to make sure they get you out of here."

"Wait—you're coming with me, right?"

"I can't. I'm so sorry." He glances at her. "For everything."

She's crying harder now. "I'm not leaving you. You're all I have left."

"You have to." Damon's eyes fill with tears. The guilt sticks in his throat. "I can't keep you safe."

"That's not your job!"

He pulls along the curb at the back of the police station. "I am truly sorry. I love you more than anything. I need you to trust me. Go inside. Wait twenty minutes before you say anything to anyone. Twenty minutes. And then tell them what happened to you. Ask them to call that number."

She clings to his hand, presses it to her wet face. "No. Please don't leave me," she sobs.

Damon's heart feels like it's ripping in half. The pain on her face—the same pain he saw when his brother died—it's too much to bear. His mind sprints through scenarios where they leave together, get new identities, move to another country, go into hiding. He's looking over his shoulder for the rest of their lives, desperately trying to keep her safe. If they find him, they find her. And then they kill her.

She's better off without him. He knows this deep in his gut, but he can't tell her; he can't explain why. He shakes his head. "I'm sorry."

"No." Her face crumples.

"You need to go. Please." He leans over and unclips her seatbelt, then opens her door.

"Damon."

He gently pushes her hips toward the door. "I love you, Mom." The second her feet touch the ground he shuts her door. Damon blows her a final kiss and pulls away from the curb, watching her shrink in the rearview mirror.

For a minute he feels numb.

And then he feels the pain. He forces back the tears, swallows the sobs. His throat feels raw, his chest hollow.

As Damon takes the corner around the front of the police station, a high-pitched beep fills the car, followed by a tiny pop, and then silence. A warm wetness spreads across his hip, seeping through the pocket of his jeans. He touches the liquid and brings his fingers to his nose. Bitter almonds.

The cyanide capsule attached to his tracking device.

Roberts just pressed the kill switch.

65 NADIA
THURSDAY, MARCH 2

Nadia fumbles for the paper clip and slips it free from the pages. Her hands shake as she straightens the metal. When she tried with the paper clip in the trailer, she failed. She folds the clip against itself and squeezes with all her might. The guard near the stairs briefly looks in her direction. Behind her back, she finds the hole in the handcuffs and inserts the makeshift key.

Roberts exits the mezzanine office and stomps down the stairs. He speaks to his guard, and together they approach. Nadia folds her hands together, concealing the clip.

The guard easily lifts her and the chair, righting her position. She glances at the papers fanned out across the ground. Her head throbs. She tries the clip a second time.

"If it's any consolation," Roberts says, "I've activated Damon's kill switch." She doesn't respond. "You're welcome."

"I don't know what that means." Nadia struggles to find the hole on her handcuffs. Her hands sweat; the paper clip slips. She snatches it just before it drops from her grasp. The bent loop will barely fit inside the hole.

"The cyanide capsule attached to his tracking device." Roberts glances at his watch. "Would you believe that Damon drove straight to the police station? He was only going thirty-five when we detonated, so it's possible his mother will survive, but who knows." He shrugs like it doesn't matter one way or the other. "In any case, he won't bother you anymore."

She closes her eyes. Tries to remember the mechanics of the handcuffs. For a second she considers telling Roberts he failed— that she cut out the tracker. But then Roberts would send a hit squad, and no matter how she feels about Damon abandoning her, his mom shouldn't have to die. And frankly, to save her own mother, Nadia would've done the exact same thing.

"Does that upset you?" Roberts asks.

Nadia visualizes a handcuff key. Tiny, compact; the end, a small ninety-degree angle.

Damon's voice in her head: *Think about the angle. That's what determines whether you live or you die.*

Her eyes open. That's why she couldn't get it. "I'll pull through."

She needs the mechanism of a pin, not a loop. Nadia shoves the straight end into the latch and presses against the metal to form a ninety-degree bend in the paper clip, using the lock as leverage. The right angle forms and she reinserts the clip. She feels it catch and holds her breath. The pin slides out of position. Back in again.

"To the matter at hand," Roberts says. "Are you familiar with Project Genesis?"

"It's come up once or twice." The key is too long, bent too far up the clip. Nadia straightens the metal and tries again, bending a smaller section on the end.

"Ah." Roberts nods. "Of course. The explosion near Langley. Well, after we lost Damon, our man on the ground, we were forced to try a more direct approach."

"How'd that work out for you?"

Roberts narrows his eyes and leans to the side, examining her forearms. Maybe he's noticed her movements. She presses the straightened paper clip between the index and middle finger of her left hand. She'll wait until the conversation ends.

He clears his throat and straightens. "Unfortunately for you, not well. Had we been successful, you would still be at school. But now I'm left with no other option. We need to compel the creator of Genesis to join our little organization."

"I gotta be honest with you. I failed cybergenetics, so I'm not really sure how I can help."

Roberts looks amused. "You remind me of your father. I used to know him very well. I only met your mother the one time. Intriguing woman; I understand his attraction. Tell me, do you know about your father's past?"

Nadia's heart pounds. She's dying to ask questions, but if she does, he'll have a negotiating tool. Worse yet, he'll figure out she doesn't know anything and lie to her.

He studies her face, then takes a deep, sudden breath, and exhales. "My interest lies in unlocking the science of Project Genesis. To that end, I need you to make a phone call."

"I can't help you."

"You will call your father, explain the situation, and then hand me the phone."

"If you know my father, then you know he's not a scientist. He doesn't have access to Project Genesis."

"I need the creator of Genesis, and I need her to be a willing participant. In order to make that happen, I will use you as my bargaining chip." He pauses for a second. "I'm explaining this to you so that you understand—"

"Did you say *her*? Who's the scientist?" Simon's mother? Didn't Roberts know she was dead? And why would Simon's mom care about helping Nadia?

He continues as though she hasn't spoken. "So that you understand that I don't mean you or your father harm. I just need a cooperative scientist. Now, you can either make the call, explain the situation, and hand me the damn phone, or alternatively, we send you home, a little bit at a time. A finger here, an ear there. It's entirely up to you."

A wave of nausea washes over her. "Who's the scientist?"

"Boss." The man guarding the stairs moves toward Roberts and speaks into his ear. "We've got a lead on Nightingale."

Nightingale. I know that name.

"A phone call," Roberts repeats, rising from his chair. "I'll give you a few minutes to think about it."

66 DAMON
THURSDAY, MARCH 2

Damon narrows his eyes and digs the tracker out of his pocket. He's not surprised that Roberts activated the kill switch, but he'd expected a longer grace period.

Doesn't matter; this works out well. Now Roberts thinks he's dead. He won't see him coming. Damon tosses the tracking device out the window without touching the brakes.

A block from the warehouse, Damon makes a U-turn and pulls along the curb. He throws the keys under the driver's seat and continues on foot. In another half block, he retrieves his silenced rifle and canvas bag from under the dumpster. Stashed inside the bag are three full magazines, a couple flash-bang grenades, and a signal jammer to block cell phones and walkie-talkies. He shoves the mags into his pockets.

Damon approaches the warehouse from the south, pausing long enough to toss the signal jammer into the bushes and shoot out the outside light. The bulb pops as sparks fly to the pavement. He climbs up the fire escape and peers through a crack in the open window, just wide enough for his long gun.

Nadia sits upright in her chair. Her lip is swollen, her head down. Above her hangs a bare lightbulb. He shoves a flash-bang grenade through the crack and turns his head, then engages the night-vision scope on his rifle.

The grenade detonates on impact—a blinding flash of light, a deafening boom.

He steadies himself and takes aim at Nadia's head.

A breath.

A heartbeat.

He adjusts and presses the trigger, shooting out the light hanging over her. Shards of glass flutter down like snowflakes. The lower level of the warehouse is pitch black.

Another breath, another heartbeat. Press the trigger. The first guard falls.

Damon adjusts his aim. The driver's in the crosshairs, pressed against the wall, blinking wildly, blinded by the flash of light. The grenade served its purpose.

Beat, breath, trigger. The driver falls.

Using the scope, he searches the warehouse for Roberts and the remaining two guards, but none are in sight.

He thunders down the fire escape and sprints toward the front of the building. As he rounds the corner, Roberts' car screeches out of the parking lot. Damon fires after him, but the succession of gunshots coming from inside the building pulls him toward Nadia. Three, then a fourth.

Damon slips through the main entrance.

The smell of acrid smoke fills the room. He can't find the shooter. He moves toward Nadia's chair.

As he nears, she stands, pulling a gun from the hand of the dead man lying at her feet. She points the weapon at Damon's head.

"Whoa—wait a sec," he says, holding up his hands. "It's me. Don't shoot."

Nadia pulls the trigger.

67 NADIA
THURSDAY, MARCH 2
(10 MINUTES EARLIER)

Nadia closes her eyes, visualizes the shim of the handcuffs. The throbbing pain at the back of her skull makes it difficult to concentrate. She's running out of time—the thought sparks a new flash of fear in her heart that quickly flares into panic. *Stop it. Focus.* She ignores the loud clang of a metal pipe as it hits the concrete floor.

A bright flash pulses through her closed eyelids, followed by a deafening concussion. Her eyes fly open—a new surge of fear as the warehouse fills with dense smoke. An unwavering, high-pitched squeal rings in her ears. The lightbulb over her head explodes. Panic closes her throat as glass rains down onto her hair and clothes. She jams the makeshift key into the lock. Her eyes sting from the smoke in the air and the pain in her fingers.

A guard materializes through the haze. He's directly in front of her, gun raised, pointed at her head.

"Wait," she cries. The paper clip is in the lock. His lips move, but she can't hear his words.

A warm, sticky spray fans across her face. The guard falls forward onto her lap, then slumps to the floor. There's a bullet hole in the back of his head. His blood is splattered across her chest.

Something hits the wall to her right. She squints through the dark haze. The driver collapses on the ground. Nadia jiggles the paper clip, searches for the proper angle.

"What the hell?" the second guard yells, but it's muffled, like underwater. He moves toward her, weapon drawn, then spins erratically, searching the dark for the shooter, backing against the wall in front of her. He fires into the open space. The noise echoes and reverberates off the tinny walls. Three, four shots. She lowers her head—he's spraying bullets.

Blood roars through her ears. The smoke fills her lungs, stings inside her chest. She struggles for a clean breath. *I can't do it.*

She's about to give up on the cuffs when a figure emerges from the smoke. He strides toward her, broad shoulders, slim waist. The silhouette of a sniper's rifle in his arms.

Damon.

With one last effort, Nadia twists the paper clip hard. The lock clicks open. Damon moves closer.

A second shadow appears over his right shoulder.

She stands, grabs the gun from the dead man's grip, takes aim.

"Whoa—wait a sec," Damon says, holding up his hands. "It's me. Don't shoot."

Nadia leans a quarter inch to her left—so slight it's nearly negligible—and fires three shots.

Damon flinches, covers his head.

She hears the *thud,* and Damon turns around. Nadia moves to his side.

Directly behind him, a guard lies dead on the floor, three shots in his throat, gun in hand, finger on the trigger.

Damon whistles. "Nice grouping."

Nadia steps away and points her gun at Damon. "Drop your gun."

"Don't point that at me."

"Put it down!"

"Okay." Damon eases the gun to the ground. "But I'm not here to hurt you. I came back to help you. I left you a way out, right?" He nods toward the handcuffs.

"Yeah, you're a real pal." She hesitates for a second, then lowers the gun. "Where's Roberts? We need to stop him."

"It's too late. He's gone." He steps toward her and brushes her hair from her cheek. She slaps his hand away. "I'm sorry I pushed you down."

She tries to shove him, but he's strong enough that he doesn't move. He looks amused, which thoroughly annoys her. "You think it's funny?"

"Are you okay?" He leans in and examines her cut lip.

"I'm fine." She swats him away.

"Come on, we don't have much time." He takes her hand and leads her to the front door. "The car's down the block. Can you find your way back to school?"

"I don't have a license."

"Not what I asked, but okay."

Outside, Nadia inhales lungfuls of the cool night air as she follows Damon to the side of the building. When they reach the back corner of the warehouse, she stops, pressing herself against the siding. Police sirens sound in the distance. She looks past him, over his shoulder. From the north come flashing lights. "Come on. We gotta go." Nadia grabs his wrist and turns toward the south.

"I'm sorry about all this. I never meant to leave you. I didn't know Roberts would have extra security." He pulls his arm away. "I'll go toward them; you double back. They'll chase me. Probably won't even see you."

"No—we can both run. Come with me."

He pulls her into a rough hug. "I knew you cared about me." Before she can answer, Damon shoves her around the side of the building.

Nadia stumbles backward. She catches herself, then scrambles in his direction. As she rounds the corner, she sees him sprinting toward the police cars.

She takes a deep breath to yell after him, but before she utters a sound, someone clamps a hand over her mouth. An arm wraps around her waist and she's dragged back around the corner.

68 DAMON
THURSDAY, MARCH 2

Damon sits in a familiar room, strapped to a familiar chair. He's never been in this particular room, but they're all the same. His metal chair is bolted to the floor in front of a bare steel table. A second chair is shoved into the far corner. A single lightbulb hangs from the ceiling. It shines in his eyes. The cinderblock walls don't have one-way mirrors, which is never a good sign. No cameras, either. He'd much rather someone look in, keep an eye on the interrogation. Make sure it stays on the up-and-up. The thick, stagnant air smells like urine.

His face throbs, which is probably a good thing, because it detracts from the pain of his arms wrenched behind his back. He can't move his left shoulder—he's pretty sure it's dislocated. And he's ridiculously thirsty.

Under the table in the center of the room is a drain. Probably to hose the blood off the floor. If he can free himself, he'll climb on the table and yank down the electrical cord holding the lightbulb. He can strangle someone with that. Damon moves his weight around in the chair, hoping to find a weak spot in the frame. It appears to be cast from a single piece of steel: no joints to exploit. He's stuck.

The door opens and a man walks in. He wears jeans, work boots, a gray t-shirt, a heavy silver watch. He's got a beard and a deep tan. Looks like special forces, maybe CIA. He pulls the spare chair up to the far side of the table, opens a water bottle wet with condensation, takes a long pull. He slams the bottle onto the table; water sloshes out of the neck. He smiles and wipes the water onto the floor. "Looks like I spilled."

"Is my mother safe?" Damon asks, his throat raw.

"I don't know what you're talking about."

"I dropped her at the police station. She needs to be in witness protection or Roberts will have her killed."

The man stands and circles the table. He grabs Damon's jaw. "That's quite a shiner." His thumb digs into Damon's cheekbone until the cut opens and starts to bleed again.

Damon winces. "What do you want?"

The man puts his face in Damon's and says, "You're a disgrace to your country. I have no intention of helping you or your mother."

Damon's pulse quickens. "Come on, she's not part of this. What do you *want*? I'll tell you anything. Just get my mother into WITSEC."

"You tried to assassinate a sitting senator of the United States."

"It wasn't me," Damon says.

"We have evidence to the contrary. My brothers are overseas risking their lives to protect your way of life. You disgust me. You're a traitor." He stands and spits at Damon's feet.

Damon turns his head. The fatigue of the last twenty-four hours catches up to him. The constant output of adrenaline has depleted his reserves. He's got nothing left. "I didn't shoot Bishop. But everything else that I did, it was for my family." The words are barely audible. "I had no choice."

The soldier sits on the edge of the table. He grabs the cord just above the bulb and shines the light into Damon's face. Damon's eyes ache from the brightness.

"Please," Damon whispers. "I don't care what you do with me. Just help my mom."

After a few minutes the soldier nods. "I got a mom. There's not much I wouldn't do for her."

A flicker of hope. Damon meets his eyes. "I'll do anything."

The soldier releases the bulb and the light swings. Shadows sway back and forth across the table. "Anything?"

"Anything," Damon says.

"Well, I can't let you walk outta here. My brothers would never forgive me. But I might be able to help your mother. If you are willing to help me."

"Whatever you need." Damon prepares himself. The next few hours, he is certain, will be spent reciting everything he knows about Agent Roberts and his operation. Contacts, procedures, meeting sites, names. The CIA's been trying to bring the Nighthawks down for a long time, but the organization is so insidious; Nighthawks have infiltrated every branch of government and law enforcement. Damon's a valuable asset.

The soldier pauses. He leans forward and speaks quietly. "What *exactly* did you tell Nadia Riley?"

Damon's blood runs cold. If this guy wanted to end the Nighthawks, that's not where he'd start. He's one of them. "Who did you say you were with?"

"I didn't."

Damon nods. "So you're with Roberts. Then you know I didn't shoot Bishop. You know it was a setup."

"I don't know anything of the kind. Tell me about the girl."

"Why does Roberts want her so bad?"

"You have my offer. It expires in two seconds."

"I didn't tell her anything. She doesn't know anything about the Nighthawks."

The soldier examines his fingernails. After a moment, he asks, "What did you tell her about her family?"

"What?" Damon asks. *Why does he care about Nadia's family?* Then Damon realizes why the soldier is asking: Damon got that intel from Roberts' thumb drive. "Is this about the drive I took from Roberts' storage unit? Because those files were encrypted. I never even saw them."

"Where is the drive?"

"My trailer blew up." Damon lies without thinking. "The drive was inside."

"So what did you tell her? What does she know?"

"That her father's CIA. That's it."

"Why'd you tell her that?"

"What do you mean?"

The soldier leans forward and raises his voice. "What was your motivation?"

These questions make no sense. Damon shakes his head, confused. "So that she'd trust me. Because Roberts wanted her alive. I needed her to come willingly."

The soldier straightened, seemingly satisfied. "Okay."

"That's it? Now my mom gets into the witness protection program?" WITSEC's good. Two US marshals will know her whereabouts—no one else. Not even this guy.

"There's just one more thing." The man stands, circles the table like a shark, sits back in his chair. "You're a loose end, my friend. As long as you're around, none of us are safe—especially your mom. She'll always be hunted, used as leverage against you. But lucky for you, I've got a soft spot for mommas." He extends a closed, upturned fist. "So this is for you." His fingers unfurl.

A cyanide pill rests in his hand.

69 NADIA
THURSDAY, MARCH 2
(2 HOURS EARLIER)

Nadia claws at the hand clamped over her mouth. She stomps the top of her assailant's foot with her heel and throws her left elbow toward his head. His hand blocks the blow, and he releases.

"Stop!" Jack whispers. "It's me."

"What are you doing here?" she whispers back.

"Saving your butt." He leans against the wall and grabs his injured foot. "That really hurt."

"So don't grab me," she says. "I had the situation well in hand."

Jack peeks around the corner. "Yeah, looks like it."

Nadia leans around the edge of the wall. Damon's face is smashed against the hood of a police car, his hands pinned behind his back. Maybe she can create a diversion, buy him time to escape.

Jack pulls her back. "I'm sure I must be mistaken, but it looked like you were about to bolt with him." Nadia doesn't answer. "I'm gonna assume Stockholm Syndrome, rather than treason. Are there any details we need to iron out before I take you back?"

Treason. Damon's committed treason. He'll be sentenced to death. He could've gotten away, but he came back for her.

"Nadia?"

The expression of hurt on Jack's face brings her back to the moment. She shakes her head. "He left with his mother. He got away. But he came back for me."

Jack grabs her arm. "He's the reason you're here in the first place. You don't owe him anything, and he didn't do you any favors. And you and I are both going to be questioned about this, so I'll ask again, you weren't helping him escape, were you?"

Nadia shakes her head and looks at the ground. Jack will be obligated to pass along any information she shares. "No, of course not. You misread the situation. He kidnapped me, then traded me for his mother. End of story." She meets his gaze.

"I thought so." His eyes bore into hers. "Come on, we gotta get out of here. I'm parked a few streets over."

Nadia follows him away from the warehouse, between darkened buildings surrounded by chain-link fence. They cross in the middle of the street to avoid the streetlamps. A few blocks later, they reach the black Avalon and climb inside. Jack drives a quarter mile before turning on the headlights.

"You'll be debriefed when we get back. Probably orally, and then you'll have to write a statement. No one knows I came for you, so if you need time to review any details, we can do that. We can stop, get your story straight. It's really important that you be consistent and confident."

She turns to him. "How did you find me?"

"Simon low-jacked you. There's a tracker in your pocket."

"Well, that explains his excessively long hug." Nadia feels around inside her jacket pockets. "How'd you get a car? What did you say?"

Jack glances at his watch. "I'm supposed to be completing my final mission, so they didn't ask any questions."

"Did you finish?"

He shakes his head. "This seemed more pressing."

"But you won't graduate. You've ruined your chance of being invited to continue on with the CIA."

"That is correct," he says quietly.

Oh no. "I'm so sorry." Jack doesn't answer.

Guilt presses onto her shoulders as the streetlights tick by at a rhythmic pace. Jack threw away his future. Damon got caught when he came back to help her—he'll be sentenced to death. Yes, they made their own choices, but they made them for her.

She closes her eyes, exhausted. But her mind won't rest.

Who paid Damon to destroy the student database? Bishop had motive, to hide his illegitimate child. That means Libby's father also knows the true nature of the Academy.

Why did her father shoot him? The *Nighthawks* wanted Bishop dead—it wasn't the CIA at all. Bishop wasn't on *their* kill list.

Nightingale. She heard the name Nightingale. A code name used in Operation Cyprus—but who is Nightingale? The creator of Project Genesis? It has to be Simon's mom.

She's not dead. Maggie Pearle is alive.

What is going on?

"Pull over a second," she says, opening her eyes.

"What's wrong?" He pulls along the curb.

"Your senior project."

"It's too late. I'm out of time."

She shakes her head. "No, not that. You know how I thought there was something more to it? Turns out I was right. The only question left is, who ordered the mission?"

Jack stares through the windshield and shrugs. "I already told you, I don't know. I'm not even sure Shepard knows. She was just acting as my handler."

"Your assignment was to alter someone's DNA, right?"

He turns to her. "How did you know that?"

"Damon made me destroy the student database. Simon broke into a lab that stores the CIA's genome data. His paternity questions were put to bed right after Alan's mission, which was to upload a strand of DNA. Your senior project was to make it look like Simon's father is dead, to hide the identity of his actual biological father. And it would've been successful if Bishop hadn't been shot."

"My mission was to hide *Simon's* identity?" His knuckles tighten around the wheel. "Wait—what does Bishop have to do with anything? Are you insinuating that Senator Bishop is Simon's father? Simon is Libby's brother?"

"I think so."

Jack shakes his head. "Why are you telling me this?"

"Because you think I'm paranoid. You think my coming here to help Damon's mom was a huge mistake. You think I'm crazy. But in this particular instance, I'm not. Can you just answer one question for me? Is the fake name of the fake agent in your fake mission Milo Riazotti?"

Jack sighs. "I can't tell you—"

"Right." Nadia looks away. "Your precious protocol."

"No, that's not—I can't tell you because I don't know." His head lowers as he stares at his lap. "I was instructed not to read the individual op-specs. All I saw was the Operational Report. The overall objectives. I was embarrassed, and I didn't want to tell you. I mean, I get the need for compartmentalization of information, but still.... For all of these missions, I've been nothing more than a glorified babysitter and chauffeur."

The disappointment on his face hurts her heart. She touches his arm. "No, that's not true. None of us could've completed our missions without your guidance."

"You seem to do just fine without me."

"If I had to get along without you, I would be sitting in a jail cell right now." He lets out a little laugh and she continues. "It's not too late—let's finish your mission. What are your op-specs?"

"I'm supposed to initiate the self-destruct on the wifi-enabled thumb drive at Gentech, then drop my operational packet at a predetermined location. I don't have time to return you to school and then drive all the way back to Tempe before the dead drop."

Initiating the self-destruct, destroying evidence that the database was altered from outside Gentech's walls, will ensure that Nadia never discovers who ordered the mission. She'll never find the connection between Jack's project and Damon's mission. The memory card in her pocket was meant to frame Oliver West-lake. It won't contain a whisper of the CIA's involvement. If Jack can't complete his mission, if she can get her hands on that thumb drive, she might actually uncover the truth.

But it also means that he won't graduate. His training will be over, his dreams at an end.

She takes a deep breath. "I'll come with you. We'll do it together. If you don't graduate because you came here to help me, I won't be able to live with myself."

He smiles a little as he locks onto her eyes. "I get it."

She smiles back at him. "I know you do."

Completely overcome with anxiety, Alan marches to Dean Shepard's office first thing Friday morning to confess his transgressions. He finds her door open and, after a curt knock, he barges inside.

"Alan, what can I do for you?" Well-formed words leave her lips like shiny little daggers. She closes the open folder on her desk and turns it face down.

He takes a deep breath, his mouth feeling desiccated. If he can get the words out without vomiting he will consider the conversation a success. What she does after that is well beyond his control. "I am afraid I have not been forthright in my communications."

"Go on."

Alan sinks into a chair. "Dean Shepard, my family is from Israel."

After a brief silence, the dean says, "My family is from Scotland."

He does not know how to begin. Should he start with the fact that he is a loyal recruit of the CIA? Should he explain the original arrangement he had with his grandfather? Should he mention that Simon blackmailed him?

"Alan?"

"Yes?"

"What do you need?"

"My grandfather is Israeli Mossad," he blurts out.

Shepard leans back in her chair and folds her hands on the desk. "I see." Her lips come together, slightly pursed. The corners of her eyes crinkle. Alan does not excel at reading facial expressions, but she appears to be amused. Perhaps she misunderstood.

"That is not all. He is here at the Academy." He wills himself to say, *to pressure me to act as his informant.* But he cannot. "Under an alias. You know him as . . . Professor Katz."

"Yes?" Saba says from the doorway.

Alan leaps from his chair and backs into the desk. "Saba. What are you doing here?"

His grandfather smiles and closes the office door. "I followed you." As he moves into the room, Alan wonders whether or not Saba will dare kill him in front of the dean. But instead of strangling him, Saba wraps his arms around Alan in a clumsy hug.

"Please, sit down," Dean Shepard says. "Both of you."

They sit. Saba appears relaxed and confident. Maybe he did not hear the beginning of the conversation. Alan's heart pounds furiously. He wonders at what point it will simply give out. He hopes it will be sooner, rather than later.

Shepard begins. "Alan, I invited your grandfather here. We've known each other for years. He taught a class at The Farm on interrogation techniques. What was that, ten years ago?"

Saba laughs. "At least. But it is not polite to point out such things."

"Anyway," she says. "After last semester's security issues, we called your grandfather and asked him to fill in until we could properly vet a new instructor."

"You knew this whole time?" Alan asks the dean.

"I did." She smiles at his grandfather. "I also know you well enough to know that you've likely been pressuring your grandson into a familial arrangement. Am I right?"

Saba shrugs. "It is what we do, eh? The life of a spy."

Shepard looks at Alan. "You have a choice to make. Do you understand?"

Alan looks to his grandfather.

Shepard continues. "I cannot have you unofficially reporting to Mossad."

Alan faces the dean. He takes a deep breath, summons every iota of courage within him, and says, "I am with the CIA."

"Eli? Will you accept your grandson's choice?" she asks.

"Of course," he says casually. Saba looks at Alan. "You have made your choice, and I will respect it."

"I intend to hold you to that," Shepard says to Saba.

"Alan's happiness is my only concern," Saba says. "After all, family is everything."

The coldness of his smile sends a chill down Alan's spine.

71 NADIA
FRIDAY, MARCH 3

Friday morning after exercises, before she even changes out of her *gi*, Nadia sprints across the cushioned lawn to Dean Shepard's office to plead her case. She knocks on the dean's open door and moves inside before she's invited.

"How are you feeling?" Dean Shepard asks, her eyes lingering on Nadia's slightly swollen lip.

Nadia self-consciously touches her face. "I'll live. Do you have a minute?"

Dean Shepard sighs. "I don't see why not. Have a seat."

Nadia shuts the door and starts talking. "I don't know if you've reviewed Jack's senior project yet, but I was wondering if you might consider grading on a curve." She sits in the chair farthest from the door. "As you know, he was late in completing his assignment because he was helping me. He chose to protect a member of his team. That's a pretty stand-up move, and I think it should be taken into account."

Dean Shepard raises her eyebrows. "According to Jack's report, it was less of a choice, and more of a necessity. He claims you were taken against your will. He received intel regarding your location—and I must say, his explanation of how *that* transpired was a bit unclear, but things aren't looking good for Simon—and Jack performed a rescue op. Would you say his report is accurate?"

Nadia falters—Jack lied to the dean. He didn't sell her out. *I didn't see that coming.* "Yes, entirely."

"Do you have anything to add?"

She can't offer anything—what if it contradicts his report? "Um, the whole night is kind of a blur. I think I hit my head. I don't remember much at all."

"Head injuries can be serious," the dean says flatly. "We should keep an eye on that. It's quite remarkable that you were able to attend morning drills at the dojo."

"Yes ma'am." Nadia drops her gaze to the patterned rug.

"Is that all?"

"Actually, no." She raises her eyes. "I have another favor to ask."

Dean Shepard leans back in her chair. "I'm not sure you're in a position to be requesting favors, but go on."

"It's about Damon. I was hoping you could call Director Vincent and ask for leniency."

"Nadia, I—"

"I know he's done a lot of horrible things, but many of his actions were taken to protect me. And the rest were to save his mother. I don't expect that he can go free, but maybe you could request that he not get the death penalty?"

The dean stands and walks to the window. She's quiet for a few moments, then turns to Nadia and says, "I have some upsetting news." She opens her right desk drawer, selects a file, then walks around the desk to sit in the leather chair next to Nadia. "I'm afraid Damon is dead."

"What? No, that's not possible. He was taken into custody."

"While in custody, he took his own life. Apparently, he had a cyanide capsule sewn into his cheek. It was a technique used during the Cold War, an out for captured agents so they wouldn't be forced to endure interrogation."

"No, no way. He would never do that. Damon doesn't believe in suicide. It's not true."

"He left a note explaining the choices he'd made. He felt

suicide was the only way to keep his mother safe. He feared that his being alive would indefinitely make her a target."

"What happened to her? What was she told?"

"She's been placed into witness protection. I don't know the details of the cover story she received, but I'm sure the explanation was as thorough as possible. I can't fathom her grief, but I do know that she's safe."

Nadia turns her eyes toward the ceiling, avoiding Dean Shepard's concerned gaze.

"I'm truly sorry. I know this must be difficult. Despite recent events, I understand that you once shared a friendship." The dean clears her throat, and then says, "His final words stated that you were, indeed, held against your will, and that you acted to protect your teammates. Apparently Damon threatened to kill Jack if you didn't help rescue his mother?"

Nadia hesitates, and then confirms the lie. "That's right."

Shepard hands her the folder. "I'll give you a few minutes." She quietly leaves the room.

It's a trick. Nadia exhales a long, ragged breath. He's not dead. He can't be dead.

She opens the report. Thin metal prongs secure the pages to the heavy cardboard file. On top is his death certificate, embossed and watermarked. Easy enough to fake. She folds it back to review the medical examiner's findings. Suicide.

She scans the autopsy report. High levels of cyanide found in his blood. Poison burns inside his mouth. Her hands shake. She turns the page and immediately recognizes Damon's handwriting. The orderly letters, all capitalized, then his signature. Paper-clipped to the note is a Polaroid. Damon's lifeless face cocooned inside a black body bag. Nadia slides the picture aside and reads his last words: formal, unemotional. A few sentences meant to exonerate her. An apology to his mother, to his country.

She closes the file and sets it on the desk.

Damon may in fact be dead, but she's certain he didn't go willingly.

After the attempt on her father's life, Secret Service demanded that Libby accept a full-time security detail. Currently, they sit in a parked car along the dusty road leading to the guard gate. Obviously, they're not helping to maintain the low profile of Desert Mountain Academy, so when Libby receives the summons from Dean Shepard, she knows it can only mean one thing: dismissal. She's been waiting all semester for this meeting, ever since her daddy announced he was running for president.

At least he's alive. That's really all that matters. And her momma's happy again—with her own personal bodyguards, she thinks she's Jackie O.

Libby shakes her head, embarrassed by her own selfishness. According to Jack, things look even worse for Simon. The dean found out about his role in tracking Nadia. Shepard doesn't know the half of it, just that Simon had an unauthorized tracking device that he somehow managed to sneak past security. As far as Shepard's concerned, that's enough of an infraction to send him back home. And that's not sitting too well with Libby.

After lunch she brushes her hair and reapplies concealer to cover the circles under her eyes. Might as well look good for the execution.

Outside, the afternoon sky is a clear, brilliant blue. She's gonna miss the perfect weather. Her friends. Classes. Sensei's brutal workouts—she'll even miss Alan. She'll be sent to some private school, probably near Washington, full of other politicians' kids: opinionated, spoiled, self-entitled.

Across the lawn she takes a tissue from her purse and wraps it around the door handle before entering the administration building. Down the tiled hall and through the sitting room, she finds Dean Shepard's door open.

"Good afternoon," Libby says.

The dean looks up and smiles. "Libby, thanks for coming. Please, have a seat."

Libby closes the door with her forearm so she doesn't have to touch the knob and settles into a chair, ankles crossed, hands folded in her lap. She concentrates on relaxing the muscles in her face.

"I've asked you here to talk about your position at Desert Mountain. Obviously, in light of your father's campaign, additional measures will have to be taken to ensure that our program remains confidential."

Additional measures. Right. *Like kicking me out.*

"We must insist that your Secret Service detail remain off campus. I've sent a proposal to Director Vincent, head of the CIA. We own quite a bit of land surrounding campus, so my suggestion is that we build several casitas around the external wall. That will provide your agents a 360-degree view, as well as close proximity, but not so close that they'll interfere with training or the covert nature of our lessons. Obviously, the proposal is also subject to the approval of Secret Service, as your safety is paramount."

"Wait—I'm not getting kicked out?"

The dean laughs. "Kicked out? Of course not. You're an asset to our program."

"I just thought with the high profile—"

"Libby," she says. "I don't think you understand the strong position your father's candidacy places you in. You'll be exposed to diplomatic leaders, heads-of-state, prime ministers, presidents, wives, children, ambassadors, attachés....And if your father wins the election, you will have unprecedented access to people, places, and parties that the CIA has never fully infiltrated."

A smile spreads across Libby's face. She'd never thought about it like that.

"I'll keep you apprised of our progress, but we should have definite answers within the next few weeks."

"I don't even know what to say. Thank you so much!"

"Of course." Dean Shepard stands, indicating the end of the meeting.

Libby rises quickly. The dean extends her hand, and Libby barely hesitates before shaking it. "Thank you again." She starts to leave, but pauses at the door. *It's now or never.* "Dean Shepard, might I be able to use a private telephone before I go? I'd like to check on my daddy, but with the hall phones being monitored and him running for office and all....It just gets sticky."

"I'll allow it this once, but we can't make it a regular occurrence. And, naturally, you cannot mention why Secret Service must remain off campus."

"Yes ma'am, I understand."

"I'll show you to Ms. McGill's—the assistant's office."

Libby follows the dean down the hall to the small office off the lobby. She's thought long and hard about making this call. Bottom line, no matter what happens to her daddy's chances of becoming president, it's the right thing to do.

The dean sets her up and arranges an outside line. After she leaves, Libby dials her daddy's cell phone.

"It's me," she says as he picks up.

"Well hey, Shug. Listen, can I call you back? I'm right in the middle of—"

"No, Daddy. We need to talk now. I need you to do me a favor." Libby drops the bomb right on his lap. She talks about her daddy's affair, Simon and his deceased mother, about what her momma said, that's it's been confirmed via DNA, the whole shebang. "Now right now, Simon and I are the only ones who know we're related.

354

Momma doesn't know about him, and I'm gonna assume you had no idea he even existed. But now that you do, I need you to see to it that he's allowed to stay here at the Academy."

He's instantly the politician. "Liberty Grace, I am shocked and appalled. Of course I didn't know—I wouldn't abandon my own child. Shame on you for thinking it. But I can't get involved in the administrative operations of my daughter's government-run boarding school just because she asked me to. How would I explain that? That's tantamount to abuse of power and ten other things. How's that gonna look to my constituents?"

"Daddy," Libby says with a steady voice. "Apparently, I have failed to make my position clear. Simon stays here with me, or every single voter in the entire country finds out about your illegitimate son, conceived while your poor wife was at home, pregnant and alone. Furthermore, I expect you will insist on creating a scholarship for his college education. And he will be returning home with me during summer break."

"I beg your pardon. Are you *blackmailing* me?"

Libby's heart is in her throat. "Yes, Daddy, I believe I am."

A full minute of dead silence follows. Sixty seconds is a God-awful long time when you're waiting on the other end of the line.

He finally speaks, his voice full of honey. "Of course, sugar. What was I thinking? I would be delighted to help that poor boy. In fact, I won't take no for an answer. I'm ashamed I didn't think of it myself."

With her sweetest tone, Libby says, "Thank you, Daddy. I just knew I could count on you."

73 NADIA
FRIDAY, MARCH 3

Friday night, well after the girls have returned from the evening's study session, Casey knocks on their bedroom door. "Nadia, Dean Shepard would like to see you in her office."

"Now? It's almost nine." Nadia locks eyes with Libby and shrugs at her roommate's questioning look. Shoving her feet into her sneakers, she grabs a sweater from the back of her chair.

"You want me to walk with you?" Libby asks, even though she's just changed into her pajamas.

Nadia shakes her head. "No, it's okay. Thanks, though. I'll fill you in when I get back."

"If you're sure." Libby looks relieved. "Good luck."

Nadia cuts across the unlit lawn. The breeze picks up, blowing tendrils of hair across her face. She sprints up the steps of Hopi Hall.

The interior is lit only by the glowing exit sign hanging in the lobby. After a deep breath, she walks to the sitting room, then on to the dean's office. She knocks on the closed door.

"Come in," Shepard calls.

As Nadia enters, the dean stands and moves toward her. Behind her, a man rises from one of the guest chairs. He turns around.

Nadia's stomach flips as her father says, "Hello, sweetheart."

"I'll give you some privacy," Shepard says. "It's good to see you again, James, and send my regards to Zaida."

"Of course," he answers. "And thanks again for the call." As soon as Shepard steps out and closes the door, he says, "How are you?"

Nadia narrows her eyes. "How *am* I? Uh, not great, Dad. If that is, in fact, your real name."

He laughs. "That's cute. Why don't you sit?"

"I don't even know what to say to you!" The anger, confusion, and deep sense of betrayal she's felt for weeks force themselves to the surface. "Why would you send me here without telling me the truth? Do you think I'm incapable of making my own decisions?"

"Of course not," he answers calmly. "You may recall, the true nature of the Academy is never to be discussed beyond these walls. I thought it would be a good fit, and I wanted to protect you. You need to be able to defend yourself if anyone comes for us."

His reasonable tone infuriates her. "Why would someone come for us?"

Her dad withdraws a folded sheet of paper from the breast pocket of his coat. "Before I can explain, you'll need to sign this nondisclosure agreement."

"Are you *kidding*?"

"It's the only way Director Vincent would agree to let me talk to you."

"Where's Mom? You didn't leave her home alone, did you? Roberts is after you, and if he can't get to me, he's gonna try her."

"Your mother is safe. I can't tell you any more if you don't sign."

Nadia strides to the desk, snatches a pen from Shepard's desk blotter, and scribbles her signature across the page.

"Don't you want to read it first?"

"You shot Senator Bishop." She hisses the accusation.

"Yes."

His honesty catches her off guard. She misses a beat, then asks, "Why?"

"We received credible intel that his life was in danger."

"So you *shot* him?"

"Well, not me personally." Her dad smiles. "It's really good to see you."

"Dad."

He sighs. "Please, let's sit down." She plops into her chair and waits while he gets situated. Finally, he continues. "A few months ago, during an overseas interrogation, the head of Mossad—"

"Director Cohen," Nadia interrupts.

"Yes, Director Cohen."

"He's here."

"I know. He and I are old friends. He came to Desert Mountain to watch over our charges until this whole mess could be taken care of."

Nadia raises an eyebrow. "Epic fail."

Her dad gives her a closed-lipped smile. "Director Cohen received intel through a reliable source that a hit had been ordered on a United States politician. Together, we investigated the specifics. I met with Bishop long before the debate and told him about the threat—along with my plan to keep him safe. Bishop wore a bulletproof vest lined with blood capsules. Our shooter targeted predetermined spots on the vest—not with lethal ammo, I might add. We staged the whole thing."

"Why?"

"So the Nighthawks aren't aware that we've infiltrated their organization. They were left believing that the shooter succeeded in an attempt, but failed at his final mission."

Nadia leans back and crosses her arms. "So you know about Desert Mountain. Alan's grandfather knows.... Libby's dad—"

"No, Senator Bishop doesn't know. He's not CIA. But we should probably brief him before he figures out Libby is rooming with the daughter of his old friend."

She scoffs. "So it's just a coincidence that Libby was recruited?"

"Of course not. I asked Sloan to look into Libby's test scores. She's extremely qualified; I just greased the wheels. I hate to tell you this, but I'm a midlevel employee at best. The CIA makes most of its decisions without consulting me."

Nadia shakes her head. "Why would you do that? I thought Senator Bishop was your friend. Not everyone wants this life for their child."

He takes a deep breath and leans forward, elbows resting on his knees. "Everyone associated with Project Genesis is at risk—therefore, their families are, too. My sole objective was to provide you and Libby with the tools necessary to defend yourselves, even if it's just a finely honed situational awareness, which you certainly learn by attending the Academy."

She looks away, considering his words. She wants to trust him—no matter what's happened, he's her *dad*. She sighs and meets his gaze. "I think Bishop knows about Desert Mountain." Leaning toward him, she says quietly, "I think he hired Damon to destroy the student DNA database."

Her father frowns. "What makes you think that?"

"Damon initially told me he wanted to destroy it to protect himself against Project Genesis—against Roberts. But then he said someone hired him—he got paid a lot of money. I think Bishop was trying to hide the fact that he's Simon's father. It would've worked, too, except that Simon entered his own independent DNA sample directly into CIADIS. And that's not all." Nadia takes a deep breath, exhales. "I heard Roberts talking—Nightingale is alive. Maggie Pearle is alive." When her father doesn't react, she says, "We have to tell Simon."

He shakes his head. "Absolutely not. The CIA is planning an operation to get her back, but if it fails.... Don't make Simon go through the pain of losing his mother a second time. It's cruel, Nadia." He sits back. "You'll have to trust me on this."

"My days of blindly following your orders are over. I want the truth."

He looks amused. "I don't recall that you've ever blindly followed an order in your life, but if you have something you'd like to discuss, by all means." He spreads his arms.

She whispers to contain the anger in her voice. "You framed Damon for shooting Bishop—and you tried to use *me* to do it."

"First of all, I didn't frame anyone. I just arranged the fake shooting. And I only did that because I wanted to ensure that Senator Bishop would remain unscathed. Secondly, you need to remember that Damon is a traitor. He was a Nighthawk."

"But he didn't *do* this. You have to clear his name. His mother thinks he tried to kill a senator."

"We absolutely will not clear his name, and neither will you. My understanding is that Damon committed suicide. And if he hadn't, he would've been executed as a traitor. To a dead man, reputation is irrelevant."

How can he be so blasé? She studies his face. "How many people have you killed?"

"I've never killed anyone," he says. "I'm not a shooter. I'm an analyst. I gather intel and information. I conduct interviews. I make friends. I advise others on how to diplomatically handle difficult situations. I don't even own a gun."

"Everywhere we've ever lived, there's been some mysterious death."

"People die all the time. Everyone you've ever met, everyone you'll ever meet."

Nadia shoots him an incredulous look. "Dad."

He pauses. His brow pulls together. "I used to work as a scout. My job was to investigate threats, determine credibility, then forward my report to Langley. I was in the counter-assassination division."

Instantly, he looks so vulnerable, so human. It's clear those deaths weigh on him. Nadia tries to lighten the mood. "Maybe you want to think about switching divisions? Because there are a lot of bodies in our wake."

He smiles a little and looks up at her. "I prevented a lot too, smart-ass. And I have switched. Someone else can chase the spies. I'm too old."

"Did you know about Jack Felkin's senior project?"

"I did."

"How could you do that to Simon? He deserves to know the truth."

"I didn't *do* anything. I heard about the operation and didn't object—not that it would've mattered if I had. I wanted Simon to have some closure—without destroying a family in the process. If Maggie had wanted her son to know the identity of his father, she would've told him."

"So you had me frame some innocent man who happens to work at Gentech?"

He points to himself. "Again, midlevel employee. And Oliver Westlake is not an innocent man. He's been selling the identity of undercover operatives living abroad to foreign governments."

"Oh." Nadia purses her lips. "Um, you'll probably want to catch him doing something else, because I didn't exactly complete that portion of the mission."

"I am aware," he says flatly. "And I have to tell you, if you find yourself unable to execute orders because they conflict with your personal beliefs or opinions, you need to find a new calling. At some point in the not-too-distant future, your choices will cease to be belligerent acts of an impetuous young adult, and will instead become treasonous crimes. Do you understand what I'm saying to you?"

Nadia drops her eyes and nods. "Yes. Though I could argue that removing any trace of our presence in that hotel room was the right call. You know, what with the dead body and all."

"And that is the only reason you haven't been expelled."

After a few minutes of uncomfortable silence, she sits back, relaxes her posture. "Tell me about how you and mom met. The real story."

Her dad rubs his face and leans back in the chair. "My team was sent to Syria. We'd received intelligence that the head scientist of the Syrian government was developing a next-generation weapon. Our job was to ascertain whether or not the intel was solid. I went in as an American grad student, set up a chance meeting with the mysterious geneticist, Zaida Azar."

"What?"

He smiles. "Your mother and I fell in love. I disobeyed orders, and we ended up exfiltrating her."

"Hold on—*Mom* is the creator of Project Genesis?" Nadia stands and paces the room.

"Why do you think she gave you all those puzzle books? Sent you to math camp? Who goes to math camp, Nadia?" He pauses. "She's why I wanted you to attend the Academy. Not because of me."

"She knows about the Academy?"

"Sweetheart, I may be CIA, but I don't have a death wish. Do you honestly think I would send you here behind your mother's back? She would *kill* me."

Nadia sits back down. "Then why did Roberts come after me and not her?"

"Your mother would give her life before betraying this country, and Roberts knows that. But she wouldn't give yours."

"Huh." Nadia slumps back and shakes her head. "Not in a million years would I have suspected Mom."

He leans forward and takes her hands. "You need to understand, our early married life was a carefully fabricated legend, but we are now, and have always been, very much in love. And we've loved our work." He shrugs. "It's not for everyone, and you get to make your own decision about whether or not you'll continue on with the CIA, but neither of us regret what we've done in the service of this country."

Nadia looks at the carpet. "Dad, I saw my birth certificate. The real one. Are you—"

"Yes, Nadia. I'm your father. We were married in London a few weeks after you were born. Wentworth—Senator Bishop—was there, and Maggie Pearle. After I disobeyed orders and extracted your mother without authorization, we were forced into hiding. Maggie hid us away in an off-books MI-6 safe house while your mom and I created her legend and negotiated terms with the CIA. We rewrote her history. Maggie saved our lives. I owe everything to her." He looks away for a moment, then back at Nadia. "My actions during that mission put everyone at risk: Bishop, Maggie, Libby, Simon, Director Cohen, Alan, you. If I'd followed protocol, if I hadn't botched that operation, Bishop and Maggie Pearle never would've met. I have a responsibility to ensure that you each have the means to protect and defend yourselves." He sighs and shakes his head. "I'm sorry, sweetheart—I wouldn't have chosen this life for you. But if I had to do it over again, I wouldn't change a thing."

A warm feeling washes over her. He sounds like her dad again. "That's why you got Simon into Desert Mountain, even though it was a risk to Senator Bishop."

Surprise flashes across his face, then he returns to neutral. He smiles. "You know a lot."

"Yeah, well. I am a spy."

74 DAMON
SATURDAY, MARCH 4

Damon's lifeless body is wheeled to a cold, darkened basement underneath the CIA-run medical center in an unassuming block of Central Phoenix. The medical examiner unzips the black plastic body bag, checks for vitals, takes two Polaroid pictures of his chalky face. She zips the bag and slides the body into cold storage.

Damon's eyes flutter open. He's lying on a bed in a dark, windowless room, his hands and legs restrained. It smells antiseptic, like a hospital; latex and rubbing alcohol mixed with pine cleanser. An IV tube is taped to his forearm. As he wakes, he hears the slow, steady beep of his heartbeat on the monitor behind him. A small lamp on a table in the corner casts a golden glow across the torso of a man standing against the wall. He wears a charcoal-gray suit, a lavender dress shirt, a striped purple tie. His face and legs are shadowed. Damon blinks, trying to adjust to the dim lighting.

"Welcome back to the land of the living," the man says. American. No discernible accent.

Damon lifts his head. The back of his skull throbs. "Where's my mom?" He tests his restraints as discreetly as possible. All solid.

"Witness protection. I saw to it myself." The man moves forward. He doesn't look familiar.

"Who are you?"

He shakes his head. "Doesn't matter. I'm not the one you'll be speaking with."

"You want to fill me in?" Damon asks, though he doesn't particularly care.

"You must be pretty important to merit a visit from the head of the entire division."

Damon sighs. He's tired of the games. He doesn't bother asking what division. The answer would probably be a lie.

The man continues. "I believe you've already been in contact. You know him as Mr. Green."

The door to the room opens, and a man walks in, five-ten, brown hair, closely cropped beard. Damon squints. There's something familiar.... *Oh no.* "You're Mr. Green? Are you kidding me?" He jerks his cuffed hands. "This is total bull. I did exactly what you asked me to—I destroyed the student database."

"You kidnapped my daughter. I didn't ask you to do that."

"How else did you expect me to access the database? Furthermore, if you'd introduced yourself as Jericho, and not Mr. Green, maybe I would've done things differently." Damon rests his head back on the pillow. "If you were trying to keep Nadia from finding out you're CIA, it's too late. She already knows."

A light laugh escapes his lips. "No, no. I wasn't trying to protect myself. I was looking out for a friend."

"So you're here to kill me?" Damon asks.

"Why would I want to kill you?"

"As you mentioned, I kidnapped your daughter. It's a reasonable response."

"I'm not here to kill you. I'm here to recruit you." Nadia's father smiles. "Consider the last few weeks your entrance exam."

Damon scoffs. He's heard this before. "Recruit me for what?"

Riley takes a key from his pocket and unlocks the handcuffs. "I run a highly specialized division of black-ops. You might say we're *black* black-ops. My unit is called Corpus Opera."

"Never heard of it." Damon rubs his wrists.

"That's because we're good at what we do. Technically, we don't exist. But then again, neither do you." Riley hands him a folder.

Inside Damon finds his death certificate, his autopsy confirming suicide by cyanide pill, and a Polaroid of his dead body. Another photograph clipped to the papers shows his old teammates standing in the desert: Nadia, Jack, Libby, Alan. The new guy. A framed picture of Damon rests on a boulder. "What the hell is this?"

"Your former teammates held a covert memorial for you early this morning."

Damon's eyes return to the picture. Nadia's lighting a candle. A lock of hair hangs along her cheek. He can't take his eyes off her. "She's not safe, you know. As long as Roberts is alive."

"What do you know about wetworks?"

"Your concern for your daughter's safety is touching." Damon closes the folder and hands it back. "I know the CIA supposedly doesn't engage in assassinations. And I know I'm not a killer."

"I think we both know that's not true." Riley's face is unreadable. "Wetworks isn't solely elimination. We also provide clean-up services for agents in the field, for situations that...get out of hand. We remove remains, destroy forensic evidence, take care of loose ends."

His mom thinks he's dead, his friends think he's dead. He might as well be dead. He's been blackmailed, shot at, framed for an assassination attempt, forced to commit suicide, played by both sides. He's done. "That's a nice way of saying I'll either be killing people or disposing of dead bodies. I'm not interested." Damon closes his eyes.

"Perhaps I've been unclear. Your options are to join us and begin a new life, or don't, and we leak the truth: that you faked your own death. You will be hunted like a dog by every organization until you are caught, tortured, and killed."

"I'll take my chances."

"We'll also kick your mother out of WITSEC."

Damon opens his eyes. Slowly, the truth dawns on him. Agent

Roberts didn't frame him for the attempt on Bishop's life. Riley did. "You set me up. You told the CIA I tried to kill Bishop."

"That is correct."

The intensity of Riley's gaze reminds Damon of Nadia. She favors her father. "Why?"

"I just told you why. You tried to kill a man running for president of the United States. You are now wanted by the CIA, the FBI, the Nighthawks, Homeland Security, and every local law enforcement agency in the country."

"*I didn't do it.*"

"I know you didn't. It was me," Riley says.

"Then why did you frame me?" Damon demands. "Don't you have a license to kill?"

Riley laughs. "No, I don't. But more importantly, I don't want Bishop dead. We found out his life was in danger, and I saw an opportunity. I bid on the contract through back channels and made it look like you were the hired gun. I've been interested in you for a while."

"You shot a man who's running for president so that you could recruit me? What if you'd missed? What if you'd killed him?"

"My operations are painstakingly thorough. Let's start with the bombing of the facility in Virginia. I sent an anonymous tip to Bishop that the Nighthawks were responsible. I love him like a brother, but Bishop is a blowhard, and I knew he wouldn't be able to resist talking about it. Makes him look like he has inside information, and voters love that in a candidate."

"Ah," Damon says. "*He's* the one you were trying to protect by destroying the student database. Because as soon as Libby and Simon turn eighteen, their DNA moves from Desert Mountain to CIADIS, a match gets flagged, and everyone learns the truth."

"See? I knew you were sharp." Riley nods approvingly. "After I heard about the contract on Bishop's life and came up with a plan to keep him safe, I knew there was a chance his DNA would be entered into CIADIS. It was a CIA mission, after all. I didn't want to destroy Bishop's family."

"You're all heart."

"Hey—I also tried to provide an orphan with closure. Simon was supposed to discover that his father was a deceased CIA operative *prior* to the student database getting destroyed. If Libby and Simon were both entered into CIADIS, Libby might be led to believe that her father was also a deceased agent by the name of Milo Riazotti, which was the information provided to Simon. I did *not* count on Simon manually entering his own genetic sequence into the main database, however. I'll have to keep a closer eye on him."

"So you're the one who called me about my mother being held in Baton Rouge."

"Guilty as charged. You arrived in Baton Rouge days before someone tried to kill Senator Bishop. It's not a huge leap to assume it was you. From the moment Bishop stepped onto that stage to the moment you woke up here"—Riley holds his arms out—"my carefully orchestrated production was flawless. Bishop suffered a tiny bruise. My doctors kept him under lock and key long enough to make the public believe it was a serious attempt. And don't think Bishop won't leverage that during the election." He pauses. "I'm telling you this as a lesson. There's not much I won't do to get what I want."

"I'm starting to understand why Nadia has such bad taste in men."

Riley's expression doesn't change. "Back to why you're here. When the CIA discovered you were the double agent, I checked up on you. You received top-notch training before you arrived at Desert Mountain Academy, but even more impressive are the skills you taught yourself after you lost your brother, before you ever got recruited."

Damon looks away. He hates when people mention Gabriel.

"The CIA wanted to eliminate you. A recruit who's actually a double agent? Talk about a black mark on our record. The Nighthawks want you dead. You know too much about their organization. But I saw an opportunity, so I framed you for the assassination attempt. Naturally, your only way out was suicide."

Damon shakes his head. "Maybe it's the morphine drip, but I don't follow."

"You tried to kill an American presidential candidate. The only way to keep your mother safe was to take your own life, or else she would be hunted and used as a bargaining chip. So now everyone thinks you're dead. Except for me. Ironically, I saved your life."

Damon clenches his jaw. He's so sick of the threats, the blackmail, all of it. "So the soldier who gave me the suicide pill—he wasn't a Nighthawk?"

"No, he's one of my guys."

That's why he asked me about Nadia. Damon glances at Riley. "So why didn't your man just kill me? Or pretend to kill me? Why the whole suicide song and dance?"

"I wanted to know how far you'd go to protect your mother. And now I do. Which is also how I know you'll do whatever you can to keep her in WITSEC."

"You're sick." Damon looks away.

"I'm thorough," Riley says, his voice cold. "My operatives are ghosts. They don't exist. And neither do you."

"Does Roberts know about you? What you do here?"

"Including you, there are seven people on the planet who know the truth about me. Roberts is not one of them. If that number moves to eight, you and I will have a serious problem." Riley drops a thick manila envelope on the bed. "I'll give you a few minutes to think it over. Review the offer: your salary, your job bonuses. Accidental deaths pay double. You'll receive a starter kit, including four identities, four nationalities, four apartments around the world. Any remaining record of your existence will be destroyed. To be safe, our plastic surgeon will alter your fingerprints. You can leave this life behind." He moves toward the door. "Obviously, you can't see Nadia again—or anyone you used to know. Damon Moore is dead."

Leave this life behind. Just like that? Pretend his little brother never existed, that Damon wasn't responsible for his death? Pretend that Roberts hadn't burned down his house, taken his mother hostage, and forced Damon to kidnap and betray Nadia? Pretend he hasn't—and this is the stupidest thing of all—completely fallen for a girl who, as it turns out, is the daughter of a government-sanctioned assassin?

It doesn't matter whose side he's on—there are no good guys or bad guys. They're all bad guys.

But truth be told, he wouldn't mind a little vengeance.

"Wait a minute," Damon says. "Do I have any discretion?"

Riley turns back. "What do you mean? Do you get to veto an assignment? No. We say who, where, and when. The why is not your concern, and the how is generally left up to you. But we don't eliminate without reason. You're not going to be hunting soccer moms and tax-evaders. We're talking worst-case scenarios: threats to the public-at-large, terrorists, enemies of the state."

"That's not what I mean. I have some unfinished business."

Riley purses his lips. "Open your envelope."

Damon slides his finger along the seal and extracts the sheaf of papers. A blank white sheet rests on top. He moves it aside and reads the name of his first assignment. He looks back at Riley. "Is this for real?"

"It's for real."

Damon's eyes return to the dossier in his hand. He nods. "All right. I'm in."

THREE MONTHS LATER

75 NADIA
FRIDAY, MAY 26

By nine o'clock in the morning, the weather verges on uncomfortably warm. Nadia sits in a white folding chair on the front lawn facing the wooden stage. Libby, in an oversized sun hat, leans against her left shoulder. Today is the actual graduation; tomorrow the seniors will join their parents at the North Scottsdale Country Club for a scrubbed ceremony—generic, but still confidential. Phones and cameras will be prohibited. In a few weeks, the professional photographer will send his apologies, describing an incident at the lab that damaged his film. There will be no group picture of the graduating class.

The commencement music begins, and Nadia stands with her classmates.

After opening remarks Dean Shepard pauses at the podium. "Esteemed colleagues, I have an announcement. This year CIA Director Vincent has chosen to honor one outstanding candidate as the recipient of the prestigious Marshall St. Clair Paige Covert Studies Award. This award recognizes a recruit who has demonstrated honor, valor, and integrity, above and beyond the Academy's rigorous expectations. Included with the award is an invitation to continue training at Langley's undergraduate program. Please help me congratulate Jack Felkin."

The applause is extraordinary, and Nadia's heart fills with an overwhelming happiness for Jack. He's getting exactly what he wanted.

Simon leans over Libby and says, "Couldn't have happened to a more worthy cadet."

The audience settles as Jack takes the stage. "Dean Shepard, Dr. Cameron, Hashimoto Sensei, professors, colleagues, classmates, and friends." He acknowledges each with a nod. "I am honored to receive this award. I pledge to you that I will strive to be an exemplary representative of the outstanding student body trained here at Desert Mountain Academy. I thank you all." The crowd explodes with cheers.

Nadia smiles and claps along with her friends.

Jack holds up his arms, his graduation gown flowing out like wings. The audience quiets and he continues. "This year has been challenging, difficult, frustrating, and completely satisfying. We've learned about friendship, country, loyalty." Jack pauses as he searches the audience. He finds Nadia and locks onto her eyes. "And love."

Nadia's cheeks warm as a few students turn to look at her.

Jack leans into the microphone. "Hey, Nadia."

"Oh my God," Nadia whispers to Libby. Her face burns hotter. "What is he doing?"

His words resonate across the lawn. "I'm not your team leader anymore."

Jack hands his award to Dr. Cameron, who happens to be sitting closest to the podium, and jumps off the stage. He strides down the aisle to Nadia's chair and holds out his hand.

Her mouth opens. She feels hundreds of eyes boring into her. She slips her hand into his.

"I'm sorry we couldn't get it together," he says.

"Just bad timing," she answers. He pulls her up, wraps his arms around her. He buries his face into her hair and her stomach jumps. Someone toward the back starts to clap. A few seconds later, as Jack picks her up and spins her around, everyone joins in the applause.

She laughs, and it's the lightest she's felt in months.

Damon's new training regimen puts Desert Mountain Academy to shame. All-day lectures about untraceable poisons, stealth kills, falsifying autopsy reports. How to befriend a target to access her twentieth-story penthouse. Advanced calculus and trigonometry, so when he arrives at the aforementioned penthouse, he can do math on the fly, a necessary skill for a sniper. Wiring bombs, breaking and entering, moving in and out of the country undetected.

He's the solitary student, granted undivided attention from the finest instructors ever to grace the halls of the CIA. Jericho created Damon's legend: his teachers believe he's preparing for an undercover black-ops mission deep inside the Middle East.

They don't even know Corpus Opera exists.

He's given a suite at the Hotel Hartford a few miles from Langley. Between twelve-hour classroom sessions, overnight survival courses, and hand-to-hand combat training, Damon barely finds time to run the decryption program on Roberts' thumb drive. But, given that his first target is his archnemesis, he makes time.

It takes weeks for the brute-force algorithm to finally break through the firewalls. He scrolls down the document titles, hoping one will catch his eye. And then one does, but it's not what he's expecting. Instead of a lead on Roberts, Damon finds *Operation Cyprus, Unredacted*. He pulls it up, skims the report.

Not believing it, he reads through a second time.

"Holy hell," he says to the empty room. *Poor Nadia.*

This is why Riley's man questioned me about what I told her. He was trying to find out how much Damon knew.

He looks back at the screen. Should he tell her? He has to—but how? He can't risk Riley intercepting a message.

Nadia's from a small town—everybody knows everybody. She's got neighbors.

He closes his eyes. She'll be devastated. Maybe he shouldn't tell her.

If it were him, he would want to know. But she's not him. His eyes open.

Damon reads the report one last time, just to be sure he understood.

OPERATION CYPRUS, 78655985
CLASSIFIED: EYES ONLY
RELEVANT FILES: 78655986
OPERATIVES: Black Sheep, Scout, Jericho, Lincoln
POST-MISSION ASSIST: Nightingale
OBJECTIVE: Elimination of SWANDIVE, declared a national threat
RESULT: FAILURE. Wetworks incomplete.
JERICHO opted for extraction (see 78655986).

> BLACK SHEEP: debriefed, deported.
> SCOUT: compromised. No longer field-eligible.
> JERICHO: requests legend for SWANDIVE.
> LINCOLN: injured. Medical leave required.
> NIGHTINGALE: success.

SUCCESS: Negative. MISSION FAILURE.
OPERATION BRIEF: JERICHO acted independently and against orders.

While instructed to eliminate SWANDIVE, the sole creator of PROJECT GENESIS, JERICHO instead exfiltrated the target, claiming the target can be further used as an asset to the United States of America. As part of the continued undercover operation, JERICHO will propose marriage to SWANDIVE. JERICHO asserts with certainty that SWANDIVE shall remain unaware of the ruse. JERICHO assures the agency that he will maintain cover by any means necessary, including children.

Damon snaps the laptop shut and stares at the wall, wondering what to do.

Nadia's mother created Project Genesis.

To gain access to the technology, Nadia's father married her, and to continue his undercover operation, had a baby.

Nadia's entire life is nothing more than someone else's cover.

Back in Virginia a week after graduation, Nadia lounges on her front porch swing reading a magazine as the cicadas hum a steady song. The humidity clings to her, leaving a sticky film over her skin. She stops reading to fan herself. It's almost enough to make her miss the 110-degree Phoenix mornings. A few minutes past noon, the mail carrier arrives with a bundle of mail. She flips through the stack and finds an envelope addressed to her from Desert Mountain Academy.

> *Dear Nadia,*
>
> *We are pleased to announce that you have been selected to serve as a team leader during your senior year. Please respond with your intention to accept by June 18.*
>
> *Sincerely,*
> *Dean Shepard, Interim Dean of Students*

Nadia smiles as she refolds the letter and slips it into the envelope. She's about to go inside to drop the mail on the kitchen counter when her next-door neighbor crosses the front yard.

Mrs. Chapman waves hello. "You look happy as a june bug sitting out here in the shade."

"Hi, Mrs. Chapman, how are you?" Nadia says loudly, knowing her neighbor doesn't hear well.

"The postman delivered your mail to me. It wasn't his fault this time, it's addressed incorrectly." She extends her hand, a postcard clutched in her bony fingers.

"Thank you," Nadia says.

The picture features Manhattan's skyline at night. Nadia flips it over and reads the single word: *Aloha*.

Her heart skips. It can't be.

She sits back down and checks the postmark. The date stamp is two days old.

A smile spreads across her face.

Damon's still alive.

ACKNOWLEDGMENTS

To my sister, Rachel Smith: once again, this book wouldn't exist without you. Words can't express my gratitude. Monica Rosen, thanks for plotting with me—for brainstorming, for encouraging, for insisting that somewhere in the stack of pages there was, in fact, a coherent storyline. Mom, though you have no free time and very few moments of quiet, you read draft after draft. Thank you for your generosity.

Jude Stone, I am grateful for your quick text responses to my redundant grammatical questions; Morgan Stone, for your indispensable advice on teenage language; Kaitlyn Kemppainen, for single-handedly increasing my readership tenfold. And for listening to thousands of variations of a single paragraph to find the one that was just right.

Details of this story were shaped across many miles of hiking through the Sonoran Desert, over the fields of wildflowers surrounding Crested Butte, and in the crevices of Antelope Canyon. Thank you to my favorite hiking partner and co-conspirator, Stu Kemppainen. I'm sorry I killed you in chapter 56, but you kind of had it coming.

As I've often discovered, it's better to be lucky than clever, and good fortune connected me to an amazing group of thriller writers—my blog sisters at roguewomenwriters.com. I am forever grateful to Gayle Lynds, K.J. Howe, Christine Goff, Francine Mathews, Jamie Freveletti, Karna Bodman, and S. Lee Manning. Thanks also to my critique group: Betty Webb, Art Kerns, Eileen Brady, Sharon Magee, and Charlie Pyeatte.

Thank you to architect Terry Stone for disabusing me of the notion that I can escape a room by crawling through the air ducts, or set off the sprinkler system in a ten-story building by holding a lighter under a single head; and thank you to Nicole and Ryan Minnick, my official munitions experts. Deniese Hardesty Reinhardt, Anna Kline, Kristy Steck, Ellen Steck, Ann Tyburski, Helen Johnston, Dr. Angela Bowers, Ian Chappel, Logan Garrison Savits, thanks for being such great sounding boards. Alan Gratz, you are as generous with your knowledge and experience as you are talented.

To my Sensei, Michael Cerpok: my editor found your koans as frustrating as Nadia found Hashimoto Sensei's. Nevertheless, I am grateful for your wisdom. Speaking of wisdom: thanks, Dad. After four and a half decades of conversations, I'm still learning new words.

Kelly Loughman, my tireless editor at Holiday House: thank you for loving these characters, and for helping shape their destinies. Sally and Pamela, thank you for your enthusiastic comments during the copyediting process, and Terry, thank you for fearlessly leading the marketing and publicity team.